Brody was asleep when he felt the mattress dip as someone climbed in with him.

For a moment, he froze, but then caught Faith's familiar mesmerising scent.

"Do you mind?"

"Uh…no. Of course not. It's your house. I can take the couch. What time is it?"

"Three. And, no, you can't take the couch. There's a power outage in the building. It's completely freezing. I think it's forty-nine degrees inside the condo."

"Nice."

"Can I just sleep with you here? Please?" She batted her eyelashes. "I promise not to hog the blankets or compromise your manly virtue. I'm even wearing flannel, see?"

She lifted the covers to give him a view of her pink flannel pyjama pants, but she'd failed to mention the form-fitting top.

His mouth went dry. "You're a nutjob. Pull the covers back up." Brody closed his eyes and sighed.

"Brody?"

"Hmm?"

"I won't lie. I sort of want to take advantage of your body heat."

First published in Great Britain 2010
Harlequin Mills & Boon Limited,
Eton House, 18-24 Paradise Road, Richmond, Surrey TW9 1SR

Second-Chance Family © Karina Bliss 2008
The Other Sister © Lynda Sandoval 2007

ISBN: 978 0 263 87938 4

23-0110

Harlequin Mills & Boon policy is to use papers that are natural, renewable
and recyclable products and made from wood grown in sustainable
forests. The logging and manufacturing processes conform to the legal
environmental regulations of the country of origin.

Printed and bound in Spain
by Litografia Rosés S.A., Barcelona

SECOND-CHANCE FAMILY

BY
KARINA BLISS

THE OTHER SISTER

BY
LYNDA SANDOVAL

MILLS & BOON

SECOND-CHANCE FAMILY

BY
KARINA BLISS

Karina Bliss figured she was meant to be a writer when at age twelve she began writing character sketches of her classmates. But a scary birthday milestone had to pass before she understood that achieving a childhood dream required more commitment than "when I grow up I'm going to be." It took this New Zealand journalist – a Golden Heart and Clendon Award winner – five years of "seriously writing" to get a book contract, a process she says helped put childbirth into perspective.

She lives with her partner and their son north of Auckland. Visit her on the web at www.karinabliss. com.

I'd like to dedicate this book to two wonderful women who saw promise in an unpublished writer and took her on board – my editor, Victoria Curran, and my agent, Karen Solem. Heartfelt thanks for everything you're teaching me about writing and publishing.

Acknowledgements

Thanks to Nancy Kashdin, who suggested the name Julia Evans, in a "Name a character" contest I ran through my website. And also thanks to my niece Cassie, and all my other nieces and nephews whose antics over the years provide inspiration for the kids in my books – the good ones, of course.

CHAPTER ONE

"JACK...WE WEREN'T expecting you in today.... Oh, Jack, I'm so sorry."

His secretary's eyes welled up as she opened her plump arms.

Jack forced himself to squeeze her shoulder as he sidestepped her embrace. "Thanks for your support, Heather. Has Mr. Yoshida arrived?"

Her mouth dropped along with her arms. "Why, yes, but surely you're not... I mean, Dave is covering for you...."

Jack dumped his briefcase on his desk and turned impatiently.

"They're in the boardroom," she finished.

"There's a lawyer called Grimble arriving in thirty minutes. Look after him until I'm free, will you? I'll be leaving after that." He pulled a crumpled list out of his pocket. "Meantime, ring the *New Zealand Herald* with the funeral notice."

Heather's eyes filled again. "Of course. Is there anything else I can do?"

His cell phone vibrated. Jack removed it from the breast pocket of his suit, checked the caller ID, then handed it over. "Yeah. Keep people off my back."

He hadn't meant to sound so harsh, but he had too much still to do to commiserate with second-tier friends and relatives. "I'm sorry." Taking a deep breath, Jack started again. "If you could accept condolences and give everyone the funeral details?"

With a sympathetic nod, Heather took the call. "Jack Galloway's phone. Can I help you?"

He'd forgotten how busy the aftermath of tragedy was. Getting the bodies shipped home, making the important phone calls and initiating funeral arrangements left no time to mourn.

Jack buttoned his suit jacket and straightened his tie, then strode down the corridor to the boardroom. Not that he had tears in him anymore. Grief had hollowed him out six years ago; there was nothing left now, except the echo of it.

And anger.

"I'm afraid I don't know any details of Friday night's accident," he heard Heather say behind him, and his fingers tightened convulsively around the boardroom's ornate door handle.

All these well-meaning people had a right to know, but to Jack they felt like rats gnawing at the corpses. He wanted to beat them off with sticks, then shake his brother's body until Anthony's teeth rattled. *You've had your joke, Ants. Now get up.*

Steeling himself, he pulled the heavy door open and entered the boardroom.

Half a dozen men looked up from one end of an enormous oval table, but Jack focused on only one. "Yoshida-san, my apologies for not being here to greet you."

The man returned his handshake warmly. "It is good to see you again, Galloway-san." They were old friends, but only in karaoke bars, belting out eighties hits at three in the morning, did they call each other by their first names.

Jack's vice president gaped at him. "I was just about to tell Mr. Yoshida and his associates that—"

"No need," Jack interrupted, "I'm here. Let's get down to business so these gentlemen can get to the airport in good time." He shook hands with the rest of the Japanese delegation. "What kind of weather will you be going back to in Tokyo?"

After exchanging pleasantries, they brought out the joint venture contracts that would take Jack's construction company into the big time—a multimillion-dollar residential subdivision in outer Auckland. He signed the papers and felt nothing.

As their lawyers tidied paperwork, he and Hiro Yoshida strolled to the floor-to-ceiling window. Twenty-five stories up, it normally offered panoramic views of Auckland's harbor, but on this early November day blinding torrents of spring rain lashed the pane. Jack could feel the last chill of a persistent winter seeping through the thick glass.

Patting his pockets, he retrieved the lighter and ten-pack of Marlboros he'd bought en route to the office. He offered one to Hiro.

One of the lawyers glanced up from the papers and cleared his throat. "I'm afraid New Zealand workplace laws prohibit—"

Hiro leaned forward so Jack could light his cigarette. "I think today," he said gravely, "we make an exception."

So he knew. Jack drew deeply, welcoming the once-familiar burn in his lungs, then exhaled. It felt like the first time he'd breathed in two-and-a-half days.

Hiro did the same, watching him through the fragrant smoke. "You should be sitting with your brother's body, my friend," he said simply, and Jack remembered the Japanese mourned their dead through wakes.

He delayed his answer by tapping his ash into a nearby pot containing a rubber plant. "He and his wife died while they were on holiday in New Caledonia. They…their remains are being flown home today."

"But you have other family, do you not?"

"No immediate family." *Not anymore.*

Hiro's black brows creased in surprise. "Your secretary said they had children."

Jack's sanity over the last horrific forty-eight hours had depended on not thinking too much about the children. "Yes, of course." He lifted the cigarette, saw his fingers were trembling, and dropped his hand. "They flew back early this morning with one of my sister-in-law's relatives. I'll see them this afternoon."

The older man took Jack's cigarette and said gently, "Go now, my friend."

Jack bowed. *"Hai,"* he said simply, then obediently left the room and headed straight back to his office. The kids needed familiar faces around them now, not some strange uncle they saw only a few times a year. He'd delegated the personal stuff to people who knew the family's day-to-day routines.

Others had gone to the house and turned on power and hot water, others had organized groceries and done the airport run to pick up the kids and their maternal aunt this morning.

But at 3:00 a.m., after lying in bed, staring at the ceiling, Jack had got up and driven to the house. He'd picked up Anthony's running shoes, still lying inside the front door, and taken Julia's apron from the hook in the kitchen. Methodically removed every sign that might suggest to their children they could be coming back at any moment.

He knew how much these things hurt.

Entering his office now, Jack saw a bald man pacing the plush carpet. He'd forgotten the lawyer. Their eyes met and Grimble immediately adopted a sympathetic expression.

Jack waved away his condolences. "Let's skip the formalities, shall we?" He gestured for the man to take a seat, but remained standing himself. "You said on the phone yesterday that I was the executor of the will...no, don't start reading the whole thing. Give me the guts of it."

Slightly flustered, Grimble cleared his throat. "The mortgage will be paid off by compulsory insurance, but your brother and his wife had no other policies."

"Teacher's salary, and Julia didn't work," Jack murmured. "It's what I expected.... So the sale of the house is the only money the children will have?" The deal he'd just signed started to mean something again. "I'll organize fiscal support through the guardian." This, he knew, Ants and Julia would have covered. "Who is it?"

"Why, you." Grimble seemed surprised he didn't know that.

Feeling as though he'd just taken a hit to the solar plexus, Jack sat down hard on the corner of his desk. "Me!"

The lawyer nodded as he checked his notes, then delivered the knockout punch. "You and somebody called Rosalind Valentine."

ROZ SAT ON HER best friend's couch in suburban Auckland, reading a story to Julia's just-orphaned three-year-old daughter. It was hard to lose yourself in a story you'd read twelve times since breakfast, but she tried.

"'The dump,'" she began, "'isn't a place most animals would choose to live, but Pinky the mouse wasn't one of them.'" On her lap, Cassie stared fixedly at the picture of the jaunty rodent, her small fingers absently pulling at a loose thread on the well-worn couch.

"Turn the page for me, honey," Roz said, to distract her, but Cassie was a multitasker and managed to keep her grip on the thread. What the hell, the foam was already showing through, anyway. It was that kind of house, unpretentious and restful, reflective of the people who—who *had*—lived here. Roz picked up her glass of water from the coffee table and sipped, trying to loosen her throat. She'd had to do it a lot since the airport run this morning. Be brave for the children.

Snatches of conversation drifted across the hall from the kitchen, where the latest bunch of well-wishers was dropping off casseroles and condolences. "I can't look at those poor kids without crying," said a neighbor.

Roz read louder. "'Pinky loved the growwwwl of the bulldozers…'" she paused for Cassie to growl "'…as they pushed the rubbish into neat piles.'" The house still felt cold from being shut up for two weeks, so she did up the buttons of the toddler's rainbow cardigan.

"I don't think," said another female voice, "that the baby understands."

Cassie growled again, with a deep, carrying ferocity that startled the unseen speakers into silence, and Roz gave her an approving squeeze. "This mini madam," Julia had always said fondly of her youngest, "is going to be an opera diva or a trade union activist."

Julia. The words on the page suddenly blurred.

"Read faster," Cassie ordered. The doorbell rang and Roz put the book aside. More flowers or offers of help.

"I'll get it." Julia's sister, Fiona Evans, bustled through the living room, pausing to pry loose the thread from Cassie's grip. "No, darling, that's naughty." A youthful forty-two, the petite salon-blonde had a refined English accent reminiscent of boarding school matrons. "Here, have one of these instead." She thrust the chocolate box on the table toward her niece.

"It's pretty close to dinnertime," Roz ventured, but cautiously, because Fee had been staking territory since she'd landed in New Zealand this morning. By 10:00 a.m. everyone had got the message—she was in charge. She was obviously using superefficiency to manage her grief. The sisters and their families had been on holiday together, and poor Fee had had to identify the bodies. But her behavior was exhausting the kids. And Roz was pretty sure that Julia would hate to see her daughter being stuffed with candy.

"Special circumstances," Fee insisted. She handed Cassie two chocolates and carried on to the door.

Roz waited until she was out of earshot. "Can I have one of those?"

Cassie popped the one she'd just licked into her god-mother's mouth.

Somewhere Julia would be laughing. "'The sea-gulls,'" Roz read, trying not to think about the soggy mess melting on her tongue, "'were rough and cheeky, but they had placed webbed feet on foreign shores, and in Pinky's eyes, that made them gods.'"

Jack came through the door. Roz gagged, then forced herself to swallow the chocolate. She'd thought she was ready for this.

Cassie cupped Roz's hot face with small, sticky hands and fixed her with a glare from eyes the same nut-brown as her hair. "Read...the...book," she said in a pitch-perfect impersonation of her Auntie Fee.

"'They liked being thought gods instead of scaveng-ing bandits, so they often visited his cardboard box home at the far end of the dump.'"

"Hey, Cassandra." Roz pinned her gaze to the page as Jack crouched down in front of them and offered Cassie a badly wrapped present. "I'm your uncle Jack, remember? I've bought you candy."

Cassie grabbed her blankie, scrunched her eyes shut and turned her head away. It was an old trick, but Jack immediately withdrew a couple of paces.

Roz fought the urge to follow her goddaughter's lead as she felt his attention swing to her. For a moment longer she stared at the mouse in the yellow-checkered waistcoat, standing proudly outside his ramshackle box.

How do you greet a man who once saw you lying on the carpet in a hysterical heap, begging him to stay? Lifting her chin, Roz eyeballed his left cheekbone and said coolly, "Hello, Jack."

A man who'd just lost the last of his generation of family? Through a throat raw from crying, she added hoarsely, "I'm sorry we have to meet under such circumstances."

"We got guardianship. Is that your doing?" demanded her ex-husband.

Startled, Roz met river-green eyes and saw the same boarded-up expression that used to throw her into gut-wrenching despair. Her control snapped. "And *bloody* sorry that we have to meet at all." Then the import of his words struck her, and she cried, "What?" simultaneously with Fiona, who'd come up behind him.

Cassie was peeking at Jack through half-closed lashes. "Where's Daddy?" she asked suddenly. The adults froze. "Oh, I forgot." She turned another page of the book with chubby fingers. "He's dead."

With a sob, Fiona fled to the kitchen. Roz gulped water, ridding herself of the chocolate's residual sweetness so she wouldn't throw up. Jack turned his back and walked to the window. Even slumped, his broad shoulders blocked out the anemic light of an overcast afternoon. "Oh, God," he muttered brokenly, "what a mess."

As she stared at him, inconsequential thoughts filtered through Roz's shock. He'd cut his dark blond hair short; it didn't touch his collar anymore. She recalled the only other time she'd seen him in a suit.

At their wedding.

Cassie growled, and automatically Roz began reading again, but her mind was elsewhere. They were *guardians?* "It's too dark," complained the little girl.

Dazed, Roz switched on the table lamp, and the mahogany coffee table gleamed in the spill of light.

Once, it had been hers and Jack's. Covered with papers, usually, because most nights he'd prepared building quotes while Roz did the books. But she'd always made him phone the slow payers. "You're a softie," he'd teased her, then bent to kiss her pregnant belly. "Except here."

They were guardians?

"'The seagulls thought Pinky was also a brave adventurer,'" Roz croaked, "'and he was, but only in his imagination.'" Needing order, she gathered loose strands of her limp hair into a tidier ponytail. "'You see, he'd lost the tip of his mousy little finger in an accident with some rusty roofing iron.'"

Out of the corner of her eye, she saw Jack straighten his shoulders. "I'll go see the other kids, then you, Fiona and I need to talk." The grimness was back in his tone.

Without looking up, Roz nodded. "'But Pinky *told* everyone he'd been in a real house, seen cheese in a mousetrap and coolly decided it was worth losing a finger for.'"

They were guardians!

Somewhere in the fear, a dangerous joy flickered to life.

CHAPTER TWO

JACK FOLLOWED FIONA INTO the kitchen and stopped abruptly. She was weeping on the shoulder of one woman, and was surrounded by others similarly afflicted. He spun on his heel, but it was too late.

"Oh, Jack," she sobbed, mascara trails bracketing her aquiline nose. "I still can't believe it. Why would they leave guardianship to you and Roz? It doesn't make sense."

He scanned the other faces and recognized nobody. "First I need to see Sam and Liam. Where are they?"

Fiona's eyes went blank and he frowned. Damn it, it was her job to know. She was the kids' rock now. It was a shame her husband, Roger, couldn't be here to add his customary steadiness.

"Liam popped next door with a neighbor," said a brunette. "Sam headed out to the garage for something."

Jack strode back through the living room, ignoring Roz. But he couldn't escape her voice. Every huskily delivered word drew blood.

"'Sometimes Pinky added a fat, black, hissing cat to his story, and everyone believed that, as well, because of his unusual roof.'"

The door wouldn't open; Jack broke into a sweat.

"'It was the rust-spotted lid of a biscuit tin with a picture of five kittens sitting in a basket….' The opening mechanism's faulty," she told him. "Hold the faceplate as you turn the handle."

Ants had always been hopeless at DIY.

"'For a mouse to choose to live under a picture of his worst enemies was considered a very brave thing to do—'"

Slamming the door shut behind him, Jack paused on the doorstep to suck in fresh air, chill with light rain. Ruthlessly, he rebuilt his self-control, until it was impregnable.

Drizzle dampened his face as he made his way to the garage. It was empty, and Jack despised himself for the involuntary spike of relief.

Of the three kids, fifteen-year-old Sam Evans, Julia's son by a previous marriage, was the one Jack knew best. And dreaded seeing most.

When at twenty-two, his baby brother had said he was marrying a woman who was not only five years his senior, but had a seven-year-old son, Jack had done his best to dissuade Anthony. Then he'd met Julia and Sam, and had shut up.

About to retrace his steps, Jack heard a cough to his right. "Sammy?" The old endearment came instinctively. For a moment there was silence.

"Over here." His nephew's voice had broken in the three months since Jack had last seen him.

Rounding the corner of the garage, he found the teenager sitting on the back doorstep, his long hands overhanging gangly knees. The hood of his dark sweatshirt was pulled over a baseball cap, hiding his lank, dark hair.

What Jack could see of his face was sunburned and peeling.

At least they'd had the holiday first.

Skirting the sagging clothesline and its load of rain-soaked beach towels, Jack sat on the wet step beside the boy. Sam's face was moist; from the shower or tears, Jack couldn't tell, and knew not to ask.

The acrid smell of tobacco hung in the air, and a mashed cigarette still smoldered by his nephew's feet. Seeing the direction of Jack's gaze, Sam covered the butt with his trainer.

"You got another one of those?"

Sam shot him a startled glance from bloodshot hazel eyes, then handed over a ten-pack of Marlboros and a box of matches. Jack lit two and handed him one.

"After the funeral," he said, returning the packet, "we give these up."

Sam's fingers trembled as he dragged on the cigarette. "I don't want to go to the funeral."

"Neither do I, but I think we're too old to get out of it."

"Auntie Fee says I have to be a pallbearer for Mum's coffin."

"You don't," Jack said harshly.

For five minutes, they sat in silence, smoking. His nephew's shoulder, where it touched his, held a terrible tension. But they didn't have the sort of relationship that would make a hug natural, and the last thing Jack wanted to do was make Sam uncomfortable.

"You need to talk?" Because talking, Jack thought bleakly, solved everything. *Yeah, right.*

His nephew shook his head, then drew a deep, shuddering breath. "If I don't have to carry one of the coffins, I'll go."

"Whatever you want, mate."

Again there was silence. Daylight was fading quickly, but Sam seemed equally reluctant to return to the house. And there was a comfort in sitting shoulder to shoulder on the step, even in the cold and the drizzle. Jack watched the cigarette burn to ash in his hand.

Yes, he still had the capacity to grieve. With one contemptuous glance, Roz had evoked emotions that he'd thought would never affect him again.

"So I guess," Sam ventured, "I stay an Evans now?"

Oh, hell. The teenager had asked Anthony to adopt him, and his brother had been over the moon. "I'll ask, but…probably." No point in raising false hopes.

"Do we have to go live with Auntie Fee and Uncle Roger? I mean, I like them but…" His voice trailed off.

Jack didn't want to hear apprehension, so he screened it out. "They seem the obvious choice."

"But not straightaway, right? I mean, we won't be going home with Auntie Fee next week or anything?"

"I'm sure she'll stay on in New Zealand for a month or so." The lower step was soft…rotten, probably, and some of the spouting looked rusty. Jack would put a crew onto it next week, get the place shipshape before it was listed for sale. The kids needed top dollar.

"No, she has to get back—I heard her tell Roz." The boy's voice rose. "I don't want to live in England."

"Hey, mate, let's calm down. Nothing's been decided yet."

"So we could live with you?" Sam absorbed Jack's

expression and immediately changed tack. "At least I could. Auntie Fee could take the small ones."

"You need to stay together. And with Fiona and Roger you'd get to live with your cousins." Jack suddenly realized he had no idea if they wanted them, and panic hit.

"They're dorks," said Sam flatly. "They were no fun on holiday."

It took Jack a second to focus. "Who? Your cous—"

"I'm not going anywhere before the end of the rugby season." Sam shoved himself off the step, eyes wild.

A light snapped on, the laundry door behind them opened and Fiona appeared. She'd repaired her makeup and her red mouth made a perfect O of shock. "Sam, are you *smoking?*"

Jack palmed his cigarette and took Sam's. "He was holding it for me while I tied my shoelace. Thanks, buddy."

"I mean it, Jack," Sam said hysterically. "I'll go live with Dad's family."

Instinctively, Jack dropped the cigarettes and caught him in a bear hug. Despite Sam's lankiness, the frame under all those baggy bro clothes was still that of a young boy. A lump caught in Jack's throat, cutting off a reassurance.

For a moment Sam let himself be held, then, with a sob, he pulled free. Furiously wiping his sleeve across his eyes, he pushed past Fiona and loped into the house.

"What's he talking about?" Her voice rose in panic. "Of course he's not living with those lowlifes—"

"Stop," said Jack sharply. "Send someone he knows well to see that he's okay. Then we'll talk this through in the study. Bring Roz."

Her shoulders squared, but her bright mouth trembled. "I want those children, Jack."

Relief washed over him, easing the ache that had begun when he'd seen Roz with Cassie. "Then I don't foresee any problem."

HE WAS GOING TO OFFLOAD the kids on Fiona.

Roz knew it as soon as she walked into Anthony's study and saw them sitting side by side on the ancient leather sofa, drinking tea. Jack hated tea.

Smiling, Fee picked up the teapot. "Roz, let me pour you a cup," she offered. "Milk, no sugar, isn't it?"

Barely knowing this woman, and without consulting Roz as coguardian, Jack was going to ship them off to a foreign country. Because he couldn't handle rejoining the human race.

Fury combusted in Roz's chest, making it hard to breathe, but she welcomed it. Angry, she could deal with him. "You son of a bitch. You're going to completely disregard what Anthony and Julia want, aren't you?"

Fee gasped and the tea she was pouring splashed into the saucer, but Jack didn't even blink. He picked up a paper napkin and began mopping up the spill.

Her color high, Fee got her breath back. "How can you talk to him like—"

"She's grieving," interrupted Jack. "We all are." He took the teapot from Fee and finished pouring with a steady hand. "Which makes it even more important to keep emotion out of this discussion."

Roz narrowed her eyes. "You'd like that, wouldn't you?" Dear God, she'd spent the last five-and-a-half years schooling herself to accept and forgive, and already she wanted to hurt him. She took the chair opposite the couch. "What about the kids…are you even going to ask them?"

His face impassive, Jack held out a cup of tea. "The children are too young to make a decision."

She made no move to take it. "Liam and Cassie might be. What about Sam?"

A flicker of emotion appeared in the green depths of his eyes and was gone. "Sam will come around." He plonked the cup in front of her. "And let's get one thing very clear before we go any further. You and I were appointed guardians. There was nothing specified about custody." Jack turned to Fee. "In New Zealand, the two roles aren't automatically synonymous."

So *that's* how he justified it to his conscience. "Of course they meant custody, as well," Roz declared.

His attention swung back to her like a club. "What makes you so sure?"

She swallowed. "It was over six years ago right after Liam was born. We were expecting Thomas and I only agreed…" Frightened by the blaze in his eyes, she rushed to get the words out. "…because we were just named as backup to your mother." Except Joyce Galloway had passed away two months ago. "For God's sake, Jack, what were the odds?"

"I knew you were behind it," he said bitterly.

"What I don't understand—" Fee adjusted her position so that her shoulder closed Roz out "—is why Julia chose you, and not me and Roger? I remember her saying you don't like spending time with the children."

Obviously, Ju had never said why. Jack's face froze and Roz intervened. "Actually, he spent a lot of time with Sam and Liam before…" His gaze flicked briefly to hers, and her throat closed.

"Before?" Fee prompted. Silver bangles jangled on her wrist as she picked up her cup…jangled on Roz's blistered nerves. If Fee didn't have the sensitivity to make the connection then Roz wasn't going to make it for her.

"Nothing." Roz sipped her tea, moistened dry lips.

Jack got up and started pacing the room. "I'm happy to take fiscal responsibility, but custody isn't even an issue." His lawyerlike detachment raised her hackles again. "Roz and I are divorced, and neither of our life-styles are conducive to looking after child—"

"Speak for your lifestyle, not mine!" He'd become a hard-partying serial dater within days of leaving her.

"Why?" The grit was back in his voice. "Have you settled down with a third husband?"

Roz smiled at him. "No, Jack. I've finally learned that if you want loyalty you get a dog. Though my second husband was a huge improvement on my first. After the divorce, we even managed to stay friends."

His mouth tightened. "These kids need what they've lost, which is a mother and a father and a stable home."

"Which Roger and I can offer them," said Fee.

Roz turned back to Fee and impulsively reached for her hands. "On the other side of the world, away from their friends, their community. I know it's not your fault—" she said, as Fee's cold fingers spasmed under hers "—but they hardly know you."

"We just spent twelve lovely days together, and I owe her—" Fee stopped. Carefully, she removed her hands from Roz's. "They're my sister's children…my blood. And their grandmother's in the U.K." Julia and Fee's elderly mother lived in a nursing home and was too infirm to travel. "You might know the children best, Rosalind, but you no longer have a relationship with them that would be recognized by law."

"All I'm asking is that we don't rush into a decision about their future three days after their parents' death."

"We need to!" Fee's cup clattered into the saucer. "I have to get back to the U.K. to my own two boys. It makes sense to take the children with me now."

As delicately as she could, Roz raised the issue that had been bothering her. "Can you really cope with raising five children?"

Julia had always described her sister as a multitasking perfectionist in need of an intervention. "I bought that because it reminded me of Fee," she'd said once, gesturing to a fridge magnet. It showed a sixties housewife with wide eyes and a toothy smile, and a caption reading, "It's been lovely but I have to scream now."

Under her foundation, red mottled Fiona's cheeks. "What are you implying?"

"Only that it's a huge responsibility. You need time to think this through."

"I know my duty." Fee's English accent grew even more clipped. "And as far as I'm concerned, if Jack's happy, that's it."

"I'm sorry," said Roz firmly, "but as a guardian, I have to be happy, too." She had no idea if that was true or not, but someone had to put these kids' interests first.

"Oh, for God's sake, Roz, get real." Jack was suddenly towering over her. "Who's going to look after them in the meantime? I've just signed a big construction contract, and you have a career. We both live in the city, miles from their schools. And employing some stranger as a nanny isn't going to help the kids."

"I'll take a leave of absence from my job and move in here for a couple of months." Roz listened to her declaration with the same astonishment as the other two. Her heart jumped into her throat, but she wouldn't renege. "They need to stay in their own home and stick to their normal routines—at least until the first shock passes. Finish the school year."

"And after Christmas they come to us," said Fee.

Roz tried to read Jack's expression, and found it impossible. "And after Christmas we make a final decision," she countered.

"No." He shook his head. "Their parents are dead. To pretend that life's ever going to get back to normal is cruel. Long term, they'll deal better with the changes if they're all made at once."

He'd done that to her, leaving her soon after the tragedy that had shattered their lives and their marriage. The clean break that had left jagged, painful scars. Roz wouldn't let him do that to Julie and Anthony's children.

"You're so wrong," she said passionately. "Right now, these kids need the nurturing only their friends and community can give them." *All the help that you and I turned down.* "Then they'll be equipped to face whatever changes are necessary—"

Jack was shaking his head again; Roz swiveled back to Fee. "And if they end up with you, well, then you've had time to make preparations." She could see the other woman was considering the idea, but then Fee glanced up at Jack for approval.

"No," he said again.

Roz grabbed the cuff of his jacket and hauled him to the other side of the room. "We can help them through this," she said in a low voice. "I know we can."

His mouth twisted. "Because we're so well-adjusted?"

"Because we know what it's like to lose the person you love most."

A muscle tightened in his square jaw. "Which is why," he said harshly, "I can't let you use these kids as surrogates."

But she'd already questioned her motives. "I can understand why you'd think that, but that's not what I'm doing."

"You'll get hurt, Roz." There was the trace of a plea in his voice.

"I know," she admitted. "But the kids' needs come first."

"Damn it, if you won't protect yourself, I will. No!"

And she knew she'd have to say the unsayable, the one thing that would rip out what was left of Jack's heart, the one thing that would kill whatever hope she'd ever had of making her peace with this man.

"You owe me." She didn't have to explain; it was always between them. The thing that had driven them apart, the thing she'd always sworn to him she didn't believe.

For a long moment, they hung on the gallows of the past.

"I always knew you blamed me," he said conversationally, but his eyes were so bleak Roz had to bite her tongue to stop herself taking back her words. If guilt would buy time for the kids, she had to use it.

"Okay." He moved away, closer to Fee. "I'll apply for temporary custody for two months. Then we reassess."

Roz relaxed her jaw and released her tongue, tasted the iron tang of blood. "Thank you."

"I need to go," said her ex-husband, the man who'd cried with her over their baby's tiny coffin. He brushed past her to get to the door. "I'll be able to give them up when the time comes," he said coldly. "Make sure you can."

CHAPTER THREE

LIAM GALLOWAY SAT in the narrow hall, his back against the study door, kicking the skirting board with the heel of his orange sneakers—same color as his hair—and getting a mutinous satisfaction from the dirty scuff marks.

Sam had said he couldn't go to Mum and Dad's funeral, and he wanted Auntie Roz and Auntie Fee to tell Sam he wasn't the boss. Except he didn't want to knock, because he could hear Uncle Jack's raised voice, and Liam was a tiny bit scared of his uncle.

It wasn't that he was so big…Dad was big, too. But Uncle Jack never smiled, at least not at Liam. He'd seen him stroke Cassie's hair once when Mum had left the room for a moment and Cassie had been asleep on the couch, but Uncle Jack hadn't looked happy doing it. Cassie probably had food in her hair. She usually did. Uncle Roger was much nicer—

The door jerked open and Liam tumbled backward, crying out in pain as his head connected with Uncle Jack's shin.

"What the hell are you doing, sitting there?"

Liam couldn't help it; he started to cry. His head throbbed, he'd had a fright and Uncle Jack sounded mad at him. He felt himself lifted in strong arms, cradled. "Mate, I'm so sorry, I didn't see you. Where does it hurt?"

But Liam didn't want a cuddle from Uncle Jack. He squirmed out of his uncle's grasp, running toward Auntie Roz—and was intercepted by Auntie Fee.

"Oh, sweetie." Liam found himself held in an embrace he couldn't shift, and gave in, resting his head against her breast and succumbing to hiccuping sobs.

"I want Mum," he wailed, even though he knew she was in heaven. Couldn't she just sneak down behind God's back?

Someone was vigorously rubbing at the sore spot on his head, just like Mum did, and Liam blinked away his tears. It was Roz, he discovered. Still, the pain went away and he felt better.

Wiping his nose on his sleeve, he sat up and shot a look at Uncle Jack, embarrassed for crying in front of him.

Uncle Jack's jaw was clenched, so Liam figured he was still mad, and ducked his head. The glimpse of his sneakers reminded him of his question.

"Sam says I'm not allowed to go to the funeral and that Cassie and me are getting a babysitter. But I can go, can't I?"

He'd asked Roz, but Auntie Fee, who was straightening the collar of his Spider-Man sweatshirt, answered. "Absolutely not."

Liam opened his mouth to protest.

"That reminds me," interrupted Uncle Jack from the other side of the room. "Sam had some crazy idea, Fiona, that you were going to force him to be a pallbearer. Don't worry, I cleared up that misunderstanding."

"Oh," said Auntie Fee faintly. "Good."

"I'll do it," volunteered Liam, though he had no idea what a pallbearer was.

"You're not going," said Auntie Fee and Auntie Roz together.

Liam stuck out his chin. "Mum and Dad would want me to go." Over the past three days, using their names had settled any argument. Sleeping in Sam's room, getting Coke instead of juice, letting Froggie out in the lounge when they'd picked the tank up from the neighbors who'd been minding him.

Auntie Roz took his hand. "Honey, funerals are very sad and you've never been to one before. Auntie Fee and I think you should stay home."

Liam scrunched up his face and tried to cry. It was strange how he kept crying when he didn't want to, but couldn't when he did.

"If Liam wants to go, he should be allowed to," said Uncle Jack.

Liam was so surprised he unscrunched his face.

"Jack, no," said Auntie Roz.

"He's too young," said Auntie Fee.

Liam went to Uncle Jack. "I'm six and everyone's been saying how brave I am. An' I have to say goodbye properly."

The tears threatened, but somehow Liam knew now was not the time to look like a baby. Uncle Jack hunkered down and put a hand on his shoulder, and Liam tried not to squirm under its weight. "You know they'll be in coffins," he said in a very serious voice, "which will be buried in the ground?"

Liam nodded and tried to listen carefully to everything Uncle Jack told him about what happened at funerals. He started to get nervous, but then something distracted him. He waited until Uncle Jack had finished before he mentioned the funny thing.

"Your eyes are the same color as James Zombie Maisy's are."

Uncle Jack blinked.

"That's our cat," Liam said helpfully. "Me and Cassie and Sam all got to choose a name. Mine's James the red engine, Sam chose Zombie because he's a Goth, and Cassie chose Maisy, which is some dumb mouse. We told her the cat is a boy," he added darkly, "but she won't change it."

He waited for Uncle Jack to say something, but he only blinked again. "Okay, I'm going to go tell Mum and Dad I'm coming to their funeral."

Uncle Jack's hold tightened painfully on his shoulder. "But, Liam—"

"I write them letters and an angel takes them every night, just like Auntie Fee said." Slowly, his uncle's gaze lifted to Auntie Fee's and Liam got a teeny bit scared of him again. "I mean, I know they're already watching us from heaven…." Liam didn't want Uncle Jack to think he was stupid or anything. "But the clouds must get in the way sometimes, right? So I have to write to them."

"Right," said Roz, when Uncle Jack opened his mouth to speak. She pulled him free of his uncle's grip and gave him a gentle push toward the door. "Give them my love, honey."

Behind him, Uncle Jack made a rude noise, but Liam found himself in the hall with the door closed before he could ask any further questions.

He heard Roz say, "Just because you don't believe

in anything anymore, Jack Galloway, is no…" Her voice faded out as she moved away from the door.

Liam considered putting his ear to the keyhole, but then thought of what Sam's face would look like when Liam told him he was—so there!—going to the funeral, and ran off to find his brother.

JACK DELIVERED his brother's eulogy with a hangover.

With every sentence, his stomach roiled and his head hammered. Cold sweat beaded on his brow and trickled into his eyes, stinging and blurring the words on the page. Fortunately, he knew them by heart.

It was a good speech, but his delivery sucked because his entire concentration was focused on not throwing up. Somewhere, his father was calling him an irresponsible loser.

His relief when he finished without barfing was so intense he swayed under a wave of dizziness and had to grip the podium.

The congregation came back into focus. Roz, dressed in a scarlet coat, because Julia had once joked that she wanted clown colors at her funeral.

Above it her face was pale, and there were dark shadows under her kingfisher-blue eyes. She looked like he felt—ragged, weary, battle-worn—though she managed a smile for Cassie, who sat next to her with the pastor's wife, happily playing with a string of shiny beads.

Once Jack had given Liam permission to attend the funeral, the adults had decided Cassie should come, too. She was too young to know what was going on.

"But," Roz said, "when she's older, she'll be glad to have been included."

In keeping with the theme, the little girl wore a garish pink fairy dress with gauzy wings, over purple-and-green stockings and pink sheepskin boots. On her head, a golden crown sat askew on a red Santa hat.

As though sensing Jack's scrutiny, she looked up. "McDonald's now?" she called hopefully. Laughter rippled through the congregation, momentarily lightening the sadness.

Even Jack smiled—until he shook his sore head. "Not yet, sweetheart." He caught Fiona's disapproving frown and straightened his lollipop tie, then made his way back to the front pew, where she sat with the boys, dressed in a severe black suit because she considered flouting tradition disrespectful. Jack was in Fiona's bad books, a situation he was keen to change.

In the last couple of days he'd made some serious errors of judgment.

The first had been to say yes to temporary custody with Roz, after she'd blindsided him with her "You owe me" comment.

The second had been getting drunk last night. There'd been too many suppressed emotions threatening to swamp him. He'd needed to release some of the terrible pressure; instead, Jack had simply passed out.

But the third mistake—the one he most regretted—had been letting Liam come to his parents' funeral.

The boy had started the service in high excitement, his eyes bright. Standing at the church door in his Sunday best, he'd handed out programs, conscious of being the center of attention, though not sure why.

Now his shoulders slumped and he leaned, bewildered, against his older brother. They made an incongruous sight. Sam, in his customary black, had painted his fingernails bright green as a concession to his mother. Liam, his short carrot-colored hair ruthlessly combed by Fiona, wore a suit and tie and looked like a miniature of his dad. *Oh, Ants.*

Roz leaned across Sam and whispered something to Liam.

"No, I wanna stay!" His petulant cry cut through the hymn, being sung tremulously by Anthony's high school class.

Jack edged past Fiona to stand next to the boy. "It's okay if you want to leave."

Vigorously shaking his head, Liam slid closer to his brother. Jack met Roz's accusing stare and turned to the front. Damn it, he'd tried. But he closed his eyes on a rush of self-disgust that had nothing to do with his hangover.

The hymn finished and there was a collective shuffling as those with seats sat down. Okay, a fourth bloody mistake—not booking a bigger chapel than the small one on-site at the cemetery.

How the hell was Jack supposed to know that Ants and Julia belonged to every social, community and sporting group in suburbia? Mourners spilled into the vestibule, where they listened to the service through hastily erected speakers.

Only the immediate family's long pew was half-empty. This was ridiculous.

Before the minister resumed the service, Jack stepped back out into the aisle. "Listen, there's at least eight seats up here. Please use them."

People trickled to the front. An elderly lady, her hat smelling of mothballs, gave him a quick hug. "Bless you."

So help him, if one more stranger touched him… He needed a cigarette, he needed a Tylenol, he needed an escape from the neediness closing around him like a trap.

The service resumed; Cassie soon got restless and was taken outside to play. The minister invited Roz to speak.

As she passed, Jack concentrated on rereading his notes in the program's margin, but her scent, faintly floral, clutched at his memory. He hadn't seen her for five-and-a-half years, and she still felt like his wife.

He reminded himself that she'd remarried within a month of their divorce; reminded himself that she'd emotionally blackmailed him now into taking temporary custody of the kids. The feeling went away.

"We're here to mourn, yes," she began in a husky voice, "but also to celebrate the lives of two very special people and to be thankful they were in *our* lives."

Fiona nudged him. "Tell Sam to uncover his head while we're in church," she whispered.

Jack leaned across Liam, wincing as the child shrank back. "It's okay, mate. Sam…your aunt wants you to lower your hoodie."

The teenager lifted his head and Jack froze. Under the hood, his nephew was crying, helplessly and silently. Instinctively, Jack pulled his sunglasses out of the breast pocket of his suit. "Forget it. Here."

Gratefully, Sam disappeared behind Jack's aviators.

Liam took one look at the tears trickling under Sam's mirrored shades, and burst into noisy sobs that ripped at Jack's conscience. One mistake he *could* fix.

Grasping the boy's clammy hand, he tugged gently. "Let's go."

"No!" Liam struggled to free himself. "I wanna stay with Mum and Dad." As Jack tried to quiet him, the child tipped into hysteria. "I want them back."

His whole body breaking into a sweat, Jack picked him up. "It's okay, son." At the podium, Roz stopped midsentence, looking stricken.

Fiona started to rise. "Stay," he barked. "I'll take care of it."

Holding the struggling child tight, he strode down the aisle, the boy screaming in impotent rage. "You bring them back. Right now! I want them now!"

His small hands pummeled Jack's face and chest, his thin legs kicked wildly, but Jack held on, ignoring the sharp nails being raked across his cheek, oblivious to the shocked faces. His tone soothing, he repeated over and over, "You're going to be okay, mate. It's going to be okay."

Outside, the gray clouds that had shrouded the city for days had lifted, and sunlight streamed over the sodden trees and gardens surrounding the chapel. Mist lifted off the dewy grass, as well as the dark earth around the newly dug graves that lay beyond a stand of trees to their left.

Jack walked away from the building to the fountain in front of it, then shakily put the shrieking child on his feet, holding Liam's arms to his sides. Eyes clenched tightly, the boy kept hollering, hoarser now, but unrelenting.

"You buggerhead, you bring back my mum and dad. You bring them back right now!"

No reassurances Jack made got through to him.

A familiar voice behind him said, "Let me take him."

Abruptly, Liam stopped his screaming and opened tear-swollen eyes. "Uncle Luke!" Wrenching free of Jack's grip, he flung himself at the other man, clutching his legs. "D-d-don't let him take me," he managed to gulp between the sobs now shaking his entire body. "D-d-don't let him t-t-take me away!"

Aghast, Jack stepped back. Luke Carter crouched down and caught Liam's face in his large hands. "Liam, look at me," he said sharply. "Stop this yelling now," he ordered. "You hear me? No more."

For a moment the little boy looked up at him, bewildered, then with a wail threw himself into the big man's arms.

"It's okay, son, we're all here for you." His gray eyes met Jack's. "It's going to be okay." They were the same words Jack had used on Liam.

He didn't believe them, either.

Jack went around the corner of the building and vomited in the flower beds, amid the yellow daylilies and purple pansies. Then he slid down the chapel's redbrick wall, warm against his back, and closed his eyes.

A few minutes later, a shadow blocked the spring sun.

"You did the right thing, bringing him out," said Luke. "Give him a couple of days and he'll forgive you."

Jack looked up at the foster brother he hadn't seen in seventeen years. Still an imposing bastard, with swimmer's shoulders and an all-too-familiar scowl.

Luke added, "What jackass let him come to the funeral in the first place?"

"Me."

"Oh." His scowl softened.

But Jack didn't want sympathy. "Where is he?"

"Liz…my wife is looking after him. He knows her. He'll be fine."

"Pull me up," said Jack. "That's the last hymn and we're pallbearers."

Luke hauled him to his feet, but didn't release his hand. Instead, he gripped it hard. "Jack."

There was such a wealth of understanding in his voice that Jack's eyes burned. How ironic that the bitter enemy of his youth was the only one who understood his loss.

And shared it.

He returned Luke's pressure. "You didn't come to the family pew."

"I wasn't sure you'd want me there."

"He was your brother, too."

Luke and Anthony had been close as kids. It was one of the many things Jack had been jealous of, once. He'd needed maturity to understand that his rival had also suffered through being bought up by Frank Galloway, who'd neglected his own sons to coach his foster one to Olympic swimming gold. Eventually, Luke had suffered Jack's earlier fate and been disinherited when he rebelled—in Luke's case by throwing away his swimming career, the reason he'd originally been fostered. But then, it had always been Frank's way or the highway.

Luke said gruffly, "Thank you, that means a lot to me." He released Jack's hand.

Their foster brother had reestablished contact with Anthony after marrying Liz, but Jack had resisted a meeting—too busy. Still, Ants and Luke had been spending a lot of time together.

Through the chapel's open window, Jack recognized

the last chorus of "Amazing Grace" and swallowed. "It's time."

Luke started walking; Jack couldn't move. His foster brother came back and put a supporting arm around his shoulders. Wordlessly, the two men made their way back into the church to carry their brother to his final resting place.

Jack could almost envy Ants the peace.

CHAPTER FOUR

"WHAT DO YOU MEAN, you can't do it?"

Hearing the rising alarm in Roz's voice, Fiona struggled to pull herself together. Using her balled handkerchief, she dabbed at the tears streaming down her face, but they came faster than she could wipe them away.

Her gaze fell on the coffins and an image of her sister emerged—lying pale and small and still on a slab in a foreign morgue. Sweat popped out on Fiona's brow and she jammed the hanky against her mouth while she forced herself to swallow rising bile.

"Fee?" Roz whispered fiercely. "We're already one short if Jack doesn't come back with Liam."

But how could she find the strength to carry Julia, when the burden was already so heavy she could barely raise her head? If only Roger and the boys were here…but she'd insisted her husband take their shocked sons straight home from New Caledonia. That would also free her to concentrate on comforting Julia's traumatized children. Fiona was always doing things "for the best" and regretting them.

Oh, so bitterly regretting them.

The tears became heaving, silent sobs. Fiona lifted the hanky from her mouth and pressed it against her swollen eyes. "I'm s-s-sorry, but I just c-c-can't."

Roz slid along the bench and started pleading. "But yesterday you were adamant about carrying Julia's casket. Remember?"

Helplessly, Fiona shook her head.

"Take a minute," the younger woman soothed. "You'll be fine." But the jerky pats on her back told Fiona she thought otherwise.

Fee stiffened. How dare Roz disapprove of her? "Find someone else!"

"Because anyone will do?" Roz's tight laugh held a touch of hysteria. "Dear God—" Her voice caught. "Do you think this is easy for any of us?"

But Fiona wasn't listening. She was staring at the pallbearers making their way to the front, and her brief spurt of anger became a terror so real she nearly ran screaming out of the church after Liam. Nothing could make her touch her sister's coffin at that moment. Because in this sacred place God would surely strike her dead—if there was any justice.

She started to whimper. "Please don't make me."

A tentative hand touched her forearm. "I'll do it, Auntie."

Some part of Fiona knew she should say no, but she was past rationality now. "Oh, Sam…" She sagged against the pew in relief. "Would you?" Raising her head, Fiona flinched as Roz's eyes blazed into hers.

"He's been through enough. Pull yourself together, *now!*"

"Roz," said Sam, "I want to do it."

SOME QUALITY IN Sam's voice cut through Roz's panic. She closed her eyes and took a deep, deep breath. *You can keep it together,* she told herself, *You have to.* Opening her eyes, she looked at Sam. "Take off those sunglasses."

Green nail polish glinted in the light streaming through the stained-glass windows as he removed the shades. Roz barely knew him these days; he spent most of his time holed up in his room with his computer. His mother had worried about his antisocial behavior. Hazel eyes met hers now, red-rimmed but steady. "I want to do it," he said again.

"Okay."

"Don't give Auntie Fee a hard time."

She made herself do the right thing. "Fee…I'm sorry." But Roz couldn't feel pity for Julia's sister. Sam's interests should have come first.

Fiona nodded stiffly. The woman looked a mess, more human than Roz had ever seen her, and suddenly pity did come. She handed over a wad of tissues, which was accepted without thanks.

Fine, thought Roz wearily. She needed her energy for other things now.

As she and Sam stood next to the caskets, waiting for the last pallbearers to join them, he surprised her by lowering his hoodie. His hair was a flattened mess, but it didn't matter. Emotion rose up and choked her. "Your parents," she managed to say in a low voice, "would be so proud of you."

He made no sign he'd heard her, but his Adam's apple bobbed convulsively as he stared down at his boots.

Jack came down the aisle with Luke Carter, the foster brother she'd only met since the divorce. But Roz didn't have time to wonder at the men's obvious rapport, because Jack had caught sight of Sam and was looking thunderous. She forestalled him by catching his hand, so warmly familiar that her heart lurched. "It's okay," she murmured, "he offered."

Jack glanced down at their joined hands and Roz broke contact. But he recaptured her icy fingers and scanned her face. "Are *you* up to this?"

His concern, so unexpected, so poignant, nearly broke the last of her control. Seeing her reaction, all emotion left his face, and a sharp, familiar pain steadied Roz. *Some things never change,* she thought bitterly, and pulled free.

"I'm fine." Furious that he could still make her feel something after so many years, she took her position alongside Julia's casket, her eyes boring into her ex-husband's back as he went to stand next to Anthony's coffin.

The minister gave the signal and Roz closed her eyes briefly to refocus—*I don't want to carry you mad, Ju*— then reached for the ornate handle. Across the polished mahogany lid, her gaze met Sam's.

Silently, she transmitted what mental strength she had left, and saw him take a deep breath. *Yes. Breathe, Sam, even when it hurts.*

Roz followed his example, then lifted her share of her best friend's slight weight and, tears spilling down her cheeks, followed the pallbearers carrying Anthony's coffin. *I promise you, Ju, that I'll do my best for your kids.*

As the procession passed the front pew, Fiona mouthed, "I'm sorry." But Roz couldn't return her tentative smile. When it had really mattered, Julia's sister had dropped the ball.

Roz fixed her blurred gaze on Jack's unyielding back. *I don't know how the hell this is going to work,* she told him silently, *but we're keeping them.*

Whether you like it or not.

AFTER THE BURIAL, Roz wandered away from the crowds to a bench under a mature oak where Luke Carter's wife sat, supervising Liam and Cassie. Roz needed a respite, and this near-stranger seemed to understand, because other than a welcoming smile, Liz made no overtures.

A young man disengaged from the mourners and loped to a low-slung Nissan Skyline—Dirk Evans, Julia's brother-in-law from her first marriage. Like Sam, he was dressed tough, but unlike her nephew his persona was real.

Sam's father, Lee Evans, had been the white sheep from a very black flock of third-generation petty criminals. A cop, he'd been killed in the line of duty while policing his old neighborhood. Dirk was attending the funeral as the family's representative, but Roz suspected he really wanted to find out if Sam was inheriting any money.

She'd let Jack handle him.

The engine throbbed to life, blue smoke pumping from the oversize muffler. Hip-hop blared through the stereo as the car accelerated and sped out of sight. Jack had obviously made it clear that Sam's interests were being protected.

Relieved, Roz watched Liam chase Cassie around some camellias. Aging petals, once white, now the color of tea, fell to the saturated ground as the kids tore past the manicured trees. Cassie had kicked off her boots and the soggy feet of her kaleidoscope stockings flicked water in her wake.

I wish I had that kind of resilience, Roz thought, then realized she'd spoken the words aloud when Liz said gently, "It will come back."

She sounded like she was speaking from experience, but before Roz could ask, there was a wail somewhere behind them. Liz looked at her watch. "Right on cue."

Rising from the bench, she walked over to a baby carriage that had been partially obscured by the tree trunk.

Roz's throat went dry and her heart started pounding. "I didn't know you had a baby." She collected her scattered wits. "How old is…?"

"Joe is two months." Liz sat down again, flicking her ash-blond hair over her shoulder as she calmed the infant. She obviously had no idea of her companion's history, and Roz was grateful.

"We had him a year earlier than we'd planned," Liz confided. "He makes the last year of my mayoralty very challenging…don't you, darling?" She dropped a kiss on the downy black hair. "I figured at thirty-five we should start trying early in case it took a while, but I got pregnant first time." Her smile faltered as she addressed someone behind Roz. "What have I said, honey?"

Roz peeled her eyes off the baby and turned to see Luke staring at her with a mix of concern and apology— the usual reaction.

"It's okay," she assured him. "Really." She turned back to a baffled Liz. "May I hold him?" She took the infant, careful to support his neck. "He's beautiful."

It had taken a couple of years of therapy to be able

to do this, but she'd always loved babies and she wasn't going to pass up the joy of holding them. Cassie had been her first success.

Yes, she was resilient.

Bubbles formed on the baby's mouth as he cooed at her, and Roz smiled. "Oh, you're a flirt."

"Hmm," said Liz. "Wonder where he gets that from?"

"His mother," Luke replied, and Liz laughed. Beyond him, Roz noticed Jack watching them—a still figure in the moving crowd—and her breath hitched painfully. He was too far away for her to read his expression, but his whole bearing was one of yearning. She lifted a hand to wave him over, but he'd already turned away.

Fortunately, because Roz already regretted the impulse.

"I TOLD YOU Liam shouldn't have come to the funeral."

Needing a distraction, Jack turned to Fiona. "You were right. I should have listened to you."

Her expression softened. "You meant well, I know. But let's face it, Jack, you haven't got my experience."

Neither had Roz, and she'd also made the right call. But he appreciated Fiona's restraint. In her place, he wouldn't have been so understanding. "No." Six weeks as a parent didn't amount to expertise. He passed a hand over his eyes, trying to erase the picture of Roz with the Carters' baby.

"I just hope—" Fiona looked at his face. "Never mind, it's not like I did so well today, either. Shall we walk?" Tucking her arm through his, she led him through the gardens. "Smell those magnolias."

"You just hope…?"

"That Liam doesn't have nightmares about this."

Jack glanced across the garden to where the boy swung upside down from a tree branch. He was happy again now, but kids expressed grief differently from adults, passing in and out of intense feelings. Jack had done some quick research, and it scared the hell out of him.

"I could still take them now," Fiona said hopefully.

He resisted the temptation. "We were awarded an interim parenting order this morning, and anyway, Sam won't go. I've already told him he can play out the rugby season. No, I won't split up the kids," he added before she could suggest it. On that point, he agreed with Roz.

"Jack, I need some reassurance before I leave tomorrow."

"What kind of reassurance?"

Her hand tightened on his sleeve. "Your guarantee that the children will come to me and Roger."

He hesitated, strangely unwilling to commit to the decision he'd already made privately. He wasn't in a fit state today.

Across the park, Liam swung out of the tree, landing in a crouch next to Cassie. "I'm a big bad lion and I'm going to eat you up," he growled, and his little sister squealed delightedly and took off.

Liam caught Jack's eye and terror tightened his expression. Scrambling to his feet, he pelted as fast as he could after her.

Fiona was watching, too. "Promise me, Jack," she said softly.

He wasn't fit to care for children.

"You have my word," he said.

CHAPTER FIVE

"MISS VALENTINE IS IN THE toilet," said Liam in his best telephone manner.

In the middle of flushing away the accident in Cassie's discarded panties, Roz gasped. A mistake. Holding her breath, she called nasally, "Liam, take a message," then went back to shallow inhalations.

"No, you don't have to ring back, I'm taking the phone in to her… Hello?" His puzzled face appeared around the bathroom door. "They hung up."

"No kidding." Gingerly holding Cassie's offending panties between forefinger and thumb, Roz walked to the back door, tossed them into the black rubbish bag outside, then pulled the drawstring tight and tied it in a triple knot.

"You're s'posed to wash them," Liam pointed out.

"And you're *not* supposed to answer my mobile. How many times do I have to…" His face fell and she bit her tongue. "Try and remember next time, hey?"

He followed her back to the bathroom and watched as she lathered up to her elbows. "You wash your hands a lot."

But she had other things on her mind. "Any idea who was on the phone?" *Please make it Jack.* He'd left for a four-day business trip to Tokyo immediately after the funeral. Was he calling in on the way home from the airport? She needed to know so she could have the house clean and the kids cute and cheerful.

"Your boss lady," said Liam.

Bloody hell. Roz was at a critical stage in several projects and had confidently assured her immediate superior she'd put in three or four hours a day at home. That had been a condition of her leave of absence.

Except Liam was home from school with a tummy ache that had miraculously cleared up at 9:10 a.m., and Cassie wouldn't nap when she was supposed to.... Wait a minute. "Cass, where have you got to? Come and get your bottom washed, sweetie."

No answer. Uh-oh. After living with Cassandra Galloway for a week, Roz knew silence meant mischief. Hurriedly rinsing her hands, she turned off the faucet. Which turned and turned. Another thing to add to her growing repair list.

"Cass, honey?" she called again, reaching for a towel. "Wait, how did *this* get here?" Freshly laundered this morning, it had a long smear of clay-colored mud across the white terry cloth.

"The model train Uncle Roger bought me in Noumea needed a wash." Liam caught her eye and obviously thought it politic to look sick again. "Are you mad at me, Auntie Roz?"

"No." She unclenched her jaw and gave him a hug. "Next time, use a rag, okay?" "Next time" had become her catchphrase.

"Next time don't put Froggie in the sink with the dishes."

"Next time put your crayons where Cassie can't find them."

"Next time tell me when you need the potty."

Cassie had regressed in her toilet training—normal under the circumstances, the doctor said. Roz had been to see him three times this week, always resisting his offer of sleeping pills to tackle her insomnia. What if one of the kids woke in the night and she didn't hear?

Sam spent all his time either in his room or with friends. Friends she knew nothing about. And he was surly when she asked about them. The boy needed a strong male to keep him in line, and whatever his faults, Jack was both that and a natural leader. He didn't suffer fools gladly, but he had endless patience with those he cared about.

Or at least he used to.

That thought was too painful, so Roz turned her mind to more practical matters. *I'll soften him up with dinner. Beef casserole with herb dumplings always used to work.* On all kinds of levels.

She caught herself checking her appearance in the mirror, and winced. The morning was already half-gone and she hadn't even brushed her hair yet. Cassie had thrust a book under Roz's nose at 5:00 a.m., and things had gone downhill from there. She promised herself a few minutes of grooming after she cleaned up madam. "Cass! Now's not the time for hide-and-seek. Come out now, darling!"

The longer the silence, the worse the damage. "Oh, hell." Roz flew out of the bathroom.

"I'll catch her with my lasso." An excited Liam disappeared into the playroom.

The home telephone started ringing, then stopped.

From upstairs, Roz heard Cassie say, "No, you can't," then the clunk of the receiver.

"Gotcha!" Taking the stairs two at a time, Roz came to an abrupt halt in the doorway of the guest bedroom—now hers. Wearing Roz's Versace sunglasses, a bare-bottomed Cassie sat on top of a heritage quilt, flicking through *Responding to Children's Grief*.

The sunglasses slid down the button nose as she lifted her head. "There's no pictures in your books," she complained. Already tossed across the carpet were *Seven Habits of Highly Effective Families* and *Toddler Taming*. Roz moaned. All the discarded library books had faint brown fingerprints on them.

She opened her mouth to gasp, "Don't move!" but Cassie had already slid across the quilt.

When she jumped off the bed holding Blankie, the diamanté lettering on her pink T-shirt sparkled: It's Not My Fault.

"You can wipe my bottom now," she said generously.

Roz URGENTLY NEEDED to call her boss and grovel, but it took her another thirty minutes to strip the bed and get Cassie cleaned up. By that time both kids said they were starving.

Startled, she looked at the kitchen clock. It was already noon and she hadn't called a single client. "What would you like?" This wouldn't take long, and then she could storm into damage control.

"Salami mayonnaise tomato sandwich." Liam swung off the back of a dining chair. "And an apple to keep me healthy." His class had been learning about basic nutrition, and he insisted on five "palm-size" servings of fruit or vegetables a day. It didn't matter how many times Roz explained that the size thing was a guide—if the fruit didn't fit in the palm of Liam's hand, it had to be reshaped.

Knowing this health obsession was a result of his new fear of death, she tempered her impatience and pared down a large apple.

Cassie held out her small fist. "Me, too."

With another glance at the clock, Roz repeated the procedure, then made sandwiches. But the little girl growled when Roz handed hers over.

"Noodles."

Roz pushed it back. "Not today," she said firmly. She had let Cass dictate terms while she'd settled in, but noodles for both lunch and dinner had to stop.

The phone rang; Roz and Liam both dived for it. She got there first. "Rosalind Valentine speaking."

"It's Jack. I'm calling from the plane. Listen, I'm exhausted. How about we reschedule our meeting for tomorrow?"

You think you're tired! She bit back the retort and said patiently, "It's not a meeting, Jack. You're visiting your niece and nephews." Silence. "They'll be really disappointed if you don't show."

"I doubt that," he said drily. "It's not like we spend a lot of time together."

And that's about to change. But she didn't want to scare him away, so she dangled a carrot.

"We could discuss renovations." She knew her ex-husband was keen to get the house ready for sale. Roz had no intention of letting tradesmen in while the kids were still living here, but he didn't know that. Yet.

"I'll be there at seven-thirty, but I can't stay long."

She hung up, feeling more cheerful. Jack would spend time with the kids; he would bond with them. He would want to keep the kids. All she had to do was to show him how easy they were to look after.

"Noodles." There was a warning in Cassie's tone.

Preempting a strike, Roz removed the plate, dumped the sandwich in the trash and mashed up some banana with yogurt. "Yummy, yum, yum. I wish *I* was having this."

Cass took one look and closed her eyes tight.

"She's a terrible eater." Munching his sandwiches, Liam watched the battle complacently from his seat at the dining room table. "Dad said he was going bald because Cassie made him tear his hair out."

"Your sister was born to collect scalps." But the un-expected mention of Anthony brought a lump to Roz's throat; she busied herself clearing plates.

"Can we look at the family photo albums again tonight?"

"Absolutely."

Cassie opened her eyes and said with great sincerity, "Daddy lets me have cookies for lunch."

Kissing the top of her goddaughter's head, Roz lifted her down from the table. "Nice try, sweetheart, but how about we wait until you really *are* hungry?"

Cassie growled; Roz smiled serenely. Her job was people management for a multinational human re-sources company. No way could she be bested by a three-year-old. Nor, for that matter, a thirty-four-year-old ex-husband.

She settled the kids with some toys and was picking

up the phone to call her boss when Sam strolled in the back door. "What time is it?" she said, startled.

"Teachers' meeting, so we got off early. Anything to eat?"

"Sure." Roz handed over the sandwich she'd made for herself. "How was your day?"

The bony shoulders shrugged under their oversize jacket. "Normal."

He started to leave the room.

"Sit down," Roz invited, hanging up the phone because the kids came first. "Let's chat."

"I gotta lot of homework to do."

"Please, Sam, just a few minutes."

He plonked himself down and stared at her.

Roz cleared her throat. "Okay, maybe *I* could start." Mentally, she scrolled through her morning. "Made breakfast, did dishes, housework, grocery shopping, read the kids stories…." Her voice trailed off as his eyes glazed over. Nothing that would interest a teenager. "It was a normal day," she finished, "like yours. But normal will do, right?"

His gaze flicked to hers in a brief moment of shared grief, then he shrugged.

Roz kept trying. "Oh, and laundry…I did lots and lots of laundry."

Sam frowned. "You didn't go into my room, did you?"

"Yes, to grab the washing." She didn't mention the mess.

He shoved back from the table and stood up. "I don't want you poking around in my room when I'm not here, Roz. That's *my* space."

"Okay, calm down."

He glared at her. "Can I go now?"

"After you've watched the kids for ten minutes while I call my senior manager."

Sam groaned and rolled his eyes.

"Thanks, Sam." Ignoring his long-suffering sigh, she picked up the phone and dialed her boss.

"I got an irate call from Quentin Gillespie a half hour ago." Chantel's normally warm voice was decidedly cool. "He said he got hung up on by a toddler." Gillespie headed a leading Internet provider, and Roz was implementing a best practices policy for his telephone help desk.

"Ouch." No point mentioning he wasn't supposed to be ringing the home line. A self-important jackass, Gillespie phoned whatever line—at any time—he wanted. "At least he wasn't redirected to the toilet."

Chantel laughed, but sobered almost immediately. "Roz, we're going to rethink your working from home."

Outside the kitchen window, Cassie trotted into view. She looked behind her for pursuers, then started picking daffodils in the front garden border. The road was mere meters away.

"Hang on!" Without waiting for a response, Roz dropped the phone and raced outside.

"You know you're not supposed to go near cars." She led Cass toward the house. "Where's Sam?"

The child thrust out the flowers. "I picked 'em for you."

Roz melted. Carefully, she took the too-short stems. "That's so sweet of—"

"Now I want noodles."

Sighing, Roz picked her up. "Let me finish my phone call and we'll talk."

Inside, she shifted Cassie to her other hip and picked up the receiver. For someone who didn't eat, the toddler was surprisingly heavy. "You're right, Chantel, this isn't working." She took a deep breath. "I have to resign."

For a moment there was absolute silence. "You sure know how to take the wind out of my sails, don't you? But let's not be too hasty here. Just tell me you'll get back to your usual efficiency."

Cassie squirmed and Roz put her down. "We both know that Gillespie's project needs someone available 24/7. But right now, so do these kids. He won't tolerate mistakes, and the contract means too much to the firm to jeopardize on my domestic learning curve."

There was a new scrawl of pencil near the skirting board, a squiggle disappearing into the worn carpet. Roz averted her gaze. "Promote Stephanie…she's been my right-hand woman on the job, and I think she's capable of rising to the challenge."

"I really don't want to lose you, Roz… How about Steph takes over the Gillespie contract, and we all pitch in with your other clients until you're back."

She was touched. Her associates already put in long hours. Still, maybe this could work.

"All I need," continued Chantel, "is your commitment to return after Christmas."

Or maybe it couldn't.

Roz slid down the wall until she was sitting next to the pencil mark. "I can't give you that guarantee," she admitted. "There are too many unknowns right now." If she succeeded in convincing Jack to keep the kids in New Zealand, she'd need to make herself available. "I think it's better for everybody if I resign."

"Be very sure, Roz. Between you and me," Chantel lowered her voice, "you're on target for a promotion."

Roz hesitated. For the last six years she'd invested a lot of energy into her career. Giving up the certainty of a great job for the long shot of convincing Jack to accept permanent custody was a huge gamble.

She took an eraser from the kids' activity table and absently rubbed at the pencil mark.

And even if he said yes to keeping the kids, then what? Was she willing to be a full-time homemaker? She stared at the smudged mess she'd made with the eraser. So far, she was useless at it.

It was one thing letting Jack financially support his niece and nephews, another to expect him to indefinitely support his ex-wife. Not that Roz would let him... she'd never accepted a penny in alimony and she wasn't going to start now. She had some savings, but when they were gone, then what?

On the other hand, she'd survived the very worst that could happen to a person—nothing could be that bad again. Oddly, there was courage in that. Life was too uncertain not to put people first. The practicalities of how to share custody with her ex could come later.

"You want to sleep on it?" said Chantel hopefully.

"No, my resignation stands." Roz got to her feet, moving the activity table to cover the pencil mark. "Just promise to give me a good reference when I need one."

Sometimes you had to burn the bridge to find the courage to jump.

CHAPTER SIX

ROZ OPENED THE DOOR, looking terrible. Jack knew his instinctive relief was unfeeling and quashed it—an attempt not wholly successful.

However bright—and fake—her smile, her hair was unkempt, she wore not a lick of makeup and there were water stains on the front of her sweatshirt.

He smiled back. If she was finding parenting tough, it would be easier for her to surrender the kids to Fiona. He handed her a shopping bag. "Presents for the kids… So how have you been managing?"

"A duck to water."

Jack looked at her sweatshirt, and his smile broadened. A waterlogged duck, maybe. Stepping inside, he scanned the living room. It was tidy, but there were suspicious bulges under the cushions. He picked one up and found Barbie in a compromising position with Teddy and Thomas the Tank Engine.

Roz dumped the bag and hastily replaced the cushion. "Obviously there are a few kinks to iron out." Unconsciously, she lifted a hand to pat her hair, and Jack's amusement faded because she wasn't wearing a bra. "But I'm coping…. What?"

"Nothing." He realized his hands had curved to the

exact shape of his ex-wife's breasts, and he shoved them in his pockets. "So how are the kids?"

"As expected—good days and bad." Poaching Barbie's pink scrunchie, Roz lifted her arms to tie back her hair, and Jack succumbed to temptation and looked. Why *wasn't* she wearing a bra?

"I'm most worried about Sam," she added.

"Talk to me, not about me," said a disgruntled voice above them, and Sam clomped down the stairs. "I'd be fine if she stopped treating me like I'm the same age as the kids," he complained to Jack.

"I don't think it's unreasonable to want to know where you are," Roz answered quietly.

"She even brought my lunch to the bus stop today."

"Okay, I admit that was a mistake, but I was running late and—"

"In a Thomas the Tank Engine lunch box."

Jack looked at Roz.

"It was all I could find!"

"*And* she's given me an eight o'clock curfew during the week."

"It's what your parents did—"

"Yeah, but now rugby training's kicked in for the reps team—"

"Which finishes at seven," Roz pointed out. "Not eight, like you told me."

"So I made a mistake." Again he appealed to Jack. "See what I mean about checking up on me?"

Jack tried to keep his tone neutral. "He is sixteen, Roz." At Sam's age, Jack had been working and living an adult's life.

Sam punched the air. "Yes!"

"*Nearly* sixteen," Roz corrected grimly.

"Oh, come on," said Sam. "Like three weeks makes a difference."

Jack looked from one stubborn face to the other. "Let's reassess on your birthday," he said to his nephew.

Roz folded her arms, throwing those distracting breasts into relief. "Fifteen or sixteen, Julia and Ants wouldn't want him out carousing on a school night."

"Carousing." Sam wrinkled his forehead. "What the hell kind of word is that?"

"Don't push it," Jack warned him. "She's in charge."

Sam opened his mouth to argue, thought better of it and shrugged. "My birthday then. I'm gonna take a shower before dinner." At the top of the stairs, he looked back with an impish grin. "Roz, got any warnings about touching the hot tap?"

"The curfew can always get earlier," Jack reminded him.

"Sheesh, can't anyone take a joke around here?"

With a glint in her eye, Roz called, "I'll be up to wash your hair in a minute."

The bathroom door slammed. Hearing the key turn firmly in the lock, Jack grinned. But the glint remained in Roz's eye. She waited until the shower was running, then said tightly, "Nice of you to remember I'm the boss—even if it was a bit late."

"Natural though it is, given the circumstances, you need to fight the tendency to wrap him in cotton wool."

"In front of the kids, you have to back me up, Jack. Besides, you haven't been here. You don't know what Sam's been like."

"I thought you said you were coping?" he challenged.

She bit her lip. "I am. Forget I said anything. Listen," she added awkwardly, "the younger ones ate early, but I waited to eat with Sam. I made enough for you."

He became aware of the scent of beef and wine wafting from the kitchen as she smiled at him, and for a split second Jack nearly smiled back before he remembered the situation. For the kids' sake she had to be pleasant. With bleak humor he wondered if she'd factored in that cost when she was bargaining with him for temporary custody.

But he had no intention of forcing his company on her or Liam. Nor of torturing himself with what he'd lost. "Thanks, but I ate on the plane. And I can't stay long. I still need to go to the office."

"But it's 7:30 p.m."

Jack shrugged. He'd begun working late the day Roz remarried, and never got out of the habit. If feeling nothing could be called balance, he'd regained his equilibrium in the years since their baby died. And he intended to keep it.

Frankly, his sanity depended on it.

"Let's talk about renovations. I want to get the place on the market immediately after Christmas, which means getting a crew in as soon as possible."

On paper it was a large, two-story brick house circa 1950 with a half-acre garden. In reality it was what estate agents always described as a handyman's dream.

It had certainly attracted a lot of dreamers, because every successive owner, including his brother, had started a renovation project and never finished it. Jack remembered Ants and Ju raving about the old fireplace, the high, molded-plaster ceilings and the wood-paneled study, and ignoring him when he'd pointed out the lack of insulation, the pokey bathrooms and the need for a new roof.

"Let's buy it if they don't," Jack's own dreamer had suggested.

"Roz, I'll build you one better than this, I promise. We have our own five-year plan." With their new baby in a pack on his chest, Jack had kissed her in this very hallway.

And just over a month later, their marriage was over.

"About the renovations…" Roz colored up in a way that immediately made Jack suspicious. "I don't want any work done while the kids are here. It's too unsettling to have strangers demolishing their home."

"But—"

"Come say hello to the children." She picked up his bag and shoved it at him with a bright smile. "They're in the family room."

"Roz!" But she was already leading the way down the hall.

Cassie and Liam were cuddled up on a beanbag chair in their pajamas, watching some cartoon. "Hey, look who's here," Roz called enthusiastically. "You guys chat while I make coffee."

Cassie took one look at him, clutched Blankie and shut her eyes, and Liam scrunched deeper into the beanbag. Jack felt like Captain Cook faced with a strange—and potentially hostile—tribe. But like Cook, he'd come prepared. "I brought presents."

Immediately he was surrounded, though both kids retreated after hooking the shopping bag out of his hands. Jack sat down and watched.

Picture books were a hit with Cassie. But he stiffened when the little girl clambered into his lap. "Read it to me."

She smelled of talcum powder and baby shampoo and dryer-warmed cotton. He read the story woodenly, every muscle tensed against memory. Thank God the book was short.

"'Nudder one."

"Maybe later." With relief, he lifted her from his lap and stood up. Liam was tugging on the stiff latch of a wooden box with shiny brass hinges. "What is it?"

"A kids' carpentry set." Jack crouched down, ignoring Liam's instinctive recoil, and opened it. "See, they're scaled-down working versions of real tools. A saw, claw hammer, mallet, plane, bradawl…"

He touched the tools as he described them. He hadn't meant to spend so much, but when he'd seen the craftsmanship Jack hadn't been able to resist them.

Across the toolbox, Liam was looking at him blankly. "I know it's a bit advanced," Jack admitted, "but you'll have them forever. One day you can pass them down to your own son. And look, there are some precut wooden pieces you can nail together to practice your hammer skills. Go ahead…."

Politely, Liam picked up the hammer and gave it a token swing. "Thank you, Uncle Jack," he said without enthusiasm.

Roz came into the lounge, holding two steaming cups of coffee. "Wow! Aren't *you* lucky."

Oh, God, thought Jack, *did I choose as badly as that?*

"Try it on some wood this time." Rather desperately, he started a nail for Liam.

The boy looked at Roz, who nodded encouragingly.

Sitting on his haunches, the wood between his knees, he raised the hammer and closing his eyes, brought it down hard. It missed the nail and cracked into his knee-cap.

Liam's eyes flew open and met Jack's in accusatory shock. Then his face crumbled and he started to howl.

Jack reached out to comfort him, and Liam stumbled backward to get away from him, tripping over the rug and landing on his bottom. Realizing he was only making things worse, Jack stepped back, watching help-lessly as Roz put down the coffee cups, then did the cuddles and consolation routine. "You'll be fine…. He's fine," she assured Jack when things calmed down. "A bruise maybe, but no major damage."

Liam glared at Jack. "I want him to go."

"Why, Silly Billy?" Roz tickled him into a smile. "It's not Uncle Jack's fault you need some practice."

But Jack agreed with Liam. He was out of place here. Loosening his tie, he stood up. "I'll leave."

THIS BONDING SESSION wasn't working out the way Roz had planned. "You haven't touched your coffee," she protested, sliding Liam off her lap. "Let me reheat it."

"No, you need dinner, anyway so…see you, kids."

"Bye, Uncle Jack," Liam said with obvious relief. Cassie ignored him.

Jack was halfway down the hall before Roz reached the family room door. Emergency action was needed. With a quick twist, she wrenched off the handle.

"Jack, wait!" Adopting a woeful expression, she waved the handle, trying to look helpless, and praying he'd forgotten how much he'd taught her. "I need some repairs done." If it was one thing her ex-husband couldn't resist, it was fixing things.

He frowned, then crossed his arms, and his biceps bulged under the fabric of his white business shirt. "You said you didn't want any renovations while the kids were in residence."

"I said I didn't want strangers here."

"Roz, I haven't got time to play handyman."

"Well, okay." Deliberately, she stood on the loose board in the hall so that it creaked ghoulishly. "I'll just keep the kids away from the danger zones." She waved the handle. "I can go through the window if the kids accidentally shut the door…and I'll use towels to stop the leak in the upstairs bathroom."

He said through gritted teeth, "What's wrong with the upstairs bathroom?"

Nothing. Yet. But surely she could loosen a nut or a washer. "Not sure," she said vaguely. "Lots of water under the sink."

His mouth tightened. "Okay, I'll do the urgent stuff now."

"Thanks, Jack."

"There are tools in my car. Go write me a list."

Oh yes, a list. A long, long list.

"And I guess whatever I do now will shorten the workload when the kids go to Fiona."

Her optimism dipped slightly, but she smiled and nodded.

"I'll start with the upstairs bathroom."

Oh, hell. "Great." Roz forced herself to hold his gaze, but folded her arms defensively. And realized she wasn't wearing a bra. Cass had called out when Roz was in the shower, and she hadn't had time to dress properly. Casually, she lifted her arms higher across her chest.

"And do something about that."

She blushed. "A gentleman wouldn't have mentioned it."

"I disagree." His smile reconnected her to everything they'd ever done together naked. "A gentleman would have told you earlier."

The front door clicked shut behind him. It took several seconds for Roz to realize she was leaning against the wall for support, having been turned on by a single look from her ex-husband. She straightened, then raced upstairs to sabotage the sink.

And find a bra.

GRIMLY, JACK HAULED his toolbox out of the trunk of the car, stripping off his dress shirt and replacing it with a T-shirt from his suitcase. A passing car honked and he muttered, "Yeah, yeah, haven't you seen a bare chest before?"

Upstairs a light snapped on, and he saw Roz haul open drawers and retrieve a pink bra. If she didn't close the curtains he doubted he'd have the moral strength to look away. Fortunately, she didn't test him. Things were complicated enough without his having to fight a sexual attraction to his ex-wife.

For another five minutes he stood by his car, battling the impulse to drive away. Finally, with an exasperated sigh, he reentered the warm house.

He hunted Roz down to the family room, where she sprawled on the carpet with Liam, photo albums open around them. Cassie sat opposite in an armchair.

"We're all looking at family pictures. You want to join us for a few minutes?"

"Hell, no!" His sharp tone drew Liam's wondering gaze, and Jack added lamely, "I remember what Ju and Ants looked like." He couldn't understand the urge to twist the knife. He hesitated, then said awkwardly, "Liam, you want to get your new hammer and come help me fix the bath?" He really wanted to repair his relationship with his brother's son.

But Liam didn't even look up. "No, thanks, I'm busy with Roz."

Cassie dropped her album and slid off the armchair, her feet landing on the carpet with a determined thud. "I'll help," she said generously.

"Umm…" Caught off-guard, Jack didn't know what to say.

"But don't you want to look at more photos, Cass?" asked Liam.

"Remember what I told you, hon," Roz murmured in a low voice. "Cassie is so little, she won't find them comforting like you. I'd be grateful," she said in a normal voice to Jack. "I'm running out of other things to give her."

"You know," he stated, searching for excuses, "some of my tools are dangerous."

Cassie eyed him. "Daddy lets me help."

"Fine, let's go."

In passing, Jack picked up the album she'd discarded on the floor, and saw it was one of Roz's. Which meant the baby pictures were… His heart started pounding in his chest and his grip tightened on the handle of the toolbox as dizziness clouded his vision.

In the distance, he heard Roz talking to Liam. "I

remember that house," she said. "It was the first one your parents bought after they got married. The wisteria was all that held it up."

Then Cassie's small hand grabbed Jack's, grounding him. "C'mon," she said, tugging impatiently. "Let's fix stuff."

In the upstairs bathroom, Jack shut the door and slid down it to the floor, then hid his face in his hands. Then silently, painfully, shoulders heaving, he cried, the pain of walled-off memories pouring out and merging with the still-raw grief for Ants and Julia.

Hadn't he and Roz suffered enough?

He could feel Cassie's curious gaze but as much as he tried, Jack couldn't stop his emotional hemorrhage, couldn't do anything but bury his head deeper into his arms.

"Are you havin' a rest?"

"Yes," he rasped.

There was a silence while she digested that. "Where's the hammer?"

Desperately pulling himself together, Jack retrieved it from the toolbox and handed it to her.

She looked curiously at his wet cheeks. "Did you hit your finger?"

Unable to speak, Jack nodded.

"Show me."

He stuck out his thumb and she kissed it. "All better?"

Her brisk sympathy moved him as much as the unexpected kiss. But then, she'd seen a lot of adults crying lately. "Yes." He smiled at her through his tears.

"Jack?" Roz tried to open the door he was leaning against. "You need some help?"

"Hang on, let me move the toolbox." After wiping his face on a towel, Jack stood up. When Roz opened the door he had his head in the cupboard under the basin.

"Uncle Jack had an owwie," announced Cassie.

"It's nothing," he said brusquely. "You're right, this is a bad leak. There's water everywhere."

"He cried."

In the semidarkness, Jack closed his eyes. There was a brief silence.

"Honey," said Roz, "go tell Liam I said you could have a cookie." The tattletale dropped the hammer on the tiles with a clunk and scampered away.

There was a tentative touch on his arm. "Jack, come out."

"No wonder this is leaking," he said. "Someone's loosened the connection on the S-bend."

"Forget the damn repairs. You're upset."

"I'm fine, and I don't want to talk about it." He re-screwed the loose fixture. "I'll tighten this to stop the kids doing this again. I just need—"

A wrench appeared beside him.

"Thanks."

He had no excuse to stay in the cupboard now. Reluctantly, he came out and returned the wrench to his toolbox. "What's next on the list?"

Her fingers brushed the tearstains on his face. "You still won't let anyone mourn with you," she said sadly.

Jack picked up his tools. "I'll fix the door handle next."

"Fine." She stood back to let him pass. "I'll stop trying to help."

Twenty minutes later, Jack had finished the most urgent repairs and was heading toward the front door.

"Why don't you stay and put the kids to bed?"

"Yeah, I can just see Liam's face."

"If he gets to know you, Jack…"

"Will you stop feeling sorry for me? It's driving me crazy."

"Will you stop pushing people away?"

With his free arm he caught her to him. "What's the alternative. This?" She'd always made him hard, and this time was no exception. She'd always softened against him and this time was no exception. "Do you really think we have any hope in hell of making this work, given our history?"

He should never have agreed to temporary custody.

She obviously hadn't thought about this complication; he could tell by the shock on her face. Releasing her, he stepped back. "Trust me," he said heavily, "It's better that I stay away. For everybody's sake." *Especially mine.*

"You're not leaving?" Sam came down the stairs, drying his wet hair with a towel. "But I thought you'd be moving in…you know, for the time we're here."

Jack looked at Roz. "Yours, I think."

She cleared her throat. "You do remember that Jack and I are divorced, don't you?"

"Oh, yeah…I guess that was a stupid thing to think." Through Sam's adolescent self-absorption, Jack could see memory start to surface. Sam had been almost ten when Thomas died.

"I really have to go."

Sam fell into step beside him. "Are you coming back tomorrow?"

"It might take me a couple of days to get a handle

on things at work. We've got big things happening at the moment."

"Oh, sure, I understand." The teenager affected nonchalance, but twisted the towel in his hands. And Jack realized Roz wasn't the only one who hadn't thought things through. What expectations had he raised in his oldest nephew?

Roz said nothing, but Jack could feel her tension as she opened the front door for him. Unable to help himself, he looked into her eyes, saw the unspoken plea, and began to drown. It wasn't a pleasant sensation. *Don't,* he wanted to say, *don't need me like this. We broke all the links, remember?*

"Good night." He could feel Sam's disappointment following him down the driveway, and tried to chase it away with rationalizations. A multimillion-dollar construction project didn't run itself. Over previous months he'd lined up designers, suppliers, construction crews and subcontractors in a finely balanced schedule that would topple like a row of dominoes if he made any mistakes.

Jack jabbed his remote in the direction of his Mercedes SUV. What Roz and Sam didn't realize was that delays on a project this size would cost hundreds of thousands of dollars—effectively, his profit margin. Opening the car door, he paused, then barked over his shoulder, "What time's your game on Saturday?"

"You wanna come watch? Really?" The teenager's face lit up before he remembered his habitual indifference. Shrugging he said, "Kickoff's at three o'clock."

"I'll *try,* okay?"

"No biggie…I mean, it would be great if you came. But whatever."

Jack waited for Roz's nod. But he wasn't expecting the smile that came with it, and its warmth hit him before he could put up a firewall. Reminding him what being loved by Rosalind Valentine had been like.

Before he'd lost the right to it.

CHAPTER SEVEN

ROZ WATCHED JACK DRIVE away, feeling a momentary wistfulness that had nothing to do with the kids' need for a father figure.

In his actions, she'd glimpsed a remnant of the soft-hearted tough guy she'd married, not the inaccessible stranger who'd divorced her. She realized suddenly that she was staking the children's future on the man he'd been, not the one he'd become.

She must need to have her head examined.

Particularly for assuming their sexual connection had been broken along with everything else.

Oh, God, I'm in trouble.

No, you're not.

Closing the door firmly, Roz checked on the kids, then went into the kitchen to dish up dinner. The casserole was perfect, the meat so tender it all but fell apart on the plate. Jack hadn't eaten on the plane; he hated airplane food.

I should have made him stay.

The serving spoon hit the kitchen bench with a clatter and she started to laugh. Like she'd made him stay six years ago? Hadn't she learned anything?

She remembered Jack in the bathroom earlier,

rugged, macho and terse—with tearstains on his cheeks. Roz sighed. The trouble was she understood him now, in a way she hadn't when he'd broken what had been left of her heart.

She understood that losing a child to crib death could make even the strong weak. They'd both been strong people before Thomas's death; and they'd both been broken by it, though she'd only fallen apart when he'd left her.

Reverting to type, her parents said, because Jack Galloway had been wild before settling down with their daughter. Thank God they lived in Australia now and couldn't disapprove of this situation.

"Gorgeous," Julia had said eight years ago of her prospective brother-in-law, "but dangerous. The kind of guy you crash and burn on."

He'd sounded like a jerk to Roz.

Recently graduated from university, she liked her men educated, and Jack Galloway had left high school before graduating. As a PR executive working for an ad agency where image was everything, what would she possibly have in common with a blue-collar construction worker?

When Jack missed his brother's wedding because of a long-standing estrangement from his aging father, a legend in New Zealand sport, her view hardened, though Julia was already expressing reservations about her new father-in-law.

Roz finally met Jack when she was twenty-four. "I don't approve of you," she'd told him, giddy on her best friend's housewarming champagne; more so on the lazy intensity in Jack's green eyes when he looked at her.

"I'm going to change your mind," he said.

She'd married him three months later, when Jack took out an overdraft to follow her to a convention in Las Vegas.

And they'd been happy. Even happier when their son was born. The first of a dynasty, Jack had toasted, and captivated by their perfect newborn, Roz had recklessly agreed to have five more.

Thomas. Through the sleeve of her sweatshirt, Roz fingered the thin silver chain around her wrist, finding the heavier link of Thomas's charm bracelet and tracing his name through the cotton.

Not that he wasn't etched in her heart. But she'd learned that embracing—not resisting—the pain was the only way to push through it. "It was worth it," she whispered.

If only his father could reach the same conclusion.

LIAM SAT ON THE COUCH with Cassie, watching a cartoon, his lower lip stuck out. Usually he liked to swing his legs, but he couldn't now because it hurt too much. He looked at the bruise, red turning purple, and it started hurting more.

It *was* big, though. Imagining how impressed his friends would be at school tomorrow, Liam cheered up. But then he thought of admitting that he'd hit himself with the hammer, and pushed his lip out again.

Cassie leaned on him and he squirmed away. "Don't sit so close!" Normally he liked how big and protective he felt when Cassie cuddled up to him; right now he felt mean.

She growled, but moved away, still looking at the picture book Uncle Jack had given her.

Liam glanced at his present, lying where he'd opened it. Dumb old tool stuff. Uncle Jack should have got him something fun, not something *he* wanted to play with.

Liam tried to think what he would have liked better. A baseball bat and mitt maybe…that's what Mum and Dad were gonna get him for Christmas.

Dad used to pitch to him in the backyard with his heavy old bat, and said Liam's swing was really coming along. Sometimes Liam even hit the ball. The urge to cry was very strong.

Cassie turned the page of her book and the heavy cardboard thwacked against his knee. "Oww," he cried, letting the tears fall, even though it didn't hurt much. "Say you're sorry."

But she was distracted. "Look." Cassie pointed. "A butterfly."

Liam glanced at the pink shimmering fabric sewn into the wings. "Dumb girls' book," he muttered, and she growled at him again.

"Dumb old Uncle Jack," he said. "He's a bum-bum," he added, and her eyes widened. She knew it was a naughty word. "We don't like Uncle Jack," said Liam.

She looked at him doubtfully, then scrambled off the sofa. "You the bum-bum."

"You are."

"No, you."

He pretended to get off the couch, and she ran out of the room. "Good riddance," he shouted after her, then sat back, feeling lonelier than ever.

He could write to Mum and Dad in heaven, and tell them about his accident, but today he resented having to. Today it didn't feel like anybody was listening.

The butterfly book lay open beside him; Liam kicked it onto the floor with his good leg, then had an idea and hid it under the couch. When Cassie was looking for it at bedtime, he whispered, "I bet that bum-bum Uncle Jack took it."

JACK ARRIVED AT Sam's rugby game at the start of the second half. He'd left an important site meeting to manage even that, and was in a foul mood.

As he strode along the perimeter of the playing field, Sam caught sight of him, and at the relief on the boy's face, some of Jack's ill humor evaporated. He gave his nephew a thumbs-up, then scanned the huddles of spectators for Roz and the other kids. He'd been up since five, yet only now did he notice the late spring sun, the smell of turf and grass churned up by rugby boots, and the light breeze, still brisk enough to make him dig his hands in the pockets of his jacket.

He passed through a group of teenage girls prematurely embracing summer in tight tees and cutoffs that revealed goose-bumpy blue flesh. Their voices rose and fell with intermittent shrieks of laughter as, flicking back hair, they glanced at the boys and practiced their flirting on each other.

Then Jack caught sight of Roz. And despite his irritation he had to smile.

She wore jeans, chunky socks, a thick jumper and a crimson beanie pulled low over her ears—and still she was shivering.

"It's about time," she hissed as soon as he was within earshot. "Sam's missed I don't know how many passes, scanning the crowd for you."

"Then leave your cell phone on so I can call you," he snapped back, taking off his jacket and placing it around her shoulders.

"What? So you could cancel?"

"Better than a no-show."

"I knew you wouldn't do that," she said. "You're too honorable." She seemed to realize she was wearing his jacket. "Jack, no, you'll freeze."

"I'm fine…. Hello, Cassandra." The little girl wore earmuffs that made her look like an Ewok, a sheepskin coat in the same pink, with fake fur trim that had turned into dreadlocks. On her feet she had a pink pair of Uggs. She sat on a picnic rug surrounded by books.

She didn't acknowledge him, but neither did she close her eyes. That was progress, he guessed.

"What's the score?" Jack asked Roz. She still looked exhausted. He reminded himself that taking the hard road had been her choice.

"No idea," she confessed, "but I think we're winning." Her eyes were very blue as she shot him a sideways glance. "Look, I'm sorry. Thanks for coming. I know it means a lot to Sam."

I also did it for you. He shoved the thought aside and turned to watch the game. "Where's Liam?"

"At a birthday party. I'm picking him up on the way home."

Jack tried to be ashamed of his relief. He couldn't seem to get it right with that kid, and Liam's continued fear of him cut him to the quick.

In Liam's world, dinosaurs, hobbits and Santa brushed shoulders with the tooth fairy, God and baby Jesus, while Ants and Julia checked the heavenly mailbox. Such blind faith made Jack uncomfortable. The sooner Liam dealt with the reality of his parents' death, the better the kid would recover from it.

Roz would disagree with him, but then she was an optimist. Which was one of the reasons he'd fallen in love with her. The wind picked up and Jack shivered.

"You *are* cold," said his ex-wife. "Look, take this back. Sam's got a jacket in his sports bag. I'll wear it until he needs it."

She retrieved the jacket and tugged it on, putting her hands in the pockets. A strange expression came over her face. Roz pulled out her hand and opened her palm, and the foil of a condom packet gleamed in the sun.

She and Jack looked at each other.

"It's probably wishful thinking," he assured her. "Most boys carry one around for years before they get a chance to use it."

"You didn't," Roz reminded him.

Jack had lost his virginity at fifteen. "Nothing about my teenage years was normal," he reminded her. "But Sam has fam…" His voice trailed off.

"You're going to have to talk to him, Jack."

"Roz, it's not my place." Damn it, he knew he shouldn't have come to the game.

"You're his guardian."

"So are you," he countered.

"Oh, yeah," she said tartly. "Teenage boys love discussing sex with mother figures. Maybe Fiona and I can set up a three-way conference call."

"What about one of the school counselors?" But Jack knew he was fighting a losing battle.

"He looks up to you, Jack," she argued.

"What am I going to say?"

"What you once said to me about it—however physically mature you are, emotionally you're still a baby."

"How about we just decide that this demonstrates a sense of responsibility?"

"I have one question for you. Did you regret having sex so young?"

"Absolutely not…at the time."

"And looking back?"

He hadn't been ready for the emotions that went with sexual intimacy, and they were messy, bewildering years. "Fine, I'll talk to him."

"Chocolate!" Cassie jumped up, practically vibrating with glee.

Hurriedly, Roz palmed the foil packet. "No, hon, it's not chocolate."

"I want chocolate." The toddler dumped the books and hauled on Roz's pocket. "I want some." Her voice rose in a wail, her face turned red and she threw herself onto the picnic rug in a full-blown tantrum.

Jack really, really wished he hadn't come. "Tell me why we're doing this again?" he asked Roz, who was crouching down, trying to pacify her goddaughter. He leaned over and picked Cassie up by her jacket, lifting her until she hung in the air like a bellowing fairy. Surprised, she stopped. "It's not chocolate," he said. "It's a preventative against accidents like you."

"I'm flying." Cassie flapped her arms. "Uncle Jack, you make me fly."

As he swung her gently around a couple of times, the final whistle blew.

Sweaty and muddy, Sam weaved his way through the

crowd, grinning from ear to ear. A few people turned to stare after him as though they could see the tragedy clinging to him; a couple whispered behind their hands. "Good God, are people always this insensitive?" Jack muttered to Roz.

"Yes," she murmured back, then overcompensated by giving Sam a hero's welcome, which the teenager shrugged off impatiently.

"We won," he told Jack.

"Great game." Jack lowered Cassie to the ground. "What was the final score?"

"Forty-thirty. But you missed the first half, right?" Sam launched into an enthusiastic account of the first forty minutes. Jack listened intently, seeing Julia in the excited gestures and passionate delivery.

Roz obviously saw the likeness, too. Her eyes widened; her hands grew clumsy as she folded the picnic blanket. His attention still on Sam, Jack took over the job. "I'll bring Sam home while you go pick up Liam," he told her. This was why he needed to stay away. She kept slipping past his defenses....

Surreptitiously, she swiped at her eyes with her sleeve. Face averted, she picked up Cassie. "Thank you."

"No problem." He watched her cross the field, carrying Cassie, who surprised him by waving. Jack waved back.

"Mind if I hang around with the guys a few minutes?" Sam gave a thumbs-up to his teammates, still milling excitedly on the pitch.

Jack thought of all the work he had to do, then looked at the longing on Sam's face. "Sure...I'll make a few calls in the car." His cell phone rang before he finished speaking. He looked at the caller ID and frowned.

"Roz?"

"Stay for dinner." Her voice was steady again.

So was his resolve. "Other plans," he said brusquely.

"Tomorrow night then?"

"My Japanese business partner is in the country for a few days. I'll be entertaining him."

Frustration mixed with the cheerfulness in her tone. "We'll expect you at six on Thursday."

"I'll check my diary and get back to you about dinner on Thursday, Roz." He had no intention of going.

"See you then," she stated firmly. Jack looked beyond the field to the car park and spotted the bright crimson of her beanie. She was trying to make him play happy family with the kids, but it wouldn't work.

After the trauma of the other night, any future encounters with the children would be on neutral ground—like sports fields and the movies. Places they didn't have to talk.

As he and Sam walked past the group of teenage girls, the greetings started.

"*Hi*, Sam!"

"Hey, Sammy, nice legs!"

"Whatever," replied his nephew. But Jack noticed his shoulders straighten, his neck flush, and hid a smile. The condom was definitely wishful thinking.

Behind them the girls giggled and whispered, then one voice rose self-importantly. "Yeah, his mum forgot she was supposed to be driving on the right-hand side and pulled into the path of a truck. It took five hours to cut the bod—"

Jack spun on his heel and cut the speaker off with a

look, but when he turned back Sam's shoulders were hunched again. Casually, he threw an arm around them. "So that drop-goal I missed. How many meters were you away from the posts again?"

"It's okay," Sam mumbled, "I'm used to it."

Jack tightened his hand on his shoulder. "They'll find something else to talk about soon." But it would be there for the rest of his life, the tragedy that marked him as different.

"Don't worry. I can handle it." Now it was Sam doing the reassuring.

"In the U.K. with Fiona, no one will know you. You can start again."

"Yeah." But the boy's enthusiasm was gone.

Brooding, Jack didn't notice his nephew had by-passed his teammates until they were almost to the car park. He stopped. "Wait a minute. Didn't you want to hang around?"

"Nah, it's getting cold. Let's just go home."

Wordlessly, Jack unlocked the car. On the drive home, he didn't raise the subject of the condoms. Didn't give his nephew the spiel that a childhood didn't last long, and when it was gone, it was gone forever. They both knew Sam's was already over.

"Next week I'll be there for the whole game."

"You don't have—"

"I want to."

He drew up to the curb in front of his brother's house; Sam got out of the car. For only the second time since his parents died, Jack saw Sam smile. "See you at dinner Thursday," said Sam.

"But—"

The car door slammed shut.

Jack waited until his nephew was inside, then punched the dashboard. "Shit!"

It looked like he was committed.

CHAPTER EIGHT

"Obviously the school's trying to make allowances for Sam's recent tragedy, but his deteriorating behavior isn't the only problem." The headmaster had left his formidable desk and sat next to Roz on low, comfortable chairs "because we're informal here at North Shore High."

Still reeling from the phone call this morning asking for an urgent meeting, she could only nod.

"In addition to being sullen and uncooperative, this week he's started skipping classes, and with final exams coming up…"

Mr. Coutts looked at her gravely. "Well, I thought the sooner I brought it to your attention, Ms. Valentine, the sooner we could up with a solution."

"Yes, of course… Shouldn't Sam be at this meeting?"

"Except he's not here, Ms. Valentine. Hence the reason for my call." There was a touch of impatience now in his kind tone.

"I'm sorry," said Roz, "I'm finding this difficult to assimilate. You see, every morning, including today, I make him lunch and give him money for the bus." Propelled by a growing anxiety, she stood up. "If he's not here, then where is he?"

"Probably hanging out at a mall or a park somewhere. If he's been coming home after school, you should see him at the usual time."

Roz bit her lip. "He's been telling me he's had sporting commitments after school…getting home around six, sometimes seven. Is that a lie, too?"

"I know he wouldn't miss rugby practice," said Mr. Coutts. "That's Mondays and Wednesdays."

"That doesn't explain the other two…"

"How's his behavior at home?"

"The same as at school. Except with Jack…his other guardian. Sam listens to him. But he's not living with us and we only see him occasionally."

Roz knew she was rambling, but could only think about where Sam might be. It was two-thirty now. She might not see him for another four hours…. Then the time registered. "Can I call you when I've had a chance to talk to Sam? I need to pick up his siblings at three."

"Of course. And if you feel a counselor would be helpful, we have a good person on staff."

For a moment Roz thought he meant for her. Because that's how clueless she felt right now. She'd had no idea that anything was amiss.

"There was bound to be some fallout after the tragedy," he said kindly, "so don't blame yourself. The important thing is getting Sam stabilized before his exams."

"Thanks for being so understanding, Mr. Coutts. I'll get back to you."

Outside, Roz pulled out her cellphone and paused. So much for her plan to show Jack how easy the children were. But she had no choice. Her relationship with Sam was too rocky to handle this alone.

"Jack Galloway here."

"Jack, it's—"

"I'm not available right now. Leave a message and I'll call you back."

"It's me…Roz." Stupid! Of course he'd recognize her voice. "Listen, call me when you can. It's urgent."

She closed her phone, curiously steadied by his cryptic tone, even on a message service. Jack had the ability to measure tough situations with a glance and do what needed to be done with a quiet competence. And he didn't mind being the bad guy when necessary. It was one of the things Roz had loved about him.

"*PLEASE* DON'T TELL JACK." Sam looked at Roz with desperate, pleading eyes. "I'll stop skipping classes, I promise."

Her heart sank. "I can't do that, Sam. This is too serious." The insolent teenager she'd been remonstrating with for twenty minutes had vanished the instant she mentioned she'd left a message for his uncle.

They were in the study, because unlike Coutts, Roz had gone for formality, sitting behind Anthony's desk and making Sam sit opposite. She'd wanted to impress her nephew with the gravity of the situation, but nothing had worked until she'd mentioned Jack.

Sam leaned forward, fingers gripping the desk. "Man, I skipped maybe four days over three weeks. Cootie's overreacting."

"He also said you have an attitude problem, disrupting the class, arguing with teachers." *Like you have with me.* She didn't say the words.

Sheepishly, Sam dropped his gaze. "I get angry when

they act like the only thing that matters is sitting up straight and studying and passing exams…like it's life or death or something."

And he knew about life and death. "I guess school feels pretty trivial right now," she conceded. And so would remembering to bring his dirty clothes down, or interacting with the family, or any of the things she'd been nagging him to do.

Sam sensed her weakening. "I'll be better," he said earnestly, "Nicer. Only don't tell Jack. I don't want him to stop lik—coming to my games or anything. Please, Roz, I'll even talk to *you*."

She laughed, but she felt more like crying. Was she really that bad? Didn't he realize that she was trying to provide a routine—a safety net—while he processed his grief? "I understand that it will take a while for meaning to come back into your life after all you've been through," she said. "Give it time, Sam, and if you need someone to talk to, I'm here for you. Maybe if we—"

Her cell phone rang and she checked the caller. "It's Jack."

The chair hit the floor as Sam sprang to his feet. "Don't tell him. Please."

"Hi, Jack, thanks for calling me back."

"What's wrong?" There was a rough anxiety in his voice.

Roz looked into Sam's pleading eyes and wavered. Jack had a right to know, but she also wanted to give the boy the benefit of the doubt. Could she trust him to live up to his end of the bargain?

"Roz?" Jack said again.

"Please, Roz," Sam whispered.

And she wanted to maximize the chances of keeping the kids in New Zealand. "Do you know where Ants keeps his toolbox?"

Sam clasped his hands together and mouthed, *"Thank you."*

"That's it?" Jack's voice took on an even rougher edge. "Yeah, okay, Glenn, I'll be there in a moment.... Your message said it was urgent."

"The door handle has come loose again and it's driving me crazy."

"For God's sake, Roz, I was imagining all sorts... Back of the garage, second shelf. It should be obvious."

"Thanks. Sorry to bother you at work. So, we'll see you tomorrow for dinner?"

She despised the neediness in her voice. But right now she longed to have another grown-up in the house.

Reluctance was rife in his tone. "Yeah, I'll be there.... Are you sure everything's okay?"

Let me see...I'm lying to you, I need you, I'm exhausted and I don't know if I've just made the right decision. I'm trying to get you to love the kids so you'll keep them, which is the right thing for them, but fraught with peril for my peace of mind.

"Absolutely," said Roz. And because Jack couldn't see her, she rubbed the back of her neck.

LIAM WOKE AT A NOISE from Sam's room. It came again, a muffled bump, and he slid out of bed to investigate. The hall light was on, because although he was too big for a night-light, he'd told Roz leaving it on would put off burglars.

Quietly, he crept along the passage and opened his

brother's door. Light spilled into the bedroom, illuminating Sam, who was half in, half out of the window.

He heard a swift intake of breath, then Sam recognized his shape and gave a muffled curse. "Sheesh, give me a heart attack, why don't you!" he hissed. "Get in here and shut the door."

Liam did as instructed and was enveloped in darkness. Panicking, he fumbled for the light switch, but Sam grabbed the neck of his pajama top and hauled him away. "Leave that off."

His eyes adjusted, helped by the streetlight shining through the open curtains. "Where are you going?"

"To a friend's house."

"But it's late…everyone's in bed."

"I forgot something…something I need for school."

"Why aren't you going out through the door?"

But Sam didn't answer. He cocked his head, listening, and Liam listened, too. A car with one of those big exhausts was coming down the street, its loud roar softening as it stopped outside the house.

Sam ducked his head out the window and gave a thumbs-up. Liam wriggled in beside him to see. "Who's that?" The person in the car was old…maybe twenty or something. If Sam was going out with a grown-up, maybe this was really okay.

"My uncle…my real dad's brother. He was at the funeral."

Liam found it confusing that Sam had the same mother as him and Cassie, but a different dad. So he focused on the immediate situation. "If you're allowed to go out with him, why aren't you going out the door?"

"Okay, I'm sneaking…so don't tell Roz. Or Jack."

Liam was going to ask if he could come, but decided he didn't like the look of the man in the car. He had big arms with tattoos and a sort of frown on his face that made Liam think he could be mean. And he was smoking, which meant he probably wasn't very smart, because everyone knew smoking was bad for your health.

The man was tapping the fingers of his free hand on the dashboard, and he jerked his head to Sam, who started scrambling out the window again.

"Go back to bed and remember what I said. You don't tell anybody 'bout this." There was a wild look in his brother's eyes that scared Liam.

"You are coming back, aren't you?" he whispered.

"Of course I am, doofus."

The familiar insult comforted Liam, and he went back to bed. But it took him a long time to go back to sleep.

"PIVOTING DECK, kick tail, inclined caster trucks…this is such a cool present, Jack." With natural grace, Sam pivoted on the Ripstik caster board, leaving black rubber marks on the lounge's hardwood floor.

"I'm glad you like it, but test it outside," Jack said drily.

"After your homework," Roz added.

"C'mon, Roz, have a heart."

"Okay," she said, "half an hour…but no more, Sam."

Bang. The front door slammed and he was gone.

Jack turned to Liam, who was looking at his matching board rather doubtfully. "What does it do again?"

"It's a cross between a skateboard and a snowboard."

"Oh," said Liam. He sat astride it and scooted across the floor.

Jack suppressed his impatience. "You stand up on it, mate."

"No thanks," said his nephew politely. "I don't want to fall."

"How about I hold your arm?" Roz suggested.

"I'm okay like this," Sedately, he rolled into the hall.

Roz looked at Jack and started to laugh. "Your face!"

"I can't seem to win with that kid," he muttered.

"Give it time," she answered softly. "Let me go finish dinner."

"Want some help?"

"No, drink your beer and relax."

Instead he sat and brooded over his continuing failure to impress his brother's son. Liam was so like Ants in looks and disposition. By rights, he and Jack should have no problem getting along. Jack noticed the family albums stacked at the bottom of the bookcase, and reluctantly picked one up. Maybe he'd find clues to a relationship with his nephew.

The album started with childhood photos of Ants, glossy small prints from predigital days. Vision blurry, Jack paused at a snapshot of two skinny kids. He and Ants were standing at the edge of an Olympic-size pool, shivering in Speedos and goggles, mimicking a dive-ready stance. Only five and six years old and already in a 6:00 a.m. training schedule.

Ants had on his "try hard" expression and a slightly anxious smile. *Shit.* Jack took another swallow of his beer. Liam had just looked at him with that same expression.

Jack's face in the photo was sullen. Ants might have the right attitude to please their father, but it was Jack who'd had the athletic potential. He also had a stubborn resistance to conditional love, as evidenced by the scowl.

As always, Mum was a blurred figure in the background. His father had treated her as a service provider, and during their childhood the boys had largely followed his example.

She'd left her husband the day Anthony started university. "He would never have let me take you boys," she'd once confided to Jack after a large sherry, "and someone had to be a buffer."

And they'd needed a buffer.

All Jack's life, his father had called him a loser because he wouldn't bend to Frank's will. In retaliation, he'd done everything he could to prove his father right—skipping school, getting into trouble. But Mum had never let Frank hit them—though he did when she wasn't around.

Only months before her death, Jack had been able to buy her a cottage in the country where she'd taken up golf and bridge and reveled in "never having to look at bloody water again."

He missed her.

On impulse, he punched Luke's number. His foster brother had left several messages since the funeral, and Roz had mentioned that Liz rang the kids regularly from their home further down the country. It went to voice mail. "Luke…it's Jack." He hesitated, feeling awkward. "I'm just keeping in touch." He hung up. It wasn't much, but it was a start.

Cassie came into the room, hefting an aged tabby that weighed almost as much as she did. It hung passively in her arms with what was obviously a long-standing resignation.

"You wanna pat James Zombie Maisy?"

Jack and the cat looked at each other warily. Liam was right; the animal did have Jack's green eyes. "How about putting him down first?"

Instead, Cassie hoisted it halfway onto Jack's lap. The cat unsheathed claws to haul itself the rest of the way up.

Jack swore, grabbed the animal and lifted it clear. "Son of a—"

"She wants to be your friend," Cassie climbed onto Jack's lap, not careful about where she put her feet. He ditched the cat to resettle her.

Liam coasted past on his caster board and said in a tormented voice, "It's a boy, Cassie. How many times do I have to tell you!"

"It's a girl!" From her position on Jack's lap, Cassie grabbed the cat, which was about to make its escape. "Pat her!" she commanded.

"Him!" yelled Liam from the hall.

This was an old warhorse of a cat. Under the soft fur, Jack felt lumps of scar tissue, and one ear had been torn in a long-ago fight. The animal closed its eyes and started to purr. "Isn't she pretty?" cooed Cassie.

Jack started to laugh. Even the animal's purr had a freighter's growl. "Very pretty," he agreed.

"She's your friend," the tot reiterated, and Jack got it.

"I'm *her* friend, too," he confirmed. Satisfied they understood each other, Cass got off the couch and, with the cat still in her arms, staggered out of the room.

Sipping his beer, Jack picked up another album, looking for more recent pictures. As he opened the cover, Roz poked her head around the door. "Dinner's ready." She glanced at the album, then at Jack, shock on her face.

"I guess I've succumbed to memories," he conceded sheepishly.

She stared at him. "What am I supposed to say to that?"

"What do you mean?"

But she'd already turned away. "Dinner's getting cold."

Puzzled, he looked down at the album. It was open at a portrait from their wedding day.

His breath caught as he looked at his radiant, beautiful bride. In addition to loving her, he'd liked so much about Rosalind Valentine.

He liked how she pretended to be a hard-boiled sophisticate, yet had the natural exuberance of a child. He liked her laugh, her quick, precise movements when she was in a hurry, and the tiny frown that drew her brows together when she was engrossed in a book.

He liked the way she'd shivered and got goose bumps whenever he came up behind her and twisted her silky black hair aside to nuzzle her neck. He liked the texture of her skin, her smell, her taste and the way they fit together—in bed and out of it.

He liked her independence, and her willingness to be emotionally vulnerable. He liked her fairness and how she'd always tried to see the other person's point of view.

He liked the way she'd seen clear through to his soul—and still loved him.

Jack shut the album. That chapter of their lives was dead and buried with their son. And just as with Thomas, regrets couldn't change a damn thing.

CHAPTER NINE

"LIAM GALLOWAY SPEAKING…. Oh, hi, Uncle Wade."

In the middle of putting a forkful of steak into his mouth, Jack froze. No, it couldn't be Roz's ex. He looked across the table, where she was trying to "choo-choo" a spoonful of peas into Cassie's obstinately closed mouth. Roz's cheeks were turning a telltale pink.

Apparently it could.

"*Uncle* Wade?" he inquired.

"Come on, hon," Roz coaxed Cassie, "the train needs a tunnel, so open up."

Liam bounced back into the dining room in high excitement. "Uncle Wade's on the phone."

"*Uncle* Wade?" Jack repeated to Roz's back as she went into the hall.

"Wade," she said in a low voice, walking as far away as the phone cord allowed, "this is a surprise."

Jack tried to read "unwelcome surprise" in her tone, and failed.

"He's ringing from China," burbled Liam, "and he's gonna send me back a dragon kite."

His nephew preferred a mass-produced dragon kite from Roz's two-minute ex to a US$100 Ripstick caster board from his *real* uncle?

Cassie squirmed to get out of her chair. "I wanna talk to Uncle Wade."

"He's not your uncle," Jack snapped.

Through a mouthful of steak, Sam said, "Technically, Roz isn't our aunt, either, since you divorced, but we—" His eyes met Jack's, and he choked and started coughing. "Can you pass the water, please?"

"Yes." Roz lowered her voice so Jack had to strain to hear. "Of course I'm glad you called."

Water splashed onto the table as Jack thumped the jug down beside his nephew.

"Oh, dear," Cassie said in her Auntie Fiona voice. "What a mess."

Jack grabbed some paper napkins and mopped up. "So," he said casually to Sam, "you know him well…? Wade?"

Sam shrugged. "I guess. He and Dad played football together on Tuesdays."

His baby brother had been like that, inclusive, generous, warmhearted…even though Wade and Roz had only been together for eighteen months. *Ants, you bloody traitor.*

"That's very generous of you, Wade," said Roz, "considering—"

"I've finished my dinner," stated Liam. "Can I have ice cream now?"

"Yes," Jack said, but he'd missed the rest of Roz's sentence. Damn.

"I want some ice cream!" Cassie yelled.

"You have to eat your dinner first," Liam reminded her.

"It's yucky." The little girl picked up the piece of

meat in front of her, licked it and put it back on the plate. "See, I don't like it."

"I wish things had worked out differently," Roz was saying, her voice rising to cut out the background noise.

Differently? Did she mean that she wished she and Wade were still together?

"But Auntie Roz said—"

"Just give your sister some ice cream," Jack barked at Liam. Because what Roz *said* wasn't half as interesting as what she was saying now.

"But that's not fair! I had to eat *my* dinner."

"So dish yourself twice as much...now just shush a minute, will you?"

"Jack wants to listen to Roz's conversation," Sam said helpfully.

"Of course I don't!"

Cassie looked at the ice cream Liam was heaping on his plate, then the meager portion he had dished her, and squawked in angry protest.

Jack grabbed the two-liter container and dumped it in front of her with the spoon still in it. "Here."

"But—"

"Quit being a baby," Sam said to Liam.

"Am not."

"Are too."

"Enough!" roared Jack.

Silence fell, except for the careful chink of spoons in bowls. "Sorry, guys. I..." His voice trailed off. What could he say? *I hate the fact that—however briefly—Roz was another man's wife?* Even though he'd left her in the hope she'd make a new life with someone else.

Liam kept spooning up his ice cream with a sullen

expression, but Sam shot Jack a look of sympathy. "Women," he said.

Roz came back into the dining room. "I had to cut the call short with all that racket," she began, then gasped.

Following the direction of her gaze, Jack saw Cassie was plastered in chocolate ice cream from hand to elbow, her lips stretched over a dessert spoon like a widemouthed frog. It was in her hair, smeared across her face, dripping down her bib into a puddle on the floor. Most of the two liters was gone.

Jack had to hand it to Cass; she knew how to take advantage of an opportunity.

"*Who* gave you that?"

"I did," he admitted.

"I told him not to," Liam said piously.

"Squealer," said Sam.

Roz tried to take the ice cream container away from Cass; the little girl growled and clutched the rim.

"Might as well let her finish," Jack commented. "It's nearly gone, anyway."

"I'll get a cloth." There was almost enough frost in Roz's voice to refreeze the melted ice cream. "Jack, can I have a word with you in the kitchen?"

She closed the door behind him. "Stop undermining my authority."

He folded his arms, leaned back against the countertop. "How does being divorced from my ex-wife entitle the professor to keep playing *Uncle* Wade to my family?"

"Oh, for God's sake. That doesn't mean anything—"

"Damn right," he said.

"I won't fight with you in front of the kids," she said

quietly, and Jack had a perverse desire to push harder, to provoke some emotion.

Instead he passed a hand over his face. "You're right, I'm overreacting."

"Wade was calling to offer his condolences from China…he's working there now. He and Ants—"

Jack's temper flared again. "Yeah, I know. They played football together. Whoopty-do." It killed him to know the man had stepped in for him on so many fronts. Judging from Liam and Cassie's enthusiasm, he'd been a much better uncle.

"You were the one who walked away," she reminded him coldly.

He barked a laugh. "And boy, was I easily replaced. The ink was hardly dry on the divorce papers."

Her eyes flashed. "A divorce instigated by you, Jack, so don't play the injured party with me. How many women had you bedded by the time I walked down the aisle with Wade?"

Far fewer than Jack had encouraged her to think. "They didn't mean anything…. He obviously did."

"Oh, so that exonerates you, does it? The fact that you didn't make any promises to anyone? Well, what about the vow to me you broke?" She stabbed at his chest. "Till death us do part?"

Death *had* parted them. "I'm not the only one who has trouble keeping vows." He caught her accusing finger. "How long did marriage number two last? Oh, that's right…excluding courtship, less than a year."

Roz yanked her finger free and slapped him. The crack resounded through the kitchen, but Jack barely flinched.

"Feel better?"

"Yes, damn you!" Her gaze shifted to something behind him, then her eyes widened.

Jack spun around to see Liam and Sam standing openmouthed in the doorway, and his anger evaporated amid overwhelming shame.

The kids gawked at his cheek. "Does it hurt?" whispered Liam.

It stung like hell. "No."

Sam pulled his shocked younger brother against him and glared at Roz. "That's so lame…hitting a guy when he's not allowed to hit you back."

"I deserved it," said Jack, "so don't blame—"

"There's a social worker's here," Sam said abruptly.

Behind Jack, Roz moaned. He turned around, and she moaned again when she caught sight of his cheek.

"We can fix this," he said, and began hauling open kitchen drawers. "Where's a cloth?"

She sprang into action and found one. "They said they'd drop by one evening when you were here to see how we were doing." She tossed the cloth to Jack, who ran it under the cold tap, then pressed it against his burning cheek.

"Keep the social worker talking at the door," he instructed Sam.

"I'll go clean up Cassie." Grabbing a dishcloth, Roz rushed toward the boys, but Sam didn't move aside.

He threw Jack an apologetic look. "You guys were yell…talking too loud to hear the doorbell so—" he stepped aside, pulling Liam with him, and a woman came into view "—I invited her in."

Somewhere in her late forties, she had a mass of

unruly dark hair over a round, kind face, a wide, warm smile and razor-sharp brown eyes. "Hello." She eyed the cloth pressed to Jack's face. "I'm Ellie Walters. I hope I haven't come at a bad time?"

CASSIE HAD HER FACE buried in the white plastic ice cream container, her sticky hands clutching the sides as she licked out the last of the contents, when Roz ushered Ellie into the dining room.

Jack stepped in front of Cassie, obscuring the woman's view. "Are you sure you wouldn't rather wait in the lounge?" He still had the towel pressed against his face. A toothache, he told Ellie.

Roz couldn't look at him directly; she was too ashamed.

She'd never hit him—or anyone—before, but he'd tapped into a rage she'd never really dealt with. Her palm was still stinging, and even now, anger simmered under her contrition. No, she hadn't forgiven him.

"I'm fine here." Ellie pulled out the spare chair at the dining table, her mild gaze settling on Cassie. "My, you have been a busy girl, haven't you?"

At the sound of an unfamiliar voice, Cassie lifted her head from the container. A line of melted ice cream from the rim bisected her hair. Seeing a stranger, she closed sticky, clumped lashes.

"She's shy," Roz explained, taking the opportunity to swipe a napkin across Cassie's face. Being cleaned up was the little girl's least favorite thing, and she emitted a warning growl.

Jack snorted—whether at Cassie's appearance or Roz's explanation, Roz didn't know or care. The other two males grinned before Liam noticed her frown and matched it with one of his own.

"Don't let us keep you, Jack," she said tartly, "if you have to go home." She concentrated on wiping Cass's face and hands, ignoring the growls, which were growing in ferocity.

"And be accused of desertion?" he countered with an answering glint. "I wouldn't dream of it. Sam, how about I reheat your dinner while Roz cleans up Cass?"

Roz registered the half-eaten food on the teenager's plate, and bit her lip. How much had the kids actually heard?

"No, thanks." Sam stared at her with accusing eyes. "I'm not hungry anymore. Hey, Liam, let's go watch *Smackdown.*" He drew out the last word and, flustered, Roz dropped the cloth, then bumped her head on the table while retrieving it.

For a moment she stayed below the tabletop, wondering if she should bother coming up.

"Wrestling," Jack explained to Ellie. "How about I make us all a coffee? Where will I find it, Roz?"

"I'm sorry, but I'm confused." Ellie drew a notepad out of her pack and jotted a few notes. "Am I to understand you're not living here, Mr. Galloway?"

"No." Jack sat down next to Ellie and Roz took a chair opposite.

"He visits," she said nervously, "whenever he can." *Oh, God!* Jack had forgotten about the cold cloth, and the red mark on his left cheek was now a perfect handprint.

Roz coughed, but he was concentrating on Ellie, who, fortunately, sat to his right.

"Uncle Jack! Owwie!" Cassie sucked her breath through small white teeth.

Casually, Jack replaced the cloth. "Is that a problem?" he said to Ellie.

"The temporary parenting order that you and Ms. Valentine applied for was for day-to-day care. That means you're both required to live with the children." She hesitated, glancing from one to the other. "I couldn't help but overhear some of your…discussion. If living under the same roof is a problem…"

Roz lifted Cassie out of her chair and sat the little girl on her lap, heedless of the ice cream. *This is Jack's out*, she thought numbly. Whatever hold she still had over him had been destroyed by that slap. *It's over.*

"If those are the conditions, then I'll move in tomorrow." Across the table, Jack's bland gaze met Roz's. "I'd hate anyone to think I wasn't honoring my commitment."

"Well," said Ellie, making more notes, "that's fine, then." She smiled at Cassie, who shut her eyes again. "Let me give you a pamphlet on dealing with shyness." She riffled through her overflowing folder. "That's odd, I can't find it."

Cassie opened her eyes. "I bet bum-bum Uncle Jack took it."

There was a moment's stunned silence. "My goodness," said Ellie, "where did you pick up that lang— agggh!" She screamed as Liam's frog jumped onto the table in front of her, and she clutched at her heart. "Oh, dear Lord."

Jack flung the cloth over the frog, then scooped it up. "Liam, come get the bloo—your frog out of here."

Liam scooted back into the dining room and took

Froggie, his eyes like saucers as he looked at the hand-print. Jack jammed the wet cloth back against his face.

"Remember," Roz said, distracting Liam, "you're only supposed to let Froggie out in your room." She reached out to ruffle his hair and he stepped back.

"It's only Uncle Jack you hit, right?"

This couldn't—just couldn't!—get any worse, Roz thought.

On her lap, Cassie said, "Uh-oh," and threw up all over the table.

CHAPTER TEN

CASSIE HAD PROBABLY SAVED the day, Roz reflected later, coming downstairs after putting the kids to bed. Because in the ensuing chaos and cleanup, she and Jack had managed to concoct a story about some computer game they all played, where Jack was the target....

Whether Ellie believed them or simply gave them the benefit of the doubt, Roz didn't know, and was too mortified to care. Right now, she had an apology to make.

Despite the chill outside, she found Jack on the deck, waiting to leave. Always waiting to leave. The porch lights were too dim to reveal much of his face, and Roz was glad. Because if you knew where to look you could still see the faint mark of her handprint.

"I shouldn't have hit you," she said without preamble. "I'm sorry."

"I provoked you.... *I'm* sorry." He stood with feet slightly apart, arms folded, the masculine stance of a reluctant apology. Roz almost smiled.

"I was jealous," Jack conceded.

"Because the kids call him Uncle Wade?"

He was silent and, realizing why, she felt her anger rise again. "Because it hurts your male pride that I found someone else." Her laugh was bitter. "Given the brutal way you ended our marriage, Jack, why would I pine for you?"

"No reason at all," he agreed, as though he really thought she could get over him that quickly. And she wanted to hurt him as much as his ignorance hurt her.

"What bothers you the most," she challenged, "that he touched me or that I touched him?"

"How much you must have loved him to marry him," Jack answered quietly.

She turned away. Wade had been a tourniquet to stop the bleeding, not that she'd acknowledged that at the time. He'd loved her when she'd needed love. Only when she'd healed, had Roz realized he deserved better than gratitude. "He's the nicest man I ever met."

"And yet you divorced him."

There was an implied question that Roz wasn't prepared to answer. Turning back, she changed the subject. "Why did you support me with Ellie? You could have got rid of the lot of us, yet you committed to moving in here."

"For the same reason I agreed to temporary custody. I owe you for Thomas."

"Thom—" Her stomach swooped and she felt nauseous. This was a discussion they should have had sooner. "The debt you owe me is for how you ended our marriage, Jack. I don't hold you responsible in any way for our son's death."

This time *he* turned away, looking out at the quiet residential street. "So you always said."

She came closer. "And nearly six years later I'm still saying it."

"Six years on, be honest with me," he challenged.

Keeping his back to her, he jammed his hands in his jacket pockets, though it was a warm night. "You never once thought, if *you'd* been there, Thomas wouldn't have died?"

"Yes, at the time I thought that," she admitted, and he turned his head. "But I never—"

"And it tortured you, didn't it?" His jaw in profile was clenched, his voice fierce in the dark. "You replayed the scenario over and over again. Staying home that morning…not going shopping or to the hairdresser."

"Yes." Her throat closed, and she had to force the words out. "I replayed it thousands of times…but it doesn't make it true, Jack. It was a fantasy that comforted me. I knew that then and I know it now."

In some terrible way, she was lucky not to have been at home with them. Because it would have happened anyway, and she'd be in Jack's situation now, unable to move past the guilt. She took another step toward him. "How could I blame you? You were his father. I knew you would have died to protect him. We should have comforted each other, Jack." He didn't answer and her bitterness returned. "Instead, you left me."

He faced her fully, leaning against the porch railing. "I couldn't spend the rest of my life watching you pretend to forgive me, Roz."

Even after all these years he wouldn't hear what she was saying. That no one held Jack accountable but himself.

"Go away," she ordered. "Go away before I hit you again."

There was a flash of white teeth, more grimace than smile. "I'll be back tomorrow night with my bags."

Halfway down the steps, he paused. "Whatever you want to call this payment for, Roz, consider the debt discharged. And if it makes you feel any better? The day you married Wade crucified me. So you got even."

And he disappeared into the dark.

LIAM WAS ON A SECRET mission.

Yesterday, he'd discovered where Roz had hidden some Christmas presents—at the top of her wardrobe— and the temptation to look had been gnawing at him ever since.

And now he had the perfect opportunity.

Roz was cooking dinner; Cassie was watching a DVD with her blankie after her bath. Cautiously, he opened the door to Roz's bedroom, and froze at the faint scent of her perfume, a sort of lemony, flowery smell. Nope, he was alone.

Ignoring his guilty reflection in the mirrored door, he slid the wardrobe open. The presents were on the top shelf, in an innocent white plastic bag, but a curl of gold ribbon hung over the edge like a fishing lure.

He'd spotted it last night while he and Cassie were playing hide-and-seek. Liam was tortured by Christmas presents—hidden around the house like pirate's treasure, waiting for an intrepid discoverer.

Last year Mum and Dad had removed his presents from under the tree because he couldn't resist poking a tiny hole in the festive paper.

Not that he'd do so now that he was six.

No, all he wanted to do was check out the size, feel the weight and maybe give the big ones a tiny shake just to hear anything there was to hear.

Quietly, he hauled the chair in front of the dressing table over to the wardrobe.

"What you doing?"

Liam jumped. Cassie stood in the doorway with Blankie, hair tufted up from lying on the couch, brown eyes sleepy—and interested.

"Go away. I'm doing big kids' stuff." He grabbed her shoulders to turn her; she screeched. Liam dropped his hands. "Shush!"

"I wanna climb the chair, too."

"You can't, you're too little." She started that rising wail that would bring adult backup, and Liam knew he'd have to do something fast. Digging into the pocket of his jeans, he felt for the last jelly bean, the black one he'd been saving. "Here!"

There was white lint on the sticky licorice coating, but Cassie popped it into her mouth.

"You can watch," he said. "But you have'ta be quiet."

Sucking noisily, she nodded.

He climbed on the chair and, on tiptoe, reached as high as he could, but his fingertips only brushed the plastic handle. Frustrated, he glanced around the wardrobe for something else to stand on.

There was a heavy cardboard box on one of the lower shelves, half-hidden by a stack of woolens. Dragging it onto the chair, he clambered on top. The cardboard sagged, but held. Again Liam stretched for the presents, fingers straining…touching. Got it!

The box collapsed, he lost his balance and fell forward into the row of clothes, landing in a tangle of fabric and presents and coat hangers.

"Uh-oh," said Cassie. A drool of black licorice trickled from her wet mouth.

Liam scrambled to his feet. "Quick, go guard the door!" He had to clean up before Roz came.

Obediently, Cassie went to stand there, but her fascinated gaze stayed on Liam.

Frantically, he shoved the fallen clothes to the back of the wardrobe and squashed the presents back in the plastic bag. "I'm gonna be in so much trouble," he muttered, grabbing papers and jamming them back into the cardboard box. He suddenly recognized what he was holding and stopped in bewilderment.

"What on earth was that crash?" Roz's voice carried up the hall, then her head appeared around the door.

"Auntie Roz is here," said his lookout.

But Liam didn't care about being caught anymore.

"Liam Galloway, are you trying to find Christmas pre…" Then Roz saw what was in his hand and stopped short, her expression stricken. Guilty.

And his whole world collapsed.

A SENSE OF GLOOM pervaded the house when Jack carried his bags and laptop through the back door from the garage that evening. He put them down in the hall and listened.

Cartoons on the TV in the family room sounded normal. Something spicy was emanating from the kitchen, and he sniffed…. Lasagna, faintly overlaid by strawberry bubble bath from the downstairs bathroom.

Cassie, her small face solemn, appeared from the living room, dressed in pink flannelette pajamas and mouse slippers, and carrying Blankie. Silently, she came down the hall and wrapped her arms around Jack's legs, laying her head against his shins. Something was definitely wrong.

"Hey, Cass." He picked her up and she cuddled against him with a sigh, her soft palms curled around his neck. Her implicit trust startled him. "Where is everybody?" With her head still on his shoulder, she pointed.

In the living room, he found Sam, Liam and Roz standing in a loose triangle around the coffee table, which was covered with letters, colorfully drawn, with childish writing.

All of them had their arms folded—Roz and Sam defensively; Liam like a judge. Fleetingly, Jack was reminded of a crime scene on one of the television cop shows. The little boy's lower lip jutted out and his brows were drawn in a ferocious frown. None of them acknowledged Jack's arrival.

"Honey, I didn't post them because I knew your parents can still read them from heaven," Roz said desperately. Against Jack's advice, she'd taken over the task from Fiona.

"Why is it such a big deal, anyway?" said Sam. "I mean, you know Mum and Dad are dead."

"But you said you'd post them—both of you—which means you lied. And anyway, how can they see through the cardboard box?"

Roz brightened. "Superman can see through lead."

Momentarily, the scowl lifted. "No, he can't!" Liam's voice grew in volume until he was shouting. "He can see through everything *but* lead." Angry tears started coursing down his cheeks. "See, you don't know anything."

"What's going on?" Jack asked quietly.

Roz turned to him, her expression pinched with anxiety. "Liam found his letters to Ants and Julia in a box in my wardrobe."

"She said she'd posted 'em, and she didn't. Mum and Dad didn't even get them." The small boy lay down on the floor and started crying sobs of despair and anger that reached into Jack's chest and clutched painfully. He knew exactly what that moment of abandoning all hope felt like.

From Jack's arms, Cassie looked at her big brother, and her mouth trembled. "I want my mummy."

Clumsily patting the toddler's back, Jack fought the urge to cut and run. Roz fell to her knees beside Liam, tears in her eyes. "Darling, no. With all my heart I believe they're watching over you and know what's in those letters."

She tried to pick him up, but he pushed her away. "You'd say anything to make me feel better," Liam sobbed. "And now I can't believe you anymore."

Despairing, she looked up. "Jack, please." But he had nothing to contribute.

Liam pushed up to a sitting position and stopped sobbing. "You'll tell me the truth, won't you, Uncle Jack? You'll tell me the truth because you don't like me." There was no judgment in the child's voice; it was said simply, as a statement of fact, and Jack squirmed like a worm on a hook.

"Of course I like you, mate," he croaked.

"You tell me, Uncle Jack! Tell me the truth!"

Hugging himself, Sam started edging toward the door, and Jack knew he had to say something.

"Actually, it's a good thing Roz didn't post them, because it wouldn't have worked."

A muffled sob escaped Roz; Jack ignored it. With his gaze still locked to Liam's, he gestured toward the empty fire grate. "You have to burn them."

Out of the corner of his eye he saw Sam turn his head.

"You burn them," Jack repeated, "and the smoke carries them up to heaven." *God forgive me,* he thought, *for this lie,* then nearly smiled at the irony of an atheist praying. He must be more screwed up than he thought.

But Ants and Julia had believed, and this was their son. Jack had no right to destroy a child's faith because life had destroyed his. Liam was still eyeballing him, so he kept his expression transparent, let the child see what Jack did believe. That if heaven existed, Ants and Julia would be there, watching over their children.

The slight shoulders relaxed in a shuddering sigh.

Shakily, Roz got to her feet and collapsed into a chair. Jack remained standing, patting Cassie's back. She was heavy in his arms and he realized she'd fallen asleep, lashes curled over her cheek.

For a long time no one said anything. They simply sat or stood numbly, like people in the aftermath of a hurricane that had razed everything to the ground, but left them miraculously untouched.

Sam was the first to move, dipping his hand into the pocket of his jeans. "I have matches," he said gruffly.

Jack made a mental note to talk to him again about smoking. "You can light them, then," he said. "That is, if Liam wants to burn them now."

In answer, Liam wiped at his eyes with the sleeve of his sweatshirt and gathered up his letters. Kneeling before the fireplace, he laid them reverently in the grate. Sam lit them.

Jack watched the edges of the paper blacken and curl, the brightly colored drawings become distorted as the crayon melted. The large words disappeared as flames consumed and then exhaled them as smoke.

Tiny fragments of charred paper rose on the updraft while Liam and Sam watched solemnly, firelight in their eyes. And strong feelings—painful from being held back for so long—came to life in Jack.

The flames ran out of fuel and died. Liam grabbed the poker and stirred until the ash crumbled and fell through the grate, and there was nothing left. Then he went to Roz and buried his face in her lap.

She leaned forward and laid her cheek over the curve of his back, her long, dark hair spread across his green sweatshirt like a protective blanket. And Jack had to close his eyes because the beauty of that image was more than he could bear.

But he still heard her softly voiced "Amen."

CHAPTER ELEVEN

ROZ STOOD OUTSIDE Anthony's study, staring at the heavy, dark oak, then knocked and went in. The younger children were in bed, Sam was holed up in his room, and Jack was in here, unpacking.

"I just wanted to say thank-you…for what you said to Liam."

Looking up from the desk, where he was setting up his laptop, Jack shrugged. "Yes, well…I did what I had to do. But I don't believe any of it, Roz."

The weariness she'd been holding at bay overwhelmed her. "Most of the time I'm faking it, too, Jack." She started to leave, but he was at the door before her, leaning on it to close it.

"What's that supposed to mean?"

Throat tight, she lifted her chin. "You don't have copyright on a bleak world view."

Shock flickered in his eyes. "Don't *you* give up," he said. "Not you, Roz."

"I'm not giving up…at least, not permanently." A sob ripped from her chest. "I'm letting them down, Ju and Anthony…. Sam hates me, and now I've traumatized Liam." She'd flung herself into taking custody, so sure she was doing the right thing. So sure Fee was the wrong person for the job. With her efficiency, at least the other woman would have posted the letters.

Knuckling her eyes, Roz reached past Jack, fumbling for the door handle. His scent, crisp and clean, enveloped her, then his strong arms. She laid her head against his shoulder and wept.

"It was never going to be easy," he soothed. "And for what it's worth, I think you're doing a hell of a job, given the circumstances."

She couldn't allow herself to rely on him like this, couldn't handle the pain of the inevitable withdrawal. Safer, far safer to fight. She pulled away to glare at him. "Say I told you so and you're on diaper detail."

"I wouldn't dare." He drew her head back against his shoulder; she felt his smile against her hair. Ah, God, she remembered that smile, so rare these days. Could feel it in her heart. Under her cheek, the beat of his was solid and familiar.

How had they fallen into this dangerous intimacy so quickly? Roz freed herself. "I'm okay."

But Jack didn't move away from the door. "Liam will get over it," he said softly, "and Sam doesn't hate you."

"He never talks to me. Every time I try to chat—"

"Guys don't chat. In fact, even the suggestion of chatting makes us run for the hills."

"Liam talks."

"Not to me."

Roz said delicately, "You want to cha…talk about it?"

"I'm handling it."

"Huh." She imbued the grunt with skepticism.

He grinned at her. "Now you're getting the hang of guy talk…. No, don't ruin it with a girlie follow-up."

She laughed and felt better. Long ago, they'd bantered like this all the time, enjoying the male-female polarity until the teasing became intimate and they took the battle to bed. A similar awareness flashed in Jack's eyes, charged the air between them.

They started talking at the same time.

"I've got a cup of tea waiting," she blurted.

"I'm going to take a shower," said Jack, "get an early night."

Neither of them could leave the study fast enough.

In the kitchen, Roz turned on the tap and splashed her face with water. "You're not the only one who needs a cold shower," she muttered, reaching for the paper towels.

Instead, her fingers touched Jack. Roz yelped and looked up, water dripping from her face.

"You…you startled me." She refused to think about whether he'd heard her or not because then she'd blush, she'd gibber, she'd sink through the floor.

"I wanted to ask where you keep the towels." His jaw was clenched as he handed her the roll. Roz ripped off a sheet and buried her burning face in it.

"Linen cupboard at the top of the stairs, opposite my…bedroom."

"Thanks." His voice had dropped so low it was almost a rumble. Instinctively, she lifted her gaze to his—and found his pupils took up half the irises. Lust jolted through her and her fingers clutched the paper towel.

"You're welcome," she whispered.

His chest expanded. "Okay if I use the shampoo in the shower? I left mine behind."

"If you like bubble-gum-scented baby shampoo." She imagined lathering it on his wet head, imagined pink bubbles running down all that strong, naked muscle.... Roz shook away the vision. "If you like I can get you something more grown-up to use."

In his eyes, she saw the something more grown-up he wanted, and she gripped the sink rim for support. Yes, she wanted to be used. There was a throb between her legs, a need she hadn't felt for a long, long time. She knew exactly how he felt gliding inside her, filling her beautifully, tortuously.

The muscle in his neck corded as though under a terrible strain. "I don't think that's a good idea."

Her brain came back to earth, landed with a bump.

Where was her pride? This man had left her in her darkest hour, then added insult to grievous injury by immediately dating other women. Yet part of her still wanted him, despite everything. "You're right," she said, full of self-disgust, "Cassie's shampoo should do fine."

ROZ KNEW TODAY WAS GOING to be a bad day when at 7:30 a.m. one week later she opened the fridge to get milk for the kids' cereal, and remembered she'd left a bag of groceries in the car overnight.

Turned out she'd left the trunk open, too.

As she approached she saw James Zombie Maisy eating the minced beef destined for nachos tonight. The frozen peas were a flabby wet packet on the suit Jack had asked her to pick up from the dry cleaners.

So it wasn't all bad.

Since the kitchen incident they'd both used the kids as human shields to avoid being alone together—on the rare occasions Jack was home. Roz suspected he worked longer hours to avoid her. It seemed a bitter irony that while her goal was getting Jack to bond with the kids, her presence had become an impediment to him doing so.

And time was running out. Fiona and Roger's weekly calls were a reminder of how fast. The temporary custody arrangement was already a month old, and Roz was lying awake at night worrying about the kids' future and trying not to worry about the fact that she wasn't over Jack.

She popped the top of the milk and sniffed, then reeled back at the sour smell. Liam's sleeping bag from a birthday overnight lay in the backseat, and as she moved it away from the soggy peas, duck down fluttered through the car. Great, there was a hole in it.

Sighing, Roz went back inside for her purse. Sam was pouring cereal into a bowl and Cassie was playing at his feet. "We're out of milk," Roz said. "Can you make sure Liam gets up and dressed while I go get some?"

"I come," said Cassie.

"No, hon, stay with Sam."

"Why?" he complained.

"Because Jack's in the shower."

"I already have to sort Liam out."

She didn't have time for this. Roz picked Cassie up— oh Lord, she needed her diaper changed—marched to the car and buckled the toddler in her car seat, still in her pajamas.

"Feathers!" Cassie cupped some in her hand and blew.

The old man behind the counter wrinkled his nose when Roz dumped the milk on the counter and counted out coins from her purse. "Kid smells worse than wartime trenches."

"Sorry," she said, "it was an emergency. Here you go."

"What about the candy she's eating?"

Looking down, Roz saw Cass stealthily chewing her way through a chocolate fish from the display at the front of the counter.

"Cassie, no!" She took the headless fish away from her, and Cass promptly threw a tantrum.

The old man yawned. "That'll be an extra dollar fifty," he said over the wailing.

Roz emptied her purse and found herself short. "Can I pay you later?"

He pointed to the sign next to the counter: Do Not Ask for Credit for Fear a Refusal Will Offend.

"It's only fifty cents."

"No exceptions," he said. "It's a slippery slope. An' you got feathers in your hair."

Anxiously, Roz glanced at her watch. She could leave and come back, but that would make Sam and Liam late for school. It was already touch and go.

"Leave your watch as security," he suggested.

"You expect me to leave my two hundred dollar watch for half a chocolate fish?" She looked down at Cassie, who was still writhing on the floor. "How about I leave the kid?"

"You think I didn't learn things in 'Nam?"

On the way home, Roz opened the windows because the stench had got so bad, and her temper was ready to blow.

Cassie stopped howling and tried to catch the flying feathers.

Jack was in the kitchen when they walked in, looking in the fridge. His hair curled damply over his collar from a shower, and a spicy aftershave cut through the smell of last night's leftovers. His broad shoulders were covered in a fine wool suit jacket that suggested he was heading for one of his corporate meetings.

No doubt, thought Roz meanly, with an interior designer in a Karen Walker suit and Manolo Blahnik heels, who'd just spent an hour buffing up at the gym and was currently enjoying a skim latte and a low-fat muffin and—

She realized she was jealous of a woman that existed only in her imagination, and not just because of her latte, but because she might flirt with Jack.

Putting the milk on the counter, Roz took a deep, deep breath and was reminded that Cassie's diaper needed changing.

Head still in the fridge, Jack said mildly, "There's no milk."

"It's here."

He turned around and blinked. "You have feathers in your hair."

Feathers in my brain, as well. "Fashion accessory," she said, shepherding Cassie toward the bathroom.

"And all over your back," said Jack, "and what the hell is that smell?"

"*Real* life."

Cassie ducked under her arm and ran to Jack.

"You mean you two went out like that?" His tone had the incredulity of a man in charge of his world.

Roz's temper rose, hot and hard. He was only in charge of his world because he refused to step outside its boundaries and get messy like everyone else.

"Yes, we went out like this! Because Sam— Wait,

where is Sam?" She checked the clock. "Oh, hell, he's left for the bus and he hasn't had breakfast."

"Relax, I gave him some money." Jack picked up the milk and poured some into his coffee. "You know, Roz, you could save yourself a lot of stress with more forward planning."

Her anger chilled to an icy rage. "What would you suggest?" Mentally, she slipped a big fat noose around her ex-husband's neck.

"A daily planner, getting things ready the night before, making sure you're always well stocked with the basic foodstuffs…"

"Gee, I never thought of that." Something in her voice—or maybe it was survival instinct—made Jack look up as he buttered his toast.

Roz smiled sweetly and fed her ex-husband more rope. "Any other tips?"

"Liam." Jack scraped the last of the jam out of the jar. "You know he's a dawdler. Maybe you should try getting him up earlier. And Cassie, well, I've been flicking through a few of Julia's books…shouldn't she be potty trained by now?"

He handed Cassie a piece of toast; she licked off the butter and stretched up, her little belly pale over the top of her pajama pants, to dump the rest on the table.

"And her eating habits are atrocious."

Roz kicked open the trapdoor and let the bastard swing. "Okay, hotshot, you've obviously got all the answers." She was tired of acting as a buffer between Jack bloody Galloway and the realities of child care. "Here!" She thrust the wet wipes and the clean diaper at him, and automatically, he took them.

"What are you talking about?"

"You know, this is my fault." With jerky movements Roz put on her coat, picked up her bag. "In trying to get you to bond with the kids I've kept all the bad, sad things from you—Cassie's toileting regression, Liam's obsession with his health, Sam's tru— All the ways they've been grieving. But I've been deluding myself, haven't I?" She picked up her car keys. "You're never going to let yourself feel anything for anyone again. If these kids were the von Trapp family from *The Sound of Music,* you still wouldn't let yourself love them, would you?"

He didn't answer; he didn't have to. The look on his face said it all.

"Well, I've had it up to my laundry-soaked elbows doing this alone. As they say on *Wrestling World* or whatever the hell that bloody show's called—" Roz tapped his arm "—tag, partner. I…give…up!"

"You can't," Jack said reasonably. "I've got a heap on today…meetings, a site visit. I can't take a pre-schooler to a construction site." He was obviously under the misconception that she'd respond to logic.

"Why not? Cass would be great at demolition."

"Roz…" Uneasiness drew his brows together. "I'll never say another word of criticism, I promise." He put his hand to his heart.

"You're in charge of the walking bus this morning, so I suggest you get a move on."

"For God's sake, you can't leave me alone with these kids. I'm not qualified." Now there was panic in his voice, a deeper thread of disquiet.

"Don't worry, you won't be in charge…they will."

She felt great—light-headed with power and vented anger. "Today you're spending time with them—whether you like it or not. Oh, and that daily planner you're so keen on is stuck to the fridge."

On her way out, she bent to kiss Cass on the top of her silky head, whispered, "Give him hell, sweetheart."

"Roz, this is crazy. Come back."

She kept right on walking. Outside, she hauled Cassie's car seat out of the back of the station wagon and dumped it in the garage.

She was backing down the driveway when she heard a small, panicked voice. "Roz!" Liam hung out of an upstairs window, alarm on his face, and she braked. "Where are you going?"

"Uncle Jack's looking after you today."

"I don't want him to."

She nearly lost her nerve. "He's...he's a good guy, Liam. You'll be fine."

"But when will you be back?"

"I'll be home in time to tuck you into bed, I promise. Now finish getting ready for school. Jack's going to need your help."

She drove two blocks and pulled over, knuckles white on the steering wheel and guilt making her stomach churn. What if Cassie didn't eat? What if Jack and Liam had a fight? What if Sam didn't come home after school? For twenty minutes Roz sat there, fighting one of the hardest battles of her life. If she went back, nothing would change. Jack was their family, and she needed a break—she'd used up all her reserves. She wasn't Superwoman; in that area Fee was way ahead of her.

Roz couldn't protect the kids—or Jack—any longer. If they were ever going to forge a relationship, they'd have to find their way together, without her interference or intervention.

She drove home to her tiny designer apartment in a tower block in the central city. The first thing she did was open all the windows to release the mustiness and let in the warm spring day.

Then she opened her mail, pulling a wry face at the half-dozen "Sorry you're leaving" cards sent from her former colleagues. Right now, quitting her job seemed like an act of sheer lunacy.

Disconsolately, she turned on the shower, then remembered she'd switched the hot water off, and swore. It was good to use rude words aloud again.

What was she going to do for the two hours the water took to heat? She pulled back the sheets on her bed and crawled in. Jet lag was like this—gritty lids, heavy limbs and a feeling of dizziness when she shut her eyes.

The apartment was very quiet. The water heater clicked and gurgled. She closed her eyes and slept.

CHAPTER TWELVE

JACK STOOD IN THE KITCHEN amid the debris of breakfast. *She'll come back. No way would she leave me alone with young children.* The thought steadied him. Ten minutes tops, and she'd walk through that door.

He sat on a stool at the kitchen counter and watched the minutes tick around the clock while Cassie pushed James Zombie Maisy around on Liam's Ripstik board.

Then realized he was being pathetic. The least he could do was get the kids ready.

"You got everything you need for school, mate?" he asked Liam, who was lurking in the hall.

"Yeah, but I can't find Froggie to put him in his tank."

Jack hid his impatience. "Okay, let's look." That bloody amphibian went walkabout so often it should have a swag on its back.

They checked the obvious places first—the sink, the bath and the toilets; anywhere there was water. Nothing. Next were the dark places—wardrobes, cupboards and under beds. On his hands and knees, Jack lifted Liam's bedspread and peered into the gloom, while Cassie jumped on the mattress. A spring hit Jack's head.

"Sh—"

"Is he there?" The cover lifted on the other side, and Liam's hopeful face appeared, upside down.

"No!" Dropping the cover, Jack stood up, rubbing his scalp. "Listen, Liam, if you're given responsibility for something, you have to look after it properly." He knew he should stop there, but he was pissed.

Ten minutes had come and gone, he was late for work and Roz should have been back by now. "This halfhearted, got-something-else-better-to-do mentality isn't bloody good enough. Froggie depends on you to keep him safe."

Jack caught sight of himself in the mirrored wardrobe—a big, angry man standing over a small boy with bowed head—and shock sent him stumbling back a step. He'd become his father. In the frozen moment that followed came another painful realization: *And a damn hypocrite.* "Halfhearted" was exactly the way he'd tackled this guardianship.

Liam shot him a scared glance that made him want to crawl into a dark hole with Froggie. "You know what?" Jack said quietly. "Most of the time you do a good job looking after that animal. He's just the Houdini of frogs. Let's keep looking." Eventually the three of them found him in a plant pot in the lounge.

Liam's watch beeped, and he glanced at it anxiously. "We need to go soon. That's my ten-minute warning for Auntie Roz."

"Maybe we'll call in sick today."

"No, we can't! You're in charge of the walking bus and I'm doing the morning talk."

"What the hell is a walking bus?"

"Parents take turns walking kids to school. Kids get collected outside their houses."

"Okay then." Jack accepted the inevitable. "What's left to get ready?"

"Make my lunch, change Cassie, sign my homework book—"

Jack raked a hand through his hair. "How about I give you money to change Cassie's diaper?"

Liam looked doubtful. "I don't think I'll be very good at it."

"Ten bucks. Fifteen if you can do it in five minutes."

Liam grabbed Cassie's hand and she growled. "If you let me change you," he wheedled, because he really, really wanted all that money, "I'll buy you a lollipop."

Obediently, she came with him to the bathroom and lay down on the changing mat.

It wasn't easy and Liam used a lot of baby wipes, but he managed. Cassie balked at the clothes he dragged out of the drawer, so he let her pick what she wanted to wear.

They were back in the kitchen in twelve minutes. "I did it!"

But Uncle Jack only nodded distractedly. He had the phone jammed between his shoulder and jaw, and was slathering peanut butter on bread. *And* using the same knife in the butter, which Mum would've told him off for. "I'll try and get on-site by ten. Find a kid's hard hat for me, will you…? Hell, I don't know. How tall are you, Cassie?"

"Free," she said proudly, giving Uncle Jack her age.

"Three…no, that's not right. About knee height."

He hung up. "What on earth is your sister wearing?"

Liam eyed Cassie. She looked all right to him, in orange jeans and a pink sweatshirt, with her sparkle shoes and yellow sun hat. "Clothes," he said helpfully, watching Uncle Jack parcel up his sandwiches, hoping he'd be able to unwrap the cling film when the time came, 'cause his uncle used so much. "I need a cookie, a drink and an apple, too."

Uncle Jack opened every cupboard, searching for what he needed, and Liam had to help him. For an adult, he really wasn't very good at this. Liam started to panic. "We're going to be very late."

"I'm hungry," whined Cassie.

"Uncle Jack, we need to go!" Liam started to feel tearful.

Uncle Jack scanned the pantry shelves. "Here." He gave a surprised Cassie an open box of cornflakes, then plonked her in the stroller in the hall.

"You have to strap her in."

Uncle Jack got mixed up with the straps and buckles, so Liam had to do it.

The doorbell rang. Uncle Jack stopped fiddling with the straps and sat back on his heels. "Of course she'd come back," he said, and gave a strange laugh. "Why was I worried?"

Excited, Liam wrenched open the door. "Auntie Ro—"

His five-year-old neighbor stood on the other side. "I brought flies," said Marcus.

Liam forgot about Auntie Roz. He took the jar and held it up, trying to count the buzzing contents. "How many?"

"Eight," Marcus stated, turning red with pride, "and one blowie. I got 'em from the compost heap. I wuz gonna bring 'em after school, but Mum wanted them out of the house…. Is that your uncle?"

Liam was still trying to count the flies. He glanced

over his shoulder. Uncle Jack was standing behind him, staring at the jar. "Yeah."

"Marcus Cunningham," said Marcus, and held out his hand. His mum was big on manners and looking adults in the eye and stuff.

Uncle Jack seemed to wake up. "Jack Galloway." He shook Marcus's hand. "The, ah…flies are for?"

"Froggie," Liam answered authoritatively. "He has one a day. If you don't catch 'em, you have to buy 'em."

"I better go to school," said Marcus.

Through the glass jar, Liam caught sight of his digital watch. "We should'a left five minutes and twenty-three seconds ago, Uncle Jack!"

Cassie said, "I want to hold the flies."

"No! She'll break it."

His baby sister started to howl. Uncle Jack gave her the jar of flies and she shut up. It was Liam's turn to protest.

"If it breaks I'll catch more," Uncle Jack promised. "Let's just get you to school…. You know where we go?" Liam nodded. "Okay, let's roll."

Outside the front gate they picked up speed, half jogging, half walking. Cassie's stroller bounced over the curbs and she laughed. "Go faster."

Liam noticed she was making a mess with the cornflakes, which bounced out of the box and cascaded down her pink sweatshirt, but she kept a tight grip on the flies. Actually, it was kind of fun, running like this, his rucksack bouncing on his back.

"This is Molly's house," Liam panted, waving to Molly, who was swinging on the gate ahead. Her mum caught sight of Uncle Jack and stopped frowning, standing up straighter, pushing her shoulders back like Mrs. White told them in assembly. It must be hard with such big bosoms.

"Hi, Liam." Molly picked up her rucksack and grabbed his hand, and he pulled free, scowling.

"You have to," she said in her bossy voice, "it's the rules."

It tortured him to hold a girl's hand; still, Liam was a great respecter of rules. Reluctantly, he let her take it again. Her hand was warm and slightly damp, and he jiggled from foot to foot. "Can we go now, Uncle Jack?"

But his uncle was smiling at Molly's mum in the way grown-ups did when they wanted the other person to do something. Liam hadn't known Uncle Jack had dimples like Dad. "So, now you can understand my predicament, Karen," he was saying. "I don't suppose you can take over the walking bus today?"

"Well, I would, but I need to get to work." Molly's mum did look sorry. "But honestly, Jack, it's so easy. They walk in front, holding hands, while you take up the rear. And there's only six kids—"

"Six?" Uncle Jack looked shocked.

"Don't worry, you'll be fine, a big strong guy like you." She laughed, tossing her head and reminding Liam of the horse in the field next to his school. Molly's hand was getting wetter and wetter; he let it go to wipe his palm on his sweatshirt.

"Can we please go now, Uncle Jack?" The next place was his friend Findley's house. He'd much rather hold hands with Findley.

Uncle Jack had lost the dimples. "Yeah, mate," he said glumly.

"So anyway, I finish work at two," Molly's mum called after them. Come to think of it, she kinda had teeth like the horse, too. "So I'll give you a call in case you still need help…with Cassie or housework."

That was weird. Liam had been into Molly's house once and it didn't look like her mum did housework.

"Will you be my boyfriend?" Molly whispered.

"No," said Liam, jerking his hand away.

"Just till you go to England?" wheedled Molly.

"I don't like girls!" And thinking about living with Auntie Fee made his tummy go funny. She wasn't like Mum or Auntie Roz. She expected kids to act like grown-ups.

"You have to hold my hand." Molly tried to grab it again, and Liam pushed her away.

"Go away, bum-bum."

"Liam, you don't push girls," Uncle Jack said.

And suddenly he'd had enough. "I can't be good anymore," he yelled. "I've used up all my goodness."

He expected his uncle to yell back, but he just said quietly, "Okay, mate," and let him and Molly hold the stroller instead.

"'THE RAIN WAS SO NOISY on Pinky's biscuit tin roof that he'd run outside with his fruit bowl, thinking plums were falling off the tree above his home.'" Jack stifled a yawn, and from her perch on his lap, Cassie elbowed him in the ribs.

"Keep reading."

"'Then the big raindrops would splash on his up-turned face, soaking Pinky to the skin. This was the only time he ever washed, so it was lucky he lived in a country where it rained a lot.'"

Across the Italian restaurant's white linen tablecloth, Liam stopped sucking up the last of his Coke through a straw. "Uncle Jack, I'm starving." The whine in his voice was getting more pronounced.

"It's been forty minutes since we ordered," Sam agreed. "I wish they'd hurry up."

"So do I. Then I can stop reading." Jack had never noticed how slow service was in his favorite restaurant. But then, he'd never been here with hungry kids. Or eaten dinner at six-thirty before. Cassie growled and jabbed him in the ribs again.

Dear God, Jack hated this mouse, but unless he read, Cassie would be getting off his lap and creating havoc. She'd already startled the wine waiter into dropping their first round of drinks by growling at him from under the table.

"'Once there'd been a drought and it hadn't rained for three weeks. Pinky had got so smelly no animal would stand downwind of him.'" All Jack's sympathy was with the other animals; he'd changed four diapers today. And Cassie smelled as if she needed another.

Surreptitiously, he turned five pages together and resumed reading. "'And so they went in and had plum jam on hot buttered crumpets and…lived happily ever after.'" Jack slammed the book shut. "Finished."

"Nooo!" Cassie took the book and, frowning at him, reopened it at the right page.

"You can't read!" Jack declared.

"She knows it off by heart," said Sam. "We all do."

"Fifteen bucks to change her diaper," he offered.

Sam leaned back in his seat, scrawny arm slung across the back of the chair's tubular frame. "Thirty."

"You did it for twenty dollars two hours ago."

Sam inspected his nails. "Yeah, but we're in a restaurant, under difficult conditions...."

"Okay, twenty-five." They both knew he had Jack over a barrel.

"I'll do it for twenty." A round-eyed Liam piped up.

Jack thought of the mountain of used baby wipes and the dirty diaper he'd found discarded in the bathroom on his return home this morning and blanched. They hadn't needed Marcus's imported flies.

"You can be Sam's assistant," he said.

"I'm not giving him any of my money."

Jack handed over another ten. Today was costing him a fortune. His conscience had prevented him looking for a babysitter, but he'd had no compunction about calling a housecleaning service—not that he was going to tell Roz that.

Getting a cleaner had been one of Luke's many pieces of advice. Jack had rung his foster brother in desperation when Cassie had thrown a tantrum in the middle of the supermarket because he wouldn't let her push the cart. After laughing at Jack, Luke had talked her down. The incident had evaporated any lingering constraint between the two men. Jack had brought the kids to Antonio's for dinner because his cooking skills didn't extend past barbecuing meat.

"C'mon, Cass." Sam picked up his sister. The three trooped off to the bathroom, and Jack found himself alone for the first time that day. Well, not quite. Cassie had left Winnie the Pooh sitting opposite, wearing a diamanté headband with pink feathery things sticking out of it.

"So, you're a girl now, too, huh?" Jack said, thinking of the cat.

He heard a cough behind him. The owner was standing there. "Apologies for the delay, Jack. The chef had trouble locating cheese slices." There was a culinary artist's disdain in his voice. "Let me buy you a drink…a glass of Chianti."

"Thanks, Dario, but if I start drinking, I'll never stop."

The old man inclined his head and gestured to Pooh. "Something for the lady, then?"

Jack leaned back in his chair and considered his old acquaintance through narrowed eyes. "It's been a long—*very* long—day."

Dario backed away, palms raised, but his liquid black eyes glistened. "Ahh, your food arrives and also your *famiglia* approaches." In an undertone he added, "And the little bella mafiosa."

Jack grinned. "Please, let me pay for those water glasses."

"No, no…I only ask you to bring her again—when she's twenty."

The kids returned to the table. Sam took a long draft from his Coke. "I undercharged you," he muttered, but brightened as the veal parmigiana was laid in front of him.

Liam looked doubtfully at his bolognese. "I thought it would be spaghetti hoops out of the can," he said.

Jack leaned over and tucked a large napkin into the kid's T-shirt. "Welcome to real food," he said.

He tried to show Liam how to twirl the spaghetti around his fork, but the boy ended up looking as if he'd been on the receiving end of a gangster drive-by shooting, splattered in red sauce.

In the end, Jack cut it up. Beside Jack, Cassie licked all the garlic butter off the dinner rolls, ate three olives and pronounced herself finished. Until Jack's crème caramel arrived and she ate the lot.

The younger kids fell asleep on the drive home. He carried them in and laid them in their beds, fully clothed, then made himself a tall bourbon on the rocks and collapsed on the couch. "Is it always like this?" he asked Sam.

"Pretty much."

Jack noticed that the school bags still needed unpacking, and remembered the other jobs on Roz's daily planner he hadn't done—the washing, the ironing, making something for a bake sale at school, buying a present for a birthday party Liam was attending tomorrow.

Over the last week he'd seen his ex-wife do so much more. The ice chinked in his glass as he took a long swallow. Kissing owwies, helping with homework, listening to troubles in addition to cooking, cleaning and coaxing Cass to eat. Being the good mother she was.

The sweet pain of watching her had driven him to take refuge in work, but today he'd realized that he owed these kids more than lip service as a guardian. No matter how hard it was being around his ex-wife.

And he had to admit, in some odd way, today had been fun.

Cassie hadn't let Jack out of her sight, but she'd been in her element, playing in a heap of sawdust on-site, and growling at any construction crew who made friendly overtures, much to everyone's amusement.

As long as Jack let her do whatever she wanted, they'd got along fine, and for the sake of his schedule he pretty much had. The stop at the toy shop, DVDs on demand, fries for lunch…he didn't fool himself that these things were anything but a stopgap. If he'd thought for a moment that he was making progress with his brother's children, Liam's disapproving face would have set him straight.

Despite Jack's best efforts, he couldn't please that boy, and it prickled him like a hair shirt. He wanted Liam to look up to him like his daddy had when they were kids. But the child—this clone of Ants—persisted in disliking him.

At least he and Sam were cool. Jack glanced over to the teenager, who was text messaging on his cell phone, and tried to think like a parent. "You got any homework you should be doing?"

"What? Yeah…it's a group project, so is it okay if I go to my friend David's house to study?" Sam waved his cell. "He just invited me and he only lives a couple of blocks away."

"Sure, just be home at nine-thirty."

When the teenager left, Jack glanced at his watch. Roz had promised to be home at Liam's normal bed-time, in twenty minutes. He picked up another album— this one of Ants, Julia and their kids. Some of the events depicted were familiar, but then the photographs be-came more recent.

Sipping his bourbon, Jack lingered over every one, hungry to know more about the years he'd avoided Ants and his family because they were too painful a reminder of what he'd lost. Yet his brother had never reproached him, and the invitations had never stopped coming, though Jack turned most of them down. How that hurt now.

But Roz was always in the background at the big occasions…clapping as the birthday candles were blown out, raising her glass in a toast. She had kept faith with them, even when Jack couldn't.

In some of the pictures, Wade was with her, but he didn't look as if he belonged, and even with his arm around her shoulders, Roz seemed just as alone. For the first time, Jack was able to look past his jealousy and see that.

Look past his jealousy and regret her failed second marriage. Because he didn't want to think she'd suffered as much as he had. He'd deserved it; she hadn't.

That big blond brainiac was meant to heal her. Otherwise what had been the point of Jack giving her up?

CHAPTER THIRTEEN

THE FIRST THING ROZ noticed about the house when she arrived at 7:25 p.m. was the silence.

Normally, Liam and Cassie were racing around in pajamas in a final play frenzy, while Sam had the sound on *The Simpsons* cranked up, trying to drown out their noise, and Roz called for everybody to please use their inside voices.

Surely Jack hadn't got them to bed early?

She dropped her car keys on the telephone table, and they skittered off the polished surface to the floor. He'd found time to clean? As Roz bent down to pick them up, she noticed the pencil marks on the skirting board had disappeared, and her astonishment grew.

Not just cleaned, but spring-cleaned?

She sniffed. The whole place had the unmistakable tang of solvents and chemicals. Climbing the stairs to the kids' bedrooms she found both sound asleep, tucked neatly under the covers. Sam's room was empty, not just of Sam, but of clutter. She'd been trying to get him to clean his room for a month.

Fighting a growing sense of failure, Roz started for the stairs. Halfway down, she caught sight of Jack sprawled asleep on the couch in the living room, and immediately cheered up—he looked as disheveled as she usually did at this time of night. On the other hand, he'd achieved a hell of lot more, so he'd earned it. Still, his success wasn't unqualified, if Sam had gone out.

Roz crouched down beside Jack and reached out to shake him awake. Then paused. How many times had she watched him sleep? His hair had fallen forward over his brow and she had to fight the urge to smooth it back, slide her fingers through that silky springiness.

But she couldn't resist a slow visual journey over his face. This close, she could see his eyelashes and brows were tipped with the same honey-gold as his hair. Once the only lines he'd had were when he smiled, that slow-burning, lip-curving grin that crinkled those green eyes and never failed to ignite a melting, come-to-me-baby response.

Fortunately, he didn't smile at her anymore.

Now new lines added harshness to the Hollywood good looks that had once bowled her over. Before Jack, she'd been dating the kind of guys who invariably gravitated to nurturers—boyish charmers with mommy complexes. There was nothing little-boy about Jack. Comfortable in his masculinity, he admired smart women and relished being challenged intellectually. During their marriage, he'd been a huge supporter of Roz's professional goals, and not the least threatened when she started earning more than his fledgling business.

Playing hard to get was the sensible course to follow with a man used to women falling all over him, and Roz had a reputation in that area to uphold herself.

But faced with the raw vitality of a man she'd instinctively recognized as her soul mate, she'd folded on the second date and all but dragged him into bed. Ironically, it was Jack—the player—who wanted to take things slowly, but Roz figured he'd had it his own way for far too long. At which point she did discover that Jack played games....

Her gaze drifted down his body with a guilty pleasure. He'd changed into jeans since this morning, the denim faded in all the right places, and the black T-shirt molded to the curves of muscle and bone. He had one arm under his head, and the pale skin of his inner biceps was as smooth and tempting as an apple.

Her throat tightened. Dear God, how she'd loved him. But a woman needed a man who'd stand by her in the bad times, one who'd let her stand by him.

Heaven knows she'd tried. After he'd left her, she'd been convinced they would get back together. She wasn't going to give up on her perfect marriage; Roz had lost enough.

Within weeks she'd heard rumors of other women, and hadn't believed them. No, he wouldn't do that to her. Couldn't. Until she'd arrived unannounced at his rental apartment after receiving notification that he'd filed for divorce.

He'd opened the door bare-chested, a thumb tucked casually in low-slung jeans, his eyes flat. Beyond him, some barely dressed skank poured bourbon into shot glasses.

"Now," he said, "do you believe it's over?"

And she'd hated him then.... Roz shut her eyes briefly, and when she opened them, Jack was awake, staring back. So close, she could see the small flecks of rust and gold suspended in the green irises. So close she could read every emotion.

He still loved her. She reeled in shock, and Jack shot out a hand to steady her.

But when she looked up, he had the customary blinds down. Nobody home…

"Don't you ever pull a stunt like that again," he said.

"I won't." Roz stood up. She'd only been imagining things. "Look, I'm sorry."

He wasn't expecting an apology; she could tell by his blink. But she was weary of conflict. And anxious for information. *Did Cassie eat? Did Sam play up? How did you get on with Liam?* She perched in the armchair opposite and asked casually, "How was your day?"

Stretching his arms above his head, Jack yawned and sat up. "Fine."

Roz waited for more; he only yawned again. She resisted the urge to shake him. "I wasn't expecting them to be in bed so early. Was Liam worried that I wasn't back?"

"No, they…it was fine."

"Where's Sam?"

"Studying at some guy called David's house."

Odd. David wasn't in the same class. She gestured to the room. "You even cleaned."

His gaze shied away from hers. "The place needed it."

The phone rang and, frustrated, she went to answer it. It was Molly's mother, Karen. At last she'd get some information.

But Karen only wanted to talk about Jack. "My God, Roz, what a hottie Anthony's brother is. You could have warned me he was doing the school run. I looked a mess. Tell me he's free."

Honesty fought with possessiveness and won. "Yes."

"Give me the guy's number."

Possessiveness made a counterattack. "He's gay."

"Really?" Karen sounded doubtful. "He's so rugged and macho."

"So were the Village People." There was a business card on the telephone table; Roz picked it up. *A1 Cleaning Services—Thanks for your custom.* She smiled. "Listen, Karen, I've got to go. I'll see you tomorrow…yes, sorry, it'll be me again."

Jack was in the kitchen making tea. She flipped the card onto the counter in front of him and he looked at it ruefully. "I meant to hide that." He put a steaming mug in front of her. "Have you noticed that the kids are sleeping in their clothes yet?"

She breathed a long sigh of relief. "I thought it was just me."

"Honest to God, I don't know how you do it."

"It has its rewards. A laugh from Liam, a cuddle from Cass—"

"A chat with Sam," Jack finished drily, and Roz laughed.

"Why aren't you madder?" she asked. "I expected a lecture at best, a flogging at worst."

Sipping his tea, Jack took a moment to answer. "Well, I did want to kill you around 8:45 a.m. But you were right. I should be pulling my weight in this arrangement."

Hope blossomed, but before Roz could ask questions, the phone rang again.

She picked up the kitchen extension. "Oh, hi, David, does Sam need a lift home? He's not there…? But isn't he studying with you tonight?" She looked across the kitchen at Jack and sighed. "I must have heard wrong. Sure, I'll tell him to call you. Bye."

"Sam definitely said David." Jack eyed her closely. "You don't seem surprised."

She busied herself with dialing. "Let me try his cell…. It's going to message."

"He doesn't know my number. Maybe I'll have better luck." Jack dialed in turn. "Sam? You're busted. I'm giving you twenty minutes to get back here. Every minute you're late after that, you'll be grounded a week." He rang off. "This has happened before, hasn't it?"

"Not since we had the talk after—" Roz stopped, suddenly in deep water.

"After?" He picked up his tea again.

She wouldn't lie to him. "Sam was skipping classes. He's not now."

"And you were going to tell me this when?"

"I wasn't," she admitted. "Because you'd see it as another reason they should go, not another reason they should stay. But now that you're considering permanent custody—"

In the middle of sipping his drink, Jack choked. "Whoa, right there. I do need to foster a relationship with the kids, but I'm not keeping them."

"Let me just tell you how I see it working." Roz almost tripped over the words in her eagerness to divulge her plan. "I'll sell my apartment and use the money to contribute to running this household—that will ease your financial burden and let me stay home

until Cassie turns five. Then I'll go back to working
school hours. The kids and I will stay in this house—
obviously it's not feasible for you and me to live here
together—but you'll be involved as much as you can.
At some stage we'll need to buy this house from them,
but..." Her voice petered out because he was staring at
her with an odd expression on his face.

"My God, you're really serious about this, aren't
you?" Jack turned and tipped the dregs of his tea down
the sink. "In terms of your scenario, I wouldn't let you
sell your apartment—I can easily support the kids. But
that's a moot point. Fiona and Roger are having them."

"Fee might have changed her mind," Roz argued.
"Or maybe she'll settle for a guarantee of contact. We
could pay for the kids to go visit a few weeks every—"

"I promised her she could have them," he interrupted.
"So there's no use talking about it."

"What?" Anger constricted Roz's chest, making it
difficult to breathe. "You had no right to make that arrangement without me."

"*We* had an arrangement, too, remember? That they
go to England after Christmas."

"Our arrangement was to discuss it again!"

"Stop splitting hairs. You always knew where I
stood."

Roz tried to calm down, press her case. "She's not
the right person to raise them, Jack."

"Why?" he challenged. "And remember, I've already
disagreed with your home and community argument."

"I'm not convinced she'll raise the kids the way Julia
and Ants would have wanted. Did you know her children go to boarding school? No, I didn't think so. I have

no idea whether she intends sending our guys…but you need to find out. And remember her behavior at the funeral? Sam's well-being came a poor second when she was under pressure. Is she capable of putting the kids' interests first? And speaking of Sam—he's made it plain he doesn't want to go to the U.K."

"Okay, let me tackle your points one by one." Jack leaned against the counter and started ticking items off on his fingers. "One. I admit Fiona can be a little uptight, but her heart's in the right place and Roger balances her out. Let's not forget he's involved in this." Jack waited for Roz's reluctant nod. "The boarding school thing we can make a condition of custody. Two. You saw how Sam was treated at the rugby game, like some kind of sideshow. England will be a new start for him. Finally, Fiona's performance at the funeral…well, we all make mistakes when we're grieving."

"But—"

"Accept that they're going to England, Roz." He turned and stacked his cup in the dishwasher. "You hit the nail on the head this morning when you said I can't love them."

"No, I said you *won't,* Jack. There's a difference."

"Then I won't," he said brutally, his back still to her. "I don't want children in my life. That desire died with our son."

There was such anguish in his voice that she reached out to touch his shoulder. Then saw a shadow hovering at the door. "Liam, what are you doing up?"

Jack turned around, consternation in his eyes.

The small boy stretched and yawned. Hopefully, he hadn't registered Jack's comment. "I meant to stay awake until you got home."

His T-shirt was covered in some kind of sauce; his pants were rumpled. Roz picked him up and his thin arms wound around her neck. "Let's get you back to bed." Passing Jack, she said quietly, "You know, you used to be the bravest man I knew."

Upstairs, she helped a sleepy Liam change into pajamas, then tucked him in. "Did you have a good day?"

"It was okay." He was nearly asleep again. "*You* love me though, right?"

Fervently, she pressed her lips to his forehead. "Always. And Uncle Jack just needs practice again, that's all."

He snuggled down. "Me and Cassie don't want to live in England. We want you." As though that settled the matter, his breathing deepened into sleep, while Roz sat rigid on the side on his bed.

Now what?

She tried to look at the progress made today. Whatever he said, her ex-husband was obviously softening. Look how far he'd come already. She could still change his mind. But if he wouldn't love them… No, that was defeatist thinking. She could still change his heart.

She had an idea of how to break through his emotional roadblock, if she could get him to her apartment. For a moment she balked at causing him such pain, then reminded herself he'd had no such qualms when he'd cut her out of his life.

This time around it's not over until I say it is.

Downstairs, she found Jack reading Sam the riot act. The teenager threw her a hostile look. "You promised not to tell."

"Hey, you're the one who can't be trusted here," said Jack curtly. "Treat your aunt with more respect."

"She's not my aunt anymore," the boy mumbled, then added with a flare of defiance, "And you're not even my real uncle."

"Fake uncle or wicked guardian, the boundaries your parents set still apply," Jack said shortly. "Roz might have the patience of a saint, but I don't. Now go to bed before I lose the last of what little I have. We'll talk again in the morning."

As Sam stomped out of the room, Roz called after him, "I know you're grieving, but we're still your family, Sam. Let's stick together."

His scornful gaze flicked from her to Jack. "What?" he jeered. "You mean, like you guys did?"

CHAPTER FOURTEEN

SAM WAS HOME FROM SCHOOL, sitting at the kitchen table eating cookies, when Roz came back from the supermarket with the kids the next afternoon.

He'd appeared contrite in front of Jack this morning, but he barely gave Roz a glance now. Did she have too much patience with his behavior, as Jack had suggested? Roz knew some of his acting out was a grief response, but at some point he had to accept her authority.

She poured everyone a glass of cold milk and they joined him at the table. "Learn anything interesting at school today?"

He upended the packet, caught the last cookie crumbs in his mouth. "No."

Liam chipped in. "I learned that Venus is the second hottest planet after the sun."

"Wow—" Sam faked a yawn "—that's *so* fascinating." Liam's face fell.

"Please," said Roz, "make an effort."

Sam rolled his eyes. "And what did *you* do at preschool today, Cassie?"

"Pooped my pants," she announced, and won an involuntary laugh from her biggest brother. Liam started to giggle.

"You're a little stinker." Affectionately, Sam grabbed a napkin and wiped a trail of milk off her chin. For once, Cassie didn't demur.

The gesture, and Cassie's response to it, suggested a history of care, and Roz wondered if she'd done Sam a disservice in doing so much for the younger ones. She'd wanted to lighten his load, but maybe he needed a sense of being necessary to his little brother and sister.

On impulse she stood up. "I need to get to the post office before it closes. Sam, you're in charge."

Immediately, he scowled. "Can't you take the kids with you?"

Roz picked up her bag and kept on going. "I'll only be half an hour. See you soon."

She shut the door on his protests, then realized she'd left her car keys inside. Going back in would be fatal. The mall was only a brisk ten-minute walk away and it was a nice afternoon. She headed down the drive and set off, trying to remember the last time she'd traveled this lightly.

Normally, there was a stroller, diapers, snacks and drinks.... It had only been a month, and already she felt incomplete without them.

What was it going to be like when the kids went to England? She stopped at the thought and, because she was alone, leaned against an oak, its mottled trunk silky smooth against her palm. *Not so brave now,* she mocked herself silently. *Not nearly so brave now.*

In the wake of Sam's home truth last night, she and Jack had said an awkward good-night. But this morning Roz had organized a babysitter, then rung her ex-husband and asked him to meet at her apartment, saying there was something she needed to bring back to the house that was too heavy for her to carry alone.

If this didn't work, then nothing would.

SAM GOT UP when Roz left, went into the lounge and turned on the TV.

"It's rude to leave the table without asking to be excused," Liam yelled after him, but his big brother didn't answer.

"I'm finished." Cassie set her glass on the edge of the table. It fell to the floor, splintering into sharp, milk-filmed shards. She and Liam looked at each other. "Uh-oh," she said, and made a move to get down.

"Stay there," Liam yelled, "you've got bare feet. *Sam!*"

His brother came and looked at the mess on the floor. "Aww, shit."

"You're not s'posed to swear. Roz says."

"Who's gonna stop me, you? Look at this bloody mess." Sam grabbed a broom and started sweeping. Cassie made another attempt to get down, and he grabbed her arm. "Stay there, dippy, till I've picked up the glass."

"Down!" she ordered.

Sam picked her up and set her in the hall. "Liam, keep an eye on her until I've cleaned up."

"I've got bare feet, too."

"Do I have to do everything around here?" But Sam swung him down from the table. "Now bug off, you two."

"Bug off," agreed Cassie, and didn't move.

"I can help if I get my shoes…." Liam offered tentatively. Maybe then Sam wouldn't be so mad. "Roz says I'm a good helper."

"Roz says, Roz says!" Viciously, Sam swept the

broken glass into a dustpan. "I'm sick of hearing about Roz. What about quoting what Mum and Dad say? Or do you want Cassie to forget them?"

"No!"

"Because she will, you know. She'll end up thinking Roz or Fee is her bloody mother…. It's not right." Sam looked at him wildly. "It's not right, Liam."

"I d-d-don't forget, Sam. I write to them every day."

"Do they ever write back? Well, do they?" He flung the broom across the room and Cassie started to cry. "Jeez, am I the only one in this bloody house who gets that they're dead and never coming back?"

Liam started to cry, too. He didn't want to, but he couldn't help it. Then Sam was kneeling on the floor and hugging him and Cassie. "I'm sorry, I'm really sorry, you guys."

"Were you tricking, Sam?" Liam pulled away. "I mean, Mum and Dad are watching over us, right?"

"Yeah, I was tricking. Is that one of your letters on the table? Can I write something on the bottom?"

With Liam and Cassie watching, he found a pen and scrawled, "P.S. Love, Sam." For a moment he stared at the words he'd written, then started to cry, big shuddering sobs that sounded like they hurt coming up, like he was going to be sick or something.

Liam got the bucket out of the laundry that Mum used to put by their bed when they had tummy bugs, but Sam only cried harder when he saw it, so Liam took Cassie out and closed the door. They weren't s'posed to watch TV during the day, but since Sam had turned it on, they huddled on the couch, watching it. The phone rang beside him and he answered it.

Ten minutes later, Sam came quietly into the room. His lids were all puffy and red, but at least he wasn't crying.

"What'cha watching?" he asked gruffly.

"SpongeBob SquarePants."

Sam picked up his little sister and sat her on his lap, taking her place on the couch. "Liam?" he began tentatively.

"I know." He didn't shift his gaze away from the TV. "Don't tell Auntie Roz and Uncle Jack."

He didn't mention that he'd just told Auntie Fee on the phone, figuring it would only get him into trouble. Just telling her Sam was looking after them had made her mad at Auntie Roz, though she'd gone quiet when he'd mentioned Sam was crying. Then she'd said it had been a mistake letting them stay on in the house.

"Who was on the phone?"

"Um…Marcus." Uh-oh. Lying was tricky. He was supposed to get Auntie Roz to ring Auntie Fee back, but now he couldn't. Besides, then she'd find out about Sam crying, and he'd get into trouble with Sam and—

Liam chuckled as SpongeBob tried to teach his pet snail, Gary, to fetch, and leaned into his brother's arm before he realized. He caught his breath, but Sam didn't shift away.

"Do you think they have SpongeBob SquarePants in England, Sam?"

"Dunno."

"I don't want to go live there. I'm gonna stay here. I told Auntie Roz."

"She can't do anything. It's all settled."

His brother's tone was brusque, so Liam didn't tell

him that he trusted Auntie Roz to change things so they could stay.

"Liam?" Sam cleared his throat. "I'm staying in New Zealand."

"But you just said we can't."

"I said you and Cassie can't…you're too young. But it's my birthday next week, which means I'm sixteen, and my uncle—my real one—says when you're sixteen you can do what you want. I'm gonna move out and get a flat."

"If Auntie Roz can't keep us, we could live with you."

"No, they won't let us, but when this house sells I'll have enough money to visit you in England, and you'll visit New Zealand."

"They're gonna sell this house?" Liam got a scared feeling in his stomach.

"It's okay, we'll get the money."

Liam didn't want money; he wanted Auntie Roz. He started to panic, then remembered she knew that, and relaxed back against his brother's arm. Sam liked to pretend he was big and knew stuff, but Liam was backing Auntie Roz. She was the boss, not Sam.

"So how long have you lived here?"

While Roz unlocked the door of her ground floor apartment, Jack studied the building. Judging from the design and materials, it had been built in the 1980s.

"Since I left Wade…" There was a loaded silence as she swung the door open.

Though tastefully furnished, the place was a shoebox compared to Jack's spacious apartment. "Why didn't you accept the alimony I offered?" Mention of Wade always made him irritable. "Then you could have bought something larger."

"This meets my needs," she said stiffly. "Besides, it's still bigger than the apartment you and I lived in."

Mentally calculating, Jack realized she was right. Yet that place had never felt cramped…maybe because they'd spent so much of their leisure time in bed. "You didn't answer my question about the alimony."

She gave him a considering look. "I wanted to hurt your pride. You'd hurt mine and I was damned if I was going to let you have everything your own way."

"It worked," he admitted, taken aback by her honesty.

"Good," said Roz, and slipped off her coat. Her high heels clicked against the hardwood floor as she walked down the hall, and Jack took note of her outfit, a soft, swinging dress in navy. His mouth went dry because she was so lovely. In their roller-coaster world of child care, he could—almost—remain unaware of the silky fall of her long hair, the curve of lashes on a smooth cheek… other curves. "You're dressed up."

"I had an early dinner with the elderly neighbor who's looking after my cat. Listen, I still have a few things to pack, but it won't take long." She paused at what must be her bedroom door. "Make yourself comfortable, and I'll call you when I need a hand."

Make himself comfortable in a place imbued with her? He even recognized the scent of the furniture polish. "I'd rather be doing something."

"You could water the plants for me." She gestured. "There's a jug under the kitchen sink."

Red geraniums wilted in their pot on the white granite countertop. Jack attended to them first, then prowled the house looking for others. He noticed she'd kept the furniture he'd made for her—an ornately carved mirror frame, a bookshelf and even a kauri dining table, squeezed into the tiny alcove posturing as a dining room.

Jack ran his hand across the table's golden, butter-smooth surface, breathing in the lemony beeswax. The smell of a world lost to him. However big his apartment, it lacked the homey touches. Who the hell was he kidding? It lacked—

"Roz," he called harshly, "are you nearly ready?"

"Five minutes."

He waited by the front door next to the hall table he'd restored for her twenty-fourth birthday. Scattered across the kauri slab top were half a dozen greeting cards, all embossed with the same message—"Sorry you're leaving." Jack swept them up and stalked into Roz's bedroom, where he tossed them on the open suitcase she was packing.

"Tell me that you didn't have to quit your job to do this."

"It's no big deal." Roz picked up the cards and threw them in the bin, then glanced at his face. "It *isn't*, Jack."

"I don't get it. Surely with your seniority, they could have managed a couple of months leave."

"They did." Roz closed the lid of the suitcase and started to lift it. Instinctively, he took it from her. "But I wanted to keep my return date open in case you saw sense and accepted full custody."

Jack dropped the suitcase. "What?"

She shrugged. "Win some, lose some."

He wanted to shake her. "Damn it, I should never have agreed to this temporary custody thing. It's got completely out of hand. And you…you're just plain crazy. You're like a moth hurtling against a hot bulb, determined to get burned. For God's sake, Roz, protect yourself."

"From what? Loving anybody again?" she challenged. "How's that tactic *really* working for you?"

It wasn't, and the sudden empathy in her eyes told him she knew it. He couldn't bear it. Jack said brusquely, "What do you want help moving, Roz?"

Oddly, her compassionate expression didn't change. "It's behind you."

He turned around and his vision telescoped to the large picture on the wall next to the door—three black-and-white photographs taken in action sequence and set in a rectangular silver frame.

In the first shot, he and Roz smiled down at their solemn baby, who was frowning at the photographer. In the second, they laughed as a bored Thomas chewed at his hands, while a blurred squeaky toy waved frantically in the foreground. Their son had been cranky that day, unwilling to cooperate. Though hilarious, the session had been a disaster.

Jack's stunned gaze shifted to the third shot. Having given up, he and Roz kissed, unaware that Thomas was laughing up at them, with a beatific gummy smile.

Jack had never seen these photographs, taken only a few days before their son died. They were funny and real and poignant, and they had the same impact as a crack on the head with a two-by-four. For a moment, the room swam and Jack couldn't breathe.

Roz came to stand beside him. "I got it out when I

came back here yesterday. It seemed like time to put it up again."

He didn't answer, because he felt as if his whole body was braced against a dam about to burst, and he needed to concentrate. He closed his eyes against Thomas's laughing face, but the image still burned on his retinas.

"Maybe I am crazy," said Roz, "but I'm tired of being scared all the time, Jack." Gently, she cupped his clenched fist. "Aren't you tired of being numb?"

He wanted to respond then, because there was a break in her voice, but if he moved a muscle, the dam would burst. And that way lay chaos.

After a few moments, she withdrew her hand and he knew this torture was nearly over. Then Roz sighed, the softest, saddest sound of defeat, and Jack could no longer stop the flood of emotion.

CHAPTER FIFTEEN

ROZ WATCHED TEARS stream from under Jack's closed lids, and a wave of love swept away everything else. She tugged his bowed head down to hers and kissed them away with an aching tenderness, her lips tracing the warm saltiness across his face to his mouth, firm, full and heartbreakingly familiar.

Though he stood stiff and unyielding, he didn't pull away, and his biceps tightened under her fingers when she gripped his arms. "Come back to me, Jack," she murmured fiercely against his lips. Cupping his face in her hands, she kissed him harder, demanding a response.

She felt the moment his control broke; a ragged sigh shuddered through his body, and then his tongue met hers with a desperate, uncontrolled yearning that rose to passion in one frantic heartbeat. They clung to each other, body to body, mouth to mouth in a savage, possessive embrace. And all the emotions Roz had struggled to suppress for six long years—love, grief, fury, compassion, revenge—rose in her like bloodlust.

Her teeth grazed his lips as she fought the urge to bite; her fingernails dug into his shoulders.

"Roz, I'm so sorr—"

"Shut up!" She yanked at his shirt until the buttons

flew open, then shoved him backward onto the bed and straddled him, her fingers tangling in his honey-blond hair to pull his head back, her mouth seeking his surrender. And he gave it to her, trusting her even in her anger until the violence seeped away and her caresses grew tender again. Roz looked at his bleeding lower lip, the ugly marks she'd nipped across his neck, and passed a shaky hand across her brow. "I'm sorr—"

"Your turn to shut up," whispered Jack. With a hand around her nape, he held her close and kissed her again, his tongue moving against hers with a devastating gentleness that made her tremble harder. For long hypnotic minutes he kissed her, and she drank in the sweetness of his taste mixed with the metallic tang of his blood, his scent, his touch on her body as he unzipped her dress, his fingers as unsteady as her own.

Her lover, her husband, the man whose child she'd borne, the man she was supposed to grow old with. She must have moaned because he stopped peeling down her dress. "I can stop if you've changed your mind."

But Roz wasn't that strong, not with his half-naked body, warm and heavy, on hers. Not with the heavy-lidded intensity in his eyes and the wet aching need between her legs.

She touched a finger to his mouth, rasped, "Your turn again. Shut up."

His lips curved under her finger; then he took it into his mouth and sucked gently. A jolt of pure lust shot to her groin. He dropped his head to her left breast and did the same to her nipple, with much more heat, and she gasped and gripped his hair. Every touch evoked a sensory memory—the slow assured slide of his hands on her body, the way he moved teasingly against her, and the intent purposefulness that made her hum with a sizzling anticipation.

With the same urgency, Roz explored him, finding and tracing old haunts—the scar on his shoulder from a childhood injury; the swell of pectorals and indentation of ribs; the hard, tight stomach scattered with fine hair. Absorbing the beauty of him, and the magical sensual connection they'd once taken for granted.

Any woman would have loved his body—those massive shoulders, the corded forearms dusted with gold, his broad chest, muscular legs and tight male butt, pale cream in contrast to the rest of his tanned physique. But for Roz the sexiest part of Jack was his eyes, and the way he looked at her as though she was everything he'd ever wanted.

The way he was looking at her now.

Their hunger grew; their caresses became more intimate; senses sharpened and merged. They stripped each other naked and threw their clothes on the floor. She could hear his heightened breathing—and hers. "Jack."

With his hand between her legs, Roz verged on coming, but she couldn't lose control before he did. She pushed his clever fingers away, pressed him back against the pillows and took him slowly into her body. Reality was so much better than memory.

"Roz." He started moving under her, and instinct and need took over.

Her orgasm roared through her, hard and scorching and fast. Dimly, she heard Jack groan, felt him shudder underneath her. With a gasp, she collapsed on his chest, lips pressed against the salty dampness right over his heart. Gradually their breathing eased. With one arm cradling her, Jack stroked her hair, then massaged her nape in the way she loved. Time slowed until she was suspended, half-asleep, in the quiet spaces between his heartbeats. Completely and utterly spent.

And everything they needed to say to each other could wait.

IMPATIENTLY, Fee stopped stirring her tea and started walking with the phone. "I thought you said you were expecting them home around seven? Well, has either of them even rung to say why they've been delayed...? No? And it doesn't bother you?"

It was eight in the morning in Surrey, England, 9:00 p.m. in New Zealand, and this was Fee's third call since getting up at 5:00 a.m. to see Roger off on his drive to London.

"I said I was happy to stay until ten," said the babysitter. "Maybe they went out to dinner."

Her girlish voice made Fee wonder how old she was. At least they'd hired a babysitter this time, rather than relying on Sam. Roz seemed to be taking her responsibilities very lightly, completely blasé about the fact that Sam had been terribly upset earlier.

Fee wanted to talk to him and confirm that he was all right, but apparently he'd been shipped off to a friend's house so Roz and Jack could go out.

"Do you want to leave another message?" asked the babysitter.

"I've already left one and she hasn't returned my call. I'll try again tomorrow." Given the thirteen-hour time difference between New Zealand and England, there were narrow windows of opportunity to phone, and she'd just missed another of them.

Irritated, she hung up, gulped her tea and went to dress. She was due at the thrift shop in twenty minutes for her volunteer shift. Opening her wardrobe, Fee chose a simple ensemble—she didn't want to make anyone in the thrift shop uncomfortable—then applied light makeup for the same reason. Was it so hard for Roz to ring her back?

Initially, Fee had used Jack as her point of contact, but he'd proved hopeless, completely vague about details, and more often than not at work, with no time to chat. So she'd been forced to start phoning Roz, who was always pleasant, but slightly defensive when Fee delved into the nuances of domestic life.

And talking to the children directly didn't furnish much information. They were clearly reluctant to be on the phone, and Roz's whispered encouragement in the background only exacerbated Fee's annoyance that her niece and nephews had to be instructed to be nice to her.

Fee realized she was dabbing on the blush with a heavy hand, and reached for a tissue to rub away the excess.

Leaving Jack and Roz with temporary custody had been a mistake; it had disrupted the tentative relationship she'd begun to forge with the children, and given her husband time to question whether Fee wasn't taking on more than she could chew. Roger meant well, but his inference—echoing Roz's—about her ability to cope, stung.

Recalling her mortifying behavior during the funeral brought a sudden and entirely natural blush to Fiona's cheeks. Thank God Roger hadn't been there to see her shameful display. Fortunately, she'd had time since to regain perspective on the accident.

Of course she hadn't killed Julia and Anthony; the truck driver and Julia's lapse of attention had. Fee started to apply mascara, but her fingers shook and she put the wand down.

Christmas would be a very sad time for the children, and it occurred to her that they might find it easier to cope with festivities here, where winter and snow and roasted chestnuts were nothing like New Zealand's summer celebrations. Her two sons would be home from boarding school and it would be a warm, welcoming introduction to their new family.

Fee phoned the babysitter back and canceled all her messages for Roz. Jack was the person more likely to say yes to allowing the children to come over earlier.

She would talk him into it tomorrow.

ROZ DREAMED.

She and Jack were skimming in a fairy tale sailboat across a moonlit sea. Traveling alongside the craft, just under the glassy water, Thomas was a dolphin baby, a pale white blur of joyous speed, as he dipped and reappeared.

Ahead was an island, black jagged cliffs rising to a plateau of lush green, where a white cottage nestled amid trees. She knew the other children were inside, waiting for them.

They sailed around the island, looking for anchorage, but the rocks were as sharp as fangs and the water sucked and spat around the cliffs' base like a malevolent mouth.

Thomas beckoned and Roz dived into the water to follow him through a safe gap in the rocks, but black seaweed tightened around her legs like cold fingers, pulling her under.

Gasping for air, she struggled free and broke the surface, but Thomas had gone and Jack was sailing on, oblivious to her plight. She screamed, "Jack, I'm over here!" But he didn't hear her. Panic consumed her. "Jack, come back!"

Roz woke up, her body rigid and heavy with dread, and cold sweat prickling her forehead. The bedside clock showed 9:00 p.m. and it took her dazed brain a moment to process why that was.

She became aware of a familiar warmth and scent beside her, of slow regular breathing fanning her right shoulder, and turned her head.

Jack.

They needed to get up, go home and relieve the baby-sitter. But Roz made no move to wake him because the dream had seemed so real—a premonition and a reminder. *Don't trust him.*

His face in the moonlight was smooth and untroubled; it tugged at her heart like an anchor. Could she risk loving him again?

She got up and dressed quietly, then stole to the door. No. She couldn't.

A gruff voice said behind her, "You're not even going to leave a note?" About to turn the door handle, Roz froze.

JACK STARED AT his ex-wife's guilty face and had his answer. He'd woken with a sense of well-being, a feeling of hope he hadn't experienced in years, to see Roz sneaking to the door.

"I told the babysitter I'd be home by ten."

He'd forgotten all about the kids. Jack shoved back the sheets. "Give me five minutes."

"I don't mind going alone if you want to take a shower...or something."

The awkwardness in her voice stopped him. He flicked on the bedside lamp, the better to see her face. "You regret what we did."

"No!" The immediacy of her response reassured him, but his relief didn't last long. "Only, it probably shouldn't happen again." She hugged herself. "We have too many other things going on." It was a lame excuse, and by the way her cheeks colored, he could tell she knew it.

It occurred to Jack that she might have slept with him to sway his decision about custody. She wanted those kids, and she must know he still had feelings for her. A little softening up might change his mind.... Then he looked into her eyes and saw the same vulnerability that was making him scramble for reasons to push her away.

But he couldn't. He couldn't do it anymore.

"I never thought I could love anyone as much as I loved you," he said. "And then Thomas was born and somehow my heart grew bigger."

Roz crept to a chair and sat down.

"When he died I blamed myself. You knew that. It didn't matter what the autopsy said, what you said, what anyone said, because rationality doesn't come into it. I had to suffer."

"So you left me," she said bitterly, "and we both suffered."

That had been his real punishment, when he'd regained sanity enough to regret it—the pain he'd caused her. "I salved my conscience by telling myself that you'd heal faster without having me around as a constant reminder."

Jack looked at the pictures on the wall. Thomas had her clear, all-seeing eyes. "In hindsight it was probably the other way around."

He owed her this unflinching honesty. His gaze traveled over her pale, still face. It was impossible to guess what she was thinking. Jack took a deep breath. "I knew you wouldn't give up on our marriage easily, so I deliberately took myself beyond your forgiveness."

Her lips barely moved. "Other women."

"When you came to my apartment, I knew I'd succeeded."

He'd thought he'd known the final dimensions of hell then, every crevice and crack of it.

Until Roz married Wade and Jack realized the very marrow of his bones could be ground down with pain until there was nothing left of hope. And in that void, he'd finally found some sense of atonement.

"Roz, I'm so sorry. I had reasons, but I offer no excuses. I know no apology can make up for what I did, but I'm going to ask anyway. Is there any way forward for us?"

"I don't know!" She buried her face in her hands and was silent for a long time.

Eventually she gave a laugh that was half sob, and sat up. "I took Cassie to see Santa this morning."

It wasn't what Jack had expected, but he nodded encouragement.

"We've been reading books about him and she was hyped. Even insisted on getting dressed up."

They exchanged an involuntary smile.

"Exactly. She teamed some of my best jewelry with a pair of antlers and a clown nose she found in Liam's toy box that reminded her of Rudolph."

Abruptly, Roz stood. "So we got there and lined up, and she watched him ho, ho, hoing and lifting kids onto his lap. And the closer we got, the tighter she held my hand. When it came to our turn, she froze."

Roz walked to the dresser, picked up some jewelry and put it down again. Her eyes met Jack's in the mirror. "Santa was so kind," she continued in a shaky voice. "Beckoning and smiling and encouraging her. So Cassie would take another tiny step, and then panic again. And she started to cry in frustration because she wanted to visit him so badly but she just…couldn't… do it."

Jack's hands clenched on the sheet as he realized what was coming.

"Right now, that's how I feel about you." She turned around and looked at him directly. "I'm a one-man nurturer who ended up a two-time divorcee. Because when my baby died, my soul mate left me."

He flinched but said nothing. Another apology would be an insult.

"And I thought…" She swallowed hard. "I thought I was going to break into tiny pieces unless I found someone to hold me. You hurt me so much, Jack—and then I hurt Wade."

Roz went to the suitcase, picked it up. "I'm sorry, but I can't do this again."

There was only one thing an honorable man could say, so Jack said it. "I understand."

And the worst thing was, he did.

CHAPTER SIXTEEN

"LIAM, YOU WANT TO COME with me and Cass to the hardware store?" Jack asked the next morning.

His nephew didn't even look up from his Lego. "No, thank you."

Jack persisted. "You know Roz is too busy to play?" She was helping Sam with his exam revisions and avoiding Jack, and he was equally intent on doing the same.

Neither of them had any idea how to take this from here.

It was Sunday, which wouldn't normally have stopped Jack going to the office, but he'd already agreed to look after the younger ones today. Which meant pretending everything was fine.

But he was a man used to going after what he wanted, so passively respecting—not challenging—Roz's decision was making him crazy. He had to get out of this damn house and think, and the hardware store was the place to do it.

Liam glowered. "I wanna stay *here!*"

Oh, great, he was in his nephew's bad books again. You'd think he'd be used to it.

"Fine." Still, Jack brooded as he bought a packet of tacks and a tube of silicon, while Cassie played with chunky reels of gold and silver chain links. He felt bad about Liam overhearing him the other night; the next present would make it up to him. He could afford to buy him a big one because the project was ahead of construction by several weeks and Hiro was talking more joint initiatives.

By rights I should be walking on sunshine, not wallowing in an emotional quagmire.

Damn it, why had Roz brought him back to life, if she was only going to stab him in the heart? Okay, she had a right to second thoughts, but couldn't she have had them *before* she made him feel again?

He rubbed the back of his neck, trying to ease the tension. "C'mon, honey," he said to Cassie. "Let's go get some timber."

Enthralled with the shiny metal, she ignored him. Jack glanced unseeing at his list. Four more weeks, he told himself, and he'd be free to crawl back into his cave and roll the rock across the door. The kids would go to England…and Roz would have her heart broken again.

Hating his thoughts, he barked, "Cass, let's go."

"I'll watch her if you like," offered the store's owner, who was standing on a ladder in the same aisle, refilling the nail boxes.

"Thanks, Phil." Jack headed for the timber supplies.

The wail started when he was at the far end of the warehouse, and rose to a scream so shrill, so petrified that he dropped the plank he held and ran.

Skidding around the end of the aisle, he saw Phil crouched down on rheumatic knees, trying to placate Cassie, who stood rigid, cheeks scarlet, screaming her head off.

She caught sight of Jack and flung herself on him, clawing at his shins until he hunkered down to her level, and then her arms closed in a choke hold around his neck. Bewildered, he tightened his grip and stood up, while she sobbed in his arms.

"I don't understand it." Phil was white-faced. "One second she was fine, then she looked around and saw you were gone, and started to scream. She bit me when I tried to pick her up." He showed Jack the neat indentation in his wrinkled palm. "I tried to tell her you were coming back."

The older man was obviously shaken. Jack felt a trifle unsteady himself. The terror in that scream had been palpable.

Cassie raised a tearstained face. "You went away," she sobbed accusingly. "You went away, Uncle Jack." Enraged now that her fear had worn off, she whacked his chest with a tiny fist. "Bad Uncle Jack."

Her parents had left her in an unfamiliar place and not returned. Horrified, he patted her back. "Shush, baby, it's all right. I won't disappear again."

Except he would, Jack realized with a sinking feeling. In four weeks, when she went to Fiona and Roger.

Grimly, he drove home and went through the motions of domestic harmony, but his anger had a focus now. After lunch, when all the kids were occupied, he dragged Roz into the study and told her about Cassie's meltdown.

"I should never have agreed to temporary custody. It's not good for them to bond with us like this."

"The kids and I had already bonded," she reminded him calmly. "And didn't you want a better relationship with them?"

"Yes, but…" It hadn't included being needed. Jack hung on to his righteous anger. "Obviously Cassie was going to become attached to the people who cared for her immediately after the accident…. It should have been Fiona and Roger."

"They had the kids in New Caledonia for three days immediately after the accident, and Fiona stayed here with Cassie for a week before she flew home."

"So Cassie hasn't spent as much quality time with them as she has with me?" Jack had glimpsed the buzzword in one of Roz's child care books. "Is that what you're saying?"

"Actually, if you add the twelve-day holiday they had together before the accident, then they're way ahead of you in terms of quality time." She was watching him closely. "Cassie loves them, Jack, but she was Daddy's girl and it's you she associates with Anthony. You should be flattered…not scared."

He ignored the last part. "This isn't right."

Roz's voice was very gentle. "Is it really such a big deal that a little girl loves you?"

Yes. "It is when we're not going to keep her. Even if I changed my mind, how can we possibly make this work after what happened last night?"

"I don't know," Roz said honestly. "I've been asking myself the same question all morning."

"Now you regret it, don't you?"

"If it's stopped you reconsidering permanent custody? Yes."

It hurt so much more than he expected. "I should never have let you put them through this," he said savagely.

Roz gasped, then went pale with anger. "I'm not

doing this for me. I'm doing it because it's what the *kids* want. And it's what Ants and Julia wanted. The reason you're so pissed is because you've realized that."

He couldn't deal with the truth, so he headed for the door. Roz was up from the desk in a flash and barring his way. "Sam worships the ground you walk on. Liam and I have always had a special bond, and Cassie considers both of us as her property." Her blue eyes flashed. "Sure, you and Liam have problems. Sam and I do, too—but you know…you *know,* Jack," she repeated in a low, passionate voice, "that we're their best option. Ants and Ju didn't just choose me, Jack, they chose you."

"They chose the person I was at the time, not the person I am now." He couldn't stop the bitter laugh. "If there wasn't a difference you wouldn't have said no to me last night."

"Don't you know how desperately I want you to prove you're still that man?"

He looked in her eyes and saw hope. The phone rang loudly beside them, and they both jumped. Roz picked it up. "What?" Immediately her tone softened. "Oh, hi, Fee. Yes, Jack's here."

He waved in dismissal. Right now there were more important things to discuss. Like what Roz meant.

"While you talk to him, I'll get the kids to come say hello," she was saying.

Reluctantly, Jack took the phone. "Hi, Fiona."

He listened to what she had to say with mixed feelings. "Let me think about the kids coming early for Christmas, and get back to you…. No, I won't tell Roz before I've made up my own mind." He hung up and turned around to see Liam in the doorway. "Sorry, buddy, I forgot you were going to talk to her."

"Does she want us to go over early?"

"Yeah." Jack hesitated. "How would you feel about that?" He'd never asked them what they wanted before, fearing the wrong answer. Now he had to know if Roz's assertion was true.

"I don't want to live with Auntie Fee," Liam declared passionately. "I want Auntie Roz."

You and me both.

"And Auntie Roz wants us, I know she does."

There was the difference. Roz didn't want him. Or had she implied Jack still had a chance? He needed to think.

Liam was eyeing him anxiously. "Sam said we get the money when you sell our house. Is that right?"

"Yes. It will go into a trust for your education." *Along with money from me.*

"Well, you know how you paid us to change Cassie's diapers?" Liam's next words came in a rush. "I'll give you our share if you don't make us go to Auntie Fee. It's okay, I asked Cassie…she said it's all right to give you the money."

Appalled, Jack stared at his earnest nephew. "Liam, I can't—"

"Don't answer now," the child interrupted. "You think about it and let me know."

And Jack didn't have the heart to tell him the answer was already no.

ROZ WAS IN CASSIE'S ROOM pulling back the curtains after the little girl's nap when Liam bounded in. "Uncle Jack's gone out."

"Go 'way." Cassie growled at her brother from her bed, where she sat with pillow hair, rubbing her eyes. With a quivering bottom lip, she held up her arms to Roz. "Cuddle."

"But he was going to look after you while I went to the market." Roz picked her up and Cass burrowed into her—a soft, warm bundle of lovable grumpiness, fragrant with soap, perspiration and damp diaper. "Was he called into work?"

"Dunno." Liam wrinkled his nose in Cassie's direction. "He said not to save dinner 'cause he doesn't know when he'll be back."

"Oh!" Roz tightened her hold on Cassie, suddenly needing the hug as much as the baby did. *I challenge him to be old Jack and new Jack runs away.* She'd thought she was getting through to him.

Last night she hadn't been thinking about the children, only about him. It had taken daylight for all the implications of sleeping with him to sink in. Along with the truth. She'd turned him down not because she was scared to love him again, but because she'd never stopped loving him, and that vulnerability terrified her.

And judging by his withdrawal now, she'd been right to protect herself. "Who wants afternoon tea?" she croaked.

Cassie perked up. "Me!"

"Okay, then." Roz made an effort to be cheerful. "Let's go. How's Auntie Fee?"

Liam scowled. "She wants us to go early for Christmas."

"What?" Roz stumbled and had to grab the upper hall balustrade. "What did Jack say?"

Liam shot her a furtive look. "Um, he's thinking about it," he mumbled. "Can I have carrot cake?"

"He's *thinking*—!" She bit her lip. "Carrot cake it is." She never said anything to raise Liam's hopes, and always talked enthusiastically about England, taking pains to foster the kids' relationship with Fee and Roger through regular phone calls.

She figured that wherever these children ended up living, they needed all the extended family they could get.

As soon as she could, Roz found a private corner and rang Jack's mobile phone. It went straight to message. She tried Fiona…no one home. For the next few hours she alternated between calm rationality—Jack wouldn't dare make that decision without her—to blind panic. He'd already made one deal with Fee behind Roz's back and was probably out buying air tickets now. And still neither Jack nor Fee answered their damn phones.

By the time she put the kids to bed, Roz was a nervous wreck, and predictably, both youngsters played up. Liam was relatively easy to settle, but at nine o'clock, Cassie was still awake.

"I'm going to bed," said Sam in disgust when Cassie came down for the fourth time, and Roz didn't blame him. She carted Cassie back to bed and lay down beside her to coax her to sleep, taking the file of custody documents with her. She hadn't read the guardianship clause in the will, but maybe it held something she could use. What she found made her drop the file and curl up closer to Cassie.

"Auntie Roz." The little girl took her thumb out of her mouth and patted Roz's cheek.

Roz closed her eyes in sudden anguish. "Go to sleep,"

she said gruffly. Her deepest belief—that her best friend hadn't wanted Fee to raise her kids—was wrong.

Cassie gave her cheek an imperative tap, and obediently, Roz reopened her eyes, but heard nothing of the little girl's chatter. Jack had said he'd relied on Grimble to give him the salient details of the will. Obviously, he'd never read the subclause appointing Fee and Roger guardians should Jack and Roz be unable— or unwilling—to fulfil the obligation in the event of Joyce Galloway, Jack and Anthony's mother, being unable to do so.

The shadows lengthened and the night-light brightened. Gradually, Cassie's lids drifted shut, and her breathing deepened to childish snores. Hearing a door close downstairs, Roz edged inch by careful inch to the side of the toddler's bed. Jack must be home.

Cassie opened sleep-drugged eyes, and she froze. When the little girl closed her eyes again, Roz resumed her incremental escape. *Quietly,* she reminded herself. *Don't hurry.* But she was impatient to hear what Jack had decided. Rolling off the bed, she began tiptoeing toward the door. A floorboard squeaked; instinctively, Roz dropped to the carpet, but Cassie only sighed and turned over.

Taking no chances, Roz stayed on her hands and knees until she was in the hall, coming to a halt in front of a pair of size eleven shoes.

"Having fun?" asked Jack.

"Shh!" Roz bolted to a sitting position and listened.

"Roz…Auntie Roz…" Cassie's wail spoke of an unspeakable betrayal.

"I'm com—"

Jack leaned down and put his hand over her mouth. "It's Uncle Jack," he called. "Go to sleep."

"Story," said Cassie.

"Tomorrow."

"Auntie Roz."

"Tomorrow."

There was silence while Cassie digested that. "Water." But it was a halfhearted request.

"Cassie," Jack said again, in a warm rumble that sent a shiver up Roz's spine, already shivery from having his equally warm hand over her mouth. "Go to sleep."

He removed his hand and pulled her, half-resisting, downstairs. Roz opened her mouth to fire accusations, reproaches and counterarguments.

"You win," said Jack. "I'll tell Fiona we want to keep the kids in New Zealand."

She sat down before her legs gave way. "But…but what changed your mind?"

"You wore me down with home truths, but I guess if there was a definitive moment, it was Liam offering his inheritance to sweeten the deal…. Oh, and Cassie's prepared to buy me off, too, apparently." His mouth twisted in a wry smile. "He was so earnest I'm pretending to think about it."

Roz was finding her victory difficult to assimilate. "Where on earth would Liam get the idea to offer you a bribe?"

"Me, of course." Jack caught her hands and pulled her up, his green eyes suddenly very serious. "I need you and they need you—at least, Liam and Cassie do. I'm sure Sam will realize he does, too, once he knows he can stay in New Zealand." Jack raised her fingers and kissed them. "I love you, Roz, and if this is what it takes to get you to give me another chance…"

Uneasiness flashed through her joy. "But you do want them, too, don't you, Jack?"

"I want the best for them and you're it," he answered, pulling her closer. "I can't fight that anymore."

He lowered his head and, as always, her breath caught in anticipation. But there was one more question she had to ask him. "You will love them, won't you?"

He paused, his mouth inches from hers. "I'm fond of them."

If he wasn't doing this for the right reasons it would never work. For any of them.

Roz turned her head so his lips brushed her cheek. "Bully for you," she said.

Jack drew back. "Why is that so important? You keep telling me this is what the kids want."

"And I do care what they want. But I care about what they need more." How could she make him understand what she only dimly understood herself? Roz could do single parenthood if she had to—but she didn't have to. The guardianship clause in the will had made that clear. "These children had two great parents, Jack. And however much I want them—and you—I'm not going to shortchange them with a father figure who's halfhearted about his commitment."

"I'm not halfhearted," Jack said impatiently. "For God's sake, Roz, they're my brother's children. Of course I'll do everything Ants would have done with them."

"But will you *be* everything to them, Jack?"

He didn't even think about it. "No. Not to the level you're asking. Not like a father."

If Jack couldn't love these kids, then morally she had no right to keep them, not when Jo and Ants had listed Fee and Roger as alternatives. Whatever Fee's faults, she and her husband loved the children and had never wavered in their willingness to raise them. They had the alternative of a loving family. The very thought of losing the children made Roz want to grab a shotgun and barricade everyone in the house. Her impartiality was long gone. Which meant she had to ask herself what she'd once asked Jack of Fiona.

When it really mattered, was she capable of putting the children's interests before her own?

Roz swallowed and stepped back. "Then let Fee and Roger have them," she said, "because that's not good enough."

CHAPTER SEVENTEEN

SHE ASKED TOO MUCH.

Jack put on his shades against the glare as he skirted the prefab classrooms on Liam's sports day. The sky was the joyous blue of early summer; the sun heated his face and bare arms. Birds chirruped with the orgiastic fervor of nest-builders and chick-raisers. Caught in an internal argument that looped and relooped through his brain, Jack noticed none of it.

He couldn't commit to loving these kids the way he'd loved Thomas, with that hurl-over-the-cliff leap of faith. With Roz there was no question of holding back, but with the kids…

Avuncular would have to be enough, and it drove him nuts that Roz insisted on more. It wasn't as if the kids noticed any difference. In the sea of colorful picnic blankets, and seething, excitable children, his gaze met Liam's.

Licking a popsicle, the boy stood on a tartan picnic blanket, dressed in his house colors—red. They clashed fiercely with his hair, which flamed copper in the sun, and his freckled face shone with sunblock.

As always, Jack felt himself measured and found wanting. Forcing a smile, he waved. Liam's expression didn't change; he said something to Roz, who knelt beside him, slathering sun lotion on Cassie's scrunched-up nose. Her own nose was pink, but she looked as fresh as a mint julep in white capris and a green-and-white-striped tee, her hair gleaming like a blackbird's wing.

She raised her head and her expression was as guarded as Liam's, but at least she waved. Couldn't she see that even being fond of these kids was a huge step for him?

He hadn't had a chance to talk to either Liam or Sam about permanent custody yet, but Jack figured once he'd marshaled his troops, they could take her. Because this time he wasn't bowing out quietly.

He hadn't wanted to be dragged back into the land of the living, but now that he was there, Roz was going to have to accept the consequences. And that was the two of them living happily ever after with Judgmental, Angry and Bossy.

"Uncle Jack!" Cassie spotted him and stood up, waving her lemon popsicle imperiously. She looked the picture of innocence in her pink overalls and white T-shirt, with her fine, light brown baby hair fluffed up in the breeze.

He was about to wave back when a female hand caught his arm. "Why, Jack, how nice to see you again." He turned politely to Karen, wishing Liam hadn't told him that Molly's mother looked like a horse. "Roz said you probably wouldn't make it," she added.

Did she now? "I had an hour free." Jack made an effort. "So how are you?"

"Oh, you know, keeping out of trouble…unfortunately." She still had her hand on his arm. Gently he freed it, only to have it grabbed by her daughter.

"Can you make Liam do the three-legged race with me?"

"Why don't you just ask him?"

Molly pouted. "I have, and he says he's not doing it with a dumb girl, but we get extra house points the more people who go in the race, and there's no one else left to go."

Jack glanced toward the picnic blanket and caught a glimpse of Liam's back as he disappeared around the side of a classroom. Roz had the innocent expression of an accomplice. "Looks like he's disappeared. Sorry, kid."

"I'll find him," Molly said with grim determination, and trotted off on the hunt.

"So, following my daughter's example…" said Karen, falling in beside him "…there's a parents' three-legged race next. How about partnering up with me, Jack?"

"Gee, I'm sorry, I'm already promised to Roz." He reached the picnic rug, leaned down and kissed his astonished ex-wife full on the mouth.

"Oh, is that how the land lies?" said Karen placidly. "I should have guessed when she joked that you were gay. But if you like, I'll look after Cassie while you two race."

With a blush spreading across her face, Roz spluttered, "I…we're not—"

Jack swung Cassie into Karen's arms. "Thanks," he said, "we appreciate it." He grabbed Roz's hand and hauled her off the blanket. "Let's go cream the competition."

"What the hell are you playing at?" she muttered as soon as they were out of earshot.

"You wanted the old Jack back…well, I'm back." He caught and kissed her again, making it thorough.

And for a second she responded with all the yearning he felt for her, before turning her head. "Please let me go."

Instead, he grabbed her hand and headed for Liam, who was hiding behind one of the silver birches shading the sports field. "Liam, come watch Auntie Roz and me in the parents' three-legged race."

A delighted grin spread across the boy's face. "You're gonna race, really?" He scampered out from behind the tree.

"You don't play fair," Roz muttered.

"I know you think you're doing the right thing, but in this case you're wrong."

"Yep, that's the way to change my mind," she began, but then Liam tugged on their joined hands.

"Hurry up, they're gonna start soon."

They jogged down to the starting line and were issued a stocking. Jack tied Roz's left ankle to his right, then looped his arm around her slim waist, scanning the competition. There were at least two couples with the smiling, relaxed smugness of regular exercisers.

"Doesn't this tell you something?" he asked as they did a quick run to warm up.

She sighed. "What's that?"

"We're in perfect step without any practice. We used to be a good team, Roz, and we can be again. You take care of the kids' emotional needs, I'll take care of the material ones."

"You mean the way you were brought up?"

Jack mistimed his step and had to catch her as they

stumbled. "Now who's not playing fair? My father didn't give a damn about us, and I do care about those kids."

One of the teachers blew a whistle. "Line up, parents."

Obediently, they toed the line. "The Jack I fell in love with gave one hundred and ten percent to everything he did," she said. "Do you really think I'm going to settle for less?"

"Love me, love the kids. Is that the deal?"

"You got it."

"I'll get back to you."

"You do that."

"Ready, parents," called the teacher. "Steady…*go!*"

Fueled by frustration, they flew down the field, passing one couple after another. Jack suddenly saw the comedy in their situation and started to laugh. Roz's arm tightened around his waist. "Concentrate!" she panted.

He'd forgotten how competitive his ex-wife was, and it only made him laugh harder. Under his arm, her ribs shook as she tried to hold back a chuckle, but by the time they crossed the finish line they were both in stitches.

Liam was almost beside himself, punching the air. "Second!" he screeched. "You came second!"

"See what I mean about teamwork?" Jack said hopefully, but she only shook her head at him as she untied the stocking from their ankles.

Karen approached, carrying Cassie, and Jack let the subject drop. For now. As the pair drew closer he noticed Cassie's face was tearstained, and he forgot his levity. "What happened?"

"We had a bit of drama with a bee sting, but she's okay now."

From her position on Karen's hip, Cassie reached out her arms to Roz. "Owwie," she said plaintively.

"I rubbed lavender on it," said Karen, handing her over. "It helps with the stinging, but I notice it's swelling a bit, so put some ice on it when you get home."

Roz looked at the puffy area and frowned. "I'll go now and drop in to a chemist for some antihistamines. Jack, will you hold her while I find my car keys?"

"I'll walk with you to the car." Gently, he took Cassie, and they headed for the exit. "Hey, baby girl," he said. "Bet you're mad at the mean old bee…. Roz, how long has she had this rash?"

Pausing from rummaging in her bag, Roz frowned at the blotches on Cassie's forearms. "The hives weren't there this morning. Could she be having an allergic reaction to the bee sting?"

"Maybe. Let's be on the safe side and head to E.R."

His tone was calm, but Roz fumbled, trying to fit the key into the lock. *Don't overreact.* This was what Thomas's death had done to her—made her expect the worst from every tiny incident.

Jack's hand closed over hers, squeezed briefly, then he took the keys. "I'll drive. Liam, jump in front with me, and we'll let Roz sit with Cass."

Roz got in and took Cassie, fastening her in her child's car seat. The little girl started to whimper. "Owwie, Roz."

"It's okay, honey, I'm here…. It's probably my imagination, Jack, but her lips look puffy."

Wordlessly, he started the engine and pulled into traffic. "I'm still putting on my seat belt," Liam complained. "And I'm not supposed to sit in the front until I'm thirteen 'cause of the airbag."

"I'll drive carefully," Jack promised. "How's our girl?"

Roz stroked Cassie's hair back from her pale forehead, unsure if the clamminess she felt was the child's or her own palms. Panic was a rolling fog around her brain, making it difficult to concentrate. Cassie had stopped whimpering, but her breathing seemed strained. "Liam," she asked, "has Cass ever had a bee sting before?"

"I don't *think* so."

"Anyone in your family, Jack, ever had a reaction?"

"No." He pulled his cell out of his pocket, keyed in an auto-dial. "Fiona, it's Jack. Anyone in your family allergic to bees...? Uh-huh. Yeah, can't talk now. I'll call you back."

He dropped his cell and stepped on the accelerator, his face grim. The car picked up speed. His eyes met Roz's in the rearview mirror, and she kept stroking Cassie's hair, murmuring foolish endearments all the while.

But even as she prayed, the small face swelled before her eyes, the gasps become a wheeze and Cassie's lids fluttered shut. "Jack! She's lost consciousness."

Roz's shoulder hit the window as Jack slammed on the brakes and swerved to the curb. He jumped out and hauled open her door. "Change places," he said. "Drive, Roz, as fast as you can."

Terrified, she scrambled into the driver's seat, flicked on the hazards and pulled into traffic, treating every set of traffic lights as a free intersection. Beside her, Liam started to cry. "Be brave for me," she croaked.

"Liam?" Jack's tone was low and urgent. "Give me your drink bottle—quickly now, son."

The road, Roz reminded herself, *concentrate on the road.*

Liam unbuckled his seat belt and hung over the back of the seat to hand him the bottle. "What are you doing to her?"

"I'm sticking the plastic tube down her throat to help her breathe."

Oh, God. With a massive effort Roz shoved the panic back, staring so hard at the black tarmac flying underneath the car that her eyes ached. Her knuckles tightened to white on the steering wheel as she fought the urge to glance in the rearview mirror, because she knew one glimpse of Cassie's face and she'd lose it. *It's going to be okay. She's going to be okay.* In her mind she chanted it, prayed it, demanded it...pleaded it.

"Why are you breathing down the tube, Uncle Jack?"

Roz's concentration faltered and the car slid into a skid; she corrected it. "Sit down, Liam," she rasped. "And put your seat belt on again."

She started to weep, lips pulled back in a silent grimace. The traffic lights ahead turned amber; Roz put her foot down and shot through them, ignoring the blare of horns. Left at McQuarrie, right into Drover Street, brakes squealing at every corner, while Liam cowered beside her...

And somewhere behind, Jack was breathing air into Cassie's lungs. Tears, hot and salty, trickled into Roz's mouth. She swallowed them and kept driving, though her hands shook so hard on the steering wheel she had to keep adjusting their position.

At last, the neon medical cross of St. Bart's, blue against white, shone through her tears and she swerved into the sweeping hospital bay, nearly sideswiping an ambulance. After slamming on the brakes, Roz shoved open her door and ran toward the paramedics milling around it.

"Bee sting allergy. Three years old. She…she's stopped breathing. Please!" A sob escaped in a strangled heave that shook her whole body. "Help us."

There was a whir of activity around her, a whir that got faster and faster. Roz put out a hand to steady herself against the ambulance, and then everything went black.

ROZ WOKE UP on a gurney in a corridor, and for a moment, she didn't know where she was. There was a crack like an earthquake fault zigzagging through one of the ceiling tiles, and she stared at it while her brain resurfaced.

Cassie.

She jerked to a sitting position, then almost fell over her knees as she bent forward to counter the wave of dizziness. A nurse approached and put a cool hand on the back of her neck to steady her. "You fainted, so take a minute."

"Cassie!"

"Your baby's been given adrenaline and taken to intensive care. Your husband went with her, so she's not alone. We're looking after your son at the nurses' station, so don't worry about him."

Roz slid off the bed. "Where are they?"

"Through the double doors, turn right and follow the signs." She smiled reassuringly. "He probably saved her life…your husband. Lucky he'd had first-aid training."

But Roz didn't hear her; she was already halfway down the corridor. She didn't need to look at the signs. She knew exactly where she was going, because she'd been here before.

Six years ago.

She recognized the sharp stench of disinfectant, the antiquated hum of the air-conditioning and the fluorescent glare reflecting off the easy-wipe walls of an interminable corridor. Her rubber-soled shoes squeaked on the pale green linoleum, while her heartbeat gathered speed like a mouse on a treadmill, racing faster and faster.

If anyone passed her, she didn't know it. Trapped in a terrible sense of déjà vu, Roz only knew one fact. Cassie was dead.

Roz stopped.

The last time she'd made this journey she'd had hope. When she'd received the brief, shocked call from Jack saying that paramedics were resuscitating Thomas, she'd abandoned a cart of groceries and sped to the hospital. Terrified, frantic, but with a heartfelt conviction that her baby would be okay. No logic held sway; she'd simply believed that if he'd died she would know. This tiny person, bone of her bone, flesh of her flesh, connected by that mysterious, symbiotic intimacy of mother and newborn.

Then she'd seen Jack. Sitting in one of the bucket chairs, elbows on knees, callused hands covering his face and his broad shoulders shaking with uncontrollable sobs. *Reaction*, she'd told herself. *He's relieved that it's over.* Until he'd lifted his head and looked at her, his eyes transmitting an agony that hit her like a thousand volts.

Roz realized she was hyperventilating now, and tried to regulate her breathing. Two seconds on the in breath, four out...the way she'd been taught to counter the panic attacks that had plagued her after Thomas's death.

Cassie was dead…but she had to make this journey.

Hugging herself, Roz took one step, then another—a condemned woman taking her last walk. She watched her feet, willing them to move, the grass-stained trainers of her fun afternoon a rebuke and an obscenity now.

There was the sound of running footsteps. "Roz," Jack called. "She's fine. Cassie's going to be okay."

"No," she whispered to her trainers. "She's dead."

Jack reached her and grabbed her shoulders. "Listen to me!" Dazed, she lifted her head and his gaze pinned hers. "The doctors have given her epinephrine. She's breathing on her own. She'll make a full recovery."

Roz moaned; immediately, his arms closed around her. "I thought…"

"I know."

She broke down. "I can't do this again, it's too hard." She buried her face in his shoulder, feeling hot tears soak and spread through the cotton of his shirt. "You're right not to take this on," she sobbed. "We'll give custody to Fee."

His hands gently circled her back. "You don't mean that."

"I d-d-do."

"No," he repeated. "You don't."

There was a utility room next to them. Jack guided her inside and shut the door. They stood in the dark, surrounded by the smell of musty wet sponge mops and cleaning products.

He gently peeled strands of hair back from her face. "I was the one deluding myself, thinking I didn't love these kids…." His voice got stuck in his throat, and Roz realized the hot tears on her face weren't all hers.

She wrapped her arms around his neck and lifted her face blindly in the dark. Their first kiss was clumsy. On the second, their mouths melded, hard, hot and honest, all about seizing life and second chances.

The nurse's words came into her mind again. *Luckily, your husband had training.* "How did you know what to do?"

He hesitated. "I took some courses in emergency first aid a few years ago."

She didn't have to ask why. Her heart broke for him. "I'm sorry," she whispered, "so sorry you were alone with Thomas when he died."

"Until it happened, I thought I was a strong man," he said. "And when I shattered, I didn't care who I hurt— you, Ants and Julia. I'm sorry, Roz, for all the pain I—"

She put a finger on his lips. "How about we just forgive each other?" Under the pad of her index finger, she felt his mouth lift in his special smile.

"I can do that."

"You're going to have to give me that smile sometime when I can actually see it," she said, starting to tremble from delayed shock. "Now I need to get to Cassie."

"I'll fetch Liam. Then I'll ring Fiona."

They stepped out of the utility room, blinking against the light. Jack's eyes were red, there were traces of tears on his cheeks and his hair stood up. Roz figured she looked as bad when he used the tail of his shirt to wipe her face. She thumbed his cheeks free of tears, finger-combed his hair. He caught her hand, held the palm against his face, and for a long moment, they simply looked at each other.

Jack brought her hand to his lips, kissed her knuckles passionately, and they parted.

LIAM SNEAKED AWAY from the nurses' station and the babyish toys they'd given him to play with, and tried to find Cassie. He had to tell her it was all right that a boy cat was called by a girl's name.

The nurses had told him again and again that she'd be okay, but he didn't believe them because his baby sister was never still, and she'd been so floppy in the car when Uncle Jack had been breathing air down the novelty straw. Liam shut the picture out of his mind because it made him want to cry again.

Uncle Jack had been very calm while he'd done it, and at the time Liam had found that reassuring, because if Uncle Jack wasn't panicking then maybe things weren't so bad. Now he thought maybe Uncle Jack hadn't been trying hard enough.

He told himself that if Cassie died she'd be with Mum and Dad in heaven, but he was so tired of everybody leaving him.

First Mum and Dad, then Sam getting all funny and not caring if they stayed together. Auntie Roz loved him, but she couldn't stop Uncle Jack from sending them to England. Liam knew Uncle Jack wouldn't say yes to taking the money. It probably wasn't enough.

Liam wandered down the hall and pressed his nose against the glass of a room, hoping Cassie would be there, but all he saw was an old man dressed in a green sheet, skinny legs hanging over the edge of a hospital bed. The old man frowned and made a shooing gesture, and Liam ducked.

"Liam, where are you?" called Uncle Jack.

For a split second he considered not answering, because he'd wandered off when he wasn't supposed to. But Uncle Jack would know about Cassie.

"I'm here."

Uncle Jack came around the corner and gave him the smile Liam had once seen him give Cassie when she was asleep. Liam's tummy went all funny, like there was a milk shake sloshing around or something, and all the worry whooshed out of him like air from a party balloon.

He smiled back.

CHAPTER EIGHTEEN

JACK KNEW IMMEDIATELY that he shouldn't have raised the issue of custody with Fiona. He should have left it a happy call, all about Cassie making a full recovery.

But euphoria and fatigue had skewed his judgment, made him utter the fatal words. "How would you feel about Roz and I having permanent custody?"

Turned out she felt a lot of things, betrayal and anger chief among them.

Now her niece had experienced a life-threatening allergic reaction. It didn't matter that this was Cassie's first sting or that her brothers had escaped the disorder. Roz and Jack should have asked the doctor about genetic predispositions at the beginning of their guardianship.

"I promised myself that I'd look after her children, and I've been negligent, Jack, as negligent as you. Well, no longer."

"Fiona, I—"

She hung up on him. Jack listened to the dial tone and thought, *Serves me right. Hitting her with a bomb-shell when she's been frantic with worry for the last...* he glanced at his watch *...hour and a half.* Of course she'd overreact.

It occurred to him that it was three-thirty in the

morning over there. He'd call her back at a civilized
hour, apologize for being an insensitive jerk, and start
again.

FEE HUNG UP and burst into tears. Roger was in London,
the boys at boarding school. She was alone in her Geor-
gian mansion in Hampshire. Outside, the first snow
dusted the hawthorn hedge with white, and the driveway
was a dirty, icy sludge under the security lights.

She fumbled in the drawer of her antique rosewood
bureau for a box of tissues and blew her nose, wanting
to call Roger at their flat, but terrified of a woman answering. He'd had an affair last year with a workmate,
a midlife foolishness he bitterly regretted, and though
Fee knew he'd never do it again…well, some fears never
really went away.

His lover hadn't been young, or even pretty, but Fee
knew her as kind. That was when she'd realized some of
the blame lay at her own door—though Roger accepted
all of it. An early menopause had made Fee shrewish and
carping; sex only happened when she thought it was
time, and the act inevitably began with her resigned sigh.

So she'd forgiven him and they'd made a new start.
Roger had been so loving since…. Odd that an affair had
repaired their marriage.

Her husband had always been forbearing, letting Fee
direct their lives, organize the boys' education; putting
up with the pokey London flat during the week and
making the long commute home on the weekends,
where she'd put him to work in a too-big garden.

The country house she'd insisted on had been a
mistake. She missed her London life and she missed her

sons. By the time she realized that giving them the best education couldn't compensate for their absence, they loved the place and wouldn't leave.

She would do things differently if she had another chance. And now she did—with Julia's children. Fee picked up the photograph of Julia and Anthony and their family, and grief washed over her. Warmhearted, easygoing Julia, effortless to love.

Fee, on the other hand, was hard to love; she knew that. An overachiever, she was smart enough to rue it, and compulsive enough to be unable to change it.

The holiday in New Caledonia had not been a success. Fee hadn't been able to relax; she'd organized tours when everyone would have been happy by the pool. It was she who'd insisted on rental cars because she had a distaste for public transport. She who'd sent Julia and Anthony on their last journey.

And the better sister had died. If only Fee had let go of the reins, it would never have happened. She felt that deeply, keenly. She would give her sister's children everything she had, because she desperately needed the chance to atone.

To hell with it. She called Roger—who answered on the third ring, obviously dragged from sleep—and told him what she wanted to do. As always, he gave her his full support. Then Fee dressed, drank tea and scribbled on a notepad in the kitchen, waiting for dawn. At exactly 8:30 a.m. she rang her lawyer.

JACK PULLED HIS SUITCASE out of the taxi. It was a fine day in early December, three days after the bee sting, and he was returning from a two-night business trip to Tokyo.

It was meant to be longer, but he'd cut it short, citing Cassie's accident—though his niece had needed to spend only one night in hospital for observation. Roz had stayed with her, and Jack had barely had time to kiss them a hasty goodbye when he dropped them home before heading to the airport.

In truth, it was Sam's sixteenth birthday, and Jack didn't want to miss it.

And he really needed to see Roz.

Stupid to worry she'd change her mind, but Jack wasn't used to happiness anymore, and he didn't trust it. Their phone calls had been frustratingly brief. And they hadn't told the kids they were keeping them, because the custody issue hadn't been finalized with Fiona. She must be away, because she wasn't returning messages.

They could set the custody wheels in motion, anyway, but they both felt strongly that they needed Fiona's approval first. It had to work for all of them.

Walking down the driveway, Jack noticed that summer had come in his absence. The lime-green leaves of the spindly Robinia tree fluttered in the breeze like pennants of welcome, while bougainvillea exploded into bursts of scarlet across the trellis to one side of the patio. On either side of the driveway, tight white buds on the standard roses gave the effect of a row of giant bridal bouquets.

And the strangest feeling unfurled in him. He no longer looked at the house as something that needed work—though God knows that hadn't changed.

For the first time, Jack saw the good bones underneath the worn exterior, the comfort and warmth. It was like noticing the twinkle in the eye of an old lady who'd lived a satisfying life and was still game for a jig, given the right partner.

"Uncle Jack! Uncle Jack!" Cassie sat in the window seat, banging on the pane. She was wearing a smart red dress, purple earmuffs and a pair of bright green satin evening gloves, the long loose fingers of which flapped as she waved, making her look like Edward Scissorhands.

He laughed. Liam came to the window, his smile more tentative, but Jack figured he had the present to turn the tide. In fact, he was damn sure he'd finally got it right.

Inside, he scooped Cassie up and kissed one round, silky cheek, breathing her in, and realized how much he'd missed her. She squirmed to be put down, intent on only one thing. "Where's my present?"

"It's Sam's birthday today, not yours," Jack teased, winking at Liam, who still stood beside the window seat. "Hey, mate." He thought about crossing the room to hug him, but as he hesitated the moment passed.

Impatiently, Cassie smacked Jack's thigh. "You been in a plane. I get a present."

"Okay, maybe I got you a small one." He dumped his suitcase on the table and opened it, handing her a parcel. "Liam, I have one for you, too."

Gloved fingers flying, Cassie ripped into the wrapping like a lioness on its kill.

"So where is the birthday boy, anyway?" said Jack. "And Roz?" Saying her name made his heart skip beats like a teenager's.

"Some urgent appointment came up," Sam said from

the doorway. "Umm, how come you're home today? We weren't expecting you until tomorrow." For some reason, he sounded nervous.

"Because today's too important to miss. Happy birthday, Sam." He gave him a hug as he handed over the present. The moment was awkward, it was uncomfortable, but hey—they'd live. His own face hot, Jack grinned at his blushing nephew. Holding his present, Liam stood watching them with a wistful expression, and Jack thought, *I should've hugged him.*

Cassie started to jump in sheer joy. "Look what *I* got." He'd bought her a hammering toy—a stand, inset with brightly colored wooden dowels that could be hammered flat with a mallet, then turned over. The perfect present.

And he had another one. "Go ahead, open it," Jack encouraged Liam.

"Sam first," the boy said manfully, "since it's his birthday."

The teenager's face lit up he unwrapped the latest cell phone. "Choice! Thanks, Jack…man, this is rad."

"It's got some weird and wonderful features," said Jack. "Read the brochure."

The home phone rang and Sam jumped. "I'll get it." Ignoring the handset in the lounge, he disappeared into the hall.

Jack turned back to Liam, who was laboriously peeling the last of the tape back from the wrapping paper. "It's a baseball training set," he said eagerly. "The ball pops up from the base, so you can practice hitting it out of the air. Then when you've mastered that, this pitching machine lobs the ball to you." He switched it on and nothing happened. "Damn, it needs batteries. I'll pick some up next time I'm out."

Liam looked at the pitching machine, then at his sneakers. "Thank you," he said in a very quiet voice.

And Jack finally accepted that he was never going to win over this kid. "Guess you should go wash your hands for dinner." Something in his tone made Liam shoot him a nervous glance. "Will you stop being so bloody scared of me?" Jack snapped. "I'm not going to hurt you!"

The kid scarpered.

Angry with himself, Jack sat down on the couch and stared moodily into space, only half aware of Cassie happily banging away on her new toy.

"I told you she's not here right now," Sam muttered from the hall. "I can take a message…okay, call back later if you don't trust me…."

Jack experienced a twenty-year-old sense of déjà vu. Himself fielding just such a call. He strode into the hall and confiscated the receiver. "This is Jack Galloway, Sam's other guardian. Is there a problem?"

He wasn't surprised by what he heard. As he listened, he looked gravely at his nephew, who fidgeted from one foot to the other, crossing and uncrossing his arms, striving to appear unconcerned and failing miserably.

"Yes, Roz and I can come and discuss the situation on Monday. Ten o'clock?" Mentally, Jack reshuffled his appointment schedule. "See you then."

Sam started babbling before he'd replaced the receiver. "They're making a big deal about nothing…a few cigarettes…anyone would think we were smoking dope. And okay, maybe we were stupid to bring beer onto the school grounds, but…man, it's not like it's hard liquor."

The torrent of words ran out, and there was silence except for the bang, bang, bang of Cassie's mallet. So this was what parenting a teenager felt like. A cocktail of frustration, worry, fury and helplessness when they repeated your mistakes. Not trusting himself to speak, Jack counted to ten.

"It's only a few days," Sam said in another rush. "I'll use them as study leave…I mean, Roz has been hounding me to put in more hours, anyway."

The front door opened; Roz came in, and Jack felt sick for having to do this to her. But she was already pale. He took three steps, shielding her from Sam's view. "Roz?"

"I've been with Grimble," she said in a low voice so that Sam wouldn't hear. "Fee's in town and she's suing for custody." As he stood, stunned, she pasted on a smile and looked past him to Sam. "Hey, *that's* not a birthday face."

"I've been suspended," said Sam.

THIS WAS THE SUCKIEST birthday dinner ever, Liam decided, washing down his dry roast chicken with a big sip of water and glowering at his big brother.

Dumb old Sam. Why did he have to go get 'spended on his birthday, anyway?

Now no one except Liam and Cassie wanted to wear party hats or play with the balloons or pull the Christmas crackers that he had begged Roz to bring out early.

The chicken caught in his throat again. "This has stringy bits in it," he complained.

"It's overcooked," Roz murmured, but Liam could

tell she didn't really care, even though she wasn't eating it, either. He felt sad. He'd made place cards and everything, and no one had even noticed.

"I can't eat it." Liam made a gagging sound and pushed his plate away.

Uncle Jack said quietly. "Now's not the time to act up."

Liam's throat tightened, this time with tears. He was tired of being the only one Uncle Jack didn't like. And he couldn't pretend he wanted a dumb old machine to throw him the ball. Baseball was something people did together. Furiously blinking back tears, he pushed the peas around his plate with the fork.

"Liam," Roz said gently, and he looked up. Her smile made him feel better. "Help me clear the table?" There was a conspirator's note in her voice that reminded him about the birthday cake.

Grievances forgotten, he scrambled off his chair and carried plates to the kitchen, where the cake sat in the pantry. Chocolate with chocolate frosting—Sam's favorite—and Liam had measured the ingredients. They put sixteen birthday candles in, and his eyes widened when Roz lit them because it seemed the whole cake was on fire.

Grinning, he pushed open the saloon doors and started singing at the top of his voice. "Happy birthday to you.... Happ—"

"Stop," shouted Sam, "I can't stand it. It's corny and phony and wrong!"

"I know that none of us is really in the mood for this," Auntie Roz said, "but it's still your birth—"

"You just don't get it," he yelled. "Why'd you have to make Mum's cake, huh? Tell me why?"

The candles were burning down, dripping wax into the icing.

"Liam said you always have chocolate cake on your—"

"You're not my mother, so stop trying to take her place!"

Auntie Roz whispered, "Oh, God, is that what all this hostility's been about?"

"Liam," said Uncle Jack, "take Cassie upstairs and play with her until we calm things down here."

Liam stared at Sam, who was all wild-eyed, and reached for Cassie's hand. "Come with me."

"No!" She pulled free of his grasp, so he grabbed her new toy, taking pride of place beside her plate.

"I'm gonna play with this," he threatened, running out of the room.

With a squeal of outrage she chased after him. "Mine."

He didn't let her catch him until they were upstairs in his room, and by that time her face was a bright angry red. When Liam handed it over, she tried to hit him with the mallet, and he had to roll across the bed to get out of range. "Okay, okay, it's yours. I was just tricking. I'm sorry."

"Don't like you," she spat, and plonked herself down on the floor, cradling her toy like a baby. Normally that would have made Liam smile, but he was too worried about what was going on downstairs.

Through the floorboards he could still hear Sam's voice raised in anger, like the rumble of a train coming through a tunnel, getting louder and louder. Liam lay on his bed, jammed the pillow over his head and started singing "Silent Night," the Christmas carol they'd been practicing at assembly.

"'Si…lent night, ho…uh…ly night…'"

Cassie started hammering in the pegs. Bang, bang bang clunk.

"'All is calm.'" Liam's voice quivered, and the tears were hot under his lids.

Bang, bang went Cassie's hammer.

"'All is bright. Round yon verssssion, mother and child.'" He remembered he wanted to ask Roz what a version was. "'Sleep in heavenly pee…eece.'" Bang, bang.

Liam lifted a corner of the pillow. Over Cassie's hammering, Sam was still yelling, so he replaced it.

"'Slee…eep in heavenly peace.'"

CHAPTER NINETEEN

ROZ STOOD QUIETLY under Sam's verbal attack, telling herself not to take it personally, but she had to clench her jaw to stop her mouth trembling. Jack had tried to intervene, but she'd caught his arm and said, "Let him finish." Jack stood beside her now, his shoulder a comforting weight touching hers.

"You may have suckered Liam and Cassie into thinking you're shit-hot," Sam yelled, "but you don't fool me. You're just some sad-ass who hasn't got a life and is taking over Mum's."

"Enough." This time Jack moved so fast Roz couldn't stop him. He pinned Sam against the wall, applying just enough pressure to hold him. "Don't you know what Roz sacrificed to keep you here? Her job—"

"Jack," she interrupted, "I don't consider it a sacrifice. By keeping to your parents' routines and rituals," she explained to Sam, "I was hoping to make the transition easier—particularly for Cassie and Liam. That's all, I promise. I never meant to take anyone's place."

Jack shifted his hand to Sam's shoulder, and his voice was deep and resonant with emotion. "You think if you act like a hard-ass no one will figure out how scared you are...how lost and alone you feel. We understand that.

But lashing out at the people trying to help you isn't acceptable. How do you think your father would feel about this behavior? Your mother?"

Sam shoved free. "Don't tell me what Mum and Dad think…you hardly ever saw them! I'm sixteen, and I don't have to do what you say anymore." He stormed out of the room and up the stairs. Then his door crashed shut.

In the resulting silence, Roz looked at Jack. "Welcome home."

He smiled and it comforted her like balm, soothing every ragged edge of her nerves. "Come here." He opened his arms, and Roz wondered how she'd ever thought she didn't need him. She walked into them, felt them close around her like a warm blanket on a cold, cold night.

"Are you sure you still want to do this?" she joked, because if she didn't she'd cry.

"Yes." One word—so much conviction.

His response gave her courage. "If Sam really does hate me, then maybe he would be better off with Fee. Which means that Liam and Cassie would have to go, too, because we can't separate the kids."

Jack drew her down to the couch. "Sam doesn't hate you," he said gently. "I think he's grappling with the opposite problem. You and Julia both have the gift of making people feel loved."

For a minute she couldn't speak. "Thank you."

"By letting you in, Sam thinks he's being disloyal. We'll talk to him again when the little ones are in bed. Now tell me what Grimble said before we call Liam and Cassie down."

She took a deep breath. "The first step is informal

mediation with a judge acting as facilitator. If we reach a consensus with Fee, it doesn't go any further."

"And if we don't?"

"Lawyers get involved, the case goes to Family Court, where apparently both sides try and present themselves in the best light by discrediting the other. And a third party—the judge—decides who gets custody."

"Mediation it is, then."

"Jack, I think we should leave lawyers out of this as long as possible."

"I agree. Fee's had a shock. When she sees we're back together and very serious about our responsibilities, she'll come around. I'll tell her that we're willing to send the kids over to England at least once a year, or bring her family over here—at my expense. I'm sure once we reassure her that she'll see plenty of them there'll be no problem."

Did he know how tightly his fingers gripped hers? "You're overdoing the calm, soothing tone."

He grimaced and let go. "I do believe we'll sort this out amicably, but…"

"But you're emotionally involved. That's okay, I get it." She touched his cheek and he caught her fingers, turning his head to kiss the palm.

"Roz, let's get married again." Her heart leaped. "Legalize your connection to them, show the judge and Fiona we're committed. It will carry a lot more weight."

The first time he'd proposed marriage he'd told her he was crazy in love with her. Couldn't live without her. "It's something to think about," she said, managing a half smile.

There was a basket of washing on the table beside

them, ready to be folded. She got up, retrieved a queen-size sheet and smoothed out the white cotton.

"You're not keen." His voice was suddenly flat.

"No, it's a good idea. Why not?" She shook it out, ready for folding, and he caught the other side, started tugging her closer.

"Talk to me."

Cassie trotted into the room, saw the sheet stretched out and threw herself into the middle. They tightened their grip just in time to break her fall. "Swing," she demanded, "give me a swing." Obediently, they swung the little body from side to side in the sheet, and her giggles drew Liam downstairs.

"Is Sam okay?"

"He's still mad at us," Roz said honestly, "but we'll fix it."

Liam looked wistfully at Cassie tumbling and laughing in the sheet. "Hop on," said Jack. When the two kids were noisily enjoying themselves, he said, "Tell me what you want, Roz."

Why was she making such a fuss about this? She looked across the sheet to Jack. "Sure," she said briskly. "We'll get married again." *For the kids' sake.*

It was naive to expect the passionate commitment of their first marriage. Not after all that had happened. Not with all these new responsibilities. Still, there was sadness in her, a very different feeling from the fizzing excitement with which she'd awaited Jack's homecoming earlier.

Later, watching him cradle Cass as he read her a story, Roz told herself not to be ridiculous. They needed some time alone together, that was all. Of course they'd go back to the way they were.

As she tidied the toys with Liam, Jack lifted his gaze without skipping a beat in the story, and smiled at her, reinforcing her confidence. "'So Pinky, that intrepid mouse, went back to his home at the dump, wiser and a whole lot smarter about seagulls….' Is it bedtime yet?" The inquiry was completely innocent, but the intent in his eyes caused Roz to drop Mr. Potato Head, who hit the floor and scattered in all directions.

Wise guy. He knew full well that they wouldn't be sharing a bed for a while. Sex before marriage got complicated with a teenager in the house. Still, she sent him a sultry smile as she and Liam collected the remains of Mr. Potato Head. No harm in flirting.

"You know," said Jack, his tone no longer innocent. "I think my next repair is the trellis outside your bedroom window."

Liam crawled from under the couch holding the toy's mustache. "Yeah! Then we can climb it again."

"I never thought of that," said Jack.

Excited by the idea, Liam scampered out to have a look at the trellis.

As soon as he'd gone, Jack murmured, "Kiss me."

Cassie hauled herself up on his lap and planted a wet one on his cheek. "Read the book again."

"When your aunt stops laughing at me." Ruefully, Jack wiped the drool off his cheek. "Can't we have a different book?"

Cassie opened *Pinky* at page one and put it under his nose.

"Maybe our next child will be open to more variety," Roz said to console him.

The smile went out of Jack's eyes, like a cloud covering the sun. She shivered. "You don't want another baby?"

"Let's talk about that when things settle down. We've got enough on our plates at the moment."

As though a child was another burden.

And she had her answer. Things were never going to be the same.

While Jack put the younger kids to bed, Roz drove back to her apartment to pick some of the legal documents they would need for the mediation in two days' time.

"I'm a glass-half-full kind of girl," she told herself, trying to rationalize her devastating disappointment. "I'll have the man I love, the kids I adore, and if Jack doesn't want to have another child together, well, that's understandable. I'll lavish love on other people's babies."

Still, she had a quiet cry in front of Thomas's picture before she locked up and drove back.

With a huge effort of will, Roz concentrated on their immediate priorities. Sam should have cooled down by now and be ready to talk, and they needed to explain about the custody issue. Through her lawyer, Fee had requested no contact with either Roz or Jack until mediation. She wanted to see Sam tomorrow, but was insistent the younger children remain ignorant of the dispute as long as possible.

The common sense in that steadied Roz. Fee's heart was in the right place; of course she'd realize that the kids needed to stay in New Zealand with Jack and her.

She was at the traffic lights waiting to turn right into their neighborhood when a youth holding a duffel bag loped around the corner and headed west. His hoodie obscured his features, but Roz knew that gait.

Where on earth was he going?

With one eye on the red light, she opened the window. "Sam!" Her call was drowned out by the squeal of brakes and tires as a Nissan Skyline accelerated from the opposite direction and pulled up beside him. The throbbing bass of a boom box vibrated across the road in waves of sound when Sam opened the passenger door of the Nissan and jumped in.

Wait just a darn minute, mister. "Sam!"

A car honked impatiently behind her, so Roz drove through the lights, then pulled over. She reached the corner at a half run, and thank God, the Nissan was still there. "Sam!"

But he still couldn't hear her over the music. The interior lamp illuminated the driver's features as he leaned across the car to light Sam's cigarette. Roz gasped and broke into a sprint.

Dirk must have spent enough time with Sam at the funeral to swap mobile phone numbers.

Dirk glanced in the rearview mirror and said something to Sam, who twisted his head to look. Roz expected horror, guilt…. What she saw was narrow-eyed defiance.

She marched up to the car and tried to open the passenger door, but he was ahead of her, locking it and opening the window halfway.

For a moment they stared at each other, and she saw immediately that anger would get her nowhere. He didn't even bother hiding the cigarette in his hand. In a low, steady voice, she said, "Sam, please get out of the car."

Dirk leaned forward, all smiles and hostile civility. "You know, it's not polite to ignore people."

Roz kept her attention on her nephew. "Come home with me, now."

"Sheesh, she's doing it again, bro." Dirk slung one muscled arm across the back of his seat. The barbed-wire tattoo encircling his biceps was the color of a cheap blue pen. He released the handbrake, gave the engine a rev. "Don't you sweat, baby doll, I'll make sure he's tucked in at night." He laughed at his own wit.

"What does he mean?" Roz said sharply.

Sam shared a grin with the young man beside him. "I'm quitting school, getting a job and staying in New Zealand—living with Dirk. You and Jack can send me my money when you sell the house."

The situation was reaching nightmarish proportions. "That's not happening, Sam." She glared at Dirk. "Jack and I are applying for permanent custody, so you don't have to go anywhere."

"You want the house, you mean," Dirk said.

"Stay out of it," she snapped at him.

"Shit, you're right, bro," Dirk said to Sam. "She is one uptight bitch."

Sam squirmed, glanced at Roz. "I didn't say it like that."

"Let's discuss this at home," she said quietly, trying to hide her increasing desperation. Dirk's eyes were clear, but he had the sweaty, sharp tang of a chronic drinker. "Please, Sam, unlock the door."

Hesitantly, the teenager lifted the lock mechanism; they were both surprised when the button clicked down again. Roz saw Dirk was using the driver's controls to override Sam's action.

"Please, Sam," he mimicked, and their nephew looked

at him uncertainly. "You wanna be pussy-whipped for the rest of your life?"

Sam's jaw tightened and he lowered his hand. "You still wouldn't let me quit school, though, would you? I'm going with Dirk."

Roz jiggled the door handle. "As your guardian, I'm ordering you to open the door."

Dirk's eyes were flat and hard as he glanced across Sam. "My man's sixteen now, doesn't have to do what you say."

"What would *you* know about the law? Open the damn door."

Dirk smirked at her. "If there's one thing Evanses understand, sweet cheeks, it's how the law works. Otherwise how can you get around it?" The window whined shut.

Roz banged on the glass. "Sam, get out of the car *now!*"

Arms folded, he kept staring straight ahead. The blue Nissan accelerated away from the curb with a squeal of tires and disappeared around the corner, its taillights flashing, leaving her standing in an acrid cloud of exhaust fumes.

CHAPTER TWENTY

THOUGH HE'D NEVER BEEN near the neighborhood before, Jack recognized the place as soon as he saw it. The overgrown lawn, the sagging chain-link fence, the peeling paint on the wooden window frames, the old sofa on the porch that obviously did duty as outdoor furniture. The young guys sitting on it, half-drunk in the late morning sun, feet up on the porch rail, countering their hangovers with a cold beer. He'd crashed in places like this through his late teens.

There would be beer in the fridge and not much else, sheets that needed washing, dirty towels and a lot of bravado masking the fact that no one really gave a shit about them.

Some things never changed.

Jack jumped the gate, having seen at a glance it was rusted shut. He ignored the Doberman tied in the yard next door, barking furiously as it pulled on its chain.

Sam straightened as he approached; the others watched him through listless eyes, yawning and staying where they were. Dirk wasn't in sight…probably still in bed, which was just as well, because right now Jack wanted to beat him senseless. But violence wasn't his objective this morning.

He and Roz had stayed up half the night trying to track Sam down. The police hadn't been helpful. Sam could indeed leave home at sixteen unless Child, Youth and Family Services thought he was at risk. Jack could go through the application process. Neither he nor Roz was prepared to wait.

Ignoring the others, he said to Sam, "Is there somewhere private we can talk?"

His nephew lounged back in the chair, an old car seat with loose springs. "There's no point. You're not going to change my mind."

Jack waited.

"I don't see why you have to interfere when you don't care," Sam muttered, getting up.

"If I didn't care I'd leave you to learn the hard way."

Sam led him into the dim interior, damp and dark because of too-small windows. The teenager's royal-blue sleeping bag, incongruous in its newness, lay on the worn couch in the lounge. He pulled it aside so Jack could sit down, moving cans and magazines off the floor to make room for their feet. "We had a party last night," he said awkwardly.

"They spend all your money yet?"

"I had to pay a bond," he said defensively, "contribute to the rent and food kitty."

Jack looked at the beer cans. "Yeah, I can see that. So you want to quit school and get a job?"

"Already got one." Sam gave a cocky grin. "Dirk has a mate who's a builder. He needs a laborer."

"You gave up school to slave ten-hour days for minimum wage?"

"You left school at my age and did okay without qualifications."

"No, I didn't do okay. I went back to night school and got them, realizing I'd made a big mistake," Jack said grimly. "I only left home at sixteen because my father didn't give a shit about me."

Sam stuck out his chin. "There's no one left to give a shit about me, now Mum and Dad are dead."

"You know that's not true. I admit I haven't been the great guardian Roz has, but that's changing as of now. I'm taking you home."

"No, you're not." Sam backed away, his eyes hostile. "I'm sixteen and I don't have to do what you say anymore."

"That's where you're wrong." Jack picked up Sam's sleeping bag and repacked it. "Ants and Ju live on through the charge they placed in me, and I'm not letting them down again." He glanced at his nephew's face and his tone softened. "I'll always regret that I missed my brother's last years because I shut out the people I loved while I was grieving…. Like you're doing now, Sammy."

His nephew folded his arms. "What? You think you can *force* me to go with you?" he jeered.

Jack smiled. "I grew up with a man who washed his hands of me as soon as it got hard, and I'm not doing the same to you. So yes, if I have to pick you up and carry you out kicking and screaming, then I'll do it." He retrieved the rucksack beside the couch. "Until the Family Court says otherwise, you're living with us and abiding by our rules. And that means exams next week."

"I hate you!" Sam started to sob with impotent rage. "You don't understand *anything*."

"Son, it's because I understand," said Jack, "that I'm

doing this." Knowing better than to offer comfort, he handed Sam his sleeping bag, and watched the teenager unconsciously hug it.

Bleary-eyed, jeans hanging around his lean hips, Dirk appeared from the bedroom, scratching his chest. "What's up, bro?"

Jack said pleasantly, "What's up, *bro,* is that I'm taking our nephew home, and if I ever see your skinny ass around the house again, I'll kick it all the way back here."

The younger man bristled. "You touch me and I'll sue you for assault."

"Do you think I'm stupid enough to do it in front of witnesses?" Jack said coldly. "It'll come down to your word against mine, which means the police will look at our records. Mine's clean. How about yours?"

FEE WATCHED HER OLDEST nephew drum his fingers nervously on a marble table in the foyer of Auckland's Grand Hotel, where Sunday afternoon tea was being served.

"You side with me," Sam said, "and I'll testify for you in any custody hearing so you get Cassie and Liam."

There was an aspect of this quid pro quo that she didn't like. But that wasn't her immediate concern. "Sam, you're too young to be on your own. Come back with me to England."

He snorted. "And do what?"

She pushed the three-tiered cake stand toward him. On it were cucumber and salmon club sandwiches, scones dripping with jam and piled with cream, and fat slices of Black Forest cake. "You can go to the same school as the boys. They absolutely love it at Harrow."

"Board," he said with a colonial's instinctive horror

of the British institution. "No way." He helped himself to a large piece of the cake and put it on the bone china plate. "School's bad enough without spending every waking hour there."

"Okay," she said, thinking hard. "I'll support your bid for independence if you go back to school here for another year—then we'll review it."

"I get to live alone though, right? With my share of the sale of Mum and Dad's house?"

Fee hesitated. He was too young to make adult choices, too young to have free access to money that should be securing his future. She began to see the problem in all its dimensions.

She'd thought she could persuade him to come home with her, if only to be with his brother and sister. "What about Liam and Cassandra?"

He'd picked up his fork; now he put it down again. "Don't you start on about family staying together and all that bull…. I've had enough of it from Jack and Roz."

"Have you?" Uneasiness snaked through her, as uncomfortable as guilt. "Well, they have a point, Sam."

"Why does everyone have to try and make me feel guilty all the time because I want my own life? I can visit once a year or something, can't I?"

"We're…" she caught herself aligning with Roz and Jack "…*I'm* just encouraging you to think things through properly. The decisions you make now will affect your whole life."

"I thought you'd understand," he accused, pushing his plate away. "I thought you'd be on my side. Otherwise what's the point of…"

"Supporting me?" Fee finished. Now she was really

worried. "I thought it was because Jack and Roz were doing a terrible job?" He'd told her some truly horrific stories over the past thirty minutes.

"Of course it is," he mumbled, but he looked down at his trainers and her uneasiness grew. What kind of Faustian bargain was she making here? This boy needed care, boundaries….

"I can't let you live alone," she said, "or have free access to your inheritance. That would make me derelict in my duty to your parents."

She ignored his exclamation of impatience. "But I'm sure we can come to some arrangement—for you to board with a friend's family, for example, and come over to England for holidays. At least that would free you of Jack and Roz's influence on a day-to-day basis…if that's what you really want, Sam. Is it?"

His blue eyes were so filled with pain, it hurt her to look at him, and Fee made some instinctive gesture to touch. Sam moved, very slightly, so he was out of reach. "Yes," he said. "That's what I want."

Two lawyers flanked Fiona.

Out of the corner of her eye, Roz saw Jack give the same start of surprise as they entered the mediation room at the Family Court with Sam.

Jack reached for her hand and gave it a reassuring squeeze, which tightened when their nephew went to the other side of the circular maple table and pulled up a chair next to Fee. Sam shot them a quick glance that was half sheepish, half defiant. Fee patted his hand, then gave them a cool nod that had nothing conciliatory about it.

Oh, God, thought Roz with a growing dismay, *we're in trouble.*

Sam had come back from his meeting with Fiona very quiet, and had slipped into his room straight after dinner, simply saying he'd told his aunt he wanted to stay in New Zealand. Given the events of the last twenty-four hours, Roz and Jack had let him be. Right now it was enough that he was prepared to go back to school when his suspension ended next week.

"What's going on?" she whispered to Jack as they took their seats.

"I suspect we'll find out," he murmured back.

Judge Sawyer was a man in his late sixties with a genial, weathered face and the kind of haircut that suggested a wife's inexpert hand. His wiry brows were equally in need of a professional trimming, jutting out over intelligent, deep-set hazel eyes.

He vigorously shook everyone's hand, then told Fiona's lawyers he expected them to behave themselves. Roz relaxed slightly.

"We're here to discuss who has permanent custody of Liam and Cassandra Galloway," Judge Sawyer began, glancing at his notes, "who have been in the interim custody of their appointed guardians, Jack Galloway and Rosalind Valentine, following their parents' deaths just over five weeks ago. Mr. Galloway and Ms. Valentine now wish to claim permanent custody of the children, as does the children's maternal aunt, Fiona Montgomery of England."

His gaze darted to all parties, seeking assent, and everybody nodded.

"During the period of temporary custody, Sam Evans

has turned sixteen. Ms. Valentine and Mr. Galloway, citing the special circumstances of his parents' recent death, are asking for an extension of custody until he is seventeen. Sam is requesting, with Mrs. Montgomery's support, that he be exempt from any final parenting order." Roz gasped. "Instead, he's asked that Mrs. Montgomery take responsibility for his well-being, though I understand relocation isn't on the cards. So this would be an advisory and support role only."

Roz couldn't stop a murmur of protest.

The judge raised his head. "This seems to be news to you, Ms. Valentine. Weren't you and Mr. Galloway informed of this in advance of mediation?"

"No," Jack answered grimly, "we were not."

Judge Sawyer frowned at Fee's lawyers and the elder of the two men cleared his throat. "The matters pertaining to day-to-day custody of Samuel Evans were only resolved between the parties, Sam Lucas Evans and Fiona Elizabeth Montgom—"

"This is an informal mediation, Bryce," the judge reminded him. "Let's leave the legalese outside the door and let the people involved speak for themselves, as much as possible. We are here to reach an amicable agreement, after all." He smiled at Sam. "And in this forum, everybody, I prefer to be called Horace."

I like him, thought Roz.

As though sensing her approval, he smiled at her. "Given the unique nature of these circumstances, all parties, including my own department, are seeking a quick resolution, which is why proceedings have been expedited."

Horace sat back and selected a mint from the bowl

in front of him. "Each of you will speak, but only I—" he looked pointedly at the lawyers "—may interrupt. Ms. Valentine, we'll begin with you."

Roz opened the folder she and Jack had sat up half the night preparing. Cassie had found it this morning, and a trail of pink marker squiggled across the page. In some strange way Cassie's handiwork steadied her.

She and Jack had agreed that honesty was the best policy, so she talked frankly about the challenges of the last five weeks, then summarized their case for keeping the children—all the arguments she'd honed on Jack.

When she'd finished, she addressed Sam directly, though he wouldn't look at her. "It's tempting to let you do what you want, so you'll like me," she admitted. "But every time my resolve wavers, I hear your mum's voice in my head, telling me to get with the program. I can't pretend I don't know what they wanted for you, Sam. And it doesn't include being separated from your little brother and sister, or living away from home before you're ready." Her throat closed up.

"The bottom line is that we're doing this because we love you, Sam," Jack finished for her. "And whatever happens here won't change that."

"Lovely sentiments," said Fiona crisply. "Now let's look at the facts. May I ask some questions?"

"Of course," said Horace. He reached for another mint, tossing one across the table to Sam, who instinctively caught it and grinned.

Frowning, Fiona nodded to her lawyers. What followed was nothing less than a mauling.

Hadn't Jack promised Fee custody? In fact, hadn't he resisted even temporary guardianship?

If the kids meant so much to him, why had his visits been almost nonexistent over the previous six years?

Oh, yes, their personal tragedy. Shouldn't they have informed Mrs. Montgomery—and social services—that their baby had died of crib death while under Jack's care?

Not that anyone was intimating neglect—the autopsy had said otherwise. They simply wondered why he'd never had counseling. Ms. Valentine had needed *lots* of it.

"For God's sake, who wouldn't?" Horace growled. A pile of cellophane mint wrappings littered the desk in front of him.

"That's our point, sir."

"And a good one," Jack acknowledged. "Roz made a faster recovery than I did as a result. But I've made my peace with our son's death."

After he answered he jotted something on a piece of paper and pushed it to Roz. *Stop gnashing your teeth. Better to know everything they've got in case this goes to court.*

Looking as sane as she could manage, she wrote back, *Then I get to kill them, right?*

Jack glanced at her note and bit back a smile. It took the edge off the dread growing inside her.

"You know," said Fee tartly, "with one divorce already behind you—two in Roz's case—I don't see your remarriage as any guarantee of security."

Sam spoke for the first time. "You guys are getting remarried?" During the discussion of Thomas's death he'd been shooting them anxious glances from under his hoodie. Now he smiled at Roz. "That's gr—"

Fiona put a restraining hand on his arm. Her nails were the palest mauve, exactly the color of her lipstick. "Roz, Sam told me you hit Jack and that Liam witnessed it." Sam dropped his head in confusion. "How does that constitute good parenting?"

"It doesn't," she replied, trying to catch Sam's eye again to reassure him. "But I immediately apologized and—"

"I provoked her," said Jack.

"And what happens when the kids provoke her? Will she hit them and then immediately apologize?"

"Don't be ridiculous," said Jack. "With that single exception, Roz has never—"

Again Fee interrupted. "What about you dragging Sam home against his will? Was that good parenting?"

"Actually," Roz answered, "it was. Dirk Evans has a criminal record."

Fee didn't know that; Roz could tell by the way her eyes widened in shock. "Of course I knew the father was bad news, but—"

Her lawyer, Bryce, cut her short with professional ease. "And what about when Mr. Galloway allowed a six-year-old to attend his parents' funeral against *your* advice, Ms. Valentine? And against my client's? I understand the child became hysterical and had to be carried out of the church. Was *that* good parenting?"

"No," said Jack, "but I've learned—"

"Learned," said Bryce. "Really? Didn't your niece nearly die under your care a week ago because neither of you bothered to find out the family's medical history?"

"Jack saved Cassie's life," said Roz hotly. Under the

table his hand came down on hers, warm and encompassing.

"*We* saved her life," he corrected. "Fiona, you've made mistakes, too, but undermining each other is not the way forward. Get rid of these guys and let's talk sensibly."

Fiona stood up and nodded to her lawyers, who did the same. "Unless you're prepared to hand over the children, there's nothing further to say. For me, it comes down to this. If you two are so wonderful with Cassie and Liam, then why is their older brother supporting me?"

CHAPTER TWENTY-ONE

SAM ASKED TO STAY with Fee and, reluctantly bowing to Roz's judgment, Jack gave permission. His nephew had a hangdog expression and was obviously feeling guilty about taking sides.

Roz saw the teenager's unhappiness, too. "You'll always be able to change your mind, Sam," she told him as they left the mediation chamber. "Like Jack said, we love you."

For a moment Sam hesitated, then, shaking his head miserably, walked outside with Fee's lawyers and Judge Sawyer, who'd also despaired of making ground today.

"Go back to your hotel," he'd told Fee sternly when he'd dismissed them, "and think very seriously about the consequences of taking an adversarial approach."

As his sister-in-law passed, Jack blocked her exit. "If we can't reach an agreement here, it will go to a defended court hearing, and the decision will be taken out of our hands. Is that what you want, Fiona? Strangers deciding what's best for the kids?"

She lifted her chin. "So let me have them."

Jack shook his head.

"I'll guarantee access." She added bitterly, "*This* time we'll put the arrangement on paper."

He met her gaze squarely. "I'm sorry for going back on my word, Fiona, but we didn't have any right to make custody decisions without Roz. And at the time I didn't think I had anything to offer these kids. I do now and, more importantly, so do they."

"Sam doesn't."

"Sam was angry at us when he talked to you. For pity's sake, you must see how conflicted the poor kid is."

She avoided his gaze. "We're all conflicted, Jack."

"I know what you're feeling guilty about," Roz said quietly.

Fiona lost her poise. "I…d-don't know what you mean."

Neither did Jack. But he trusted Roz's instincts. "What is it?"

"Ju and Ants died on the way to something Fee arranged for them. Liam mentioned it once." She turned back to Fiona, and the movement released the faint scent of her apple blossom perfume. "But until today I'd never made the connection with your need for custody. You're looking to salve a guilty conscience, aren't you?"

"That's ridiculous," Fiona snapped. But her strained expression said otherwise.

Jack suddenly felt immense sympathy for her. "Fiona," he said gently, "guilt is a corrosive emotion that skews your judgment and ruins your life. Believe me, I know. After Thomas's death, I lived with it for six years."

Until Roz dragged him kicking and screaming back into life. Thank God for her. On a surge of emotion he watched his ex-wife touch his sister-in-law's hand, concern in her blue eyes.

"Come and stay with us," Roz suggested. "See for yourself how the kids are with us."

"My lawyers have advised me—"

"Screw the lawyers," Jack interjected. "We can solve this as a family."

She shook her head and her mouth set in a stubborn line. "I want my sister's children."

Jack's sympathy evaporated and he put a hand under Roz's elbow. "Then we'll see you in court."

JACK WATCHED AS Roz filled the kettle at the kitchen sink, her head bowed. Under the shiny black ponytail, her neck seemed unbearably fragile.

He came up behind her and enfolded her in his arms, resting his chin on her hair. "We need to talk about the worst-case scenario."

"If Fee wins," she said steadily, "I don't want to appeal, drag this out for months, years…. It will be too hard on them, Jack."

He'd been thinking the same thing. "She hasn't won yet."

"But she has a good case."

"Yes." Still holding her, he took the kettle out of Roz's hand and set it on the counter. "Go sit on the porch where the kids won't overhear us." Cassie and Liam were in bed, but it was safer to take no chances. "I'll finish making the drinks, then we'll talk for five minutes about losing, before strategizing for a win. Agreed?"

He could feel her shoulders relax a little. "Agreed."

When he followed ten minutes later, Roz was so still in the shadows, sitting in a cane chair, that Jack thought she must still be inside. Then Thomas's bracelet glimmered as she moved her hand.

Tea slopped out of the mugs as Jack placed them unsteadily on the table.

Roz began speaking in a rush. "Once I'm working again, I figure I should be able to save enough to go see them once a year. And if we keep this whole court thing civilized, maybe Fee will let them come to New Zealand for a holiday…in a year or two when they're older. By then I should be able to afford a bigger apartment."

"What the hell are you talking about?"

She started twisting the bracelet again, around and around her wrist. "There's no hurry to get remarried if we lose custody, is there? If you want more time to think about that kind of commitment."

His astonishment gave way to a gut swoop of fear. "Are the kids the only reason you agreed to remarry me?"

"Aren't they the reason you suggested it?"

"Hell, no!" How could she even think such a thing? His gaze fell on the bracelet. *She thinks I'm going to leave. Because that's what I do when things get bad.*

"I want to marry you because from the minute I saw you I loved you," he said passionately, "and I'll love you until the day I die."

Her eyes widened; she swallowed.

Jack caught her wrist and dropped to his knees in front of her. Under his fingers, the metal was smooth and warm from her skin. He lifted it to his lips, kissed Thomas's name, then the jumping pulse point underneath it. "In my heart, you never stopped being my wife."

"Then why," she cried, "did you give up on us?"

"Because…" he forced himself to expose his deepest shame "…because I couldn't fix it for you."

"Some things can't be fixed, Jack, and…" her hand crept back to the bracelet "…love doesn't conquer all. Our divorce proved that."

"You're right," he said simply. "It doesn't." Pulling her out of the chair, Jack took her place, then gathered her onto his lap. "My love couldn't save Thomas. Your love couldn't stop me self-destructing." His gaze stayed unwavering on hers. "But you've made me believe that love's still worth everything you have to suffer for it. And if the worst happens, and we lose custody of these kids, then I'll pay that price again, willingly. And if you want another baby, then we'll have another baby, because life with you is all about courage."

Tears filled her eyes; she buried her face in his shoulder and said in a muffled voice, "I love you so much, Jack."

He lifted her face, holding it between his hands, and his voice was unsteady as he told her, "Whatever happens with custody, I'm not going anywhere. We're getting remarried and I'm going to wake up beside you every morning for the next fifty or sixty years, until one day, Roz, you forget I ever left."

The last strain on her face relaxed into a tremulous smile. "How about I just remember you came back?"

His throat tightened. "That will work."

LIAM KNEW EXACTLY WHERE the courthouse was because his class had been on a tour there once. Molly's mum, who could type in stuff as fast as people talked, worked there part-time, and his class had been learning about how laws worked so they could make some up for the school. He'd come up with "No borrowing other people's rulers without permission."

Cassie started whining as they got to Dunlop Street, but he'd put some shortbread in his pocket. She quietened when he handed over a biscuit. He figured they had to keep moving because he didn't want to leave the babysitter locked in the bedroom for too long in case she ran out of oxygen.

He would tell the people at court to go and let her out. Maybe they'd put him in jail, but this was too important, and Liam felt very strongly that he had to go by himself to show he wasn't being made to do anything he didn't want to.

Seemed people worried about that a lot.

In the last few days he'd been asked a lot of questions 'bout stuff by strangers, and he'd answered truthfully, like Auntie Roz and Uncle Jack had told him. "I want to live here with them." He even told about the deal he'd offered Uncle Jack, to show how serious he and Cassie were about staying.

"And what did he say, son?" said Ellie Walters. She was the only one of the social services people he knew, so Liam turned to her with relief.

"He said he'd think about it, but I haven't had time to ask him since then." The way she'd looked at the others gave Liam a bad feeling in his tummy.

Yesterday he'd remembered again to ask Uncle Jack about the deal, but he'd only laughed and ruffled Liam's hair. "I'd never take your money, mate. Incidentally, I couldn't get batteries for that baseball pitching set I bought you. Is it okay if I just throw the ball to you instead?"

"Yeah!" said Liam.

On their way out he'd seen an album opened at a picture of Dad pitching to Liam in the yard. "That's my favorite," Liam had exclaimed.

"Mine, too," said Uncle Jack. "You know, the clues were always there. I just wasn't ready to see them."

"Huh?" said Liam.

"It doesn't matter. Let's play ball."

Now Liam wanted to tell those people what Uncle Jack had said about not taking the money. He'd overheard Uncle Jack say that the court made the decision about who got to take care of him and his sister, so he and Cassie had to go speak to the people there.

Cassie started whining and dragging on his hand again, and Liam gave her another biscuit. "Nearly there," he coaxed, because he could see the big redbrick building at the end of the street. As they trotted closer, a meter maid stopped him.

"Hey, there, dude. Where's your mummy?"

"In heaven."

Cassie nodded solemnly. "Heaven."

The woman looked startled. "Well, who's looking after you and your sister? You're too small to be out walking by yourself."

"I'm sorry," he said politely, tugging on Cassie's hand, "but we're not s'posed to talk to strangers."

"Little boy, wait a minute."

"Run," he whispered to Cass, and she did, shrieking with joyous terror. At the courthouse, they had to slow down because Cassie needed to plant both feet on each broad step before tackling the next one. Glancing over his shoulder, Liam saw the meter maid still watching them. With a faint frown, she started to follow.

So now he had no time to stop at the big doors leading to the dark interior, which he wanted to do, because he was a teeny bit scared.

A Maori lady in a uniform sat at a desk inside the door. She peeked at him over her reading glasses, then looked around for a grown-up. Liam stood up straighter when her attention came back to him, curious now. "Yes, young man?"

"I have to speak to somebody," he said, "about a cus…a cust…" He racked his brains. "A custard issue." *Issue* was an easier word to remember because it reminded him of a sneeze.

"I see." Wrinkles folded into deep creases at the sides of her brown eyes as she smiled. "Your name?"

"Liam Jack Galloway."

She wrote it down, then took off her glasses and regarded Cassie, who was sucking her thumb. "And who is this with you?"

Liam yanked on his sister's arm and her thumb came out of her mouth with a soft popping sound. "My witness."

FEE AND SAM WERE DRIVING to her lawyers' office when her nephew's cell phone rang.

"Tell whoever it is you can't chat now, Sam," she said impatiently. "We've got too much to do." She hoped to talk him into a haircut and some new clothes after the appointment, get rid of that neglected look that Sam seemed to think was so cool.

Over the couple of days he'd been staying in the hotel with her, she'd grown increasingly worried about him. He was sullen, uncommunicative…even depressed, a far cry from the staunch, convincing ally who'd bolstered her conviction that she was doing the right thing in pursuing custody.

Last night she'd steeled herself to ask him if there was something he'd like to tell her. It was the closest she could come to asking if he'd had a change of heart, because the thought of not getting the children was too painful to contemplate.

"No," he'd snapped, and gone back to watching TV. A few minutes later he'd added moodily, "What good would it do now, anyway? Roz and Jack hate me."

He seemed to have tuned out what Fee grudgingly admitted was a surprising maturity on his guardians' part in handling his defection. But it wasn't in her interests to remind him, and self-preservation won. Although her conscience still prickled her.

In the passenger seat beside her now, Sam jerked upright and gripped his cell phone. "You're *where?* Yeah, sure I'll come get you. Um…" Out of the corner of her eye she saw him dart her a worried glance. "I'll get there as soon as I can."

Fee shifted down a gear as the city traffic started to thicken. "Is something wrong?"

"Yeah. A friend of mine's got an emergency and I said I'd help him out. Can you drop me at Main Street as you drive past?"

She tried to keep the exasperation out of her voice. "Sam, we're due at the lawyers for an important meeting! Ring him back and tell him you can't make it."

"I don't care about the lawyers! Lia…my friend needs me."

Fee wasn't the wife of a barrister for nothing and she had the truth out of him in five minutes. Liam and Cassie had run away from their babysitter and were at the courthouse. Liam had called Sam in a naive belief that their big brother could prevent Roz and Jack from finding out. Fee took great pleasure in calling them at *their* lawyer's office and telling them to go rescue their elderly babysitter while she collected the children with Sam.

"This is one more example," she fumed thirty minutes later as she buckled the young offenders into the backseat, "of totally inadequate supervision."

Cassie growled.

"I'm never gonna tell you anything again, Sam," Liam said hotly to the back of his brother's head. "You're the meanest, horrible-ist bum-bum and I hate you!"

Sam said nothing and, glancing up, Fee saw he was hunched in the front passenger seat. "Liam, don't talk to your brother like that. He's doing what he thinks is best."

"So was we," Liam said sullenly. "We want to stay with Auntie Roz and Uncle Jack, but no one will listen to us 'cause we're little."

In the process of getting into the driver's seat, Fee bumped her head when she raised it in shock. "Oh, my God, they've turned you against me."

"No, they haven't!" Sam snapped. "They always say nice things about you…and Roz makes us phone you even when we don't want to. You're the one who made a war out of this." His Adam's apple bobbed as he swallowed. "And now I can never go home."

Fee took her hand off the ignition key. "Is that how you really feel?"

Liam misinterpreted her. "We do want to talk to you sometimes," he said, "only not when you're trying to make us do stuff we don't want to—like you did when we were on holiday. Mum said you can't help it and—"

"Shut up, Liam," Sam interrupted savagely. "You're hurting her feelings."

"Sorry, Auntie Fee," Liam mumbled.

She made a massive effort and smiled. Because Julia was wrong. Fee could help it. She started the car.

"Where are we going?" Liam asked warily. "To your hotel?"

"No," said Fee. "I'm taking you home."

Liam and Cassie tumbled out of the car as soon as she parked in the driveway, but Sam balked when she told him to join them. "What will I say to Jack and Roz?"

"'Sorry' is always a good start. Then tell them you'll accept an extension of the parenting order. And that I'm letting them have custody."

"Will you come in with me?"

I've done enough damage. "Darling, some things a man has to do on his own, and making amends is one of them. But they love you. It'll be fine."

To her surprise, he leaned over and gave her a fierce hug. "Thank you."

Fee fumbled for her sunglasses, her composure starting to unravel. "All right, off you go."

Still, she waited until the front door opened. Jack caught the younger ones up in his arms, and she could hear him doing the relieved rant of a father. Climbing up on the porch, Sam started to stammer something about giving up smoking, and Roz cut him off with a fierce hug.

"So," said Fee, "that's that." She started the engine and began backing down the drive, her eyes so full of tears she nearly ran Jack over when he suddenly blocked her route. Slamming on the brakes, she steeled herself for a verbal onslaught as he came around to the driver's window.

His eyes were moist. "Thank you."

"I'm sorry," she croaked, "that it ever came to this. I won't bother you again."

He reached through the open window and took her car keys. "You're not leaving, Fiona. You're staying with us until you fly home, and while you're here we're going to organize when your family next sees the kids."

She couldn't bear his kindness. "Jack, you don't understand. Their death *was* my fault."

Instead of stepping back in horror, he opened her door and guided her out of the car with a firm hand under her elbow. "I doubt that, but talk to me."

"I kept telling them that they should go out for a romantic dinner and spend some time on their own…. I all but pushed them out the door. 'Go and have a good time,' I said, 'and I'll look after the children.'" Her voice dropped to a whisper. "It was the last thing I said to them. 'I'll look after the children.'" Blindly, she groped for the door handle, and instead found herself enfolded in her brother-in-law's arms.

He held her very tightly, but his voice was calm and sure. "It's only takeaways for dinner tonight," he said, "but I know you won't mind the informality—being family."

CHAPTER TWENTY-TWO

ROZ WOKE FROM a lovely dream about Thomas, and thought she was still in one. Jack lay beside her, his shoulder a broad cliff in the dark, rising and falling with his deep, even breathing.

In the hall a night-light glowed a pale blue, and downstairs she could hear the sporadic hum of the refrigerator, the fall of ice in the icemaker. Beside the bed, the cat stopped licking its paws and stared at her for a moment before returning to the task.

It was instinctive to turn, still half-asleep, and slide her hand down the slope of Jack's shoulder and back lower to the swell of tight buttock. *Mine.*

Waking, he flung a protective arm across her upper body. "I love you," said her new husband.

Burying her nose in his shoulder, Roz breathed in the clean scent of him and the fainter saltiness of hot sex and crisp, cool cotton. "'Behold, thou art fair, my beloved,'" she murmured, "'yea, pleasant: also our bed is green. The beams of our house are cedar, and our rafters of fir.'"

"Acutally," Jack said sleepily, "the beams are kauri and the rafters are macrocarpa."

Roz grinned. "'For, lo,'" she continued, "'the winter is past, the rain is over and gone.'" Now she knew why the verse had come into her head. Because of its joy. "'The flowers appear on the earth, the time of the singing of birds is come, and the voice of the turtle is heard in our land.'"

There was a croak from under the bed and they both laughed. "That bloody frog," said Jack. Wide-awake now, he asked curiously, "What was that?"

"Song of Solomon. I learned it by heart when I was twelve for a bible class speech competition. It was *so* romantic... 'Many waters cannot quench love, neither can the floods drown it: if a man would give all the substance of his house for love, it would utterly be condemned.'"

"I would give all for love," said Jack, "particularly this house."

"Quit teasing your wife." Roz picked up his hand and kissed the warm knuckles, suddenly deeply, intensely grateful. "'Set me as a seal upon thine heart,'" she finished, "'for love is strong as death.'"

Jack was silent a moment, then cradled her against his chest. "No," he corrected gently. "Stronger."

Twelve months later

IT WAS CHRISTMAS EVE and the arrival hall at Auckland International Airport was packed. People jostled and queued and griped amid the decorations and tinny carols played over the loudspeaker between flight announcements.

It was also raining as Jack strode out of the entrance's double doors with his suitcase. "Guess we won't be having Christmas at the beach this year," said his companion.

They'd sat next to each other in business class on the flight home from Tokyo, and Jack wished he'd lost Damien Stanhope in customs because the guy was a card-carrying grinch.

"Actually, I will be at the beach," he replied. "We're driving down to Beacon Bay to spend Christmas with my foster brother and his family."

Damien shuddered. "So you've still got a three-hour drive ahead of you. Rather you than me."

The two men moved out of the human tide, staying under the shelter of the building's overhang.

"Well, I guess this is where we part ways," said Jack. "Merry Christmas."

They shook hands. "Don't talk to me about Christmas," Damien started, then his eyes fixed on something over Jack's shoulder. "Bloody hell, will you look at that menagerie!"

Jack turned and grinned.

Six months pregnant, Roz—his wife of seven months—came toward him pushing Cassie in a luggage trolley. Cass was dressed like a Christmas fairy and held a sign: Welcome Home, Uncle Jack. Where's My Present? Beside her Liam hung on to the trolley, being dragged along on his skateboard.

Sam walked behind, in full Goth regalia wearing a Christmas tree ornament in his left ear and bright red nail polish. He was hand in hand with a very pretty girl also dressed all in black.

Jack saw a condom talk looming in his near future, but even that couldn't stop a surge of pure unadulterated happiness. "That's not a menagerie," he said, "that's my family."

* * * * *

THE OTHER SISTER

BY

LYNDA SANDOVAL

Lynda Sandoval is a former police officer who exchanged the excitement of that career for blissfully isolated days, creating stories she hopes readers will love. Though she's also worked as a youth mental health and runaway crisis counsellor, a television extra, a trade-show art salesperson, a European tour guide and a bookkeeper for an exotic bird and reptile company – among other weird jobs – Lynda's favourite career, by far, is writing books. In addition to romance, Lynda writes women's fiction and young adult novels and in her spare time, she loves to travel, quilt, bid on eBay, hike, read and spend time with her dog. Lynda also works part-time as an emergency fire/medical dispatcher for the fire department. Readers are invited to visit Lynda on the web at www.LyndaSandoval.com, or to send mail with a SAE for reply to PO Box 1018, Conifer, CO 80433-1018, USA.

This one is for Barbie,
referee of many condiment and bratwurst scandals.
Don't know how you do it, but better you than me!

Chapter One

"**W**hy here?" asked Ken Hayward, the chief of Troublesome Gulch Paramedics. He flipped through Brody Austin's job application and résumé, then peered at him over the top of his half-perch reading glasses. "That's the million-dollar question, son. If we were FDNY, Chicago—even Denver—it'd be a no-brainer, but—" He spread his arms to indicate the mishmash decor, circa 1980, that comprised their headquarters.

Perspiration gathered beneath Brody's collar, despite every vow he'd made to keep his cool. He'd figured the topic would come up eventually.

Of course. But he still felt unprepared to address it, even after all this time, which had to say something negative about his character.

"Well…" He cleared his throat—the standard stall tactic. Luckily the grizzled old medic went on, affording Brody time to concoct some sort of explanation that didn't make him seem as if he were hedging, which he was, or worse—that he'd completely lost his mind. And the jury was still out on that issue.

"Not that we won't be thrilled to welcome you." Hayward held up a hand. "Your training is extensive, and I'm even more impressed by your experience. Large agencies, Flight for Life, the U.S. Army for cripe's sake."

"Thank you."

"How's your skiing?" Hayward asked, out of the blue.

Brody blinked, thrown by the seemingly unrelated question. "Ah…a little rusty, I guess. Used to be good."

Hayward indicated the mountain range looming outside his office window. "We work with Alpine Search and Rescue as part of our duties. They're always abysmally short on trained volunteers. So you'll pull some tours as ski patrol. But don't worry—it's like riding a bike. Few weeks on the slopes, and you'll be fine."

Brody swallowed and leaned slightly forward. "Does that mean I have the job?"

Hayward's chair creaked as he tipped back and braced his hands behind his head. "Hell, I'm not going to beat around the bush. You want it, it's yours. Most of our applicants are fresh out of EMT-Basic and don't know PVC from PMS."

Brody chuckled.

"We welcome someone with your experience. I guess I'm just curious what would make a young guy like you want to move way out to the north end of Timbuk-nowhere."

A small measure of relief trickled through Brody knowing he tentatively had the job offer, but he still had to tackle the unanswerable question. Everything could change if Hayward knew the whole truth. Brody nodded. "The thing is…"

Silence.

What *was* the thing, dammit? Any idiot knows you can't start out a statement with that phrase when you have no clue about the *thing*. Against his will, his jaw clenched, and so did his fists. He was blowing this. And he couldn't. He had no explanation for why, but he just…couldn't.

"Frankly, our salaries don't even come close to

those in the city," Hayward prompted, inordinately patient.

Brody acknowledged by lifting his chin. "I'm aware of the pay scale. Money isn't why I do this job, Chief. It never has been."

"That's admirable, and I share your feelings." Hayward raised one bushy eyebrow. "But, just to play devil's advocate…it's expensive living in a Colorado ski town." He gave a rueful half smile. "Even a redheaded stepchild ski town like Troublesome Gulch. We're not Aspen or Telluride, by any means. Hell, we're not even Keystone, but the going's still rougher than you'd imagine. You independently wealthy?"

"Not that. I *wish*. My needs are simple." He didn't bother mentioning the blood money settlement he'd received from the state all those years ago, or the fact that he hadn't been able to touch a dime of it. Consequently, it had grown over the past ten years, and the interest alone provided a cushion of security that allowed him to work for a smaller salary than he might otherwise have to.

Hayward chuckled and glanced toward a framed photograph on the corner of his desk. "*Simple needs* definitely means you don't have a wife or kids at home."

It wasn't a question, but Brody answered anyway. "Not sure I'm the marrying type, if you ask my former girlfriend's opinion," he said, wryly. "But, no. It's just me. My folks live in New Mexico. Brother's in Iraq."

"God speed to him."

"Thanks."

"Which brings us back—again—to my original question." Hayward flipped his hand casually. "Why Troublesome Gulch Paramedics?"

It took some effort for Brody to appear nonchalant. Somehow Hayward had pinpointed the sore spot on Brody's soul, and he just kept jabbing it. Brody wanted to answer the man's question. He really did. Problem was, he didn't think he could make anyone understand what drew him back to Troublesome Gulch, after a decade trying to erase the godforsaken place from his memory altogether. Hell, he barely understood it himself.

All he knew for sure was that something in his life needed to change, and if his ex-girlfriend, Kelly, knew what she'd been talking about the day she'd unceremoniously kicked his ass to the curb, all Brody's "issues" started and ended in this place.

But he couldn't say any of that.

Not during a job interview.

And, frankly, he wasn't sure what it meant anyway.

He went for a bland explanation that would hopefully pass. It even held a bit of truth. But it wasn't the whole truth, nor was it anywhere close to the bottom-line reason he'd come back. "I think," he started slowly, "all towns, no matter how big, small or remote, should have great emergency medical care." He hiked up one shoulder. "I know it's difficult to draw qualified medics out to these smaller departments. And you're right. A lot of guys couldn't afford to live in the high country on the salary you offer—no offense intended. I can manage, so here I am."

Hayward steepled his hands in front of him on the desk blotter. He inclined his head and smiled. "A guy willing to take a hit in the wallet so the residents of Troublesome Gulch will be safer. You don't come across that kind of dedication very often."

The implication of some superhero devotion or personal sacrifice made Brody's skin hot and itchy. His decision had a helluva lot more to do with atonement than altruism. "I don't mean to imply I can single-handedly—"

"No, no." Hayward brushed the notion away. "I didn't misunderstand you, and I appreciate it. Before you accept the position, though, I want you to be absolutely aware of what you're getting into, because we need commitment. We have enough turnover as it is, Brody. We can't take another personnel hit if you decide three months down the road that the town is too restrictive for your tastes."

"My own personal work ethics wouldn't allow me to do that. But fill me in on the cons, anyway."

"Winters can be hell. Tourists. Or 'tourons,' as some of the locals call them, which is a hybrid of tourist and moron. Ski traffic. Not to mention the cold."

"I served a tour of duty in Afghanistan before leaving the army. Trust me, you haven't faced a cold winter until you've weathered one in those godforsaken mountains."

"I'd heard that," Hayward said. "I bet you have some stories."

"That I do."

"Weather aside, housing prices are ridiculously inflated. Whether you can manage them or not, it rankles to pay several hundred thousand dollars for a prefab shack."

"I can deal with that."

"And your social life will suffer, too."

Brody lifted one ankle and rested it on the opposite knee. "How so?"

"Well," Hayward drawled, "you must know we're not exactly a bustling metropolis, especially in the off-season. As old Betty at the phone company loves to say, 'If you didn't bring her with you, you sure as hell ain't findin' her here.'"

Brody smiled. Luckily, he wasn't in the market for yet another relationship to overload with his baggage until it broke beneath the weight, so old Betty had nothing to worry about on his behalf. "Frankly, my last relationship was a disaster to the power of ten. I'm looking forward to some time alone here."

"Man can't live on work alone. The nights get chilly."

"I'll deal," Brody said, fully planning to give the alone thing a fair shot. If it got too cold, he'd buy a big old dog who could curl up on his feet. But he didn't want to talk about his private life anymore. He wanted to sign on the dotted line and get on with it…whatever *it* was. "I just—" he blew out a breath "—I'm not generally this inarticulate, but I don't know that I can adequately explain why I'm here."

"Give 'er a shot."

Brody just couldn't understand why Hayward was making this so difficult on him. "I'm a good medic, and I love what I do. Yes, I've worked in big cities. I've worked with the military. I've taken advantage of a lot of great opportunities." He paused, pressing his lips together as he gathered his thoughts. "But I'm twenty-nine years old, Chief, and I feel rootless."

Hayward nodded.

"I want to work someplace where I can make a difference, where I can build...some kind of life. I have no idea why, but it feels like I might be able to do that here. So I'll answer your question with a question. You ask, why Troublesome Gulch? I ask, why not?"

Silence ensued.

"That's it?"

Brody hesitated, thinking that wasn't *it* at all, but he settled for a terse nod.

Another silence yawned. The older man's piercing gaze never left his face, and, not knowing what else to do, Brody held the stare. He couldn't stand much more of this.

Finally Hayward sighed, removed his glasses, rubbed the bridge of his nose wearily, then replaced the glasses. "Son, listen. I was there." He paused, and when he spoke again, his voice came out huskier. "That night. We were a volunteer battalion then, but...I was there."

Brody's stomach clenched. He knew exactly the night to which Hayward referred. How could he not? To him, the word *prom* had become synonymous with *death*. Dread drizzled over him, cold, ugly and oh so familiar, as resignation settled on his shoulders like a shroud. Okay, so he wasn't going to skate out from under the crush of his past like he'd hoped. His body sagged. "I...I don't remember you. I'm sorry."

"Of course not. I don't expect you to. The scene was swarming with emergency personnel."

"Eventually," Brody said, and the words came out more bitterly than he'd intended.

A shadow of pain crossed over Hayward's face. "Yes, it did take a while for help to arrive. I'm sure it seemed like forever to you kids. But we did finally get there. God, what a scene."

Brody closed his eyes for a moment but forced himself to open them again. He didn't care to expose how much that night had affected his life. Jaw clenched, he stretched his neck to one side, then the other.

"I've never forgotten any of your names. Those who passed, of course. But the survivors', too." Hayward absentmindedly tapped a pen on his desk. "Especially yours."

"Why mine?"

"Isn't that obvious?" Hayward's eyes narrowed thoughtfully. "You haven't been seen nor heard from since you were released from the hospital the next morning. That's a mystery, boy. Everybody loves a good mystery."

Brody swallowed and shifted his gaze to the

sweeping vista of mountain peaks and valleys outside the window behind the older man's desk. "It's been a long time. I just want to get on with my life. Or, I don't know, *get* a life. I figured…or maybe hoped people would've forgotten by now," he added in a low tone.

"How could we forget? That tragedy was the worst Troublesome Gulch has ever seen. It changed emergency services here forever. In a damn good way. We're one of the top battalions in the state now, and High Country Medical Center has been upgraded to a level-two trauma center. Two choppers and a plane."

"So something positive came from that nightmare," Brody said in a pained monotone.

"One thing, yeah. You could say that." Hayward's thoughts seemed to move inward for several moments, but then he shook it off and refocused on Brody. "How about for you? How have you gotten along since—"

"Fine," Brody said. Immediately regretting the rudeness of his interruption, not to mention his clipped tone, he added, "Thank you for asking, sir."

Hayward didn't press, but his expression said he knew "fine" didn't come close to explaining anything about Brody Austin's life. "You seem to have done well for yourself."

"You do what you have to do."

Hayward sighed. "Look, I'm not a big talker myself, and this isn't a therapy session. But if you want to work for me, I need to make a few things crystal clear. Understand?"

Brody's heart revved, but he forced a nod.

"If you've come back because you want to help make sure that kind of devastation never happens in Troublesome Gulch again, I understand the desire. Hell, that's why I'm still here. But ultimately? That's up to God, son. Despite all our hard work, public-service announcements about drunk driving, high school visits, heavy road coverage on prom night and homecoming—all of it— bad things do and will happen. Here or anywhere else you might run to."

Hayward leaned in, adamant, impassioned. "You can't escape it. And by God, Brody, as dedicated as you seem, you can't prevent it, no matter how desperately you want to. *You can't.*"

He didn't want to go down that road. Not yet. Not here, of all places. It was that one "issue" of control he couldn't quite pry out of his clutches. "Of course not."

"You've got to let that unattainable need go, or you'll make yourself crazy."

"I'm trying. Maybe that's why I'm here, who

knows?" He spread his arms wide. "What is there for me here? I didn't even live here when it… when it happened. I was the outsider, the only one who didn't go to TG High School." Brody pressed his lips into a thin line and calmed himself. "I don't know why I returned, except that my life's at a standstill and I'm out of options. For no logical reason, this seemed like the proverbial end of the long, long road to who knows where."

For a long moment, he didn't think Hayward would accept the simple answer.

Finally, the man nodded. "It's good to see you again. Really good, son, and I mean that. Always wondered where you'd gone."

To hell and back, thought Brody.

"Everyone else is still here, you know."

Not everyone, Brody thought bitterly. Four of them were dead. And yet, still so alive in Brody's mind. "I didn't know. We haven't really…kept in touch."

Hayward acknowledged the admission silently. "It's the damnedest thing, I tell you. Every one of you kids has ended up working in the field."

Brody blinked as surprise riddled through him. "In emergency medicine?"

"Not just. Police, fire, emergency communications. The whole gamut, basically. Lots of interagency cooperation up here, though." He cocked his head to one side. "You'll probably run into them from time to time on calls and such. That won't be a problem for you, will it?"

His stomach soured, and he didn't know if it was nausea or fear. "Not at all. I left, sure, but I don't harbor any bad feelings toward any of them. It's just…they weren't my circle of friends. They were—"

"Michelle Montesantos's friends?"

"Mick."

"Excuse me?"

"Mick. She hated the name Michelle." That familiar knife of pain pierced Brody's heart at the casual mention of the best friend he'd ever had, and he couldn't go on. After all these years, he still couldn't hear the name Mick—or Michelle—without suffering a powerful, almost debilitating surge of guilt. Naturally.

Since her death had been his fault.

"Her folks still live here," Hayward said softly.

The statement hit Brody like a boot to the gut. Why had his brain blocked out that inevitability?

"It's a small town. They'll hear that you're back."

He swallowed. "I'll tell them myself."

"I'm sure they'll be glad to hear from you."

Yeah. Right. He could just imagine. *Remember*

me? I'm the guy who basically killed your brilliant, amazing, funny, exuberant daughter. He hadn't been behind the wheel when they'd crashed, but what the hell did that matter? He was the one who forced her to go to the stupid prom in the first place. Oh, well. He'd chosen this path. Facing the Montesantoses on his own terms would be better than dreading it every day until the inevitable occurred, and he ran into them somewhere awkward. He'd rather control the when, where and how. They might not even want to talk to him. Who knew? But however they chose to react, he deserved it.

"Any other issues we should get out in the open?"

Brody pushed out a breath, then ran his palm over his face. He couldn't take much more of this. "None. Chief Hayward, look. Can I be honest?"

"Been hoping for that this whole time."

"I swore I'd never set foot in this damned town again after that night. The only thing for me here was Mick, and she was gone. Dead. Forever. I wanted to forget…." He paused and clenched his fists, unsure how to proceed.

"You didn't, did you?"

"God…I tried," he said, his words coming out stiff and halting. He never talked about this with anyone. Well, except Kelly, and look how that had turned out. "I did everything I could think of, got as far away as I could. You want to know the worst thing? I prayed every day that I'd get killed in Afghanistan—" His words caught, and he clenched his jaw. "And that's damned disgraceful to admit, considering all the soldiers who've lost their lives, and for what good purpose? My own brother off in Iraq. But it is what it is."

"Survivors' guilt."

Brody flicked the psychobabble away with his hand. "Whatever you want to call it. Mick shouldn't have died. Period." He pressed his lips together for a moment, then lowered his tone and went on. "If I had it to do all over again, I probably would've stayed here, dealt with things better than I did."

"You did what you had to."

He lifted his arms, then let them drop helplessly to his sides. "I was a kid…." A piss-poor excuse, he knew, but it was all he had.

"I understand."

"But I'm here now. Baggage and all, I'd like to accept the job if your offer still stands."

Hayward searched his face for a moment, then nodded once. "You'll talk to me if things get to be too much? What is said in this room stays here. That's a promise, man to man."

"I will."

The older man extended his hand. "Welcome to Troublesome Gulch Paramedics, Brody. And get your ass on the slopes as soon as possible. Hone your skills."

Brody stood and reciprocated. "Will do. Thank you. You won't regret it."

"I don't expect to, but that's not the issue." Hayward released Brody's hand and crossed his arms over his barrel chest. "I'm more concerned with what *you* might regret."

Brody wanted to say he'd learned to live with regrets, but it would've been a lie. Truth was, here he stood, twenty-nine-years-old, and he hadn't yet learned to live at all.

"Don't worry," he said instead. "I'll be fine." Even as he said it, he wondered at his word choice. If history were any indication, "fine" was just another lie he told himself to get through each day. But more than ten years had slipped through his fingers, and frankly his life was a mess. So, regardless of the personal risks, here he was.

Troublesome Gulch. And now, with a job.

Permanence.

God, he thought, as he walked down the hallway and then out to his truck in the parking lot, he should be happier that he'd gotten the position.

But he couldn't help but wonder, was he making the hugest mistake of his life coming back?

Everything here reminded him of her.

The streets, the smell of the air, the mountain peaks.

Mick Montesantos had been a different sort of girl, a raucous, athletic tomboy, full of life and laughter and more daring than any guy he'd ever known, before or since. She was beautiful, but she never gave a damn about that. Also, she wasn't his girlfriend—she wasn't *anyone's* girlfriend, thank you very much—and that was just fine with her. She was his pal. His closest pal.

From the first day they'd met in their coed rugby league down in Golden, they'd been as inseparable as two teens who attended different schools could be. They could, and had, talked about anything and everything, from the mundane to the deepest secrets in their souls.

The absolute worst part? Mick hadn't even wanted to go to prom that night, claiming it was an outdated, exclusionary ritual that reinforced stupid male/female societal roles and *blah-blah-blah,* typical Mick stuff that Brody had never tired of hearing. She was passionate about her beliefs, about who she was—he liked that. He felt like he'd learned more about life and humanity and society in the "Mick years" than he'd learned before or since.

But still, Brody had cajoled her. *You'll always regret missing your senior prom,* he'd told her. *Come on, Mick. What can it hurt to go with a friend? It'll be a kick. Besides, if it's horrible, at least we can make fun of people and eat free food.* So she'd relented—even bought a dress. It had looked great, but she groused the whole evening that it was about as comfortable as a layer of wasps coating her body, and half an hour into the evening, she'd ditched the tiny, strappy, heels in favor of bare feet, handing the shoes unceremoniously to Brody to carry. They'd headed off to the dance with three other couples, someone's dad's Range Rover, and a cache of smuggled booze. Hell, they were all eighteen years old and invincible, right? They'd planned on making it a prom night to remember.

Famous last words.

Now, instead of Mick, it was Brody living with regrets. Not to mention guilt and anguish, the nightmares, his so-called control issues and the inability and lack of desire to get really close to anyone. Mick and three of the others had died in that horrific crash and the subsequent fire. One split second had ended their lives and changed Brody's forever. All he had left of her was one stupid strappy high-heel shoe that she'd *never* have worn voluntarily. The other one had burned to ash in the fire.

Shave it right down to the bone, and the truth was, he'd killed his best friend. He should've died, dammit. In a lot of ways he had, but not in the ways that counted. Mick had had so much more to offer the world than he did. More than anyone else in the world, Mick never, *ever* should've died so damn young. And he didn't give a rat's ass what anyone said—it was *his fault*.

So, scared or not, confused or not, skeptical or not, here he stood in Troublesome damn Gulch, the mountain town where all his nightmares started and ended, where all his ghosts remained. It was way past time he faced his demons.

Chapter Two

What was the worst that could happen?

Faith Montesantos stood at the top of the professional downhill ski run, the site of an international event that had taken place there earlier in the day. She braced her poles in the crook of one elbow, then adjusted her goggles with her free hand. Dang, did that ever look steep, icy and hilly from her vantage point. But really, how hard could it be? Wouldn't gravity take care of most of it?

She inhaled slowly, then blew out a plume of breath that froze and hung in the air like a wraith. Despite the low temperature at the moun-

tain peak, bright winter sunshine glittered dia-
mondlike on the snow, which glowed even whiter
than normal, thanks to the cloudless, deep-blue
sky above.

Mick would've loved this day.

Then again, Mick loved every day.

Faith thought, as she always did, of her sister, and
thankfully, doing so now brought a smile to her face
rather than tears to her eyes. It had taken her years
to work through the grief, to come to the realization
that Mick might not be on this earth physically, but
she was absolutely, without a single doubt, Faith's
guardian angel. Big sis had her back in every situation. She had actually *felt* it on several occasions.

The first time had been during college. One
night, driving home from her part-time job, exhausted to the marrow of her bones, the motion and
the warmth of the car began to lull her to sleep. As
her small car drifted toward the oncoming lanes, she
felt her sister's arms around her from the back, both
holding her and shaking her, and she heard Mick's
voice clearly. "Faith! Wake up. It's not your time."

That jolted her awake enough to make it home
safely.

It freaked her out initially, but then she came
to a peaceful understanding of what had happened and why. And from then on she knew. The

best of all angels was, and always would be, watching out for her.

Shaking off the memories, she bit her lip and forced her focus back to the steep, hilly ski run facing her.

Yikes, should she?

Mick would never have hesitated. *Never.* Her life may have been short, but she'd lived every minute of every day of it full-out, start to finish. Mick would've taken one look at this run, let out a whoop and gone for it. Of course, Mick had been a pretty dang good skier. Given more time, she probably could've gone pro.

Faith had watched the competition earlier in the day, marveling to herself over how much life the professional skiers exuded, how filled to overflowing they seemed, thanks to the simple magic of *doing.* They'd reminded her of her sister, which is what drew her back to the empty run now. The race had ended and all the pros and spectators were long gone, probably hitting the bars lining main street in town.

Here she stood. Alone.

A smattering of skiers still dotted the late-afternoon slopes, grabbing a few extra runs before the sun dipped behind the peaks, but no one paid a lick of attention to her. All that remained was the mountain and her insane urge to conquer it like the ski racers had. Like her sister would have.

The rub was, did *she* have the guts? By no possible stretch of the imagination was she an experienced enough skier to attempt this run, but she didn't want to let that stop her. Life was too damn short, and if anyone knew the truth of that stupid, annoying cliché, she did.

In all seriousness, what did she have to lose? Would she die? Not likely. Besides, Mick would never have turned down the chance to hit a professional run, to cheat death one more time. Or even to take one last walk, to feel the dry, cold Colorado mountain air against her cheeks.

So, even though doing it scared Faith spitless, she had to. Taking another deep, calming breath, Faith set her jaw with determination. "This one's for you, sis." She laughed nervously. "But you'd better damn well be down at the bottom to scrape me up."

Then she launched.

It took only seconds for the trees lining the run to meld into dark, whipping blurs in her peripheral vision as she sped almost instantly out of control. Her arms flailed, her legs flailed—she had to be a wild sight. She would've loved seeing the playback of this; too bad nobody was filming it. As the first jump point, or big giant cliff, or whatever the heck the huge scary thing was called, raced up to catapult her, Faith realized three things with crystal clarity:

One, she was *way* out of her league.

Two, the inevitable wipeout was going to suck.

And, three, too bad, because at this point, there was no going back.

Brody wasn't on duty that day and had no plans whatsoever beyond having no plans whatsoever. The perfect kind of day, if you asked him. He set coffee on to brew and headed to the hideous orange plaid couch that had come with the place, preparing to chill there with a book all day.

But when he pulled open the dusty curtains on the ramshackle A-frame cabin he'd bought from an old-timer who was more than happy to dump it when Brody offered far more than it was worth, that Colorado sky beckoned like a blue-eyed centerfold. A bed of fresh powder adorned the ground, laid over with a blanket of shimmering crystals.

A perfect day to ski.

Man, he'd missed that stupendous contrast from sky to earth the Colorado high country offered. He just hadn't realized it until he'd come back.

In any case, with nothing penciled in on his nonexistent social calendar besides sitting on the couch, he suited up quickly, grabbed his gear and headed out of the cabin in record time, travel mug of coffee and a CLIF bar in hand.

Within minutes he was slopebound.

He spent the entire morning tackling the various runs, and darned if Hayward hadn't been right. All the moves were coming back to him as if they'd somehow seeped into his DNA. Awkwardly at first, and then smoother as he kept it up, pushed himself. He threw back a quick lunch at noon, but didn't even stop to watch the ski races that afternoon, loving how it felt to move his body like this again.

The sun started to dip and the slopes had cleared considerably. His day had been so phenomenal, though, he wanted to give it one more run.

From the lift, a lone woman standing at the top of the competition course grabbed his attention. Why, he didn't know. Something oddly familiar about the way she stood? About her solitude? He supposed it could simply be her knockout shape that even those looser black snowboarding pants couldn't hide.

But he didn't think so.

It was more than a lust thing. He wasn't in a lust frame of mind these days. It was more of a warning-bells-in-his-head sort of thing. But why? He jumped off the lift and moved out of the way of the other skiers, unable to take his eyes off her. This woman. This petite, curvy woman *looked* like she might be contemplating that unbelievably difficult world-class ski run, which, of course, would be pure insanity. Unless her name happened to be Peekaboo Street, and she was way too tiny for that to be the case.

So, it couldn't be true.

His pulse revved. Damn.

She was going to go for it. He could feel it.

"No way," Brody said quietly to himself, every muscle in his body tensing. He almost called out to her.

It would be feloniously stupid. Dangerous. It could be fatal. And if not fatal, at least injury causing or—

But then she launched anyway.

Frozen with shock, he watched the whole horrific debacle as if it were in slow motion, but *slow* didn't come close to describing her speed as she careened, completely out of control, down that run. She started to tumble—maybe *windmill* was a better choice of words—at the first jump point. She lost one pole, then the other. A ski went flying like a javelin. Finally she came to a bone-jarring rest on one shoulder, spiraling down, down, down until her momentum waned enough for her to slide to a dead-still stop.

Without hesitation Brody took off. Wisely, he chose to ski adjacent to the pro run, snowplowing to a stop right next to the still woman. His hands shook, but his brain automatically kicked into paramedic mode. He snapped out of his skis, planted his poles and crouched down beside her.

"Hey, can you hear me?"

"Yep."

His gaze moved over her body, checking, assessing, which was more than a little difficult with all the outerwear. "I don't want you to move, okay? How's your breathing?"

"Wind knocked out of me when I struck that landing, but it was so...so worth it." She blew some snow off her lips, then grinned. "That freakin' rocked."

"Are you out of your mind?" he asked, astonished. He frowned down at her. "Do you have any clue how dangerous that little stunt was?"

"Newsflash—life's dangerous, buddy." She huffed a tired-sounding and humorless laugh. "And short. Trust me, you have no idea how dangerous and short it can be."

"Yeah. I do have an idea." Brody gulped, thrown slightly by the unexpected reminder. He sat back on his haunches and forced his mind back into medic mode. "Well, you're conscious. Breathing. That's a start. Do you hurt anywhere?"

"Busted my right clavicle, that I'm sure of. Other than that, I'm in one piece. I mean, I'll feel like a truck hit me in the morning—just your garden-variety soreness—but I'm intact." She reached up with her left hand to release her helmet and remove her goggles.

Brody grabbed her arm. "No. Leave them on. In case of a neck injury. Alpine Rescue will be here soon."

"And you know this because?"

He shook his head. "Sorry. I'm a paramedic in town. We work with them, but I'm off duty today."

"So, how will they know? Telepathy?"

"I'll call them in a sec."

"Gotcha. However, before you do so, and as much as I respect your expertise, I need you to listen closely to me for a moment," she said in an almost forceful tone that sounded both sure and eerily familiar. "My neck? Totally fine. My head is perfect. My mental status is sharp as a damn ice pick, enough to know that my ego is bruised, but not that much, because at least I didn't chicken out. What I have is a broken collarbone, okay? That's it. Sum total of my injuries, Para-doc. I'm going to take off my helmet and goggles so I can freakin' breathe. Is that okay with you?"

He paused. No stopping this one. He almost

smiled at her grit. "Will you at least let me do it so you don't accidentally aggravate the break."

"Whatever rocks your world."

Brody gingerly unsnapped the helmet and lifted it carefully off her head and set it aside. He eased her goggles off next. She shook out her thick black hair, and stared at him from grass-green eyes. "Thanks."

Stunned, in truth almost frightened, Brody stumbled backward in a sloppy crab crawl until he literally fell to the ground, holding himself up with one hand and his other elbow. His heart didn't so much pound as punch him, repeatedly, from the inside, killing him, trying to get out, escape, avoid being shattered again. He reached for her, then pulled back. "Mick?" he half whispered.

She pinned him with a quizzical stare.

With shaky hands he removed his own helmet and goggles.

Her eyes widened. "Oh my God, Brody? Brody Austin?"

He scrabbled to his knees. "Mick, God, I swear—"

"Where the hell have you been?"

"Everywhere. Nowhere. I'm sorry." He held up his palms, and his words came in an agonized tumble. "I thought you died, Mick, I swear on my life. I never would've left. Never. They told me you died at the scene, pulled me away from you and strapped me to a backboard. I mean, I saw you there with my own eyes, in that stupid dress you hated—" His voice caught, thickened. "I'm so sorry I made you go. Sorry for…for everything. I'm—oh my God—I'm so glad I was wrong, but I just can't believe—"

"Brody," she started, her voice level and modulated. Favoring her right side, she half sat, then reached out and touched his knee as if to harness his attention. "Take a breath."

He did.

"Listen to me, okay?"

He nodded.

"I'm not Mick." She paused to let that sink in fully. "Mick did die at the scene. You did see her in that stupid dress she hated. Honey, Mick…is dead."

"B-but then—" He gestured vaguely toward her.

"I'm Mick's little sister. Faith." She smiled sadly. "Remember me?"

Shock stomped his gut. Repeatedly. He wasn't, in any possible way, ready to face anyone in Mick's family.

Not now. Not like this.

Especially the kid sister he'd barely given the time of day back in high school. Why was she smiling at him? Talking to him all…normally?

Where was the hate? The blame? His throat tightened, and he seriously didn't know if he could hold his emotions in check. His fists clenched.

"Faith," he said, almost in a whisper. "Little bookworm Faith?"

"The very one."

He swallowed, knowing he had to straighten things out, prepared or not. "I'm so sorry about Mick. I don't know what to say, even. *Sorry* is so inadequate and my stupid apology is…so late. I can't explain—"

"No need."

For a moment, they just stared at each other.

"You look…God. Just like her."

"Thank you. I'll take that as a compliment."

"You should. I meant it that way." He frowned, dazed, nearly incapable of wrapping his brain around any of this. He gripped his forehead with the heel of one hand.

Mick's little sister had been a kid. Not even in high school yet. Twelve or something, if memory served, all gangly knees and awkward preadolescent bookworm girlishness. Nothing whatsoever like the confident woman before him.

"How'd you get to be so…old?" he asked, almost to himself, even though anyone with a lick of sense would know how stupid that question was.

She laughed, a bittersweet sound. "Honey, almost eleven years have passed, I hate to break the news to you. I'm the ripe old age of twenty-four now."

"Twenty-four?" Wait. She'd only been five years younger than him and Mick? They'd seemed generations separated back then.

She nodded. "I have a master's degree in counseling and I'm a guidance counselor at the high school."

"At Troublesome Gulch High School?"

"The very one."

He blinked. Twice. "A guidance counselor?"

"Yep."

"You work at the high school." She'd progressed from skinny kid to high school guidance counselor, and he felt like he was stuck in the nightmarish memories of those years. She'd lapped him. How ironic was that?

She nodded.

"But you're...a kid."

She smirked. "That's just how you remember me. I drive and vote and everything. Even own my own condo. And, get this—"

He raised his eyebrows.

"It's furnished with my own stuff and everything."

He scrubbed his hand through his hair. "I'm sorry."

"It's okay. Memories are weird. Stop apologizing."

Stop? "No." To his ultimate mortification, an uncontrollable rush of tears blurred eyes. "I mean about Mick, everything."

"Everybody's sorry about Mick. It's okay. She's gone, but she's really still here in our hearts." She smiled softly at him. "Don't forget that."

"Believe me, I haven't."

"I know, but we all need a reminder of it now and then." She adjusted slowly, extra careful with her right side. "Uh, Brody?"

He ran a hand down his face, hoping to wipe away any tears before they betrayed his weakness. He cleared his throat, telling himself to cowboy the hell up. "Yeah?"

"Much as I'm psyched to catch up, chat, prove to you that I'm really and truly past my prepubescence and all that, my collarbone hurts like a mother. Any chance we can get a move on with that rescue effort?"

Catch up? Chat? And here he'd expected her to pummel him with her fists, enraged, screaming at him, *"KILLER! KILLER!"* like she had in his dreams for so many years. He couldn't fathom her bland, normal, indeed almost positive reaction toward seeing him again.

"Brody," she said, snapping her fingers. "Focus. Broken bone. Pain. Alpine Rescue."

He shook his head as if to clear it, hauling his cell phone out of an inner pocket of his parka. "Of course. What was I thinking?"

"You were thinking I was my sister, which was totally freaking you out—completely understandable. And, Brody?"

He glanced up at her from his dialing.

She smiled, and his heart clenched. "Being mistaken for Mick? That's more than worth a busted collarbone."

Faith shared her sister's ability to sharp-talk her way out of anything, Brody realized, when she somehow convinced the ambulance crew who showed up for transport that she was *fine,* that Brody could give her a ride to the hospital, and no way in hell was she being strapped to a backboard. They'd have to knock her out first, and—injured or not—she'd fight back.

He didn't mind taking her, of course. In fact, he was glad they had more time together so his brain could start to accept what seemed so surreal. She didn't hate him.

Mick's sister didn't hate him.

Incomprehensible.

He took the roads gingerly, glancing over to make sure Faith was okay each time he hit a bump or a dip.

"Can I use your cell phone?" she asked, partway down the mountain, wincing as a switchback jostled her collarbone.

"Of course." He handed it over.

"I just want to let my parents know what happened so they don't worry." She held the phone in one hand, dialing with her thumb.

Brody's body went ice-cold and rigid. He clutched the steering wheel tighter, then swallowed thickly, knowing he had to say something. Anything. "I, uh, was planning on calling them to let them know I was back in town. Maybe warn them would be a better way to phrase it," he said, ruefully.

Faith laughed softly, hanging up before the call went through. "*Warn* them? What do you think they're planning to do—lynch you?"

"Truthfully? Not sure."

She stared at him, wide-eyed, for a good long time, and her expression moved from disbelief to sadness. "Don't even *tell* me you blame yourself for Mick's death."

He shrugged one shoulder.

"Brody. Come on. Do you know how long it's been?"

To the minute, he thought. "That doesn't matter."

"It does. If you felt some responsibility at the beginning, I get that. Even though you bear no blame for what happened. But now? People heal, honey. We have to heal or how can we live?"

That's what he was trying to figure out. "You don't understand. We wouldn't have been there if I hadn't forced her to go."

Faith laughed. She actually *laughed*. "Uh, hate to bust up your endearingly testosterone-fueled God complex, but no one ever forced my sister to do anything she didn't want to do, and as her *best friend*—" she paused to let those emphasized words sink in "—I know you're well aware of that."

"But—"

"No," she said, with a definite finality in her tone. "The accident wasn't your fault. Mick wasn't your fault. All eight of you kids made stupid decisions that night, drinking and driving, don't get me wrong. Stupid, irresponsible, life-altering decisions, but Mick's death is *not* on your shoulders. It's not on anyone's shoulders. It just is."

She paused until he shot her a quick glance. "And my parents, contrary to your skewed opinion, will be thrilled to see you. They always loved you. They still talk about you. You're like the son they never had or something."

"Right."

"It's true. We've all missed you, you big dummy. Wondered where you were. Having you around is—" she pushed out a melancholy sigh "—well, it's almost like having Mick back again."

Thankfully they pulled up at the hospital right about then, so Brody could avoid having to comment, because he didn't think he could form words past the tightness of his throat. He jumped out of his side of the SUV and ran around to assist Faith. The parking lot had been cleared, but icy spots remained. He held her uninjured arm and guided her toward the entrance doors. Just outside them she stopped. "Hang on. Let me make that call. I'm not sure you're supposed to use cell phones inside the hospital."

The call. Darn. He'd hoped she'd forgotten.

She dialed and listened as the phone rang, obviously. Her face lit up when someone answered. "Hey, Mom. First, I'm totally okay," she enunciated clearly, "but I just wanted to let you guys know I fell skiing and broke my collarbone, and I'm at the hospital." She paused to listen. "No, no, I swear. Nothing else is hurt—it wasn't even that bad of a crash. Just an unfortunate landing."

Brody snorted beside her. She narrowed an eye at him.

"But, hey, there's a great side to this story. You're not going to believe it. Ready?" She gave Brody a reassuring look and laid a hand on his forearm. "Guess who came to my rescue up on the mountain?" Pause. "Brody Austin." She listened, then laughed. "No, I'm not hallucinating. He's back, Mom, working for TG Paramedics. I swear! He's a paramedic, here in town." More silence. "I know, it's so... Okay, I'll tell him. Yes. We'll see you soon."

She clicked off.

"Did I hear you say, we'll see you soon?" he asked, his tone funereal at best.

"Mom was overjoyed to hear you're back. She started crying. And yes, she and Dad will be here soon. To check up on me, of course, but they're so looking forward to seeing you, I can't even tell you."

He shook his head, truly baffled. "Why?"

She stared at him, round-eyed for a moment. "Is that an honest-to-God question?"

"Yes," he said, his voice husky. "I don't understand why any of you would ever want to see me again."

She stood a moment longer, then shook her head, grimacing at the collarbone pain the movement caused. "Whoo-boy, you're in a bad way, Austin. If you don't get it at this point, honey, I can't explain it to you right now. I might be taking some creative license here, but I'm pretty sure pain drugs come before absurdly obvious explanations on Maslow's Hierarchy of Needs."

"Come on." He placed his hand at the small of Faith's back and guided her gently into the emergency room. "Let's get this process started. It can take forever when you don't come by ambulance," he said pointedly.

"And yet, it's so worth it."

Brody settled Faith into one of the intake nooks, then took a seat in the lobby, slouchy, with his legs sprawled. The optimum brooding position. So much for setting up the "reunion" with Mick's parents on his own terms. Brody blew out a resigned breath and squeezed the bridge of his nose.

Fine. Okay. He'd roll with this unexpected event—especially since he had no choice. Pretty soon it'd all be over, and he could check one item off his monumentally long dread list. That was something, at least.

When Faith had finished with the intake paperwork, she joined him in the waiting room. She turned in her seat so she could face him directly. "Brody?" she asked in a soft tone. "You're not truly nervous about seeing my parents, are you?"

"Of course not. Don't be ridiculous," he lied, stretching his neck to one side, then the other.

Faith studied him, her "bull" detector clearly in full operational mode, then smirked. "Anyone ever mention you're the worst liar in the world?"

"Only one person." Brody said.

Then they smiled at each other. Some things just didn't require explanation.

Chapter Three

As luck would have it, the emergency room didn't seem to be wall-to-wall busy. Not too long after Faith had finished the paperwork part and sat down next to Brody, she heard her name called out and glanced up to see a red-haired older lady with a file clutched to the front of her purple scrubs. The nurse waved at Brody.

He lifted a hand in reply.

Faith raised an eyebrow at him.

He shrugged. "Paramedic. Small town. We all get to know each other pretty quickly."

"Ah." She stood, started to walk toward the

nurse, then turned back gingerly to look over her shoulder. Brody just sat there.

"Come on."

"Me?" he asked.

She gave him her best *Duh* look, the one that always made her students laugh. "You think I want to be back there alone while Nurse Ratchett tortures me? This is the high country, bucko. You catch it, you clean it."

That earned her a bit of a smile. She watched him push up from the chair. He'd removed his parka and sweater, and she could see well-defined shoulder muscles flex through his thermals. Whoa….She'd always thought he was hunky back when she was just a kid and he was her sister's friend who ignored her, but he'd been just a boy then. Absolutely no doubt in her mind, Brody Austin had somehow become All Man.

And then some.

When he caught up with her, they resumed trailing the nurse and she turned her thoughts away from him as much as she could. Not an easy task. Why was that?

"You know, Faith," he said out of the side of his mouth, "just an hour or so by your side, and I can already see looks aren't the only trait you share with your sister."

She widened her eyes, intentionally feigning misunderstanding. "Oh, Brody. You mean I'm as skilled a skier as my big sis?" She laid the hand from her uninjured side lightly on her chest. "How sweet of you to notice."

He snorted. "No. What I meant was beautiful, bossy and sarcastic. The Montesantos female trifecta."

She laughed softly.

He patted her lower back. "You did all right for yourself, Faith, with that whole growing up thing. But your skiing?"

She glanced up at him as the nurse ushered them into a curtained-off room. "Yeah?"

One corner of his mouth quivered. "Let's just say Mick's on a cloud somewhere up there laughing her ass off."

Faith scowled playfully. "I'd punch you if I wasn't injured, you know. Don't underestimate me just because I'm small and female."

He tipped his head to one side, eyebrows raised. "Oh, believe me, I don't."

The nurse whisked the curtain closed in one practiced move, then patted the gurney. "Sit on up here, hon. My name's Sheila, and I'm going to take your temp and blood pressure, all that good stuff." She smiled, then glanced at Brody. "Day off?"

He nodded. "Just scooping up overconfident skiers attempting stupid things they shouldn't be doing. You know how it is. Never off duty."

Faith let out a *hmph!* and pointedly ignored them as she struggled her way up onto the gurney, thankful it was in a partially upright position. She crossed her ankles. Meanwhile, Brody took the chair in the corner and folded his hands in his lap.

A simple motion, but one that mesmerized Faith.

"First, let's get you some pain meds and then we'll get you out of that parka."

"Thank God for Sheila." Faith tore her gaze away from Brody as the nurse handed her two white pills and a little cup of water. She knocked them back in one swallow, not even asking what they were. Who cared at this point, as long as they did the trick?

As the nurse went through her required steps—temperature, pulse, blood pressure, etc.—Faith found her gaze returning repeatedly to Brody's hands. The man had hands that said he worked for a living. Strong, wide, dusted with a bit of brown hair on the backs. Perfectly clean, short nails, but they had a rough and rugged edge to them. And they were still. So still. Confident. He definitely wasn't a fidgeter.

Sheesh.

It had to be the pain drug the nurse had given

her, but Faith couldn't help wondering how those hands would feel on her body. All over her body.

Stop!

Okay, dammit, that did it.

She was officially spending way too much time on her students and not nearly enough on her love life, such as it was, or wasn't. She quickly cut her gaze away, and her heart set off on a sprint. Her breathing chased right after it. Good thing the nurse had already taken her pulse and pronounced it normal, or they'd be getting out those shock paddles and calling a code blue or whatever-the-heck. Faith swallowed.

"What's wrong?"

She shot a sharp glance at Brody, noting the line of worry bisecting his brow.

"Nothing," she lied, surprised by his perceptiveness. Most of the guys she'd dated in college had been majoring in *Duh* with a minor in *Huh?* "Why?"

"You looked pensive all of a sudden."

A feeling she couldn't name coiled inside her center. Why this weird awareness? This pull? This knowledge somewhere deep down in her soul that she didn't want to let Brody Austin slip away again now that he'd come back? Was it just his connection to her sister? She wasn't sure. But she wanted to grab hold of him and never let go, which scared the everloving crap out of her. So, naturally, she whipped out her best diverting defense mechanism: sarcastic humor. "I might look 'pensive,' cowboy, but I'm actually cheap." She winked. "Easy, too, if you want the full lowdown."

Brody blew out a big long breath and crossed his arms. He raised his eyebrows at the nurse. "Sheila? I believe we have confirmation that those narcotics are on board."

Sheila laughed, but Faith didn't fail to notice Brody had turned a little red.

Ha. Got him.

Still laughing, Sheila gathered up her things. "The doctor will be in to see you soon, hon." She rested a hand softly on Faith's foot. "Do you need a blanket?"

"No, I'm fine."

The nurse nodded once and patted a well-worn white hospital gown with small, faded, multicolored dots on it. "I need you to take off everything except your underpants and socks and slip into this, okay? Ties in the back. I'd help you, but we've got two nurses out sick, and although we don't look busy, I've been chasing my own rear end all day long. Brody can help you change, though." She lifted her chin toward a certain drawer. "Trauma shears are in there, Brody."

Then she left.

Dead silence.

Faith looked over at Brody, who sat there like some freakin' bug-eyed-fish ice sculpture on a buffet table. She sighed dramatically, even though the thought of him taking off her clothes wasn't helping these weird feelings. She couldn't let *him* know that, so she opted for blasé.

"Oh, for God's sake, you ignored me like a brother for years. I'm sure you're capable of helping me out of my clothes."

"If…if you're sure."

"Brody. You're a paramedic, aren't you? It's for medicinal reasons." She leveled him with a bland stare. "Hurry up. I don't want some doctor to walk in and see me in the buff. He'll probably be the father of one of my students. It's that small-town, Murphy's Law thing. Divert your eyes at the key moments if you feel the need to maintain your choirboy status. But I guarantee, I've got no surprises under here. You're what now…twenty-nine?"

His Adam's apple rose and fell as he stood. "Yes."

"Then, surely, you've seen your fair share of naked women. So, get on with it."

Brody retrieved the weird-looking scissors from the drawer and came toward her.

"What are you doing?"

"I'm going to cut off your shirt layers."

"Cut?" she enunciated, with disbelief, emphasis on the *T*. "They're brand-new, and they weren't cheap."

Brody raised his eyebrows. "Can you lift that arm over your head without passing out?"

She sighed. "No."

"Then, suck it up. I'll cut as close to the seams as I can, and just on your injured side. A good tailor can fix everything. Trust me."

"Okay. But, I can't look."

"Women," he said in a light, disgusted tone. "Know what happens when you cut a shirt off of a guy?"

"What?"

"He buys another shirt."

She clicked her tongue. "That's just twisted. Guys are freaks. And there's nothing wrong with being emotionally attached to your garments."

"If you say so. Just, whatever you do, don't move your arm or try to help me. Sit still."

"Can I have another pill?"

Brody huffed a small sound that could've been a laugh. "Like you need one."

Her unharmed parka laid aside, thanks to the zipper, Brody just needed to get through her sweater—which would be irreparable since it was knit—thermal turtleneck and silk long underwear.

And bra.

Her tummy swirled again.

Both of them were silent as he held her hand gently and sliced up the seam of the sweater. When he'd cut through the neckline, he said, "I'm going to pull it off your good side now. You doing okay?"

"Physically, yes. Clothingwise, I'm in mourning," she said in a breathier tone than she'd have wanted.

That completed, he took up the shears again and cut the seam of her expedition-weight thermals. The routine continued with her silk long underwear, but he hesitated before pulling it off her other side. The tension in the room buzzed, leaving her drunk with it. Both of them knew what she wore underneath that final layer. She could always blame the nipple thing on being cold, she supposed….

Brody cleared his throat. "Do you want something to, ah, cover up with?"

She masked her shallow-breathed attraction with a braveness she didn't really feel. "Ever been to the beach?"

He looked confused. "Uh…yeah?"

"Well then, you've seen plenty of bikinis that covered far less than my bra does." Her breath caught, and she swallowed. Looking away from him, she said, "Just...take it off."

Brody slipped the white, long-sleeved shirt from Faith's shoulder, exposing a fiery red, lacy bra that did amazing things to her cleavage. He tried not to look. Really. But it was red.

He hadn't expected red.

Could she not have warned him about the *red?*

He forced himself to ignore the creamy expanse of her exposed torso and focus on the telltale bump of broken bone at her clavicle. She had goose bumps. "You're cold."

"I'm naked. It's a common correlation."

"I'll get you that blanket. First we need to..." He did some half-assed gesturing at her bra.

Red.

He shook his head. "I'll go around and undo it from the back, okay?"

Faith's throat moved on a swallow. He could see her pulse, rapid in her neck. "No can do, cowboy. It's a front clasp." Long pause. "I'm sorry. I know you don't want to be doing this."

"No," he lied. "It's fine." Strangely, he wanted to be doing this. Hell, yes. And he hadn't wanted to be doing anything like this with anyone since he and his last girlfriend split. Faith somehow made him want to…just not under these circumstances.

He snatched up the gown and put it in her good side hand. "I'll undo it, and you can cover yourself with that. Just move slowly, okay?"

She nodded. She might be acting brave, but Brody got the impression this was just as difficult for her as it was for him. Probably more so.

His body reacted as he reached in and clasped the center hook of Faith's bra. The backs of his hands rested lightly on the powder-soft curves of her breasts; there was no avoiding it. He finagled the thing open as quickly as he could, brushing the straps carefully off her shoulders. The cups, inevitably, fell away from her body.

Her breasts were the perfect fullness—high and round with tight, mesmerizing nipples he could almost feel against his tongue.

What was he doing?

This was Mick's baby sister, for God's sake.

Averting his eyes, he eased the strap off her injured side, then walked around the gurney and stood behind her to get the other side. Releasing a huge breath, he reached around her and helped her slip her bad arm into the gown, then held it while she followed suit with her good arm.

He tied the top into a bow at her nape. "I'm sorry about that," he said, his tone husky.

"It's okay," she said, equally subdued.

"We'll get your pants and boots off after I tie you up back here, okay?"

"Wow, that sounded kinky!" she said with a nervous laugh. "Kinky, but fun."

It's the drugs. Ignore it. "You know what I meant." He squatted down to tie the second bow, and that's when he saw the tattoo at the small of her back. A red heart with an arrow through it. The arrow looked like wrought iron, bent so as to spell MICK as it pierced the heart. He touched it. Couldn't stop himself.

She shivered.

"Didn't mean to surprise you."

"You didn't. That's just one of my…spots. You know what I mean."

He did, God save him. But right now, he was focused on the tattoo. He couldn't stop looking at it. "It's…beautiful."

"Thanks."

"When did you get it done?"

"The day I turned sixteen."

He ran his fingers over it one more time, tracing the arrow with his index finger. Faith shivered again, and he regretfully pulled his hand away. He tied the bow in the gown and then moved back in front of Faith. Their eyes met.

"I loved her," Faith said, simply.

"I did, too."

Faith rewarded that with an angelic smile.

Brody removed her boots, then reached up under her gown and felt for the zipper. He undid it, then did the same for the zippers on the outside of each pant leg. They managed to wriggle her out of them without much trouble. He wondered if the bikini underwear he'd felt were that fiery red, too.

Now she really looked cold. He could swear her teeth were almost chattering.

"I'll get that blanket."

She grabbed his hand before he could turn away, clutched tightly. Her eyes looked wide and troubled for the first time since their reunion.

He cocked his head to the side. "Faith?"

"The sheet's fine. I'm not cold. I'm just…I don't know."

He frowned. Was she shocky?

"Can you…stay with me? Please. Don't go."

His heart clenched, and he squeezed her hand back. Unable to stop himself, he reached out his other hand and brushed her hair back from her face, tucking it behind one ear, letting his fingers linger there, against the softness of her jawline. "I'm not going anywhere."

And that's when her parents walked in.

Chapter Four

Brody and Faith wrenched apart like two teenagers caught buck naked on the family couch, but neither parent seemed to notice. And why did he and Faith react so guiltily anyway? Maybe because he'd just undressed their baby daughter? Maybe because she was feeling the same sort of…attraction…that he'd been feeling? He didn't know.

Mr. Montesantos had always been the perfect daddy to his girls, so when he moved immediately to Faith's bedside, concern and fear creasing his face, Brody wasn't surprised.

What did surprise him, however, was the fact

that Mrs. Montesantos, tears in her eyes, rushed toward him rather than her daughter.

"Brody," she said on a sob, and pulled him into a huge hug, resting her wet cheek against his chest. "You rotten boy, disappeared for so long from us. *Dios mio,* I prayed you'd come back. And here you are."

It stunned him.

This was 180 degrees from the "greeting" he'd imagined, for eleven years, that he'd receive should he ever show his face in Troublesome Gulch again. He somehow wrangled control of his senses and wrapped her in a hug, too. Tentatively, at first, and then more tightly as his omnipresent grief resurfaced. "I'm so sorry."

"Shhh, *m'ijo,*" she said, pulling back. "There are no *sorries* with family. Let me just look at you." She searched his face with her jade-green eyes, squeezing his shoulders, arms, hands. Laying her palms on his chest as if he might be an apparition who could disappear at any moment. She touched him as though he were a precious thing; he couldn't understand it, but damn, it felt good.

He was ashamed to admit he'd even been somewhat distant from his own family since the tragedy. In any case, he hadn't received this kind of motherly attention in far too long. Maybe never, except during the Mick years from this very woman. His own mother, wonderful as she was in her own way, had never been as demonstrative as Elisa Montesantos.

Brody knew how much he missed Mick every day, but he hadn't realized how much he'd missed her family, too. It felt amazing just being amongst them.

"Look at you," she said, on a sigh. "Just look at you. All grown-up, such a strong, handsome man. And a paramedic," she exclaimed, as though he'd become a medical researcher solely responsible for curing cancer, AIDS and the common cold all at once. "I'm so proud of you, Brody."

"Thank you." He swallowed with more than a little difficulty. Loss and time had etched lines around her eyes, he noticed, but it only made her more lovely. Some women aged angrily, the wrinkles emphasizing a lifelong scowl of discontent and disillusionment, but not Elisa Montesantos.

Her face had aged to show her happiness in life, despite every storm she'd weathered. Feathery crow's feet framed the outer edges of her eyes—a look he'd always found astoundingly beautiful—and smile lines grooved around her mouth, emphasizing the left-side dimple she passed on genetically to Mick.

Both of her daughters resembled her in appearance, but took most of their personality traits from their headstrong, outspoken father. Most, but not all. It was, he thought, an absolutely perfect mix.

With a jolt, Brody wondered what Mick would've looked like now, what her life would've been like, who she would've fallen in love with. Would they still have been best friends? His chest clenched, but only momentarily. Yes, he decided. They would always have been best friends.

"I didn't plan for us to reunite this way," he said, his voice unable to hide the shame he felt. "I was going to call as soon as I got settled."

Elisa shook her head. "All that matters is that you're here. We've missed you. Both of you," she added in a voice that only wobbled slightly.

He clenched his jaw to contain the emotion that threatened to overtake him. After a moment, "I…miss her every day. Every minute."

"Of course you do, *m'ijo*. We know. We all do," she said, rubbing his hands between her own as she spoke. "But it helps to remember that she's here with us, always. It's hard to reach that place of understanding, of serenity with what is, but once you do…" She sighed.

He pressed his lips together. "I'm not there yet."

"I know, *pobrecito*."

He nodded. It really seemed like she did understand the depth and breadth of his loss, despite her own. And she didn't seem to fault him for being so…stuck. But he still felt the need to atone or explain. Something.

He lifted his arms and let them fall loosely at his sides. "It's so late in coming, but how can I convey to you how sorry I am? About Mick. The prom. The drinking and…the rest?"

She tilted her head to the side and studied him with wonder. "What makes you think we don't understand that?"

After thinking about it a moment, he shrugged. "She died. I lived. If I could change places—"

She laid her fingers on his mouth to stop the words. "God chooses his angels, Brody. You had nothing to do with that. And why wouldn't he choose our Mick? She was more enlightened and at peace with herself than any eighteen-year-old young woman I've ever known." She took his hands in hers and squeezed. "You loved our girl, Brody. Horrible things happen every day. Not just to our family. We move through. We continue to live. Not just for ourselves, but for those we've lost. We owe Mick that much."

His eyes filled, and he closed them, not

wanting—*God,* desperately not wanting—to be the weak one here. "How? How do we do it?"

She reached up and grabbed both sides of his face. "Brody Austin. You listen to me, young man. We never, ever, not for one moment blamed you. Not a moment. And had you stayed, you would've known that."

Guilt backhanded him.

"But you had to go. It hurt, I won't lie, but we understand that, now, too. We love you like a son. That has never, and will never, change. Your healing will come, love. Just let it come."

One tear escaped, and Mick's mother reached up and brushed it from his whisker-roughened cheek with no fanfare whatsoever. They studied each other for a bubble of time, and then he pulled her into another hug, different this time. Lighter, happier. He lifted her off her feet until she laughed and smacked at his back.

When he set her down, she kept her hands on his arms and angled her head toward the bed. Lowering her voice, she said, "Okay, the truth. This one. Did she really just land wrong or was she doing something…"

"Stupid? Dangerous? Impulsive?"

Elisa chuckled. "I figured."

He leaned in. "Well, let's just say it could've been much worse. But, she's a tough one, your Faith."

Elisa clucked her tongue and shook her head. "I tell you, she turns my hair gray. Determined to be as gutsy and crazy as her older sister ever since... But she's not made of the same stuff."

"Some of it," Brody said, with admiration. "A lot of it, actually."

"Yes. But not all of it. I know you understand what I mean. Every child comes with different skills." She squeezed his arm. "Let me go give her a stern talking to and a big kiss." And then she moved to Faith's bedside.

Brody's heart started a hard, slow dirge in his chest. Facing Mick's sweet mama was one thing, but it was always more difficult to confront a girl's father. Every guy in the world knew that from about age thirteen, if he had any brain matter whatsoever.

Abel Montesantos leaned down and placed a kiss on Faith's cheek, then stood. The two men's eyes met across the gurney for one frozen moment. Instinctively Brody knew he needed to be the man and make the first move. He strode around the room with more confidence than he felt until he stood before the Montesantos patriarch, shoulders straight, head held high. All that military bearing stuff coming back like pure instinct.

He extended his hand. "Sir—"

Abel brushed Brody's hand aside and pulled him into a bear hug that knocked the wind clear out of him.

"Welcome home, son." His voice was shakier than his wife's had been, by far, and watery with tears. Brody blew out relief. Knowing Abel Montesantos was man enough to not only feel emotions, but show them as strongly as he himself did lifted a huge weight from Brody's shoulders. With this family, he didn't have to pretend it didn't hurt.

"Welcome home, finally," Abel repeated, in a choked voice. The two men pulled apart, and Abel wiped at his eyes. "You've been missed."

Brody didn't speak, because he couldn't. The whole situation was too overwhelming, too far removed from the nightmares he'd imagined for the past eleven long years.

Home? Everyone kept using the word.

It sounded, *felt* so enveloping.

He'd never even lived in Troublesome Gulch, so it technically wasn't his home, but did that matter? What was the meaning of home, anyway? Four walls and an orange plaid couch that sagged in the middle like a sway-backed nag? These people he'd feared for so many years were welcoming him unconditionally, pulling him into their fold as if he'd always been a part of them. Maybe he had, and he'd just been too damn blinded by grief and fear to realize it.

Now the question remained…could Troublesome Gulch actually become his home? He hadn't had anything resembling *home* in a long, long time, but right then, in the curtained-off room of High Country Medical Center, he felt it.

A sense of place, of belonging.

A grounding that he'd lacked for far too long. The earth seemed to steady beneath his feet, and his heart eased. Home.

He hadn't realized how much he wanted it.

And he'd never imagined it might be right here.

Brody stayed awhile longer, filling in the Montesantoses on bits and pieces of his life over the past eleven years and hearing about theirs. They talked about Mick, but shared only stories and memories that made everyone laugh or smile. Finally, it seemed time for Brody to go, leave Faith in her parents' care and head back to his cave to recover from the emotional white-water rapids he'd been through today.

He slapped his hands on his thighs and stood. "I think I'm going to get out of your hair for now. I work early tomorrow morning." He cocked an eyebrow at Faith. "Do what the doctor says for your shoulder, so it heals right, no matter how you feel, understand?"

She went bug-eyed. "Geez, you act like I'm some kind of wanton rule breaker. I mold the minds and hearts of young people every day, I might remind you."

"Yeah, don't worry. We won't alert their parents about the real you." He scoffed and shook his head. "Anyway, they're called after-care instructions. Follow them. *All* of them."

She scrunched her nose at him.

"How will we get in touch with you, *m'ijo?*" Mrs. Montesantos said, scrabbling through her purse for a pen and something to write on.

In touch? "Oh. Uh, well, I haven't hooked up phone service yet, but I bought Mr. Norwood's A-frame out on—"

"You actually paid money for that old grouch's pile of rotting wood?" Faith asked, incredulous. "What are you, some kind of an idiot?"

"Faith!" her parents said in unison, clearly stunned by her rudeness.

Brody, on the other hand, found it amusing, not to mention quite Mick-like. "Don't worry," he told them. "It's the narcotics. I'm sure she's usually polite as can be, the very picture of demure femininity."

Abel snorted.

"It's a good thing she doesn't take those pills every day," Elisa said, scowling playfully at her daughter. "Rude girl. You should apologize."

"What for? It's only *Brody*. It's not like some stranger. And besides, it's the truth. The place is a dump and Norwood *is* a grouch."

"Was," Brody said.

"Huh?" Faith asked.

"Norwood was a grouch because he wanted to move into the assisted-living complex closer to town, have some folks his own age to interact with, which is totally understandable. He couldn't handle the upkeep on his A-frame any longer, so he couldn't unload it."

"For obvious reasons," Faith said. "He needed an out-of-town sucker like you."

"Faith!" her parents said at once. *"Callaté,"* her mother added in a rasp.

Brody remained unfazed and amused. "He needed a hand, is all. The place has good bones and it's structurally sound. I can do what needs to be done, and Norwood's happy as a clam in his new condo."

"Those new places aren't cheap," Abel said, thoughtfully rubbing the backs of his fingers along his jawline. He looked up at Brody with an interested but knowing gleam in his eye. "Norwood must've bloated the price on his old place."

"Not really. Let's just say I gave him full price for the house and bought all the furnishings for, ah, a little more than they might be worth."

"Sucker," Faith teased.

He made a face at her. "Maybe. But the old guy needed a break."

"Always tenderhearted, our boy," Elisa said to Abel.

Brody basked in the warmth of inclusiveness but burned a stink-eye at Faith. Ruefully, he said, "So, I guess you know where my humble abode is, and—" he wrestled his wallet out of his back pocket and extracted a business card "—this has my numbers at work. I'll write my cell phone number on the back and let you know when the real thing is installed."

Elisa Montesantos handed over her pen, and he scribbled down the digits, then handed them both back to her.

She clutched pen and paper to her chest, looking almost winsome. "We'd love to see you. Have dinner. You'll come to the house, yes, so I can cook for you?" she asked, with hope in her voice.

His stomach fell from a cliff.

The house.

Mick's house.

Another emotional hurdle he was wholeheartedly unprepared to jump.

He'd spent so much time there in his teens, and yet at that moment he felt incapable of walking through those doors again. Dizziness assailed him. "Sure. Or, hey. How about if I save you all that work and take you out to dinner someplace nice?"

"Nonsense," Elisa said, with a sniff. "You must eat out all the time. A bachelor, living alone."

"In that freakin' tar paper shack, too. Do the appliances even work?" Faith asked.

Everyone ignored her.

"You need a home-cooked meal." Elisa's statement didn't allow for any argument.

"Of course," he said, acquiescing because what else could he do? He patted his stomach. "That sounds wonderful. I look forward to it."

Abel and Elisa said their goodbyes to Brody, then left briefly to get coffee from the vending machine, promising to return before the doctor came in.

Brody grasped the metal sides of the gurney with both hands and looked down at Faith. He took in a big breath, then exhaled through his nose. "If you need anything, you know where I am."

She smiled. "Yes, but until you've fumigated,

exterminated and disinfected, you won't see me darkening your doorstep."

Brody smirked. "Your loss, smart-ass. The orange plaid couch is a must see. It's vintage."

"I think the word you're looking for is vile. Possibly vomitous, if you're using teenspeak. I'm bilingual in English and teenspeak, you know, being a high school counselor. So, yes, let's go with vomitous."

"Hey, I'm a guy." He shrugged. "Furnished house, turnkey ready. It works for me."

She shook her head with pity. "Okay, you need cable television, too, and a healthy dose of the decorating shows. Turnkey ready doesn't mean— You know what? Never mind. Too hard to explain. What you need is a woman with some sense to help you with the important aesthetic decisions."

Brody felt itchy and looked away. After a moment he forced himself to meet her eyes again, this time with challenge. "Well, you're a woman."

"Thanks for noticing."

Oh, he'd noticed. Stupid red bra. "If you're so damned up in arms about my place, then why don't you help me fix it up?"

He'd expected her to give him a "no way, José," but her green eyes actually lit up. "Really?"

He'd only been joking, but he shrugged, as

though it were nothing. His heart pounded. This felt dangerous, this invitation. The two of them transforming his ramshackle abode into a real home. Dangerous…and yet alluring. "Why not? It's your issue."

"Excellent. Can't wait."

"We'll start when you're healed."

She smiled, but then her expression moved into something more vulnerable. She pulled her bottom lip in between her teeth, a move that made Brody's skin tingle.

"Brody?" she said, her voice softer. She reached out and laid her warm hand on his. "Can you make me one promise?"

He hesitated. He'd never been good at promises, ever since prom night, when Abel Montesantos told him, "Take care of my girl," and he'd said, "I will."

Then failed in the worst possible way.

He hadn't made many promises since then.

"I can try," he said.

"Please…please just tell me first if you're going to disappear again." Her tough-girl eyes filled with tears until one spilled over and ran down the soft curves of her cheek. "I can't lose both of you twice."

Something unexpected swirled through Brody, a sense of protectiveness, but even more than that. He couldn't understand it, much less explain it.

With the pad of his thumb, he brushed away the tear. "I'm not going anywhere, Faith. I think I'm right where I belong. At least for now."

"For now?" She bit her quivering bottom lip again. "What does that mean?"

"Give me time, okay? I just got back." He leaned down and kissed her forehead. "And—" he made an *X* over his chest "—you'll be the first to know my every move. If it'll make you feel better, I'll even wear one of those prison tracking devices on my ankle."

"Oh, be quiet. God! Who's the smart-ass now?"

But he'd coaxed out her smile again. That made it all worth it. "Takes one to know one."

"I know you are, but what am I?"

He shook his head, a smirk on his face. "Are you ever going to grow up?"

"Not if I can help it. Forever young. That's my goal. Just like Mick."

"Just like Mick," he replied, softly. "It's a good goal. Although, not to burst your bubble, but I don't think you're going to ski as well as she did. Ever. In fact, you might just want to stay off the slopes completely so you're not a danger to yourself and others."

She sighed, with feigned annoyance. "That again. Not everyone's a jock, you know. Doesn't mean I can't still have fun. And I saw you whispering with my mother, so don't think you're sly. I know you ratted me out."

He spread his arms, feigning complete innocence. "She wanted to know if you'd been reckless. You want me to *lie* to your mom?"

She leveled an unblinking poker face at him. "You know I'd be punching you right now if I wasn't hurt, don't you?"

He held up both palms. "Let's just say, I'll remain duly informed about your penchant for violence at all times from here on out."

"Smart man." She held the back of her good hand over her mouth to mask a big yawn. "Go on. Scurry off to your creepy-old-man house. I'm tired. But…I'll see you soon?"

"Soon. Don't worry. To fix up my place, remember?" He winked, tweaked her nose and then walked away.

The weirdest part? Walking away from Faith Montesantos turned out to be the most difficult part of one hell of a stress-packed day.

That, he hadn't expected.

Chapter Five

Brody had worked three straight weeks of as much overtime as he could possibly get, and there was a lot to be had since they were understaffed. He needed all the money he could stockpile for this overambitious Extreme Home Makeover Faith had been busily planning. He'd figured, a little paint here, a sheet thrown over the plaid couch there and call it good. Oh, no. Faith had vastly different aspirations from his own, and basically he'd given her free rein. Like he cared. Money wasn't too much of an issue thanks to all his overtime earnings, but she didn't know that and planned to go mostly on the cheap anyway. He did throw in for new flooring, kitchen countertops and a mattress, and he told her he'd pay her back for any paint, supplies and fixtures she needed to buy.

He'd just gotten off his twenty-four-hour shift, but though they usually got to sleep quite a bit at night between calls, last night they'd run call-to-call until their relief showed up—thank God—at 6:00 a.m. Nothing spectacular had happened— just your garden variety medical calls, but after more than twenty-four hours awake, he was bone-deep exhausted. The three weeks with hardly any days off were catching up to him big-time.

He opened his front door at 6:30 a.m., slid his gear bag from his shoulder, then undressed as he walked through the house, dropping pieces of his uniform wherever the hell they landed. One boot landed on the couch, the other hit the ugly paneled wall. Socks on the scarred linoleum floor in the kitchen, belt and pants in the hallway. Being a bachelor did have its perks.

Wearing nothing but his boxer briefs, he entered the creaky bedroom and fell facedown on the uncomfortable mattress imagining the hellish, sagging thing cradled his body like a bed of clouds, he was so tired. In truth, he'd slept on comfier cots in Afghanistan. But right then, he didn't care. All he wanted to do was sleep the whole day away, wake up when it was getting dark outside and have a bowl of cereal for his breakfast/dinner, do a little reading, then go back to bed.

He drifted into oblivion thinking first of Mick and then of Faith. What a pair, those two. So alike, and yet so very different. Both, however, were extraordinary women. He couldn't be sure, but he thought he fell asleep with a smile on his face.

"Brody, get up!"

He groaned. Why a nightmare now? he wondered, snuggling back into his pillow. Just when he'd hit the deepest sleep. He was used to nightmares—or daymares, if he wanted to get technical—however, today was not the day. He covered his exposed ear with one hand.

Something shook him. Earthquake? No, he was in Colorado. It could happen, but be real.

"Brody!"

Like a bucket of ice water to the face, Brody realized he wasn't alone in his bedroom. He flipped over and scrambled into a sitting position, his legs and hips tangled in the sheets and blanket.

Faith stood before him, fists on her hips, hair in a messy ponytail, and a breast-hugging T-shirt that read, Take Me, I'm Yours cradling every delectable curve.

Maybe this was a dream. He almost reached for her. With an offer like that on her shirt, who was he to argue?

Mick's baby sister, he reminded himself.

Right.

"How did you get in?"

She waggled a credit card at him. "Slipped the lock. You need a dead bolt. Anyway, that's for another day. Come on," she said. "It's already late."

He glanced at his clock and groaned. He'd only been asleep for an hour and a half. He scrubbed his hand through his bed head. His eyes felt like someone had poured salt into them. "Faith, can't this wait? We were up all night last night. I just want to sleep."

Looking crestfallen, her shoulders sagged. "But, it's Take Me, I'm Yours day, and I'm finally healed." She touched her collarbone. "You promised. If we miss it, we'll have to wait another month."

"Take me, I'm…huh?"

She blew out an exasperated sigh. "I left you a voice mail, remember?"

"Right," he said, slowly and mystified. He made a mental note to start checking that more than once a week.

She crossed her arms. "To reiterate, Memory Man, it's the day when everyone in Troublesome Gulch drags all the furniture they no longer want out onto the curb, and you can take whatever you want or need. Free! Whatever's left over, the charities pick up tomorrow morning."

She glanced around, her upper lip curling slightly. "Though they might want to take most of this stuff directly to the dump."

"Oh. That." Now he remembered. As if Troublesome Gulch's own tweak on Dumpster diving was worth waking up for. "I'm okay with next month," he said, lying back down and pulling up the blankets to his chin.

"I'm not, so get up." She yanked them down to his feet. "You promised. Besides, I can't stand the thought of you living in this flea-bitten flop house any longer. You can sleep tonight."

He held out his arms. "Can a guy have a little privacy? I'm in my underwear here, Faith."

"So freakin' what? You *removed* my bra, need I remind you, which required actually touching my breasts."

No. No. He definitely needed no reminders of that.

She stooped and swiped a pair of wrinkled jeans up off the floor, chucking them at him. "Man, you're a slob. I'll make you some coffee while you get dressed. And hurry up, because the kids will be here soon."

Brody groaned, but he got up and jammed his legs into the jeans, skipping the shirt for now. "Stay away from my coffeemaker," he called out. "I've tasted that beige water you call coffee. I'll make my own." His brain went through a quick rewind. "Wait a minute, what kids?"

"Some of my students are coming over to help. It's part of their detention."

"You've invited hoodlums into my home?"

"They're not hoodlums," she said with a decided edge of protectiveness in her voice. "They just don't get the concept of actually completing homework or showing up to class. Besides, cut them some slack. Not every kid had a good childhood. And we need them." Fists on her hips, she surveyed the area. "Not only do we have to drag every stick of junk in this place out to the curb, but we have to take time to treasure hunt through town before all the good stuff is gone. Chop-chop." She clapped twice. Loudly.

He cringed. "I hate you right now, you know."

She shrugged, nonplussed. "Whatever. Hate's better than apathy."

As he ground the beans, he watched her glance

around his living room like a vulture, tapping the pads of her fingers against her luscious lips, then moving through and sticking little round red dots on various things.

"I'm thinking we'll have the kids move the big stuff first…couch, those heinous log coffee- and end-tables, the Formica dinette, or should I say the For-make-me-hurl dinette. And that recliner. Shee-zus, who'd ever buy an acid-green-and-orange-striped recliner."

"That stays."

Faith spun toward him, horrified. "You've got to be kidding. Brody, you can't keep that in the room. It'll ruin the whole vibe we're going for."

"First of all, *you,* not *we,* are going for a vibe. I'm just humoring you. I don't even know what a decorating vibe is, much less how to go for one."

"But, that recliner." She pouted. "I mean, isn't it Naugahyde? What the hell is Naugahyde anyway?"

"I don't know," he said, with feigned serious-ness, "but a lot of naugas sacrificed their hydes to create that masterpiece. Have a little respect."

She stared him down.

"I'm not keeping it in the room, but it's not going out on the curb. Okay? I have plans for it. So just push it off in a corner and leave it alone. And do me a favor. Stop detailing your grand plan for a few minutes, at least in that rapid-fire 'chop-chop' tone of voice. I've had one hour of sleep and no caffeine."

"Touchy, touchy," she teased, but she went through the house, happily tagging stuff in silence.

While his coffee brewed, Brody escaped to the bathroom and did a quick washup with the coldest water he could. He brushed his teeth, found a T-shirt and some sneakers, clapped a baseball cap on his head and called it good. By the time he emerged, six gangly, bleary-eyed, baggy-clothed teenage males were systematically emptying his home, at the direction of one small, curvy, bossy-ass woman.

One of them, hat on backward, hiked a soul-patch-sporting chin at Brody from one end of the plaid couch they were carrying out of his house, as though this were all normal. "Hey."

"Hey," Brody replied, feeling a twinge of nostalgia for that sofa. Faith was right, though. The thing was ugly and way past its prime. It smelled of mothballs and take-out Chinese food, and you could actually feel springs poking you in the butt when you sat on it. Still, this whole Take Me, I'm Yours tradition in Troublesome Gulch was a bit creepy, especially when coupled with sleep deprivation. The town wasn't *that* large; it seemed a bit like wife-swapping. So you go for dinner at a friend's house and *your* old sofa is in their living room. Weird.

He crossed to his cupboards and grabbed out a mug, pouring himself some joe. As he sipped, he leaned against the chipped, woodgrain Formica countertop that would soon be replaced, and crossed his ankles. Faith bounced back inside and favored him with a tentative smile. "Good coffee?"

"Like you'd know the difference. What do you want me to be doing?"

"Nothing. Just relax there, drink your anally-prepared, free-trade, freshly ground Mr. Perfect coffee. And, Brody? Become human if at all possible. That's all I ask at this point."

"Tone down the perky factor, and you've got a deal."

"I am not *perky.* I'm efficient."

Brody snorted.

"Anyway, the plan. Shall I whisper?"

He angled his head toward her. "Just tell me."

"These guys owe me, so they're going to do the grunt work. Your part will come in when we head out hunting for new stuff to go with our new *vibe,*" she said, with playful emphasis.

He hiked his thumb over his shoulder toward the bedroom. "Swell. Mind if I go lie down until we're ready for that particular circle of hell, then?"

She quirked her lips in apology. "Bed's already out on the curb, sorry. You can sleep out there if you want, but people in town will gossip about you."

He shook his head, still exhausted but amused. "What is it with you Montesantos women?"

She grinned. "Go hard or go home. That's what my sis always said."

"She did, didn't she?" Brody smiled. "Who knew Mick's knock-kneed baby sister was paying attention all that time, nose stuffed in a book or not."

She raised her chin. "Who knew Mick's best friend even noticed her knock-kneed, bookworm, baby sister," she quipped, giving his body a long, suggestive once-over.

Or had he imagined that?

In any case, he may have noticed the kid back then—barely—but he was finely tuned in to the woman she'd grown into with a whole different *vibe*.

And that kind of vibe he *definitely* understood.

"People have no vision," he said in a glum tone, when they returned to his A-frame late that afternoon, his pickup truck filled with curb finds. Almost all of old Norwood's furniture sat just where the teens had placed it, not even picked through.

"Honey, his stuff was just gross."

Brody felt a twinge of compassion. "I'm sure it was cool when he bought it. He's a nice old guy."

"I'm not doubting that, but it doesn't negate the grossness of his retro—and not in a good way—belongings. All good furniture has to go to that great big living room in the sky sometime or the other."

"So, let me get this straight." Brody shifted in his seat. "We removed all of Norwood's old crap just so we could go out and pick up other people's old crap?"

"It's not *crap*," she said, peeved. "The items we've carefully chosen have potential, they just need a little bit of our elbow grease."

Brody quirked an eyebrow. "By *our*, I assume you're meaning *your*."

She sighed. "Yes, I realize I've forced you into this and that you're working a ton of hours."

He cupped a hand around one ear. "Wait. Is that empathy I detect?"

Her eyes narrowed. "*But* by the next time you get off work—when do you pull a twenty-four again?"

"Tomorrow, hence the need for sleep."

She nodded, decisively. "Sunday. Perfect. When you get home on Monday morning, your place is going to be so revamped, it'll blow your mind. My detention kids are going to help me scrub this sucker down and paint. That friend I told you about has the countertops ready to be installed. Floors, too. It'll be a whole new house."

"Yippee. One question."

"Whip it on me."

"Where in the heck do you expect me to sleep? My bed is gone. I've had one hour of sleep." He opened his eyes wide. "I have to sleep before tomorrow, Faith, not that I've mentioned this before, or anything."

She had the audacity to look excited. "Oh, that's perfect!" She wrestled her keys out of her purse. "You sleep at my condo. That'll give us the rest of the day to get the cleaning and masking done on this place so we can paint bright and early to-morrow. And don't worry, the kids will help me unload the truck."

Brody stared down at the keys in his hand, attached to a fob that read Chicks Rule. Sleep. In Faith Montesantos's condo. There was that clutchy feeling in his gut again. But he was too tired to even argue.

"Okay. Let me get my gear and go. I'm thrashed."

"Drive my car. In fact, you can just drive it to work tomorrow, too."

A perky yellow-and-black Mini Cooper. "Not."

She frowned. "Why not?"

"Girly car. Sorry, I should be man enough,

but—" He shrugged. "Apparently I'm sadly lacking. I'll drive it to your condo now, but not to work. Besides, you need somewhere to sleep, right?"

"Sure."

He flipped a hand, as though the solution was obvious. "When you're done with my truck, just bring it and we'll swap in the morning. You can leave the keys outside the guest room door."

"Uhhhh…" Her gaze moved off to the side.

"What?"

"I don't have a guest room. It's a one-bedroom condo. I work in the school system, remember? We're even more underpaid than you guys or the cops."

Brody scrubbed his hands over his face. These details were killing him, right where he stood. What was it with women and irrelevant details? He didn't care about the where, the how, the what-the-hell-ever, he just wanted *sleep*. "Then on the coffee table. The doormat. My forehead. Wherever. I'll hit the couch."

"No need—just take my bed. I have a tiny condo, hence a small couch, and I don't even think you'll fit on it, actually."

He couldn't argue. He could barely think for being so exhausted. "Your bed. Fine. If that's okay with you, I'm out."

She rattled off the address. "You know where it is?"

He gave her a droll look.

"Gotcha. Paramedic. You know where everything is."

"See you tomorrow. I wake up at five. My shift starts at six."

"No sweat! I'll be up early, too, so we can have tons of time to transform your house."

He held up a hand. "Please, God, don't go all Suzy hostess on me and make coffee."

She planted her fists on her hips. "What is so wrong with my coffee?"

He looked up and off to the side. "Um…it sucks?"

She laughed. "Fine. Someday you can teach me to make it how you like it."

Brody thought about how good that sounded. The implication of mornings spent with Faith was something he'd never expected, but just couldn't get out of his mind. He wasn't even sure he wanted to.

"Can you do me one favor?" he asked.

"Sure, name it."

"Load the Naugahyde recliner into the shed. And cover it with a tarp, in case we get weather. That shed's not altogether waterproof."

Faith held up her hands. "As long as it's not in the room, your wish is my command."

He winked. "Yeah, I have that power over women."

She shoved him. "Oh, please. Get out of here, Austin. The sleep deprivation is jacking with your brain."

Chapter Six

Brody didn't know how long he'd been asleep in Faith's comfortable bed when he felt the mattress dip as though someone had climbed in with him. For a moment he froze, but then he caught her familiar mesmerizing scent. He turned over to find Faith shivering next to him. Her wide green eyes looked up at him through the moonlight, wary and apologetic.

"Do you mind?"

It took him a minute to fully realize what she was asking. "Uh…no. Of course not. It's your house." He raised up on one elbow and ran his hand through his hair. "I can take the couch. What time is it?"

"Three. You have a couple more hours to sleep. And, no, you can't take the couch. There's a power outage in the building because of the wind and it's completely freezing out there. No lie, I think it's forty-nine degrees inside the condo."

Come to think of it, his nose did feel rather cold. But the woman had an alternate heat source. Had she forgotten that? "I'd be more than happy to fire up your pellet stove."

"Uhhh…"

"What now?"

She grimaced. "I'm out of pellets."

"Faith," he chastised.

"I know, I know. First rule of living in the high country—never run out of wood or pellets. But I couldn't carry the forty-pound bags with the whole collarbone thing."

"Ni-i-ice."

"Can I just sleep in here with you? Please?" She batted her eyelashes. "I promise not to hog the blankets or compromise your manly virtue in any way. I'm even wearing flannel, see?"

She lifted up the covers to give him a view of her pink flannel pajama pants, but she'd failed to mention the form-fitting top with the skinny little velvet straps that matched them. A wave of cold air invaded the bed, and her nipples hardened into tight, luscious points.

His mouth went dry. He shook his head and lay back down on the pillow, facing away from her. "You're a nut job. Pull the covers back up. It is damn cold in this house."

"Thanks."

Brody closed his eyes and sighed, preparing to take full advantage of his remaining two hours.

"Brody?"

"Hmm?"

"I won't lie. I sort of want to take advantage of your body heat."

It shouldn't sound as good to him as it did. And he absolutely couldn't let her detect the level of desire that rushed through him. "If you're going to snuggle in, Faith, then snuggle in. I'm not afraid of you."

That silenced her. But when she pressed her shapely body against his bare back, he felt the round softness of her breasts and her warmth. Her breath tickled him between the shoulder blades, and suddenly he *was* afraid. Of her, of this. Everything.

She laid her arm casually over his waist and shivered. "This is so much better. My teeth were chattering out there."

And it was so much better. He damn well hoped

her hand didn't accidentally move a little lower, though, or she'd find out just exactly how much better it was for him.

"'Night, Faith," he said, struggling to sound nonchalant despite his racing pulse. He couldn't say much more, because all the blood in his body had flown south for the cold winter's night, and the words just weren't there.

"'Night, Brody." She kissed him softly on his bare back, just a sweet, innocent good-night kiss. But the way it affected his body was neither sweet nor innocent. More like high-voltage shock.

Good Lord, what was he doing here? Playing with fire? Testing his resolve?

Mick's baby sister, he reminded himself.

But—unbelievable as it was to him—the mantra was losing its punch.

Mick's. Baby. Sister.

He waited. Nope. Didn't change the effect she was having on his body or his brain. The absolute truth was he wanted to roll over, right that moment, feel Faith's body beneath his. Bury his face in her neck and inhale that unique musky floral scent of her. He wanted her to feel just how much she turned him on.

The shock of it hit him. He wanted Faith.

Faith Montesantos—yes. Mick's baby sister.

He wanted to taste her, touch her, feel her body clench around him as he pushed inside her. He wanted his lips against the pulse in her neck as her body clutched his in climax. He wanted to hear her pant and moan. He wanted to taste her, make her scream. He wanted her nipples against his tongue and her mouth on him. Everywhere. He wanted her legs wrapped around him, his hands beneath her as he pushed into her deeper, and deeper still.

Not only that, but he wanted *this*. Faith snuggled against his back, steady puffs of her warm breath against his skin. He wanted it all—all of her. He'd even suffer through that dreck she called coffee if he could have the rest. And *that* above all else, meant one thing.

He'd fallen hard under the lust spell. But lust wasn't what this particular woman deserved. She deserved love and commitment and so much more. He just wasn't there yet. Who knew if he'd ever be?

Mick's baby sister.

Part of him felt like mourning all over again.

He'd come back to Troublesome Gulch to heal, to get his head on straight, not to put another Montesantos sister in danger, not to break her heart—which he absolutely would. How could he offer himself to another person when he didn't feel complete himself? Suppose he did put the moves on Faith and she reciprocated? He was still only half a man, and no damn good for anyone. If she made the mistake of falling in love with him, he'd wind up hurting her. Ugly, but true.

And in the meantime, while he was satiating his rampant lust, how would he ever keep her safe? How could he live with worrying about her? How would he take care of her, fulfill the promise to Abel that he hadn't been able to with Mick?

Take care of my girl.

A sword of pain lanced through him.

Was it even fair for him to ask that of Mr. Montesantos after all Brody'd put them through? To trust him with another daughter—his only daughter left? Absolutely, no questions asked, *no*. Especially in the context of a simple fling.

No way.

This thing with Faith just couldn't happen. It couldn't, and yet his feelings were what they were, absolutely beyond his control. He wanted it— wanted her—more than he'd wanted anything for a long, long time. But that didn't matter.

Tension rocked through him as the depth of his dilemma became clear. He would have to do everything in his power to remain detached from these unexpected feelings for Faith, from Faith herself.

Friendship. Friendship was a good thing.

He'd been friends with Mick, but of course that had been a different case. Mick had no interest in dating guys, which was all good. He and Mick, they understood each other, soul deep. He'd never harbored romantic feelings for her, because that wasn't what they were about. Buds, pals. Rugby and skiing and just hanging out.

But, Faith? Faith was a whole different story, and he was terrified to turn the next page, to find out just what part he might play in the tale. He was sure making love to Mick's baby sister hadn't been in the plan.

Because he hadn't had a plan.

He'd been winging this whole, damn "find yourself in Troublesome Gulch" thing, and somehow he'd wound up in Faith Montesantos's bed, with her spooning him and him so rock hard and desperate with wanting her, further sleep was impossible at this point.

God, he was screwed.

Staring into the darkness, he weighed his options as minutes, then a half hour, then a full hour ticked by.

He'd have to avoid her, he decided.

It was the only solution. After the house decorating was over, he'd thank her profusely, he'd have dinner at her parents' house, and then he'd make himself scarce. She was young and beautiful. With any luck, she'd find some other guy, the type who was actually capable of falling in love with her, and then Brody would be safe. And, okay, the thought of that made him feel ill and vaguely violent, but there really wasn't another choice.

Yes.

Avoidance.

The perfect answer.

Being a hermit was one of his specialties, after all. He'd honed that skill for eleven long years. The only variable in his grand plan was Faith herself.

As if she could read his thoughts, she snuggled closer in sleep and sighed.

What did she want from all this? Was she up for a meaningless, purely physical tumble?

No. Stop. His brain shouldn't even travel down that road, because it wasn't going to happen. Ever. Faith deserved more than what he could offer, and wherever Mick was, he absolutely knew she would never forgive him for breaking her baby sister's heart.

Faith had been preoccupied all morning, thrown by how natural, how wonderful it had felt to share a bed with Brody. Okay, it had been a while since she'd had a serious boyfriend, but it was more than that. Being with Brody felt like…fate. So natural and comfortable. Completely different from any other experience she'd ever had with a man, not that there'd been so many. But there was none of that first-night awkwardness.

Several of her detention boys were outside sanding, priming and painting the furniture they'd scored on Take Me, I'm Yours day. One surprised her by offering to make some throw pillows, and she hadn't even known he could—or would admit to being able to—sew. So far, so good. The countertop had been installed and the carpet ripped up. Later that afternoon, the professionals were coming to install the new bamboo floor. It wouldn't take too long, they assured her. The place was small.

"So, Miz M, can I ask you something?"

Faith jumped. She hadn't realized she and her best painting apprentice, Jason Cole, had fallen into an unusually long silence.

From the top of the ladder where she was cutting in the new slate-blue-accent wall color along the angled ceiling line, she looked down at him. "Sure. Ask away."

He dipped his roller and started on another section of wall, with care and precision. "You got the hots bad for this ambulance guy, don't you?"

Her face flamed, and for a long few moments,

she just kept painting. At last, when her pulse was under control, she said, "First of all, Jase, that's an inappropriate question to ask your guidance counselor, wouldn't you think?"

He shrugged noncommittally.

"And secondly, it would be 'you *have* the hots,' not 'you *got* the hots.'" What could she say? Her undergrad was in English.

"Sorry," he said, clearly not. "But you do, right? *Have* the hots for him," he said, emphasizing the grammar.

"He was my sister's best friend."

He rolled his eyes. "I get that part, brah. I mean, Miz M. But it ain't what I asked."

She half laughed. "I have to say, it's that exact snarky attitude that your English teacher doesn't appreciate, which is why you're always hanging with me."

He frowned. "What, asking questions? That's her definition of *attitude?* How else are we supposed to learn about the world?" He spread his arms wide, paint dripping from his roller onto the drop cloth in a big blue splat. "Figure out our own heads and where we stand on things?"

"I hear you. I'm not saying I agree, I'm just telling it like it is."

"She wants me to take whatever she says as gospel and I'm just not down with that."

"I understand. Really, I do." Jason was far too brilliant for high school and had just about zero support from home. That was his main problem.

"Besides, I don't mind hangin' with you, even if I have to be your painting slave," he said, as though it were pure torture.

Faker. She could tell he was enjoying the process.

He paused, and when he spoke again, his tone was lower and huskier. "Anyhow, anything's better than being home with the 'rents."

Her heart squeezed. "Well, thank you. Although I wish you were happier at home."

"Don't matter," he said, in his tough guy tone. "Can't pick your family, ain't that right?" He turned back to his painting.

"That's exactly right. But when you grow up, you can choose how you want to live *your* life, apart from the family into which you were born. That part is all you."

He watched her out of the corner of his eye.

"And, just for the record, you're right, Jase. About the questioning."

Now she had his full attention.

She smiled. "We should question what we're

told and not just believe something because someone in authority says it's so."

"Duh," he said. "Ever heard of Hitler?"

"Exactly. Great example, by the way, smart
guy." She shrugged. "But unfortunately, the high
school mentality hasn't come that far in all
schools. Some teachers—not all—want you to
listen to what they tell you, do your work, behave
and show up to class on time. There's the whole
tangle of state standards and required curriculum.
It's just the way it is."

He met her gaze, his eyes filled with disgust and
anguish. "Don't they get that that ain't what the
real world's about? I mean, what the hell kind of
Disney movie do they live in?"

Faith just shrugged, didn't even remind him to
please not swear. They were connecting on a far
more important level, and she didn't want to break
that. "You're ahead of the curve, my friend."

"Whatever. Alls I know is it sucks."

"It'll get better once you're in college."

He scoffed. "Right, like I'm goin' to college.
I'm sure Mom and Dad have the funds all ready
to go, if the old man hasn't spent every dime on
hooch already."

"Your grades are more than good enough to get
into college. When you apply yourself," she added

pointedly. "And I'm sure you probably won't admit it to me, but I know you love to learn. It shows. I can't think of another student more deserving of a college education than you, Jason."

"Yeah, well, sucks to be me then."

"I know you think you can't get in, you can't afford it, *blah-blah-blah*."

He smirked. "Is that proper English?"

She flicked some paint at him. "There are financial aid programs, scholarships, grants."

"I don't know nothing about all that."

"Anything," she corrected automatically. "And it doesn't matter, because that's what I'm here for." She aimed her finger at him. "I'm going to get you into college, smart-alec. Your parents won't have to contribute a dime if they can't or don't want to, and you're going to study and grow and become an amazing adult. Believe me. Because you're already an amazing kid with a brilliant mind and unlimited potential. You just don't hear that enough, and for that I'm sorry."

Jason shrugged as though he couldn't care less, but she knew better. The blush all the way down his neck gave him away. She loved building these kids up. It gave her life purpose and meaning, warmed her heart.

"Anyway," he said, as if all her compliments

bored the living crap out of him, "nice try at changing the subject, or…what is it you say?"

"Deflecting."

"Right, deflecting. So back to ambulance bro."

"Ah, yes. About that line of questioning." She
held up a palm in anticipation of his calling her out.
"This might seem like a contradiction to everything
I just said, but it's not. You can talk to me about absolutely anything on your mind and in your life, but
my private life is off-limits. Sorry. It has nothing to
do with you personally, but I'm on the faculty and
you're a student. There's always a line."

Jason took off his baseball cap and resettled it
on his head backward. "That's cool. I get that. But
can I tell you one thing?"

"Go ahead."

"If you do want to hook up with the dude, you
should just tell him. Because—" he whistled
through his teeth "—he's all kinds of down wit'
you, if you know what I'm sayin'."

For a split second, Faith lost her guidance counselor cool. In fact, she almost fell off the ladder.
After she regained her balance, she shot a glance
at Jason. "He is? Really? How can you tell?"

Jason laughed. "I'm a guy, dude. I mean, Miz M.
We know things."

She shook her head. "Wait, wait, wait. Back up

a sec. Can you please not use that whole 'hook up' terminology to describe…well, you know? It's just so crude."

"Sorry."

They painted in silence for a few moments, after which Jason said in a smug, quiet tone, "I knew you was into him."

"Were," Faith corrected, with a smile. "Now be quiet, Mr. Thinks-He-Knows-Everything, and paint."

"See? I rest my case."

"Jason."

"Sorry, brah. I mean, Miz M."

The worst part was, Jason Cole was dead-on right. Perceptive little bugger. She did have feelings for Brody. But she didn't think they were mutual, and she didn't want to embarrass herself. "Don't say a word," she told Jason finally, with a narrowed gaze.

He had the audacity to look both offended and self-satisfied. "You think I'd front you like that?" He clicked his tongue. "Man, and here I thought you and me had an understanding. Ain't no love up in here, man. Ain't no love at all."

Chapter Seven

Brody was packing up his gear Monday morning, preparing to head home for a much-needed day off. The shift had been considerably slower than his previous one, so he felt well rested, and—if he was honest with himself—psyched to see exactly what transformative miracles Faith had pulled off with his house.

Luckily for him, old Mr. Norwood had replaced the ailing shingle roof with a sleek metal one after the blizzard a few years back, so it was in perfect shape and likely to remain that way for the next twenty years. But the exterior cedar planks were in dire need of restaining and weatherproofing, and his property could use some tree grooming to provide more defensible space before fire season was in full swing. Now that the inside was finished, maybe he'd feel the urge to put his stamp on the outside. Make it a real home—something he'd avoided for way too long.

Just as he hiked his bag onto his shoulder, his cell phone rang. He pulled it off his belt and answered it on the second ring as he headed out toward the parking lot. "Hello?"

"Where are you?" Faith asked breathlessly.

His heart tugged just hearing her voice. Bad sign. He reminded himself of his midnight vows. *Friendship. Avoidance.* Schooling his voice into nonchalance, he said, "Just leaving the station. Why?"

"You can't come home yet. We pulled an all-nighter, but they're still working on the floor. Almost done, though."

His level of disappointment surprised him. He stopped where he stood, in the middle of the parking lot. "Almost. How long are we talking about?"

"Hang on."

She'd covered the mouthpiece, but he could hear muffled conversation.

"A couple hours?"

He sighed. "Okay. Are they going to call you at school when they're finished, or what's the deal?"

"No need," she said. "It's a teacher planning day. The boys and I are off."

"I think you told me that. I've been working too much." He thought a moment. "Well, I guess I'll just hang out here, maybe get a workout in. You can call me when they're done."

"I have a much better idea," she said, in an enticing tone.

"Is that so?" He adored her enticing and playful tones, whether he wanted to or not. And he was so damn susceptible to them. "Well, lay it on me."

"How about you meet me downtown at the Pinecone Diner for breakfast? It's right on Main."

"I know where it is."

"I keep forgetting, sorry. Anyway, I'll even let you treat me, since you owe me big for making your place livable."

He laughed. Despite all his fears and resolutions, what could a meal out hurt? He had dinner to survive that Friday night at the Montesantos's house, anyway—which, incidentally, he dreaded with every single fiber of his soul. Not because of the family, whom he adored, but because of the house. The memories. Would he still sense Mick there? Would it reopen all the wounds that had just recently begun the slow healing process?

After this proposed breakfast, the "reveal," whatever that meant and the dreaded dinner, he would book a one-way ticket directly to hermitland where he'd be safe from his feelings for Faith. He may as well enjoy one last chance to hang out with her before Operation: Avoidance went into full effect. Breakfast in a public place seemed relatively harmless, and he was starved. "Okay. Meet you there in fifteen minutes?"

"Perfect. If you beat me there, grab a booth."

The place was packed, and he'd lucked into the last available booth, at the back. The sizzle from the kitchen grill carried into the dining room, which smelled of bacon and pancakes. Fresh, hot coffee scents permeated the air, too—everything that made small-town diners so very popular and timeless. The acoustics were such that he couldn't hear every syllable of chatter from the other tables, but he did catch the occasional holler from a waitress to the cooks, or vice versa. It only added to the charm.

Faith showed up a few minutes later.

"So, how did it turn out?" Brody asked, as the waitress poured their coffee. From the looks of Faith, they'd worked hard. Her perpetually messy ponytail was even messier and dotted with flecks of paint that looked sort of bluish, others that looked like a cup of coffee with the perfect amount of cream. She was a mess. An absolutely gorgeous mess.

She yawned against the back of her hand. "Sorry, my turn to be fried. You'll find out soon enough."

"Come on. Throw me a bone."

"Well…my boys gave it the thumbs-up of approval, if that eases your mind at all."

"It does. Unless they're into goth."

"Goth, no. Emo, a couple of them."

"Whatever that means."

She shrugged. "Teen-guidance-counselor speak. However, not to worry. They were my worker bees, but I was the sole designer."

Brody took a sip and felt the warmth of the brew all the way down his esophagus and into his chest. "So you didn't go all chintz and pink and girly on me?" He knew she hadn't, thanks to the hints of paint in her hair, but he just felt the need to get under her skin.

Faith scowled at him. "You know, I might not play rugby like Mick did, but I'm not exactly a high-maintenance girly-girl, if you haven't noticed."

Brody held up both palms. "Whoa, Nelly. Teasing. I didn't mean to offend you. Please accept my apology."

She pouted for a moment, but then smiled. "Okay, you're forgiven. And no. It's very masculine, don't worry. It's probably the hottest bachelor pad in all of Troublesome Gulch. I would quit my job and get my own decorating show on cable if I didn't love the kids so much."

Brody chuckled. "I should invite Mr. Norwood back up to take a look at the place."

"I don't know. You might give him a heart attack," she said. "But he'd probably be tickled to see it. He's lived there since the dawn of time."

Brody decided that's exactly what he'd do. Invite Norwood up for dinner and a game. A guy's night. He had plans to see the old guy soon anyway, see how things were going in his new place.

Behind Brody, the bell over the diner door chimed as someone entered. Dang, the Pinecone did an impressively brisk breakfast business, that was for sure. All the tables were filled except for a round one up front with a reserved sign on it, which everyone, it seemed, respected. Only in a small town...

Faith glanced up, and her face paled. Brody watched her swallow tightly.

He reached out and covered her hand with his own. "What's wrong?"

She gave a weak wiggle-finger wave at someone, then leaned in. Her words came rapid-fire. "Okay. Listen fast. The front table's reserved for the firefighters, and they just walked in. Heads up, Erin DeLuca is headed this way to say hi to me. She was the girlfriend of—"

"I know who she is." His heart revved. Another of the survivors. A perky cheerleader type, if he remembered correctly. But not one of those stereotypical phony rah-rahs. Much more down to earth. Nice girl.

"Does she know you're back?" Faith asked.

"No. None of them do. I've sort of avoided everyone."

"You okay?"

He opened his mouth to speak just as Erin DeLuca arrived at the table. She looked a lot like the Erin DeLuca he remembered from the couple times he'd met her, except for the fact that she wore navy blue uniform pants, a navy blue fire department T-shirt with the sleeves rolled up a bit, and she was a stone-cold hard body.

Damn.

No mistaking a woman who took her workouts seriously. She'd been athletic in that soft, curvy cheerleader way back in the day, but this was a whole different version of Erin.

"Hey, Pipsqueak," Erin said, punching Faith

lightly in the shoulder. "Hope I'm not interrupting one of those morning-after dates, if you know what I mean, although God knows you're due for one."

"Erin!" Faith's face reddened. "Sheesh."

"Sorry." Erin glanced leeringly at Brody, and then shock registered in her expression. She stumbled back a half step and laid her palm over her heart. "Holy— Talk about a ghost from lifetimes past."

"Hi, Erin." He stood and gave her an awkward hug, noting the defined musculature of her back that he could feel easily through her T-shirt. Man. He was no shrug in the workout arena, and yet she made him feel like hitting the gym again. Maybe a twice-a-day schedule.

They broke apart, and she studied him. "I can't believe you're actually standing here like it's just normal and stuff." She smacked him in the shoulder. "Scoot a cheek."

Brody obliged and slid to the inside of the bench seat. Meanwhile, Erin called out to her crew. "Hey, Cap?"

Brody turned around. A forty-something, totally in-shape woman lifted her head from the menu she'd been studying and raised her eyebrows at Erin.

"Mind if I eat over here?" She hiked a thumb at Brody. "Old friend I haven't seen in years."

"Go for it," the captain said.

Erin sat down. "She rocks. I just recently got moved to her station house. My old captain was a micromanaging jerk. Little-man syndrome," she said with a shrug, by way of explanation. She signaled the waitress for a cup of coffee. "So, Brody Austin." A pause. "Wow. What brings you back to our quirky little enclave after all these years? A sudden urge to slum with the lifers?"

"Lives here," Faith said. "He's a paramedic."

Erin shot a glance at Faith, then back at Brody, a line of confusion bisecting her brow. "What do you mean, a paramedic? For TG?"

"Yep," Brody said, wrapping his hands around his mug and feeling kind of…outed.

"Well…shoot. Unreal. How come I didn't know?" She spread her arms and widened her eyes at Faith. "Whatever happened to the small-town grapevine? Did I get kicked out of the loop? That so sucks."

Faith laughed.

"I haven't been here long," Brody said. "I guess it hasn't gotten around. We would've run into each other on a call sooner or later."

"Sure, but that's no way to find out." Her voice lowered. "I mean, we owe each other more than that after everything, don't you think?"

Brody didn't have an answer. At least not a good one. An uncomfortable pause ensued, while they all sipped.

"How've you been, Erin?" he asked, trying to keep the conversation light. But it wasn't. How could it be? The last time he'd seen her had been a night that changed both their lives forever.

Her gaze dropped to the table for a moment as a shadow of pain crossed her face. She covered it just as quickly and looked up. "Peachy. I've been a firefighter for seven years. I'm an engineer now."

"That's great. Do you enjoy it?"

"Well, the twenty-four-hour shifts can suck sometimes, but you know all about that. My dog has abandonment issues and occasionally goes through destructive phases."

"I told you he could come to my condo on your workdays," Faith interjected. "I love dogs."

"He's too big for that, Pip, and you know it. Besides, you're not allowed to have pets in your place."

"A fact which sucks, incidentally. But Finn never makes a sound. They'd never know."

"He's huge. They'd think a horse was walking around in your living room."

Brody had been considering the dog idea, but there was that twenty-four-hour shift consideration.

He supposed he could fence off part of his property and put in a dog door. Bringing himself back to the conversation, he asked, "What breed is Finn?"

"Irish wolfhound."

"Definitely huge."

"Tell me," Erin said, with a huff. "His destructive phases can mean, like, the whole couch."

"Yikes." Brody hitched his chin to one side, eyebrows raised. "You have to admit, Finn's a pretty big dog for your condo, Faith. He'd take up your whole bed."

Erin's gaze ping-ponged between the two. "Bed? Did I hear the word *bed?* Uhhh, anything I need to know, here, boys and girls?"

Brody and Faith realized the implication seemingly at once. "No!" they said, in stereo.

"Brody just had to stay at my house last night because—oh, it's a long story. Anyway, back to your job." Faith, blushing strawberry-red, practically buried her face in her coffee mug.

Brody picked up the train, focusing on Erin and stupid work small talk. "I admire your ability to navigate all those switchbacks in a big old engine."

"Takes some getting used to, that's for sure." She still didn't look convinced that there wasn't something more between him and Faith. He could tell by the way she studied them.

The waitress interrupted briefly and took their orders.

After she'd left, Brody laughed softly, glancing at Erin's well-defined biceps. "Please don't punch me, because I have a feeling it would hurt—"

"It would."

"—but I never would've imagined you becoming a firefighter."

Her eyes took on a distant look again. "Well, life has a funny way of leading you off in strange directions, as you well know. I was going to study child psychology in college as a backup, but I really just wanted to be a mom. I don't know." She shrugged. "Life's weird."

"That it is." He glanced at Faith, who seemed engrossed in watching the two survivors reconnect. "And if you want to know just *how* weird, I actually let Faith pull a makeover on my house. With a bunch of Take Me, I'm Yours crap we picked up the other day."

"Gems, not crap," Faith said, in an annoyed tone.

"I was wondering why you looked so trashed, Faith. Although the homeless look sort of works for you because you're so damn cute." She shook her head at Brody. "She's so damn cute."

"No arguments here."

Faith reached up self-consciously and tried, in

vain, to smooth her hair. "We pulled an all-nighter, speaking of twenty-four-hour shifts. Give me a break. I wasn't exactly thinking fashion, I was thinking food."

Erin laughed. "So, the big makeover, huh?"

"That's why I needed a place to sleep night before last," Brody said, realizing it was the perfect opportunity to lay the rumors to rest. "I got kicked out of my own place so they could work."

"Ah." Erin sipped, looking almost disappointed that there seemed to be no illicit affair in the offing. "So where do you live?"

"Old Norwood's shack," Faith interjected.

"Seriously?"

"No lie, Erin, you should've seen it. It was like 1976, but in a bad way." She shuddered. "Now it's 'da bomb,' according to one of my detention kids who helped me with it."

"You haven't even seen it yet?" Erin asked Brody.

He shook his head. "They're finishing the floors. Hence the 'killing time at the diner' idea."

"Ah, full mystery solved now. Well, you do have to eat," Erin said.

"You'll have to come over and see it," Faith said, in a gushy tone. "It turned out so great." She caught herself, then blushed and looked at Brody. "Listen to me, acting like it's my house. Sorry."

"No," Brody said, although he felt a little uncomfortable with the idea. Inviting people over was diametrically opposed to his hermit plan, but he couldn't say no now. He smiled tightly at Erin. "You're more than welcome to come see the transformation whenever it's convenient for you."

"Thanks. I'd love to. We should all get together there, like a reunion or something."

All.

Meaning the survivors.

Brody's throat closed. He didn't know what to say to that. Another awkward conversation lapse ensued, but it was conveniently covered by the arrival of their food.

Erin cleared her throat and forked into her egg-white omelet. "So—" she cut him a glance "—you married, Brody? Two-point-five kids? Dog? Cat? The whole nine?"

"Nope." He took a bite of his French toast.

She chewed, studying him, then swallowed. "Never?"

"Never. Not yet, at least. I've been…sort of all over the world. Afghanistan, other places. Working. How about you? Ever reach that mommy goal?"

Brody caught Faith's barely perceptible cringe out of the corner of his eye, but he didn't understand what he could possibly have said wrong. Erin brought up the mom thing in the first place, right?

"Not quite, no," she said quietly. "Like you, I'm work, work, work."

As if on cue, the engine company's fire tones went off, clearly audible through the pac set Erin had slung over her shoulder. She was up in an instant, glancing around for the waitress, who waved her off and called out, "Don't worry, honey-bunch. We'll keep it warm or make you a new one when you're able to come back."

Erin raised her hand in thanks, then quickly turned to Brody and Faith. "Sorry. Duty calls." They all glanced at her crew, who were scraping their chairs back and stuffing in last bites.

Brody could relate.

"Listen," she said to Brody. "It's really good to see you back. I know we didn't all get to really know each other…back then, but I hope we can now. Any friend of Mick's is a friend of ours."

He nodded.

"And…I hope…I hope it feels that way to you, too. Good to be here, I mean. With friends."

"I'm getting my bearings. Go."

"See you soon?" she said, hopefully.

"Sure," Brody said, noncommittally.

"Bye, Erin," Faith said with a finger wave.

Erin winked. "See ya, Pipsqueak. We still on for lunch Friday?"

"Wouldn't miss it."

And just like that, the engine company was gone. Brody and Faith remained quiet until the sound of the retreating sirens faded into silence. They turned back to their meals.

Faith cleared her throat. "Erin and I have lunch together once a week, whenever she gets her days off."

"Mmm," Brody said.

"So that wasn't so hard, huh?"

Brody didn't answer, because it had been hard. "She is seriously buff. I wouldn't have expected that. Does she compete in bodybuilding competitions?"

"No way."

"Why 'no way'?"

"Well, she was burned pretty badly in the accident."

"Oh. I didn't know. I didn't see any of the others before I…"

"Left," she said, with absolutely no judgment in her tone. "I know. Anyway, when she healed enough for physical therapy, she went at it hard and never stopped. I think it was her way of coping with the losses. But she's not one to show off her body."

"The losses of her boyfriend and friends?"

"Well, yeah, that. But, you obviously didn't know the other part, or you wouldn't have asked that question."

"Which question?" He remembered her wince. "Oh. Uh-oh. How far did I stick my foot in my mouth?"

"It's not your fault. But Erin was pregnant at the time of the crash."

He closed his eyes briefly. "Oh, no. I wish I'd kept my damn mouth shut. Mick never told me."

"I'm not sure she knew." Faith twisted her mouth to the side sadly. "It sort of all came out after the accident. She and Kevin were going to elope that summer and go to CU Boulder together, live in family housing."

"Her 'be a mom' comment takes on a whole new light." Brody's appetite fled. He pushed his plate away and concentrated on his coffee. "Lost the baby?"

Faith nodded. "It was really awful. Her burns were all to the torso, but they didn't affect any of her internal organs."

"So, can she still realize that mom dream?"

"I don't think so. But Kevin was her soul mate. I don't know that she has the heart for it with anyone else, anyway. At least, not so far." Faith shrugged. "I guess she's pretty badly scarred. Which is why she isn't the show-your-body type."

We're all scarred, Brody thought, in one way or another. "God, that's rough."

"All four of you had it rough. The whole community had it rough, really, but you four most of all."

He didn't want to ask, didn't want to know, to feel their pain as if it were his own. But he had to ask.

"Is Sexy Lexy still around?"

Lexy's boyfriend had been driving the SUV before it rolled. Last he could remember, she was practically crawling on his lap to kiss him. They didn't call her Sexy Lexy for nothing. She'd been a curvy little bombshell. In fact, she'd reminded him of a dark-haired Marilyn Monroe back then.

"Of course she's still around. Don't you recognize her signature bedroom voice?"

He frowned. "What do you mean?"

"She's the supervisor of the communications center for you guys. Police, fire and EMS. I'm sure you've heard her voice a million times over the radio."

"Wild. I had no idea. I haven't been inside the dispatch center itself."

"She's a paraplegic." She raised a hand. "Just so you know. I didn't want it to come as a shock."

"Oh. That's…awful."

"Believe me, it doesn't hold her back. She drives a specially outfitted car, competes in wheelchair races and on a competitive wheelchair volleyball team, and lives fully on her own. She's amazing."

"So, she's doing okay?"

Faith tilted her head to the side. "In most ways."

"What do you mean?"

"Well, she's still Sexy Lexy, but she doesn't date. Refuses to. Believe me, she has interest. I don't know if it's because she uses a chair or because…well, she really feels culpable for what happened. To this day, she takes full, unwavering responsibility. I sometimes think she's punishing herself for what happened by denying herself the chance for love."

He blew out a sigh. He'd have to stop in to dispatch soon and say hello to Lexy.

"What about Cagney? They still call her that?" She was the police chief's daughter at the time of the accident. Her real name was Casey, but her nickname had been Cagney since she was about five, an homage to the old popular cop show, *Cagney & Lacey*. If he remembered correctly, she hadn't gone to prom with her boyfriend, who'd been a rebel from the wrong side of town. Her dad hated the guy. Instead, for no logical reason, she'd gone with some other fill-in, a friend of hers, he guessed, although it had seemed as though they barely knew each other.

"They do still call her that. She's a cop."

Brody inhaled at the wrong time and aspirated some coffee. As far as he could remember, she and her dad got along about as well as water and electricity. She'd refined covert, passive rebellion to an art form back in the day. In fact, she'd been the one to provide all the alcohol for prom night. He had no idea where she'd gotten it, unless she swiped it from the chief's liquor cabinet, which he wouldn't have put past her. She'd been so upset about not getting to go with her boyfriend.

After he'd coughed until his eyes watered, he exclaimed, "What?"

"I know. Shocker, isn't it? All she wanted was to get away from her dad and everything about his authoritarian ways, but after…well, it was like she lost all her fight."

A sadness enveloped him. "Didn't she want to be a writer or something? A dancer?"

"An artist, sort of punk-retro. She paints. And sculpts. And a whole bunch of other artistic stuff, or at least she used to. But her dad always wanted her to be a cop. Or something—" finger quotes "—practical." Faith shrugged. "He won, I guess."

Brody couldn't help but feel a little angry about

that. Her father had been heavy-handed, according to Mick. "Is she happy?"

"Are you?"

Brody cut his glance to the black-and-white-tiled floor briefly, then brought it back up to Faith's face. "At this moment, yes."

She graced him with a smile so ethereal, his gut squeezed. "You're so sweet, Brody Austin. But you're also as evasive as one of my detention kids."

He hiked one brow. "You're way too astute for me."

"I've had a lot of practice." She leveled a stare at him. "Just answer my question. Generally, Brody, are you happy?"

He shrugged. "As happy as you can be when you're…well, not."

"Why aren't you?"

"That's what I'm trying to figure out." He pulled one leg up and rested his foot on the banquette seat. "I mean, there's the obvious. Guilt. Regrets. All that. I'm a little lost is all."

This time she reached for his hand. He knew he should give hers a friendly squeeze and break the contact, but he just couldn't. He missed human connection, touch, and hers felt so sincere, so filled with caring. Hers felt like exactly what he needed. It was as if he were a dying plant, and

Faith had somehow become his water, sun and soil.

"I'm so sorry you feel that way, honey."

"It's nothing for you to apologize for. I made my own misery."

Her face brightened. "But see, that means you can end your own misery, too. You just have to find out how, and then do it."

"I wish it were that easy."

"I'll help you in any way I can."

"You do help."

"Everyone should have a chance to be happy. Blissful, actually." She leaned in. "Life, liberty and the pursuit of happiness, right?"

"Well, if you want the truth, that's why I came back." He shook his head. "I know. It doesn't make much sense to me, either, considering I swore I'd never set foot here again. But here I am. Searching."

She cocked her head to the side. "Which of those inalienable rights are you searching for?"

He thought about it a minute, then squeezed her fingers. "You know? I guess I'm looking for all of them." A life, freedom from the prison of guilt he'd been locked in for far too long, and—if he was lucky—maybe even a little bit of happiness along the way.

Chapter Eight

"Okay, keep your eyes closed."

"I am."

"All the way."

"They're closed, they're closed," Brody said, as he stumbled over a rock and flailed out blindly for her shoulder to steady himself. He almost knocked her on her face before he felt her brace herself.

"Oops. You okay?"

"Yeah. But, just a thought. It would help if you watch where I'm walking, since I can't."

"Sorry," Faith said, slowing down a bit. "I'm just so excited. I can't wait for you to see the place."

"Don't ever apply to be a seeing-eye dog," he muttered. "You'd fail miserably, and not solely because you aren't a dog."

He heard her working the key into the lock, not once, but twice. "Did you buy me a dead bolt?"

"Brody Austin, are you peeking?" she demanded.

"No, I'm using my keen deductive powers, otherwise known as ears. You unlocked two locks. Previously it was just the one."

"Oh. Smart-ass. Well then, yes. Never can be too safe. I knew you'd never get around to it, so I went ahead and did it for you."

As they stepped over the threshold, he didn't even have to open his eyes to sense the change. The whole place smelled different. First of all, it smelled cleaner than he or Norwood had ever had it, which he hated to admit. But above that were the mingled scents of fresh paint, new rugs, wood. He even detected the scent of plants and—he stopped breathing for a second to listen—was that gurgling water? "Can I look?"

"Take off your shoes first."

"Huh? I'm not going to have one of those no-shoes-in-the-house places, if that's what you're thinking."

"I'm not, Brody, for God's sake. Do you think I don't know you at all? Just do it."

With a sigh, he toed off one running shoe, then the other. "Happy?"

"Socks, too."

He reached down blindly and obliged, feeling some sort of squishy doormat beneath his soles.

"Okay, step forward."

He stepped forward onto sleek hardwood…but it felt warm. "What's this?"

"Radiant heat. It's under all your floors, which are bamboo throughout, incidentally. A totally environmentally-friendly, renewable source. Anyway, this place is pretty drafty, but you will never have to walk on cold floors again."

"It feels great. Good idea." He did need to upgrade the windows to keep winter's chill out, but with summer coming, he had time for that. "Can I see the rest now? Please?"

"Okay, on a count of three. One, two, three—"

Brody opened his eyes and felt like he'd been zapped by a stun gun. It was so completely transformed, he could hardly recognize it. "Wow." Long pause. "Faith."

She stared up at him with happiness and expectation in her eyes. Her hands were clasped tightly at her chest. "What does that mean? What do you think? Do you like it? Do you want to kill me? Say something."

He held out a hand. "Hang on, let me take it all in. There's so much to look at."

The large arched wall with the fireplace had been painted a slate-blue color that made the floor-to-ceiling river rock stand out in a way he'd never imagined. He'd hardly noticed the ugly, sooty thing before, but now it was a clean, pristine showpiece.

"We had it cleaned and checked. It works for when you need it."

"Thanks." For now, she'd put some kind of multileveled candle thing inside the firebox, with fat gold beeswax candles letting off a flickering glow. She'd added a dark, polished-wood mantel that matched the new dark-stained bamboo floors, but strangely, the large space above the mantel remained empty. It seemed like a weird detail for them to have missed, but maybe they wanted to give him the chance to find a piece of artwork that spoke to him to fill the space.

The other walls were no longer cheap paneling, circa 1970, but smooth drywall in that coffee-with-cream color. The place looked so much brighter, so much homier. All the windows had bamboo rolling shades, but they were flanked with slate-blue drapes banded with the coffee color at the bottom.

"The drapes are all thermal."

"That's perfect."

The countertops had been replaced with a creamy granite and extended out to provide bar space. Three bar stools perched beneath it.

Brody pointed. "Did we find those on the curb?"

"Yep. Amazing what a can of brown spray paint and some new fabric for the seat cushions can do, huh?"

The floral couch and love seat he'd stridently protested against were now unrecognizable. They'd been reupholstered in a soft-looking, simple blue-and-brown fabric that pulled together all the other colors in the room, and at right angles to each other in front of the fireplace, they made a cozy conversation area. "I can't believe you transformed those ugly couches. They don't look at all like they used to."

"That was the point, smart guy." She shrugged. "I took an upholstery class through adult ed. It was fun. See all the pillows?"

"Yeah. You bought those, right?"

"Not." She grinned smugly. "My detention student, Jorge Gabaldon made every single one."

"Dang." He studied them anew. "Under duress?"

"Nope, he volunteered. I didn't even know Jorge could sew. The kid's talented. Of course, they're all talented in one way or another," she said like a proud mama.

He smiled at her. She'd make a great mom someday.

He axed that line of thinking immediately.

Instead, he turned his attention to the plush area rugs here and there, the curbside table and chairs they'd somehow transformed from out-of-style to state-of-the-art. Even the ugly lamps they'd collected were redone and beautiful. "What happened to that square coffee table we snatched?"

She pointed to a leather-upholstered ottoman in front of the couches, with a wooden tray angled on one corner. "Repurposed. You can put your feet on it, or use the tray to set drinks."

They'd even mounted a copper-backed, lighted fountain on the wall next to the front door, hence the gurgling. He'd never lived anywhere as beautiful.

"Faith, this is amazing. I don't even know what to say. Except maybe you *should* quit your job and go into this professionally."

She beamed. "Wait, you haven't even seen it all. Come on." She took him by the hand and gave him a tour of the new appliances, the updated bathroom, new washer and dryer, spare bedroom, which they'd set up as a small office, and finally she unveiled his bedroom.

The focal point was a king-size platform bed they'd built and stained themselves, backed by a toffee-colored, leather-upholstered headboard. The medium-chocolate walls had been treated somehow to make them resemble suede, cream-colored bedding—very sleek, nothing fussy—muted lighting, unobtrusive candles, and not a flower in sight. Masculine with a definite sexual undertone, the room exceeded his expectations. "This is unbelievable."

"Unbelievable good or bad?"

He looked at her as if she were joking. "What do you think? Look at the place."

She laughed. "We bought you one of those Tempurpedic mattresses. Expensive, but worth it. Well, *you* bought it." She waved her arm toward the bed. "Give it a try. It conforms to your body."

Brody sat on the edge then flopped back. The comfort of this bed was so far removed from the horror of his previous inherited bed, he didn't even think they should be called the same thing. He groaned with pleasure.

"Like it?"

"Love it."

"Can I try?"

An alarm bell binged in his head. "Sure."

She flopped down beside him. "Ahhh. I should splurge on one of these suckers myself."

Or just sleep over here with me, Brody

thought, before he could stop himself. He sat up suddenly, then stood and ran a hand down his face slowly.

Faith sat up, too, bracing her hands behind her on his mattress. The position emphasized the amazing curves of her body. A few locks of her silky dark hair draped over one shoulder, teasing the top curve of her breast. "What's wrong?"

He managed a sincere smile. "Nothing. I'm just overwhelmed by all of it, by the fact that you did this." He laid a palm on his chest. "For me."

"I wanted to."

"I honestly don't know how to thank you."

She stood. "I'd settle for a hug."

Brody hesitated only briefly before wrapping his arms around her small, shapely form. She reached up and wrapped her arms around his neck, and they fit together like two halves of a whole.

He studied her face, trying not to focus on her bare, moist lips. But, damn, it was difficult. She seemed to sense it, flicking her tongue to moisten them.

His gaze shot to hers, and held. His own heart pounded, and he could see the pulse quickening in her long, sexy neck. He loved that pulse in her neck.

"Thank you," he said, his voice coming out in a tone that totally betrayed his lust.

"You're more than welcome." Faith stood on her tippy-toes and moved closer. She hesitated, as though waiting for him to protest.

He wanted to. Needed to. But couldn't.

So she kissed him softly on the lips. Shyly, testing.

He tried to pull back. He did. But he couldn't. Instead, he kissed her back, deepened the kiss into something that had nothing to do with their history or anything else, other than pure, searing, explosive attraction.

He pulled her body up and closer to his, with one hand wound through her long hair and cradling her neck and the other at the small of her back. He wanted to press her against him, meld her softness with his instant hardness. She tasted like candy and smelled fresh as the air after a rainstorm, even after pulling an all-nighter. This was no perfume or lotion or soap. It was all Faith, all natural. And he loved it.

An image of Mick slashed into his brain without warning, shocking him into reality. He pulled away so quickly Faith stumbled. She righted herself and brought the back of one hand to her full bottom lip, plumper now and redder from the kiss.

Her eyes widened, became wary. "Wh-what's wrong?"

"Nothing, I—" He didn't know what to say.

The hurt showed plainly in her eyes, but she

braved her way through it and smiled. When she spoke, though, her tone was overly bright. "Well, I suppose you had a long night at work, and I definitely need a nap. I think I'll head home and let you enjoy the place alone."

"Wait—" He reached out and grabbed her hand. She watched him, expectantly.

"I'm…sorry. I didn't mean—"

"It's okay."

"No. It's not. Everything's a jumble in my brain, Faith. I'm just not—"

"Brody, I understand." She tilted her head to the side slightly and smiled so sweetly, it pierced his heart. "Really."

He caressed the back of her hand with his thumb. "I'm not so sure you do."

"Well then, someday when you're ready, you can explain it to me. Okay? See you Friday." She kissed the pads of her fingers and blew him the kiss, then she was gone.

Brody sat on the edge of his new bed and buried his face in his hands. He had never felt more alone in his life.

Faith sat in her office at school the next day, staring at the framed picture of Mick that had claimed the prized corner spot on her desk since the day she'd moved in. She tried to find an answer to her current *man-tastrophe* in her sister's beautiful eyes.

That whole kiss thing? Disastrous.

The verdict was in. Faith had absolutely no guy skills. She might resemble her sister, but inside she was still that geeky, clueless, bookworm she'd always been. Most women could tell when a guy was interested, and there were only, like, a zillion articles on the subject in every single women's magazine, every single freaking month.

Not Faith.

No matter how hard she tried, how many articles she perused, she inevitably read guys totally wrong. It was as if they were written in Greek, and she was never going to learn that language.

Hello, she knew Brody wanted to kiss her. At least at first. One thing about the male physique, it gave off, well, *signals* that were impossible to hide when their bodies were pressed against yours.

Maybe that just happened, though. Autonomic response or something, like blinking or sneezing.

Still, just as the coals were heating up between them—she'd thought—he'd pulled away so abruptly, you would think they'd been doing something illicit. Criminal, even.

For God's sake, he wasn't one of her students. And now he probably thought she was some trampy guy hunter, throwing herself at any available male with a pulse and a ringless left hand. She groaned, threading her fingers into her hair. If it wasn't totally against her personal and professional ethics, she'd tell Jason Cole that he'd been completely wrong about "the paramedic dude being all kinds of down wit' her."

Whatever.

Brody Austin was the first guy she'd been truly interested in for a couple of years at least, and he wanted *jack* to do with her. Life sucked.

Her glance lifted to the photo of Mick again, forever suspended in that moment, and a needle of guilt poked at her.

No. Life didn't suck. Life was something to be treasured and savored every day. But her current situation—or as her kids would say, her *sitch*—sucked.

Her door banged open and Jason sauntered in, then stopped in his tracks. "Man, brah—I mean, Miz M. Who peed in your Cheetos?"

He caught her off guard, and Faith smirked. "Jason, can you please find a more socially appropriate way of expressing that question?"

"Hmmm." He grabbed his chin and rubbed his

soul patch with one finger. "Who urinated in your crunchy, cheese-flavored snack food?"

She shook her head. "That's not exactly what I meant."

"But it was funny, huh?"

"Hilarious. Have a seat. What's up, buddy?"

He slouched into the chair opposite her desk, legs sprawled wide, then squinted up toward the corner of her office. "Let's see…Pops is still drunk, Mom is a doormat who won't do a thing about it, my teachers—especially that English-teaching Nazi—think I have a 'tude, when all I have are questions. And nobody thinks I'll amount to anything. Except you, but we all know you're delusional. So I guess it's biz as usual."

She smiled.

"Oh, and I did turn sixteen yesterday."

Her jaw dropped. "Jason, why didn't you tell me it was your birthday?"

"Who cares?"

"I do. What did you do to celebrate?"

His eyes widened, incredulous. "Celebrate?" He waved his hands in front of her slowly. "Hello, Miz M, wake up from your Disney life. The only good thing that happened on my birthday was that Pops didn't kick my ass for once. Passed out before he got the opportunity."

Sadness overwhelmed Faith so unexpectedly, tears stung her eyes. She was usually able to remain detached, but her feelings were raw at the moment, and she really liked Jason Cole as a person.

She gulped, got a rein on her emotions. "I need you to stay after school today. Meet me in the cafeteria."

"Aw, man." He slumped further. "What I do now? I turned in my stupid English paper. I didn't even title it Another Stupid English Paper like last time."

"You're not in trouble, goof. We're going to throw you a birthday party."

His face reddened, but he tried to look bored. "I don't want no party. I've never had one before."

"Well, there's a first time for everything." She narrowed her eyes and aimed a finger at him. "You're staying."

"Fine." He released a dramatic sigh. "Speaking of staying…there was something I wanted to talk to you about."

"Whip it on me."

He fidgeted in his chair. Cleared his throat. "Well, now that I'm sixteen, I'm thinking of dropping out, getting a job so I can move out."

"Not happening, Jason, and don't bring it up again."

The speed and certainty of her response seemed

to throw him. For a moment, he just blinked at her, openmouthed. "B-but, the law says I can leave school at sixteen."

"And Ms. Montesantos says you can't."

"But—"

"No! No buts." She aimed a finger at him. "I'm not going to let you ruin your life. Don't you see, if you drop out, you're going to follow in the footsteps of your father. Is that really what you want?"

He sulked. "No."

"Then you'll be at school every day for the next two years unless you're puking sick or in the hospital, understand?" She smacked her palm down on the desk. "And don't make me embarrass you by driving to your house and dragging you out of bed if you don't show. Because, trust me, Mr. Man, I will."

For the fleetest of moments, his eyes showed little-boy fear. "But what if…what if you aren't here in two years."

She knew, right at that moment, that she had become the hand grasp for this kid. She had a chance at changing the direction of his life, and she couldn't blow it. Wouldn't. No matter what it took. "I am absolutely not going anywhere. And when you graduate, I'm going to be the one to hand you your diploma."

"Swear?"

"I try not to—" she winked "—but you have my promise." She made an *X* over her heart.

A small smile teased one corner of his mouth. "Cool, then. If you'll show, I'll show."

"Deal." Faith reached her hand across the desk, and they knocked fists on the agreement, then Jason stood up. "And don't forget to show up this afternoon."

"Oh yeah, I forgot to ask. How'd the ambulance dude like his crib?"

"You can ask him yourself. He's coming to your birthday party." I don't care if he wants to kiss me or not, she thought to herself, if I have to drug him and drag him here, he'll be at this kid's party.

Jason tried to hide it, but he looked pleased. "Dang. Musta dug it then."

"Oh, yeah," Faith said. "He agreed. Da bomb."

"Smell ya later," Jason said, raising his hand as he left.

The minute he was gone, Faith picked up the phone and dialed Brody's number. When he answered, she said, "Hey, it's Faith. I need a favor, and it's an emergency."

Chapter Nine

All the detention kids who'd worked on the house makeover, some of Jason's other friends, a couple of the office ladies, one of the cafeteria ladies, the principal and Brody showed up for Jason's impromptu birthday party.

As promised, Brody had picked up a great ice-cream cake and some other beverages and snacks, including Cheetos—Faith's little private joke with Jason. He'd also stopped at Altitude Books on Main Street, and found the book on quantum physics Faith wanted to give Jason as a gift. He'd even had it gift-wrapped and bought a birthday card for Faith to sign.

Beyond that, Brody himself had gotten Jason a thank-you birthday card for the work he'd done on the house and included a $100 gift certificate to the bookstore. It was, Faith thought, the perfect gift for a kid who read voraciously on the sly and wanted to learn so much, so fast, that he actually annoyed many of his teachers.

He brought smaller thank-you gift cards for the other five boys who'd transformed his house—to the arcade, the movies, the coffee shop, the bookstore—and he let them pick what they wanted.

They made Jason suffer through an off-key rendition of "Happy Birthday," forced him to make a wish, then strong-armed him into blowing out the sixteen candles. Of course, Faith could tell he was enjoying every moment, in spite of his dramatic eye rolling and sighing.

After the histrionics, there wasn't any hesitation about digging into the cake and the other snack foods, though. The principal had brought in a boom box so the boys could play some music while they sat around, jaw-jacking and laughing.

After a bit, the other adults left one by one until only Brody and Faith were left with the kids. They sat in a couple of cafeteria chairs a few feet away from the sprawl of boys.

"You have no idea how much I appreciate you doing this for me on the fly," she told Brody, her focus on Jason across the way.

"No problem. He and the others did a great job on my house. I owe them. And you."

Faith crossed her arms over her torso. "I mean, the kid's never had his birthday celebrated at home. Ever." Her lips pressed into a thin line, and she shook her head. "I think that's criminal. And he's such a good kid underneath all the bravado. Tenderhearted and scared, too. His intellectual potential blows the AP kids' out of the water. I just wish he could get it all in sync."

Brody rested his elbows on his knees, hands wound loosely together, and studied her. "You really love them, don't you?"

She glanced at Brody with a flicker of a smile. "Yeah. I do. It's never fun to be the forgotten one."

"You never felt like that growing up, did you?"

Her eyes widened. "No. No. Don't misunderstand. My parents are great. But I wasn't in the popular group like Mick. Star athlete, center of every party, friends with all the various cliques, student council. I mean, she was Mick Montesantos, know what I'm saying?"

"I know exactly what you're saying."

"Same as you, probably, at your own school."

He shook his head. "Mick outshone me, too. But I do get it. She was one of those standouts."

"I know. And I loved that about her. I wasn't ever jealous—I thought it was cool. We were far apart enough in age that there wasn't any competition. But me? I was a dork, and so were most of my friends."

"I can't believe that."

"It's true. You've seen my athletic prowess up close and personal. My friends and I weren't even fringe popular. We were invisible. I was probably the most visible, but only because I was—" she made finger quotes "—the dead girl's sister."

"Ow. Harsh."

She shrugged. "It just was. But the point is, school is one thing. Some of my friends faced the same kind of thing at home, though. I felt terrible for them. I guess that's what drew me to this career. Plus—" She pressed her lips together.

"What?"

"I just know what a pivotal time adolescence is. A trauma—any kind—can lead you down a healing, transformative path, or a perilous, destructive one."

"You chose correctly."

"Eventually." She huffed out a humorless laugh.

"Believe me, after I lost Mick, I was so damn angry, I had to fight the urge to go the destructive route—to myself, my life, my education. Drink, smoke, sample drugs, slut around. I mean, who cared? My sister, my best friend was dead."

He felt her words like a punch. "Did you do that?"

"I dabbled," she said unapologetically. "Then, one day, for no particular reason, I woke up with the clear realization that continuing down the wrong path would've broken Mick's heart. She didn't want that for me. She wanted the world for me." She glanced around the room. "And I want the world for these kids, even if the other adults in their lives don't seem to care. I eventually got it together, then I chose to show other kids how to make that same decision, what kind of personal power it can bring to their lives."

For a long moment, he just stared at her, thinking about his own poor choices after the trauma. She may have been a knock-kneed little bookworm when it all happened, but she was a hell of a lot stronger than he had ever been. "You're an amazing woman, Faith," he said.

Then why can't you love me? she wondered. But she looked away from him quickly and shrugged. "Nah. I'm just human. I do my best, day by day, same as all the rest of us."

* * *

"Okay, spill. You're falling for Brody, aren't you?" Erin asked pointedly, almost the moment their Diet Pepsis had been delivered to the table. She popped the paper off one end of her straw and blew the rest of it toward Faith, who laughed when it hit her in the cheek. "Not that I blame you. He is smokin' hot."

"Falling? More like fallen. And he is incredible." Faith felt glum and ugly and forgotten, just like those lovely high school days. She blew her own straw wrapper toward Erin, who caught it in midair. It was nice not always having to be the adult. "But it doesn't matter. He hates me."

"Oh, shut up," Erin said. "He doesn't hate you, freak. How could he possibly hate you?"

"Okay, maybe not *hate,* but there is zero reciprocal interest, trust me."

"And how, exactly, do you know that?"

Heat rose to Faith's cheeks. "Well, the other day after I showed him his place…I…I kissed him."

"What?" Erin shrieked, before glancing around apologetically at the nearby diners. She leaned in and lowered her tone. "What happened? Tell me everything."

So Faith did, start to finish, ending with her regrettable braveness. "I only hesitated a second, but then I said screw it and kissed him—"

"That's awesome!"

"—but he pushed me away."

"Oh. Like, pushed, pushed? Harsh-o-rama."

"No, it was more like he pulled away so fast, I almost lost my balance."

Erin frowned, perplexed. "Do you think he's gay?"

"Oh, no." Faith sipped her soda, then lifted an index finger. "Let me clarify. He didn't pull away immediately. In fact, he kissed me back, and it wasn't some chaste, brotherly, forehead kiss either."

Erin waggled her eyebrows, her mouth spreading into a full grin. "Details, details, please."

Faith laughed nervously, but Erin was the only female friend with whom she discussed this kind of thing. "We're talking, his hand threaded into the back of my hair, pressing me into him, full body, passionate kiss. And…let's just say, it certainly *felt* like he was able to be turned on by a woman, if you catch my drift." She sighed. "Just, apparently, not by boring old *moi*."

"Forgive me for pointing out the obvious, but it was you, your kiss, that gave him the—" Erin rolled her hand in the area of her lap.

"Shh. Cut it out. People will notice."

"No, they won't. But you have to admit it."

Erin had a point. "Then why did he pull away?"

A paused ensued, while they both thought about this. "Do you think it has something to do with Mick?"

"Why would it?" Faith shrugged. "They were inseparable friends, but they were never involved. Not like that."

"Well, *duh*. But I guess I meant…I don't know, just the trauma of the whole thing. I'm sure you're a huge reminder."

"Well then, I might as well write it off." Faith threw her hands up in the air. "I'll always remind him of Mick, so I'm screwed."

"Don't jump to conclusions—"

They clammed up while their lunches were delivered, and they smiled their thanks at the waitress before resuming the conversation.

"Give him time, Pip. He's obviously going through some heavy stuff being back in the Gulch. Stuff the rest of us have had years to deal with. He chose to run rather than deal, and it's all catching up with him now. That's some serious healing." She tilted her head. "He'll come around. Who could resist you?"

"And if he doesn't?"

Erin patted her hand. "Then he's an idiot and I'll beat him up for you. Don't worry. He's a big guy, but I fight dirty. I seriously think I could take him."

Faith laughed. "You always know how to make me feel better."

"So, when's the big family dinner?"

"Tonight," Faith said, tucking her hair behind her ears. "Poor guy, I know he's dreading it. Not dinner, per se. He loves my parents. But just coming into the house." She crinkled her nose with sympathy. "Talk about reminders of Mick. He'll be smothered by them. You know my parents, they never change anything."

Erin hiked her head to the side. "It's just another hurdle. I hate to go all tough love on the guy when he's obviously still so vulnerable, but he needs to jump the hurdles, one by one, if he ever wants to heal completely from what we all went through. It's the only way."

"Are you healed completely?" Faith asked, in a soft voice.

Erin hesitated, swirling her straw through the crushed ice in her cup. "Mostly. Not completely. But I'm not exactly sure what'll do it for me." She paused. "I guess I'd like to get married someday, but I picked the wrong job for that."

"What do you mean?"

"Men are intimidated by female firefighters. Either intimidated or turned on in an icky way. Plus…I guess the bottom-line reason is, there's just nobody who measures up to Kev, and unfortunately, I'm still using him as my yardstick. Pathetic, I know."

"It isn't. I love you, Er. You've been like my big sister since I lost Mick. I want you to be completely healed. I want you to fall in love and get married. All of it. You deserve it. And Kevin would've wanted it for you."

Erin's eyes misted. "I know. Someday. Maybe." But she sounded doubtful.

"For now, I'm happy enough. And I love you, too. Now let's talk fun stuff for a while."

They finished their lunches discussing more upbeat topics like kids ditching class and the ridiculous uproar at Erin's station house because someone on the previous shift had opened a new ketchup when a half-used bottle was clearly visible in the fridge, like it freakin' mattered. They compared the *new* self-tanners and dished celebrity gossip. After they'd paid and walked out together, the two of them hugged by Faith's Mini Cooper.

"Call me tomorrow morning after the dinner, okay? Or tonight even, if it's not too late. I want to know every detail."

"I will."

They broke apart. Erin lowered her chin. "And as for Brody—"

"I know, I know. Give it time."

Erin grabbed both her hands and lowered herself to meet Faith eye to eye. "No, listen to me. If he really feels like the one, Faith, don't give up. Give him time, but go for it." Her eyes misted over again. "You don't get the chance to find your soul mate all that often in this jacked-up world. If you believe he's truly the one, then jump in with both feet. If not for yourself, then for me and Kev, and all we could've been."

It smelled the same.

How could a house smell the same after more than a decade? He couldn't pinpoint the scent as something exact, but whatever it was catapulted him right back to the good old days. It reminded him of friendship and laughter, carefree, endless futures and open arms. It reminded him, stupidly, of heated air hockey tournaments in the basement and movie nights with enough heavily buttered popcorn to make them all want to gag.

His gut swirled.

How was he going to make it through this evening when he couldn't even take a step off the tile entryway and go farther into the house? He clutched the bottle of wine and bouquet of flowers like weapons, as Elisa fussed around him, welcoming him in and exclaiming over the bouquet. Abel thanked him for the wine and went to uncork it so it could breathe.

If only I could breathe.

Faith, he noticed, leaned one shoulder against the archway that led to the kitchen and family room, one bare foot resting atop the other. She wore jeans and a casual T-shirt. Her hair hung loose, and her only jewelry was a leather ankle bracelet. She stood there, arms crossed. Watching him, assessing him.

She knew.

She knew exactly how difficult this was for him, even if the elder Montesantoses hadn't caught on to his extreme stress. Faith, he realized suddenly, was his safety net, and knowing that eased his anxiety level a bit. Especially because things had been so weird between them lately, thanks to his stupid issues.

He smiled at her.

She winked back. "Come on in," she said, softly, so her parents couldn't hear. "It's okay."

"In. Right." He took a deep breath and blew it out, then stepped forward into the living room that, as he looked around, made him realize it hadn't changed a bit since the last time he'd been there.

Faith pushed off the wall and sauntered toward

him. He couldn't figure out how a five-foot-nothing woman could manage to look like she had model long legs, but Faith pulled it off. She leaned in and whispered, "As soon as I can talk the 'rents into it, I'm pulling an extreme makeover on this place, too."

The coil of tension in his chest loosened, and he laughed. "You're horrible."

"Well, it's no Norwood Nightmare, but come on." She waved her arms around at the pristine but, admittedly, dated decor.

"I hope you're hungry," Elisa called from the kitchen. "I made your favorite. Well, your old favorite."

Faith took his hand and tugged him toward the kitchen, reassuring him with her sweet glances.

"Chicken enchiladas?" Brody asked, hopefully.

"You still like them, *m'ijo?*"

They entered the kitchen together as Elisa pulled a bubbling casserole dish out of the oven. "I love them. I can't believe you remembered."

"Don't be silly. Of course I remembered."

"I can't wait." Brody laid a palm on his abdomen. "Nobody makes them like you do."

Elisa laughed. "Oh, you sweet-talker. Go on, kids. Sit down and relax. Abel, pour us all some of that wine while I finish up here."

Abel did his wife's bidding, handing everyone a glass. "Come to the table for a minute, honey," he said to his wife. "Let's make a toast."

Elisa dried her hands on her apron, then joined them, all smiles. Faith and Brody stood. Abel put his arm around Elisa's waist and looked from his wife to his daughter to Brody. "Here's to family. To having our boy back with us. And, as always, to our beloved Mick."

A huge lump rose in Brody's throat as they clinked glasses. He didn't think he could manage a single swallow of the wine, but he did. Somehow.

Afterward, he cleared his throat as the panic descended upon him. He needed to get away, to breathe. "Do you mind if I use the restroom to wash my hands before dinner?"

"Of course not, *m'ijo*," Elisa said. "The plumbing in the powder room down here is acting up, but just use the girls' bathroom upstairs. You remember where it is."

Brody froze.

Beneath the table, Faith squeezed his knee. He glanced over, and she nodded. *You can do this,* she seemed to be saying. *You can handle it.*

He took in a huge breath and eased it out. "I'll be right back."

Dread beating in his chest, Brody climbed the

stairs to the second floor. He knew exactly which steps would squeak, and they did. He almost expected Mick to pop her head out of her bedroom and say, "Hey, jerk. It's about time you showed up."

He held his breath as he passed the closed door to her old bedroom, releasing it as he entered the restroom and locked the door. For a moment he just braced his arms wide on the sink counter, hung his head and took some deep breaths. When his brain stopped swirling and he had a handle on the panic, he splashed his face with ice-cold water and dried it on the embroidered guest towel. Looking at his face in the mirror, he barely recognized the man staring back at him. He looked pale, shaky. He needed to cowboy the hell up and enjoy this evening with people he loved. He owed that to Mick.

He stood up straighter, stretched his neck side to side, washed his hands and then left the bathroom. On his way back down the hallway, he stopped in front of Mick's door. *Breathe in. Breathe out.* Reaching out, he laid his palm on the door, just to see if he could somehow still feel her there. But it was just a door, like any other door.

"You can go in if you want."

He spun around to find Faith coming out of her parents' bedroom carrying a huge, wrapped package. "Sorry. I didn't mean to surprise you. They sent me up to get this."

He concentrated on the package and not her suggestion. "What is it?"

"A housewarming gift for you. But you can't open it until after the pineapple upside-down cake—Mom's rules." They stared at each other for a minute.

"Anyway, really. You can go in."

"I don't know."

"Whenever I'm especially missing her, I go in there. Sometimes I just take a nap on her bed."

He wanted to. But terror clutched him all of a sudden. "Will you…come with me?"

"Of course." She set the cumbersome package aside, then joined him in front of Mick's door. They didn't move for a moment, then she looked up at him. "You open the door, Brody. I think it's important."

He gave a jerky nod, then reached out a shaky hand and turned the knob. As the room came into full view, his knees almost buckled. They'd left it as Mick's room, just the way he remembered it.

"Come on, honey. Just come in. You can feel her in here. It's beautiful. It really is."

Grasping tightly to Faith's hand, he walked into the middle of the room and did a slow circle, taking it all in. The snapshots stuck in the edge of her mirror, rugby stuff here and there. The guitar she'd never really learned to play.

He had the urge to go to her closet, smell her clothes to see if any essence of her remained. It had been too long, though. The realistic part of him knew that. "God, Faith," he said on a pained exhale. "How do you stand it?"

"You work through your grief, that's how. You remember the good times. You talk to her, as if she were sitting right next to you." She faced him and took both of his hands in her own. "And actually, some spiritual beliefs say she really is right here with us, like nothing has changed for her. Only for us. You remind yourself daily that she loves you, and she's looking out for you. She *loved* you, Brody. You were the best friend she'd ever had in her life."

He clenched his jaw so hard, but he couldn't hold the wave of grief-swirled emotion back. Silent tears began to stream down his cheeks. He could feel his whole body tremoring with the effort not to sob.

"Come here." Faith pulled him into a hug and held him tightly as his tears soaked the shoulder of her T-shirt. Racking sobs broke free from his chest.

"It's going to be okay, Brody. Just let it out. Let it out. We all have to go through this part."

"I'm...so sorry. You're so strong and centered, and I'm a mess. A weak mess."

She hugged him tighter, and he hugged back. "You're not. You're normal. If you hadn't come back, if you'd never faced your grief, that would be a problem. This part sucks, but you *have* to let yourself go through it, Brody. You can't run forever."

"I don't want to run anymore."

"I know." She smoothed one hand down the back of his head. "But you're home now. And you're dealing with it. I'm so proud of you. So proud."

They pulled apart, and Brody smeared away his tears with the backs of his hands. "I should go splash my face or something. I don't want your parents to see me looking like some kind of an emotional wuss."

She laughed, softly. "Want me to wait for you?"

He managed a wistful smile. "Is it a wuss signal if I say yes?"

"Of course not, dummy."

He reached a hand for her, and she grabbed it, held on. "You're the best person I know, Faith."

A look he couldn't decipher flickered over her face, then she hiked her chin. "You're pretty tolerable in small doses yourself, Austin." She squeezed, then released his hand with a flirtatious smile. "We'd better get down there before Mom starts squawking about dinner getting cold, *blah-blah-blah.*"

He nodded, and they left Mick's room one after the other. Faith snicked the door shut as Brody, once again, splashed his face with cold water in the bathroom he knew so well.

With a great deal of his pain released, his chest felt lighter, and his stomach had settled enough to send up hunger signals. He was more than ready for dinner. He came out of the bathroom and found Faith standing at the top of the stairs waiting, the large package resting against her leg. She lifted it. "Ready?"

He nodded. "Thank you."

"Of course. I'd do anything for you, Brody. I don't think you've accepted that yet—" she held up her palm "—but I'm willing to wait until you figure it out."

Chapter Ten

They'd enjoyed a delicious dinner together,
laughing and passing stories back and forth about
the past, the present, Brody's home makeover,
Faith's students. Finally, stuffed and happy, they
settled into the living room with cups of coffee
that, thankfully, Elisa had brewed instead of Faith.

In light of all his fears, the evening had turned
out better than expected, thanks to Faith bringing
him into Mick's room and comforting him when
he couldn't manage to get his emotions in check
alone. Simply entering the room had felt like a
huge, healing step.

At a lag in the conversation, Faith glanced over at her parents, anticipation sparkling in her eyes. "Mom, should we…?"

Elisa nodded. Abel, too, and then he stood and walked over to the wrapped package and lifted it carefully. He brought it over to Brody and set it down.

"We had a chance to take a peek at your house before it was finished, and we asked Faith if we could contribute the artwork for above the fireplace. Our gift to you, to warm the house."

Brody looked at Faith. "That explains the big blank spot. You were so meticulous, I wondered what had happened with that detail."

"Open it," Faith said, her eyes serious.

That put his brain on alert.

He cleared his throat, then carefully peeled back the taped corners of the brown wrapping paper. The painting, or whatever it was, had to be about twenty inches by twenty-four unframed, because the package was huge.

When he finally had the paper off, he turned the frame around to look at the image it held. What he found was a huge, double-matted photograph of him and Mick after the nastiest, muddiest, most fun rugby game they'd ever played. The officials had wanted to call it on account of an unexpected torrential rainstorm, but the players begged until the officials and coaches gave in. Sure, it probably wasn't regulation play, but if the kids wanted to slide around on the soggy field in the mud, they might as well.

It had been sloppy and slippery and so damn fun. They'd won, and this photo was snapped just after the victory. Both of them soaked to the bone and literally covered in mud, Mick had jumped up and Brody caught her around the hips with one arm. His other arm and both of Mick's were raised in exuberant victory as they faced the camera. It was one of those spur-of-the-moment snapshots that ended up looking like a professional photo. He'd never seen an image with their grins so carefree, so well deserved. So grimy. So unbelievably young.

It was as if this single photograph perfectly encapsulated their entire, irreplaceable friendship.

The double matting matched Faith's color theme, and the frame complemented the dark bamboo floors.

Simply stated, it was perfect.

He glanced up from the photo to see tears running down Abel's face despite his smile. Same with Elisa, and even Faith. It brought tears back to his own eyes. "I will treasure it forever. It's the best gift I have ever received. Thank you."

Brody set the photograph aside and stood, embracing Abel. Elisa rose and hugged them both.

"Group hug!" Faith said, joining the clump, and for a long moment they held on to each other silently.

"She's here," Elisa said softly, her eyes meeting Brody's. "Our Mick. Can you feel her hugging us, too?"

Brody went still for a moment, and an inexplicable warmth surrounded him from behind. "You know what—? I can." He'd never been completely convinced about the woo-woo stuff, but there was no denying what he felt at that moment. And it was as if his soul exhaled, right then, deep and restorative, something it had needed to do for a long, long time.

"Hey, jerk." He heard Mick's voice inside his head, like a whisper. "It's about time you showed up."

Brody started laughing, and the entire Montesantos clan laughed with him, without even knowing why. Or maybe they did know. Even Mick was there laughing along with everyone else. Somehow, he felt sure of it.

It had been a week and a half since the completely successful dinner at her parents' house and, call her a paranoid, lovesick whack job, but it sure seemed like Brody was doing his level best to avoid her. She'd called him for breakfast—busy. Lunch—gosh, swamped. Dinner—laundry night, but maybe some other time? Like they couldn't eat a meal while his whites tumbled in the dryer? Please.

She'd even asked him just to hang out that very evening, watch TV, play Monopoly—whatever, and he'd hedged, finally admitting that "he kinda had other plans." When she'd asked him, innocently, what he was up to, he'd been evasive, eventually changing the subject.

She couldn't believe it!

Sad fact was, the eligible-guy pickings in the Gulch were slimmer than a twenty-something Hollywood starlet. Had some other Troublesome Gulch lifer swooped in and dug her talons into him already? And if so, why hadn't she heard it through the grapevine?

She'd vented at length about the whole situation with Erin at their weekly lunch earlier that day, which was how they ended up parked a little ways down from Brody's house in Erin's blacked-out car, preparing to do a little impromptu sleuthing. Erin always had been, shall we say, a tad on the impulsive side.

It had sounded like a good idea at the time.

Daylight was holding on for dear life, but everything was turning that pale-lavender hue that hinted of the darkness to come when the sun finally lost her grip on the day. It was so peaceful and quiet up here, unlike the hustle and bustle of her centrally located condo. Faith enjoyed being in this neighborhood in the evenings, but she had reservations about this whole surveillance thing....

She sighed, then bit the corner of her bottom lip.

Erin gave her a don't-wimp-out look. "What now?"

"I'm not so sure about this after all, Er." She grimaced. "It feels so high school."

"No." Erin held up a finger. "High schoolers would just TP his house. This is more *Fatal Attraction*."

Faith groaned. "You're supposed to be making me feel better, not worse. I'm not even dating the guy and now I'm some bunny-boiling stalker? That's just swell."

Erin widened her eyes. "Do you want to know what's up with him, or not?"

"Well, yes, but—"

"Get down! Here he comes."

They both slid down in their seats. Too late. She was deep into it now. Faith craned her neck to get a glimpse of him. If Brody did have a hot date, he sure wasn't dressed for romance. Hope floated inside her heart. That was something, at least. He wore jeans, lightweight hiking shoes, and a well-worn Gramici T-shirt, untucked. Granted, he looked totally, edibly hot in his casual wear, but still. It didn't look like date clothing. Then again, with her luck, he was probably dating some athletic type to whom that sort of outfit spelled date with a capital *D*.

Groan.

They watched Brody back his pickup out of the driveway, do a quick three-point turn and then reverse it *into* his driveway again. He cut the engine and got out of the driver's side.

"What on earth is he doing?" Erin wondered aloud.

Faith shrugged and shook her head simultaneously. Call her clueless.

They watched in silence as he opened his shed and disappeared inside. Moments later he emerged, wrestling out a heavy, tarp-wrapped object that Faith knew to be that ugly-ass old recliner.

"Holy—" Erin's eyes widened as she glanced at Faith, then back at the action in the driveway. "What *is* that? A dead body?"

Faith laughed. "You've been watching too much crime TV, Erin. It's a recliner."

"Oh. I couldn't tell."

"Uh, newsflash, you're a firefighter, AKA

'recliner monkey.' You damn well know you spend the majority of your shift with your butt planted in a one of those."

"Shh, the general public doesn't know that."

Faith barked a laugh. "Covered or not, you should recognize one from way off."

Erin glanced over at her with a smirk, but still seemed confused. "Just explain the recliner connection, smart-ass. I thought he had a date."

"Who's to say he doesn't? I have no idea what the recliner angle is. Anyway, the chair. It is green and orange—oh, and *Naugahyde,* I might add. The man refused to put on the curb for Take Me, I'm Yours day. With no explanation whatsoever." She shuddered. "It was so hideous, I almost had to look at it through a pinhole in a shoebox to keep from permanently damaging my retinas."

"Wow." Erin grinned. "This is getting more interesting by the minute. Dude's got a freaky side. I can get behind that concept."

They watched him struggle to get the chair up onto his tailgate. Faith remembered how heavy that horrible thing was, and sympathized silently.

"Man," said Erin. "I almost feel like asking him if he needs a hand. Should I? I can say we were just passing through the neighborhood."

Faith gripped her forearm and spoke through

clenched teeth. "Don't you dare. You'll bust my cover and I'll never forgive you."

"Okay, okay. Just a thought."

"Well, unthink it. He's almost done anyway."

Brody jumped up into the bed of the truck and slid the chair in, his arm muscles flexing to the max.

Faith felt that all-too-familiar swirl of attraction in her middle, just watching him.

Erin whistled low through her teeth. "He's a top-shelf hottie, Pip, I'll give you that."

"And then some." Faith sighed miserably. "But he's so much more than just hot, that's the thing. He's smart and kind and emotional. Not afraid to show it, either. His obvious assets are upstaged by those you can't see."

Erin's mouth lifted into a wistful half smile. "The best ones always are that way. Hot fades. It's the inside stuff that counts in the end."

Faith knew how much her friend still missed Kevin, and she reached over and squeezed her hand.

Brody took his time securing the chair into the truck bed with jute and bungee cords, and then he jumped down, closed the tailgate, climbed back into the cab and fired up the engine. Erin waited a few moments after he'd pulled out before she crept away from the curb behind him as stealthily as possible.

"You stay down," she said. "He'll never recognize me in this ball cap and glasses, and he doesn't know what kind of car I drive."

"Okay."

They remained a safe distance behind Brody's truck as he meandered down the mountainside into town, then turned onto Main Street, where the majority of the shops and restaurants had been since the dawn of time.

They'd slapped up a Super Store and some of the other generic chain stores on the outskirts of town, an "improvement" which had caused a huge uproar in the community. They were the subject of a year's worth of explosive city council meetings packed with angry TG lifers who didn't want the Gulch to turn into just another look-alike town in the United States of Generica. But so far, the unwanted shopping area hadn't forced any of the small local businesses to shut down. One thing you could say about the Gulchers, they were loyal.

"Um, Pip?" Erin said, in a half grossed-out, half intrigued tone. "When I said the guy had a freaky side, I'm not sure I knew *how* freaky."

"What do you mean?"

"He's turning into that new retirement community."

"The retireme—" She stopped short, and a smile lifted the corners of her lips. A huge feeling of relief washed over her, and all her muscles relaxed. She almost groaned. "Thank God."

"What?" Erin pulled a face. "You're okay as long as he's boinking an octogenarian?"

"Don't be gross. That's not what it's about."

"So then…?"

"You'll see."

Brody, she now realized, had a "date," but it was with grouchy old Mr. Norwood. Hence, the recliner. Her heart expanded when she realized the full picture of what was happening here. What a sweet, thoughtful gesture, bringing Mr. Norwood that hideous chair from hell. The poor old guy had left everything behind. Maybe, unbelievable as it seemed to her, that Naugahyde monstrosity had been his favorite. Men were strange like that. It took a really special guy like Brody to think of such a personal gift, if you asked her. "Just find a spot down the way from wherever he's parked, and we'll watch him. I know what he's doing."

"And, what, exactly, would that be?"

Faith sighed. *Oh, just making me fall more in love with him every second, the jerk.* "I told you. You'll see. Just wait."

They watched Brody muscle the chair out of the truck and remove the tarp, then polish it up with a rag he'd pulled from inside his pickup. He lugged it to the side of the front door on one of the patio homes, started to reach for the doorbell, then snapped his fingers and headed back to the truck.

The two women looked at each other.

"What the—"

"Beats me," Faith replied. "Like I know how to read the guy. Or any guy. Please. I'm illiterate in *Guy*."

He exited the truck with a white, plastic grocery store sack, out of which he lifted a huge, orange bow. He stuck it on top, and the women released simultaneous, mushy "Awwwws."

Brody wadded up the shopping bag and stuffed it into his back pocket. Faith found herself holding her breath as he rang the doorbell. It seemed like forever before Old Norwood answered, and when he did, Faith was shocked to see him looking happy and healthy and even tanned. "Wow. I guess the move down here really did do him good."

"People need people." Erin shrugged.

Faith narrowed her eyes at Brody. "Except for certain people, apparently."

"He'll come around."

"Right."

"Besides, Norwood only got really grouchy after his wife died. Cut him some slack. It's hard to lose the love of your life, believe me. Remember how fun he used to be when we trick-or-treated at his house as kids?"

Faith thought about that, and her stomach sank. "You know, you're right. Thanks for making me feel guilty for every single time I've called him a grouch."

Erin shrugged, nonplussed. "Karma."

Faith punched her in the biceps, but Erin only flexed against the ineffective impact and then laughed.

They watched as Brody stepped aside to reveal his surprise, and laughed when Mr. Norwood actually threw his hands into the air with sheer delight. The two men did that half-hug/back-pound thing, and then Brody began hauling the chair into the patio home.

Faith sighed. "Let's get out of here. I've seen enough."

Erin started up the engine and turned in the opposite direction. They'd make a full circle through the complex to avoid getting busted at the eleventh hour. "So? What's the verdict."

Faith laid her head back and groaned. "The verdict? One, I'm in love. Two, my life sucks because he doesn't want anything to do with me. So, three, let's go drink."

"You got it, Pipsqueak. I'll be your designated

driver." Erin reached over and patted Faith's knee. "But don't give up yet. Our Brody might just—"

"—see the error of his ways and come around eventually, *blah-blah-blah.* I suppose you think the more times you tell me that, the more likely it is to come true?"

"Can't hurt."

Faith scoffed. "I've practically thrown myself at the guy, and *nada.* Let's just say I'm not holding my breath, and not just because doing so would make it hard to suck down the gigantic margarita I have in my crosshairs."

Herman Norwood settled into his ancient recliner with a sigh of contentment. "Now this hits the spot." He gazed over at Brody with true warmth in his still-bright eyes. "Thank you, son. This is just about the best housewarming present I could've asked for."

"My pleasure. I had an inkling you felt a special kinship with that chair." Brody grinned as he took a seat on the sofa.

"That I did." He looked chagrined. "But with the price you paid me for that place, I just didn't feel right about asking to keep it, or any of the furniture, for that matter."

"I would've let you keep whatever you wanted.

You didn't hear me complaining about the price. Sometimes we men have to help each other out."

"I appreciate that. You're a good man."

"You, too."

"Ahhh, comfortable. This new stuff looks nice, but nothing is as comfortable as my recliner." Herman shook his head and sighed with exasperation. "A woman, no matter how loving, just doesn't understand the time and care it takes to perfect the personalized butt-dent in a man's favorite chair."

"I hear you, Herman."

"My late, lovely wife, Emaline, God rest her soul, despised this chair for years. Ugly, she called it, as if that matters." He huffed in disgust. "Tried to make me throw it out, slip-cover it—whatever the hell, you name it. It was the subject of many an argument, son, believe you me." He held up a palm as if to prepare Brody for his next words. "She actually wanted to get the seat refilled with goose down so it was plump."

"No," Brody said, with disbelief in his tone.

"Yes. After all those years to get it just so, she wanted to take it off to some upholstery shop and ruin it." He paused, shaking his head again. "Women. Indecipherable creatures."

"Ain't that the truth?"

"Wonderful, indecipherable creatures."

"Again, ain't that the truth?" Brody groaned.

Norwood peered over at him, sidelong, with a gleam in his eye. He sucked his teeth. "You sound like you've got yourself a lady on the hook, Brody. Been doing some fishin' in the Gulch?"

"No." He paused, considered it. "Well, not intentionally. There is someone I'm interested in, but it's one of those impossible relationships. It'll never happen."

Norwood kicked up the footrest and settled in for some guy talk. "Now, nothing's impossible. What's the gal's problem? Want a beer?"

"Sure."

"Good, they're in the fridge. Get me one, too."

Brody obliged, and when he was back on the couch, beer in hand, he continued. "About the girl. It's not her, it's me." Brody blew out a breath. He wasn't sure if he wanted to burden the old man with his issues, but his whole hermit plan left him short of friends, and he needed to get this off his chest. What the hell? He started haltingly. "I don't know if you remember the prom night tragedy about eleven years ago."

"'Course I remember it, boy," Herman said in a voice both gentle and testy. "Do I seem the least bit feeble-minded to you?"

"No, sir. Not at all."

"Then? Out with it."

Brody paused again, struggling with his story. "I was in that crash. My date—and three others—died."

"Girlfriend?"

"No, no. It wasn't like that. She was my best friend in the world, but we never dated." He didn't feel the need to lay Mick's whole story out on the line. It didn't matter anyway.

"That's a tough one. Tough loss."

Brody nodded, raising his eyes toward Herman with shame. "And it gets worse. I ran. Never even talked to my best friend's family before I escaped the Gulch, didn't attend the funeral. I just couldn't."

Herman's bushy eyebrows raised, but Brody didn't sense any judgment in the expression. "And this gal you're interested in?"

"She's my late best friend's little sister."

"Aha."

Now that it was out, Brody found he really did want to talk about it. Herman was the perfect sounding board. "All grown-up now, of course, but still. I mean, how can I possibly become involved with her?"

Herman said nothing, just took it all in, sipped his beer, watched Brody.

His anguish returned, fresh and painful. "Do you

know what her father's last words to me were on that prom night when I escorted her sister? 'Take care of my girl.' And I didn't, Herman. I failed."

Herman rubbed his chin, thinking back. "It was an accident, yes? If memory serves, the driver himself died in that accident, so that couldn't have been you."

"No, I wasn't driving. But that doesn't matter. We were all drinking. All of us. And it doesn't bring Mick back to life." He flexed the muscles in his jaw. "She didn't even want to go. I convinced her."

"Well, nothing wrong with that. You couldn't see into the future. You had good intentions, I'm sure."

"Of course." He twisted his mouth, trying to put it all into words. "But, good intentions or not, how could I possibly ask Mr. Montesantos to ever trust me again? With another daughter?"

Herman nodded, sagely, but said nothing.

Brody felt the need to fill the silence. "As a result, I've been avoiding her. Faith, the little sister. Which isn't the best solution. I get the feeling she's attracted to me, too. And she's been so good to me." He blinked. He'd almost forgotten to tell him. "Oh. She redid the whole house. You'll have to come for dinner and have a look. It's amazing."

"Love to. My Emaline would've loved to have seen it, I'm sure. She was always after me to freshen up the place, but I had no fire for that kind of thing. There's something to be said for a man set in his ways. But, back to the women problems."

Brody smiled, then rubbed his palms together, elbows on his knees. "The only solution I could think of was making myself scarce, because every time I'm around Faith, I just want to grab hold of her and never let go, you know?"

"And she wants the same thing?"

"Well, I get that impression." He shook his head and sighed. "She's amazing. Beautiful, smart. So wise for her age. But most of all, she's got this incredibly empathetic heart and soul. It just bursts forth from her in everything she says and does."

Again Herman nodded.

Brody waited.

Nothing.

He cleared his throat. "So…you don't owe me anything, but you've lived a full life already and you're still living one. You've been in love."

"Desperately. Blindingly. Best years of my life."

"Any words of wisdom?" Brody laughed self-consciously. "Brilliant suggestions for my solving my moral dilemma?"

"Your moral dilemma is your own to puzzle through, I'm afraid, as all moral dilemmas are," Herman said, in his gravelly voice. He pursed his lips for a moment and steepled his hands on his lap, tapping the pads of his fingers together. "'Spose the only words of wisdom I have are, true love—the lifelong kind—doesn't come around all that often. For some folks, never, sadly. And of course that old chestnut, 'Life flies by.' Unfortunately, it's true."

Brody nodded, watching his new friend intensely. He appreciated Herman's words, but they didn't really offer up a solution. He wanted more.

"I look like an old man to you, son, but I feel as young as you on the inside. The body ages, but the mind and heart remain young." He held a liver-spotted fist to his chest. "This avoidance garbage you're doing is a bad way to go, bound to leave you with even more regrets than it's obvious you already have."

"I was afraid you'd say that."

"Deep inside, you know it's true."

"So, what do I do?"

Herman pondered the question for only a moment. "Figure out what you truly want, then grab it, risky or not. Because it sneaks up on you."

"What does?"

"This," he explained, spreading his arms wide. "Old age. The twilight years. Before you know it, you'll be planted in the well-worn butt mark of an old recliner. Alone. Like me." He smiled. "But don't waste a moment feeling sorry for me. People die," he said plainly, with a shrug. "It's the way of things, and it's not easy for those left behind. I wake every morning thinking of Emaline and fall asleep thinking of her, too. But I've got forty years of memories with my sweet Ema, and no one can ever take those away."

Brody swallowed against the lump in his throat. "You're a lucky man."

"Yes," Herman said simply. "And you can be, too."

"Do I deserve to be?"

Herman exhaled. "Stop thinking so damn much, Brody, and go make yourself some good memories for your recliner years. You say this older sister—"

"Mick. Mick Montesantos."

"This Mick was your best friend?"

"Ever," Brody said.

"Well, I don't believe in coincidence, and I do believe in fate." He leveled Brody with a challenging stare. "There's a reason you decided to return to the place of your life's biggest trauma. No family here, you told me. No friends, really. No ties, except the painful ones."

Brody thought on this. "True."

"Why?" Herman demanded.

"That's the part I can't figure out."

Herman struck a fist on the arm of his beloved chair. "Which means that's exactly what you need to figure out. And avoiding things that put the itch under your skin isn't going to do you any favors. Face it."

"My unfinished business? But what is it? I've apologized to the family. They accepted me unconditionally. And something's still missing."

Herman nailed him with a wise stare. "Have you ever considered that your own Mick drew you back here? For a reason?"

Brody felt like he'd been zapped with a stun gun. "I never...I never thought of it that way."

"She loved you, yes? As best friends do?"

Tears threatened. "Yes," Brody said.

"And no doubt she loves her baby sister."

"Definitely."

Herman took a sip of his beer and stared at Brody for several long moments. He covered a belch politely with the side of his fist. "Any of this clicking in that overthinking brain of yours yet?"

Shock zinged through him.

Mick.

Having a hand in bringing him back to Troublesome Gulch. *For* Faith. Unbelievable, but—

Brody stood and crossed the room in two strides. "Herman, I owe you."

They shook hands. "You owe me nothing, my friend. When you're an old man, all alone, you do the same for some confused young man comes to you for some wisdom. It'll happen, no doubt. It's the way of things. Fate, remember?"

Chapter Eleven

Brody was flipping through the channels on his television, uninterested in any of the morning offerings. He wasn't much of a television guy, anyway. Maybe he'd go for a run, burn off some of this sexual tension. His dreams had been fraught with images of Faith. And him. Together in ways he couldn't seem to remove from his brain, didn't *want* to remove.

He wasn't able to get Herman's words out of his mind, either. He knew the old man was right about going out and making new memories, about his avoidance idea being stupid, but he didn't know how to proceed from there. He felt immobilized.

Scared, if the truth were told. What if he was wrong, and Faith had no interest in him? Or if Abel and Elisa were totally against it?

Herman was right. Brody needed to stop thinking so much and figure out his next step.

Loud knocking, punctuated by the ringing of the doorbell, interrupted his thoughts. Alarmed, he crossed to the door and pulled it open. Faith stood there, her face flushed, eyes both flaming and worried at once. She was breathing as if she'd just run a mile.

He reached out for her instinctively, pulling her into the house and into a hug. "What's wrong?"

"I need a huge favor." She squeezed him once, then pulled back, clearly appreciative of his comfort, but all business, too. "Are you on your four days off?"

"I am." He guided her toward the couch. "Come in and sit down. Take a deep breath and tell me what you need, okay? I'm right here."

They settled onto the couch and she gulped a few times, worrying her hands into a knot in her lap. "One of the kids who helped with your house, Jason Cole—"

"The birthday boy?"

"Oh." She shook her head and gripped shaking fingers to her temples. "Yes, I'd completely forgotten that. Sorry, my brain is racing. Anyway, Jason is in a world of trouble. His parents—" She pressed her lips together and her chin quivered. She pounded her fists on her thighs once. "Dammit, I've got to pull myself together before I go back out there. He can't see me like this. I'm supposed to be the stabilizing force in his life."

Brody glanced toward the door. "He's out there?"

"Yes. Listen." She reached out and grabbed his forearm. "It's not the first time it's happened, but his dad beat him up good this time, and legally I have to report it to the police and Social Services."

A flame of anger rushed through Brody. "Bastard."

"Yeah. They'll take one look at his face and remove Jason from his home, but he'll also get thrown into a system that will do him *no* good, believe me. Sometimes the system punishes the child, and Jason doesn't deserve that. It doesn't happen intentionally, but—" Tears welled in her eyes, and she spoke with a conviction that hit him right in the gut. "This kid, Brody, he's amazing. He's got a chance. Not all of them do, and I understand that, but Jason. I can't even tell you—"

Brody scooted closer and put his arm around her.

"He's a good kid with a rotten lot in life, that's all. He's brilliant and funny and—"

"Faith. Honey, what do you need from me? Name it."

She swallowed back her emotion and took a deep breath. "I have a friend in Social Services, Tisa." She clasped her hands together, her gaze beseeching. "It's not standard operating practice whatsoever, but this is a small town and she owes me a favor. Long story. Anyway, she'll get you certified as a foster parent immediately if you say yes, so Jason can stay here with you."

"With me?"

Faith held up her palms. "Just for a few days. That's all. I know it's a lot to ask, I know you like your alone time, but you're the first person who came to mind. He needs to see an example of a good man, and you're the best man I know next to my dad." She sniffed as the tears finally won their battle, then glanced around for a tissue.

Brody jumped up from the couch and brought her a whole box of them.

"Thank you. Wonderful as they are, I just don't know that Mom and Dad could relate to a surly kid Jason's age as well as you could." She blew her nose and dabbed at her eyes. "I'd have him stay at my house, but I'm his guidance counselor and I'm a female. Plus, I only have one bedroom. Totally inappropriate."

"Yeah, that wouldn't work at all."

She flailed her arms, and her words came in a torrent. "You have the office that we can set up as a guest room. All I need is a few days to get his emancipation papers rolling so we can take him out of that toxic situation, Brody, before they throw him into a foster care group home, or worse. The system does its best, but kids fall through the cracks all the time, and that's not good enough for Jason. I wouldn't ask if I didn't really, truly believe in this kid. In his potential. I really care about him. He's hanging on by a thread now and—"

"Faith. Faith, shhhh." He laid a finger on her lips to stop her rambling. When she silenced, he cupped her face in his hands. "Take a breath, okay? You had me at 'I need a favor.' Of course I'll take Jason in. Just tell me what to do."

She went dead still, blinking at him a couple times. "Really?"

He brushed the hair back from her face, caressing her cheek with his thumb. "I'd do anything for you. I'm a sucker for a beautiful woman, especially if she's crying, didn't you know that?"

That won him a small smile.

He glanced around. "He's not a thief or into drugs, anything like that, is he?"

"No, no, absolutely not. He's a giant sarcastic smart-ass, but I figure you're used to that, having been friends with Mick—"

"And you."

"Whatever." She gave him another half smile. "You just have to call him on it."

"Smart-ass. Check. No problems there. So, what do we do next?"

"I have the paperwork in the car. All filled out, call me optimistic." She gave a small shrug. "You just need to sign on the dotted line, and I'll bring Jason in. I can stay for a little bit, help you guys get settled in and break the ice, but I have to be back at the school after lunch."

"Let's get going, then." Brody stood, rubbing his palms together.

Faith stood and tilted her head back to meet his eyes. "Thank you. I owe you. So much."

"You owe me nothing." He held her chin gently and kissed her softly on the lips, surprising himself. Thinking of Herman's words of wisdom, he stared deeply into her eyes, then kissed her again, with a little more passion. "Go splash your face with cold water. I'll get Jason and the paperwork. Where is it?"

"Just bring in my whole briefcase," she said, heading toward the bathroom, sounding a bit breathless. "It's in the backseat."

Brody heard the water turn on in the bathroom just as he headed outside. Jason slumped in the passenger seat of the Mini Cooper, hiding his face without trying to look like he was. He peered up slowly when Brody rapped gently on the window, and Brody's gut clenched. God, his dad had done a number on his face. Brody'd love to give the dad a taste of his own medicine, even though he knew that would help nothing. Violence never solved violence. Instead he'd focus on the kid.

Jason pushed the button and rolled the window down.

"Hey, buddy." Brody smiled. "Grab your bag and come on in. Looks like you and I are going to play bachelor pad for a while."

"Really?" Jason asked, facing Brody head-on now. "Are you a foster parent?"

"I am now." He lifted his chin toward the fire-engine red, leather briefcase in the backseat. "Grab Ms. Montesantos's briefcase while you're at it, too."

Jason wasted no time getting out of the little car and shouldering his duffel. He reached in farther and carefully grabbed the briefcase, turning instantly to hand it to Brody as if it were a priceless thing.

"You're going to have to help me turn that office you guys decorated into a second bedroom," Brody said, clamping Jason on the shoulder with his palm.

"That's cool. I can sleep on the floor, too, or the couch. Ain't no problem."

"Nah, we'll set you up better than that." He gave Jason's shoulder a quick squeeze, then released it. "Everything's going to be fine, okay?"

"Sure, just…"

"What?"

"Don't feel sorry for me. Okay?" He indicated his face. "This ain't nothin' but a thing. Business as usual in the Cole household," he said, bitterly.

"You got it. No pity." He paused, considering his next words. He wasn't a counselor, after all. But he was a human being. In a flash, he realized perhaps he was getting his chance to be that wise old man in a recliner early. A half smile lifted one corner of his mouth at the thought. "But you have to know, Jason, it shouldn't be business as usual. Fathers don't have an open-ended option to beat on their sons and daughters. It's wrong. On every level."

"I know," Jason said, quietly. "But I'd rather have him hit me than mom, so I took it more than I probably would have." He shrugged. "I always hoped he would straighten up, stop drinking, become normal. But that ain't gonna happen. I get it now. I just want out of there. I'm sixteen now, so I can get emancipated and get a job."

"*And* finish school."

"Yeah, that too. Miz M and me, we have a deal, because she's just about the only adult who thinks I'm worth a damn. So she shows up to school, I show up to school, which means I'll probably graduate." He shook his head with a huff. "Thank God for her, because the 'rents don't care if I go to school or not."

"Well, you can worry about school in a few days after your face has healed a bit." He stepped aside and let Jason precede him into the house. "And just so you know, she's not the only adult on your side."

Jason smiled through a grotesquely puffy, cut lip. "Thanks, brah. I mean, um...what should I call you?"

"Well, I've been called a lot of things in my day, but how about Brody. Brah works, too. Or whatever, as long as it's polite."

"Cool." He held out his hand.

Brody shook it, thinking this was going to work out just fine. It would do him good to focus on someone besides himself for a while. *That* was getting tedious.

Near the end of her seemingly endless work day, Faith's phone rang. She answered it by rote, completely distracted by thoughts of Jason and how he and Brody might be getting along. Or not. "Ms. Montesantos."

"Wow," Erin said. "Someone's all business."

Faith smiled, always happy to hear her friend's voice. "Hey. Sorry. It's been the worst, never-ending work day of my entire career."

"Anything you want to talk about?"

"Not now. What's up?"

"Just making sure we're still on for tonight."

Faith's brain blanked. "Tonight?"

"Hello! It's live-band night at the Horseshoe," Erin said with more than a tinge of sarcasm. "You know, that once-monthly event we've attended together every fourth week since you turned twenty-one?"

Faith swore in her brain. "Erin, I'm sorry. I completely spaced."

"You're tellin' me."

"I can't make it tonight. Everything's just—" Her voice caught. She grabbed her forehead with one hand, wishing away the headache that had been forming all day.

Erin dropped the joking tone altogether. "Okay, Pip, what's going on?"

Faith filled her in on everything that had happened with Jason and Brody, on all the red tape she'd had to cut through today with Cagney at the police department and Tisa in Social Services. "I just feel like I should go over there and help out in the evenings. He's doing me such a huge favor. I don't even know if he *likes* kids."

"Yes, you do. Or you never would've left Jason there."

Faith sighed. "True. I went on a feeling, I guess. That makes me feel better. Anyway, looks like the Horseshoe is out. I'm sorry."

"No, of course. I understand."

"But you have to go and tell me how it is. I've wanted to see Opie Gone Bad forever, dangit."

"I will," Erin said. "We can always drive into Denver some weekend and see them at Herman's Hideaway."

"That's true."

"You have to do me a favor, too, though."

"What's that?" Faith asked, standing to gather the papers she needed and stuff them into her brief-case. She wanted out of there ASAP, so she could get home, take a long, hot shower to become human again, and then head over to Brody's.

"Give that hottie a big ol' kiss that'll knock his socks off. Better yet, his pants."

"Right." Faith looked heavenward and shook her head. "Totally appropriate under the circum-stances, Erin, thanks for the advice." But the thought made her laugh, and she appreciated having her mood lightened, if even for a moment. "Love you, Er. I'll call you tomorrow."

"Okay. Love you, too."

"Have fun, and be careful."

"Gotcha. As for you, have fun and be daring. Anything worth having is worth taking a risk for."

Before Faith could protest, Erin had hung up. Faith turned off her lights and, thanks to friendship, left her office with a smile on her face.

On her way home, Faith called Brody on her cell phone. When he picked up, she heard laughter and the *thump-a-thump* of loud music in the background. It sounded like…rap?

"Austin's Poker Palace, how can I help you?"

She paused a moment, startled. "Brody?"

"Hey, Faith," he said, in a breezy, casual tone. She could hear the smile in his tone.

Her spine straightened. "What's going on over there?"

"Just playing poker with my boys."

"You're playing poker with Jason?"

"Jason and Herman. My boys. And in case you're wondering, Herman is wiping the floor with us. His stack of pinto beans is more of a mountain. Man's got a poker face you wouldn't believe."

Faith blinked, her mouth spreading into a smile. "So, let me get this straight. You're playing pinto bean poker with Jason and Mr. Norwood."

"That's about the size of it. And Jason is educating us on the so-called virtues of rap music."

She laughed. "Well, I'm glad everything is going okay over there," she said, ruefully. "No problems?"

"None whatsoever."

"Brody, you're…amazing."

"Likewise," he said, in a gentle, flirtatious tone.

She cleared her throat. "I was thinking of coming over for dinner, if that's okay. I mean, I don't want to interrupt your guys' night…."

"Let me ask the guys. Hang on." He held the phone a little away from his face, from the far-off sound of his voice. "Jase, what are you making for dinner?"

"Making? Dude, what're you smokin'? I don't cook."

"Herman?" she heard Brody say. "You have the menu planned?"

"No, sir. It's your house now. You cook."

"That poses a problem, my friends, because I'm not cooking either. However, Ms. Montesantos would like to join us for dinner. That okay with both of you?"

"Sure, sounds perfect," Jason said, in his signature smart-ass tone. "Tell her I like thin crust, and no green peppers."

"Or green olives," Herman added. "They give me gas."

"And extra cheese," Jason hollered.

"Gotcha. Thin crust, extra cheese, leave off all green stuff, just to be safe." Brody came back to the phone. "Okay, Faith, you're all in for dinner, assuming you can provide it. I assume you heard everyone's preferences on the pizza you're bringing with you?"

She groaned, but with a smile on her face. "Men are so pathetic. And groups of men are pathetic to the power of ten."

"Admit it. You love us."

"Whatever. See you in a few, after I pick up the pizzas. Anything else?"

"Just you," Brody said, in a tone that made her tummy flop.

Brody headed off to the restroom, leaving Jason to present his case for why Eminem was a song-writing genius, misunderstood by the masses. Instead, Herman leaned back in his chair and took a swig of his rootbeer. "Who did that to your face, son?" he asked, flat-out.

Jason dropped his gaze. "My dad."

"Helluva thing," Herman said, keeping all pity out of his voice. He had a sense this kid wouldn't need, nor would he appreciate it. "It's best you're here with Brody. He's a good man."

Jason looked back up at him. "Yeah, he's cool. I think he's got a thing for Miz M."

"I think you're pretty astute." Herman winked.

"They oughtta just hook up and get it over with."

"Agreed." Herman paused. "So, what about other family? Your grandparents?"

Jason shrugged. "Don't have any. Least, I never met 'em."

"Most likely your dad's father did the same sort of thing to him. Those sort of penchants for violence can carry on in a family."

"Not with me," Jason said almost angrily. "I'd never hit my own kid."

"'Course not," Herman said. "Do I look like an idiot to you, boy?"

Jason gulped. "N-no. Not at all."

Herman nodded with confidence, then held up one knobby finger. "Takes a smart one in the family chain to break such a cycle. Seems to me, you're man enough to do it."

"I am. And I will." Jason stared at him a few moments and then hitched his chin. "What about you? Any kids? Grandkids?"

Herman sighed. "Unfortunately, no. My late wife, Emaline, God rest her soul, was never able to conceive."

"Helluva thing," Jason said.

Surprised, Herman smiled at him.

Another pause ensued.

"Have any interest in an honorary grandson?" Jason blurted suddenly, immediately turning red and looking like he might die if Herman said no.

A clutch of emotion tightened Herman's chest, but he didn't let it show. "Listen here, son, if you think I'm going to take you to the county fair and let you eat junk food until you puke in my car—"

Jason laughed. "I'm past that stage, brah. But we could go to an Eminem concert together or something. You could bring earplugs if you wanted. I wouldn't mind. And I could come to your place. Hang out."

A moment of silence hung between the two.

"I'd be honored, my boy." Herman reached out his hand, and Jason shook it, then stood, and gave Herman an awkward hug.

After that had been settled, Jason sat back down, clapped his hands together once and rubbed them like a miser. "I know we've reached a new level and all, but you'd better guard those beans, Gramps, because I'm going to win them all back from you. Your old butt's gonna be thrashed all over this floor."

Herman snorted. "Give it a try, whelp. Just give it your best shot."

Both Jason and Herman cracked up, just as Brody returned to the living room. He looked from boy to man, both of them beaming. "What did I miss?"

"Nothing," Herman told him, with a gleam in his eye. "Plant your butt. Let's get this game back on. The cocky youngster here thinks he stands a chance against my formidable skill and experience. I want a chance to put him in his place without having to do so in the presence of a lady." He winked at Jason.

Chapter Twelve

Faith watched with a mixture of horror and wonder as the two younger men pounced all over the pizzas like hyenas on antelope road kill. She hovered in the background with her empty Chinet, taken aback by the testosterone overload. "Geez, you'd think you guys had never had a meal in your lives."

"Step aside, you rude heathens," Herman barked at Brody and Jason, who immediately backed off. "Let the lady get through and pick a slice." He turned to Faith with a wink. "Bad breeding. In my day, a man would never step before a lady at mealtime."

"Sorry," said Brody and Jason in stereo.

Herman touched her back. "You just go on in and take whatever you'd like, dear. They're just ravenous because I've beaten them so badly in poker for the last several hours."

She shouldered between Brody and Jason and picked out a slice of pepperoni and a small slice of mushroom and extra cheese, then turned back toward Herman with a smile. "Thank you, Mr. Norwood."

"Please, call me Herman. Mr. Norwood makes me feel so old."

She laughed. "Can I grab you a couple of slices before the hyenas descend again?"

"A couple of the mushroom slices would suit."

She retrieved them, handed them to Herman, then settled into a chair at the table, tucking one foot beneath her. Brody and Jason hit the pizza boxes again.

"You know," she said to Herman, looking at him through her lashes. "I used to be afraid of you."

He nodded with understanding. "I went through a period of, shall we say, unapproachability after I lost my Emaline, God rest her soul." A flicker of regret showed in his eyes. "I suppose I wasn't the friendliest Gulcher those first couple of years."

She tilted her head to the side. "I'm so sorry."

"I understand you've had your share of loss,

too, so I suspect you understand the emotional roller coaster one rides in the aftermath."

"That I do."

He nodded once, like a gentleman. "But I apologize if I scared you."

"No. I apologize for being judgmental rather than understanding. It's not usually how I am." She took a bite of pizza, chewed, swallowed. "So, what do you think of the transformation of your old place?"

He quirked one bushy eyebrow. "Hear tell you weren't fond of my old scheme?"

Her face flamed, and she glared up at Brody, who just shrugged, trying to look innocent.

Herman laughed. "Not to worry. My Ema hated it, too. I was more of a creature of habit than I'd like to admit, and then, after she was gone, who cared?"

Faith's heart clenched for the old guy.

"Your changes have made the place right nice. But thank you for keeping the chair."

Her stomach plunged. For a split second she thought she and Erin had been busted stalking Brody. But no. Herman had the chair now, that was all. She realized all she had to do was play dumb. Nobody had seen them scrunched down in Erin's car watching the whole chair reunion happen. She widened her eyes. "Oh, you have the recliner?"

He nodded. "Your Brody brought it to me." He

leaned in so only she could hear him. "He's a good man, that one. A catch, I think you young women say."

Faith sighed, against her will, and love blossomed in her heart again, as it had all day thinking of Brody's kisses earlier that morning. She knew he'd just been trying to comfort her, but still. "I know he is. The best, actually." She glanced up at Brody, embroiled in conversation with Jason, who looked more animated than she'd seen him in a long time.

With Brody, he stood straight and showed his confidence. He talked, debated. He looked challenged and contented, unafraid, despite the wounds on his face. God, how much farther could she fall in love with Brody before she just died from the pain of it?

"I'm so glad you're happy with the chair," she told Herman.

"Come on, now. You're just happy to be rid of it. I know how the fairer sex thinks."

Faith held up her hands. "Guilty."

They both laughed.

After dinner Brody and Jason cleaned up. No need to wrap any leftovers, because they'd made short work of the three pizzas Faith had donated to the cause. He'd tried to pay her, but she refused.

"So, what's on the agenda for the evening?" Faith asked, looking at three generations of men before her. "More poker?"

"Jason and I thought we'd watch a movie, isn't that right, boy?" Herman said. He settled onto the couch, kicked off his loafers and lifted his feet to the upholstered ottoman with a groan of pleasure.

"That's right. You two won't be interested in it, though. It's a young-dude, old-dude kind of thing." He glanced quickly at Herman, then back at Brody and Faith. "Why don't you two go out or something?"

Faith's jaw dropped. She blinked over at Brody.

"Now that's a grand idea, sonny," Herman said, stretching one arm along the back of the sofa. "Isn't it some special night down at the Horseshoe?"

Faith gulped. "Yeah, it's, uh, live-band night."

"Opie Gone Bad," Jason said to Herman. "They're tight, but I'm underage." He shrugged.

"Tight?" Herman asked.

"It means...they're good."

"Then why don't you say they're good, for cripe's sake? Tight makes them sound bad," Herman asked him, in his classic grumpy-old-man voice.

"Yeah, but bad can be good, depending on how you use it," Jason countered.

Herman shook his head. "You kids, and the destruction of the English language. Shameful."

Jason clicked his tongue. "You're way old-school, Gramps."

"If old-school means I speak the language properly, then I'm proudly old-school."

"Herman," Brody said, interrupting their banter. "I can't ask you to stay here with Jason while we go out."

"No," Faith agreed.

"Geez, Miz M, I'm sixteen," Jason said, with disgust. "I don't need a babysitter. We're just a couple of dudes taking in a flick."

Herman hit Brody with a glare. "Besides, who said you asked me? This young man and I have an agreement, isn't that right, Jason?"

"Yup." Jason smiled shyly at Faith. "He's my honorary grandpa, since I don't have one. We shook on it earlier."

"Oh, Jase." She raised both hands to her mouth. "That's wonderful, buddy. Herman, I—"

"None of your mush now, young lady. It was an agreement between two men. Nothing further to discuss." He flicked away her unfinished comment with one hand. "Brody, pop your head out and take this woman to the live-band show, for the love of Pete. Don't make me feel like I've been talking to a brick wall," he said pointedly.

Brody's turn to look embarrassed. "But, if we're late—?"

"Then sleep on the couch when you get back," Herman said, picking up the remote and starting their movie. "Everyone knows a decent host gives the most comfortable bed in the house to the person with the oldest bones, and that would be me."

"But—"

"Shhh," Jason said to Brody, looking exasperated. "Brah, step up, geez. We're giving you every freakin' opportunity here. So git. But be quiet about it. The first five minutes of this flick are unreal."

Brody looked at Faith.

Faith looked back.

They both shrugged.

"Herman, you have my cell phone if you—"

"Shh!" Herman and Jason admonished, simultaneously. Clearly, they'd been dismissed.

Brody took a moment to change into perfectly faded jeans, a button-down shirt and boots. Faith was wearing jeans and a floaty turquoise top herself, so she felt appropriately dressed for the unexpected night out. "You look awesome," she said.

"That's what I thought when you walked in," he

replied, both of them keeping their voices low so as not to interrupt Herman and Jason's movie.

"See you later," Brody called out as they left.

"Yeah, yeah, yeah." Herman waved him off without his eyes leaving the screen.

When they reached Brody's truck, he opened the door for her. "I think we were set up."

"I suspect you're right."

Brody shook his head. "You just can't trust the younger generation. Or the older generation, for that matter." But he said it with a smile. Tonight he planned on testing out Herman's advice, for better or for worse. Time to make some new memories for his recliner days.

"Wow, this place is packed," Brody said, scanning for an open parking spot. The bass of the music throbbed out onto Main Street, and some of the shops and restaurants offered extended hours, hoping to cash in on the foot traffic.

"Yeah, live-band night is a huge monthly thing in the Gulch. Erin and I haven't missed a single one since I turned twenty-one."

He did a quick double-take at her. "What about tonight?"

She shrugged. "Jason was my priority, so I begged off." A shiver of excitement escaped her as she smiled. "But I do have to say, I'm psyched to be here. I've wanted to see Opie Gone Bad live for a long time."

"They sure sound like they're rocking the house from out here."

"Yeah." She paused. "How sweet was that grandpa thing between Jason and Herman?"

"Very cool."

"How do you suppose that came about?"

"I don't know. I was out of the room, and when I came back, they were laughing and Jason was calling him Gramps. I thought it was just another of his nicknames, like dude and brah and so on." Brody smiled and pulled into a recently vacated spot on the street. "Herman's an honorable man with a good head on his shoulders. Very sharp, despite his age."

"Yeah, I'm still paying penance in my head for all the times I called him a grouch."

Brody patted her knee. "And despite what Jason's been through, the kid's solid. I think they'll be good for each other."

"Definitely."

He cut the engine and pocketed his keys. "Ready?"

Her huge green eyes met his gaze in the dark car. "Brody, I don't know how to thank you enough."

His heart started to race. *Cowboy up.* "I'd settle for a kiss," he said, taking Herman's risk advice. He ignored all the warnings and red flags and fears roiling inside him and leaned a little closer, then hesitated.

Faith, however, closed the distance between them with no hesitation whatsoever, laid her palm on his chest and kissed him so tenderly, so lovingly, his limbs went weak.

"Damn," he whispered against her lips, threading his fingers into her hair. "Any other favors I can do for you?"

"Be careful with your questions, honey." She laughed, giving him one last kiss. "You're going to make a girl want to miss Opie Gone Bad altogether, and that's just wrong."

A rush of yearning surged through his body, but this time it felt different. It didn't feel like a lust thing. Well, it did—he definitely wanted her. But it had somehow morphed into something much deeper than that, to a place where he knew he'd never intentionally hurt this woman. Faith had become imbedded in his soul just as deeply as her sister had so many years ago, but in a different way.

Would Mick be happy about it? Is this what she would've wanted for her baby sister and her best friend?

He pulled himself together, opened the door, and rushed around the back of his truck to open Faith's door. He took her hand to help her out of the tall vehicle, then didn't let it go. They started toward the club, a few blocks down, and he lifted their clasped hands up and glanced at her. "This okay with you?"

"Yes, Brody. It's okay if you hold my hand," she said, her tone teasing.

He grinned. "So give me the lowdown on Opie Gone Bad before we get in there."

Faith had a little skip in her step, clearly a huge fan. "You'll love them. It's four guys, Jake, Randy, Windall and Scott. They've got this great rock/soul/funk vibe, and they're totally indie, which I love. They're a Denver institution. In fact, they won the Westword's Best Soul/Funk Band category recently. And they raise money for charity and stuff. They rule." She smiled up at him, and he realized he was watching her, mesmerized. "What?" she asked.

He shrugged. "I just love watching you speak passionately about...well, anything. The kids you help, decorating, bands. Mick. Your passion is infectious."

She turned suddenly to face him and kissed him solidly, finishing off with a little nip of his bottom lip that set his blood rushing. Running a finger all the way down his chest until she hooked it in his waistband and pulled him more tightly against her, she said, "Watch out, Brody Austin, or I might just infect you." Her tone was so seductive, he couldn't even formulate a reply.

The mutual attraction thing? Confirmed.

What to do about it? Still up in the air.

But he had a feeling tonight was his chance, and he didn't plan to let another eleven years slip through his fingers. When she unhooked her finger from his waistband and turned toward the club, he grabbed her wrist and pulled her back against him. Her arms went around his waist, and he held both sides of her face, and their gazes locked.

"God, Faith," he said, "I think you already have infected me. And I think…I don't want to be cured," before leaning in and kissing her thoroughly, exploring the softness of her mouth like he'd been dreaming of since the first time he saw her on the ski slopes. They kissed and touched, he ran his fingers through her long, silky hair, and she gently ran her hands up and down his back. When they finally broke apart, Brody felt as disoriented as Faith looked.

"Brody," she whispered, her voice shaky, her pupils enlarged with passion.

"Opie Gone Bad," he reminded her.

"But—"

"Later," he said, leaning in to kiss the pulse in her neck, before taking her hand and pulling her toward the almost forgotten club. "That's a promise."

They paid their cover and then shouldered their way into the crush. Faith leaned up toward his ear. "Erin's here somewhere. Let's find her."

Brody nodded, indicating that she should lead the way. Up on stage, Jake, Randy, Windall and Scott were seriously rocking the house, and the Gulchers were showing some major love.

They located Erin off to one side at a tall bar table with some other firefighters Brody actually recognized from calls they'd been on together. They all shook hands, knocked fists, hellos all around, and then Brody leaned down to Faith.

"Want a drink?"

"Sure. I am feeling a little…parched," she said, giving him a private, seductive look. "How about a radler?"

"Huh?"

"It's a German thing. The word actually means biker, but Gabi will know."

"Gabi?"

"The bartender?" she said, in a *Duh* tone, shaking her head. "If you're ever going to be a real Gulcher, you seriously need to get out more, honey. Everyone knows Gabi. Anyway, a radler is half German beer, half Sprite."

"That," he said, cringing, "is vile. Or would that be vomitous," he added in a teasing tone. A real Gulcher, huh? The thought wasn't altogether unappealing. He hadn't been a real anything in a very long time.

"Neither. It's yummy. You'll have to try it."

He gave her a dubious look. "What's in it for me?"

She swayed into him, their bodies touching from hip to chest, and met his gaze directly with that sexy, sultry look that could bring him to his knees. "I guess we'll have to find out, won't we?"

"Are you flirting with me, Faith Montesantos?"

She paused, pretending to consider the question seriously. "I think I'd use the word…seducing," she said, raising a brow. "Is it working?"

Grinning, Brody left to get the drinks.

When he returned, the firefighters remained, but Faith and Erin were gone. Brody set the drinks on the tabletop and hiked his chin in question at Dave, the guy next to him.

"They had to do that chick thing where they to go the bathroom together." Dave shook his head, clearly baffled. "I never have understood that."

"It's strange," Brody agreed. "I think they go to talk about us."

"They talk while they're…? Never mind." Dave took a long pull of his beer. "So you and Faith got a thing going on, huh?"

Brody bought time by taking a swig of his own. "I'm not sure yet. Hopefully."

"Lucky man. I wish my guidance counselor in high school had looked like her instead of that blue-haired old ex-nun we used to have." All the guys nodded. "I would have screwed up a *lot* more just to end up in Faith Montesantos's office, that's for damn sure."

The table of men laughed, clearly knowing exactly how Dave felt.

"Well?" Erin demanded. "What is this? A date?"

Faith had filled her in on the whole chain of events that led them to the club. She shivered with a mixture of excitement and apprehension. "I think so, although we were sort of tricked into it, so I'm not sure. We kissed, though. In the car and on the street. I mean, big-time, the real-thing kissing. And the mutual flirt thing?" She hugged her arms around her and twisted side to side with happiness. "All indications point toward more to come later."

"It is *so* on, girl. Definitely a date, and a hot one to boot." Erin leaned into the mirror and refreshed her understated lip gloss, pressing her lips together and then wiping the excess from the edges of her lips with her pinky. "He is big-time into you."

Faith's tummy flopped. "You think?"

Erin half laughed, half groaned. "No, I don't *think*. I know. It's painful to watch, if you want the truth. It's like Kevin and me, back in the day."

"Oh, honey." Faith hugged her friend. She knew exactly how difficult that had been for Erin to admit. When they pulled apart, she bit her bottom lip. "If you want us to tone it down in front of you—"

"Don't you dare." Erin narrowed her gaze. "I'm living vicariously through you."

"So, what should I do now?"

"Dance."

"Dance?"

"Yes. Dance with the man, and make your desires clear without uttering a single word. It's the oldest trick in the book, and it's not even a trick. It's just sexy, raw body talk. If you want him—"

"I do. Oh, I do."

"And if he wants you, which anyone with a brain can see he does, tonight's the night." Erin messed up her casually hip, messy hair, then turned to Faith. "Don't screw this up, Pipsqueak. These chances don't come around every day. You guys are *meant* to be together. And Mick would've wanted it."

"Really?" Faith bit her bottom lip.

Erin sighed. "Yes. It's completely obvious to everyone except you two dolts."

"Thanks a lot," Faith said, laughing.

"I'm trying to help you. I want for you what I had with Kevin." Her eyes clouded, but she made an effort to brighten them almost immediately. "Be bold. Make it clear what you want. And go for it. Herman and Jason will be absolutely fine together for the night. Take the man back to your condo and ravish him before I have to kill you for being timid."

"I'm *not* timid."

"I know." Erin spread her arms. "So what are you waiting for?"

Faith took in a deep breath and eased it out. "I'll do my best." She gave her own appearance a cursory glance in the mirror, but she'd never really been a primping sort. She shared that trait with her big sis. "What about you?" she asked, as they left the bathroom. "Any of those firefighters out there on your list?"

Erin pulled a horrified face. "Are you freakin' high? I'd never date a firefighter from my own department. Or any other department, for that matter. They're just friends. Firefighters can be really annoying. Like kids. I haven't even regaled you with the latest 'someone on A-shift ate my bratwurst' scandal."

"Oh, come on," Faith said in a dubious tone. "Everyone thinks firefighters are hotties."

"That's because they don't live with them for twenty-four long hours at a stretch." She criss-crossed her hands. "Not interested. Period."

Faith reached out and rubbed her palm up and down Erin's supertoned arm as they made their way through the crowd. "I just don't want you to be alone forever. I know Kevin was your soul mate, but you're young, Er."

"Yeah, yeah." Her eyes went dead. "Tonight's your night, not mine. We'll worry about my issues at a later date. Way later. Okay?"

"Okay. But I'm not going to let the issue drop."

"Like I thought you would." Erin threw an arm around Faith's shoulders. "Come on, Pip. Let's head back out to your man."

Her man.

Faith's tummy flopped for about the hundredth time that evening. She prayed Mick was with her right then. And more than anything, she prayed Mick approved, as Erin had suggested. They got stuck in a crowd bottleneck, and Faith closed her eyes and concentrated. A sudden radiating warmth in her chest made her realize that, yeah,

Mick was there—as always—and she approved wholeheartedly.

With that knowledge, Faith's whole body relaxed.

It was time to grab for what she wanted in life.

Chapter Thirteen

Opie Gone Bad finished a high-energy song, and the crowd around them went wild. Faith turned to Brody and threw her arms around his neck. "Take me home."

He blinked, concerned. "I'm sorry, Faith. I should've asked earlier. I know this has been a really long day for you. Are you exhausted?"

She held his unwavering gaze. "*Exhausted* isn't the word I'm thinking of, sweetheart, when I say take me home," she repeated, making her meaning clear by pressing her body into his.

Desire flowed through his veins like liquid fire. "Are you sure?"

"I've never been more sure of anything in my life."

They said goodbye to Erin and the others as quickly as they could without making it obvious that they *really* wanted to leave, but Brody didn't miss the little gleam and eyebrow waggle Erin gave Faith.

It was a short drive from the club to Faith's condo, and they made their way silently. Faith kept her hand on his thigh, but said nothing.

So many thoughts jumbled through his brain, Brody didn't know what to think first. Above all of the worries and reservations and stressors, however, was a solid core of desire for Faith.

This woman.

Not because she was Mick's baby sister, his link to the past and the grief they shared. Not because Jason and Herman had set them up, or even because it was obvious Erin was on their side, too.

He wanted Faith, he realized, because he loved her.

Every single thing about her.

With her, he didn't feel that empty gnawing in his soul that had plagued him for so many years. She filled that, and then some. He didn't know how to verbalize all this yet, but he could certainly show her.

Faith fumbled with her key opening the door to her place, but as soon as they were inside and the dead bolt had been thrown, Brody pressed her back against the door, his hands braced by her head, and kissed her. Their mutual need was like a caged animal tearing its way out of confinement, and she moaned against his mouth as she reached in between them to unbutton his shirt. She pulled it from his waistband and pushed it off his shoulders, breaking their kiss to press her lips to his naked chest, nibbling here and there.

With a groan, Brody pulled the turquoise top over Faith's shoulders, missing the contact of her mouth with his skin, even for that brief moment.

"Red," he said, his eyes on her bra.

"I like red."

He half laughed. "So do I, babe." He reached in and unclasped the bra, freeing her beautiful breasts. He lifted them in his hands, astounded at how perfectly they fit his hands. Leaning down, he pulled one of her tight nipples into his mouth and worked his way around it until Faith was whimpering and writhing, her head thrown back against the door. "Brody, stop," she begged. "I can't feel my legs. Bedroom."

Brody wasted no time in swooping her up and carrying her into the bedroom. He placed her on the bed, following her down to continue his explorations of her breasts with his hands and mouth.

He felt her reach between them and fumble with the button fly of his jeans. She got them open, and reached her warm hand in, wrapping it around the hard length of him and squeezing lightly. "Faith," he groaned.

"I want you," she whispered, kissing his chin and neck in the moonlit room. "Inside me. Now."

They tore at each other's clothes, all animalistic need and desire, sharing moans and kisses as they fumbled out of their remaining garments. At last they were skin to skin, and the relief of it slowed them down a bit. He explored her mouth with his tongue, smoothing his palm down her body until he reached between her legs. She spread them slightly, inviting, and he slid two fingers inside her. Slick, wet, hot. She contracted around him and responded by lifting her hips to increase the pressure. He rotated his thumb over her little rock-hard center until she was panting and groaning, reaching back to brace herself on the slats of the headboard.

She cried out as she climaxed around his fingers, and he closed his eyes against the rush of unexpected emotion he felt. When he felt her body relax beneath him, he kissed her on the lips and met her gaze in the full-moon darkness their eyes had adjusted to. She studied him. "What's wrong, honey?"

"Nothing." He kissed her. "Absolutely nothing. But I need to say something to you. Before we…"

She hesitated, then leaned over to the night-stand and lit a candle so they could see each other better. "Talk to me," she whispered, with so much love in her eyes. "Whatever it is, it's okay."

"I…I just need you to know." He swallowed. "Mick and I, we never—" This was harder than he'd expected. "This thing, between you and me, is all about us. Totally unexpected, but completely about you…and me. I loved Mick with my whole soul—still do. But I was never, not once, intimate with her."

Faith laughed softly. "Is that it?"

He paused, then nodded.

She ran her fingertips lightly over his skin, which was supersensitive from his arousal. "Sweetheart, do you think I don't know who my sister was as a person? We were close, she told me everything about her feelings, her crushes, how she needed to live her life. We didn't have any secrets."

Brody nodded. "I wanted to make sure you knew. This is real. You aren't some sort of…substitute."

"Honey, do you want to know one of the last things Mick told me before…that night?"

He nodded, swallowing against a tight throat.

"She said, if it was possible for her to fall in love with any guy on this earth, it would be you."

That touched him, warmed him in ways he'd never expected. "Really?"

Faith nodded, moving against him suggestively. "And she told me her wish was for me to find a guy just like you. So we can do that one better. Because there are no other guys like you, Brody Austin. And I only want you." She kissed him softly on the lips. "I really think Mick knew that, too."

"So she wanted me…for you?"

Tears came to Faith's eyes, and she nodded. "Fate."

"Fate," he repeated, remembering Herman's use of the word. Maybe it was more than just woo-woo.

"I love you, Brody."

"I love you, too, Faith." His eyes misted over. "I never knew…I never imagined…how much."

"Show me," she whispered, through her tears.

Their gazes locked, his tears mixing with hers, as he entered her in one passionate motion, felt her close around him. They moaned together, in sync once again. They made love slowly, but rife with an intensity he'd never felt before. He rested his forehead against hers, and they gazed into each other's eyes, saying everything with their bodies that was too emotional to say aloud.

When they climaxed together, both of their faces wet with tears, Brody knew, finally, what being home really meant. They wrapped their arms around each other, and he stayed inside her, never wanting to leave. They fell asleep just like that, in each other's arms, bodies connected, hearts beating together.

The way fate had intended all along.

Brody sat on his couch, staring at the framed photograph of him and Mick—the crown jewel of his home. It wasn't remorse for making love with Faith that he felt. Not at all. He was more in love with her than he even knew possible. But there were certain issues he hadn't yet faced, and he couldn't move forward until he faced them.

No time like the present. He might as well find out sooner rather than later whether this thing with Faith would ever turn into something permanent.

"Love you, Mick," he whispered to the photo, as he pushed up off the couch and palmed his truck keys. "I hope you'll be with me now." He didn't think he'd ever needed her more.

Twenty minutes later he pulled into the Montesantoses' driveway and cut the engine. He'd hoped he'd feel more positive at this moment, but he didn't. He still didn't know exactly what to say, how to broach the topic, but he knew he needed to face it like a man.

He pulled in a deep breath and rang the door-bell. As he heard footsteps approaching from the other side of the door, he suddenly felt like an awkward teenager again.

The door opened, and Elisa's face broke into a smile filled with sunshine and love. *"M'ijo!"* she exclaimed, pulling him into a bear hug. "Abel!" she called over her shoulder. "Our Brody is here." She turned back to Brody, threading her fingers with his and pulling him over the threshold.

"How good to see you. To what do we owe this honor?"

"I'd hoped to speak to Abel for a few minutes."

"Is everything okay?"

"Everything's great," he lied. "Just a little man-to-man talk, that's all."

She wrung her hands together. "Can I get you something? Coffee, water? Are you hungry?"

"Coffee would be great if you have some made. Don't go to any trouble."

Elisa laughed. "Oh, silly one. You're never any trouble. One thing you can count on is a fresh pot of coffee in my kitchen at any time."

"Your daughter sure didn't take after you in that respect," he said wryly.

Elisa pulled a face. "Awful stuff, I know. I don't know what's wrong with that girl," she added, with a laugh.

Nothing, Brody thought. *Absolutely nothing was wrong with Faith.*

Abel came in and the two men exchanged a hug. Elisa fixed them both cups of coffee and ushered them out to the back patio. She was going upstairs to do some cleaning, she told them.

For the first few minutes Abel and Brody exchanged Gulch gossip and sports commentary. After a bit, though, Abel sat back in his chair and crossed one ankle to rest across the other knee. "What's on your mind, son?"

Now or never.

Brody brushed his palms together, elbows on his knees, and hung his head for a moment. When he started to speak, his tone was low. "A long time ago I made a promise to you, Abel. And I broke that promise." He clenched his jaw, then looked up to meet the older man's gaze. "I walked out the door with your beautiful daughter, Mick, and you told me—"

"Take care of my girl," Abel said, emotion making his voice shake.

Brody nodded for a moment until he could find his voice again. "Yes. 'Take care of my girl.'" A pause stretched between them as Brody contemplated what to say next. "I failed to keep that promise."

Abel leaned forward and laid a palm on Brody's shoulder. "It was an accident."

"Still. It's the single biggest regret of my life, Abel. I don't know if I'll ever get over it."

"If you've come to ask my forgiveness, you already have it. You've always had it."

"That's not exactly why I've come."

One of Abel's salt-and-pepper eyebrows raised. *Hey, jerk. It's about time you showed up.*

He heard Mick's words in his mind, and he smiled. "Abel, I'm in love with your daughter. I'm in love with Faith. And she's in love with me, too." He shook his head, marveling at that fact. It still blew his mind. "So, what I've come to ask you—" he held out a palm "—and I will respect your feelings no matter what they are…"

"Go ahead, son."

"Mr. Montesantos, I know I've failed you before, but I came back to Troublesome Gulch for a reason. I just didn't know what it was. Now I do." He cleared his throat. "Sir, can I take care of your girl? For today, for tomorrow, for the rest of our lives? I love Faith more than I ever knew I could love anyone, and I can't help but think that Mick would be thrilled for us, but I can't do anything without your blessing."

Tears glistened in the older man's eyes. "I would trust you with my beloved Mick again, were she alive, Brody. And you're right—she would be thrilled for you and her sister."

Brody gulped, feeling hopeful.

"As for my blessing, I can't think of another man I'd feel more comfortable saying this to. Son, take care of my girl."

"I will."

Brody held out his hand, but as usual, Abel stood up and pulled him into a hug. "Welcome to the family for real this time, son."

Brody laughed. "Don't welcome me too soon, Abel. I haven't even spoken to Faith about our future yet."

Abel clapped him on the back as the two of them headed inside the house. "I know my girls. Not to worry. There's one thing we're going to have to do for each other, though."

"What's that?"

"Commiserate through the wedding planning." He raised his eyes heavenward. "Elisa and Faith will go absolutely nuts, mark my words. Rehearse this line, and your life will always run smoothly— 'Yes, dear. I love it. Your taste is impeccable.'"

Both men laughed, sharing another hug before Brody headed home. He had some serious planning to do.

Chapter Fourteen

At work, Faith's phone rang. "Ms. Montesantos," she answered.

"Hey, sweet thing," Brody drawled.

She set her pen aside and leaned back in her chair, a smile on her face. "Hey. Where have you been? I talked to Jason earlier and he said you'd been running around 'like some kinda crackhead,' and that's a direct quote."

"That kid," Brody said, with clear affection in his tone. "Speaking of Jase, he has a dinner and movie date with Gramps Herman, did he tell you that? Herman's picking him up from school."

"He did tell me," she said, a seductive note entering her tone. "What did you have in mind?"

"I was hoping you'd come over here for dinner. I have a surprise for you."

She crinkled her nose. "You didn't redo the place in orange and green, did you?"

"Ha, ha— No. It's just a little present I thought would be perfect for you. And I'm cooking dinner."

"Wow! Of course I'll be there. How about I make the after-dinner coffee?" she teased.

"I love you, but no."

"You're such a snob."

He didn't deny it. "When can you be here?"

"When do you want me there?"

"Now." *Always. Forever.*

"Oooh, I'm intrigued."

"Seriously, when can you be here?"

She glanced up at the clock on her wall. "I don't have any more appointments today, and I do have comp time. I could probably leave now." She cocked her head to the side. "That'll be an early dinner, though."

"Oh, I can think of an appetizer or two that could take up some time," he said, in a sexy growl.

Her chest clenched. "I'm so in. I can be there in twenty minutes, tops."

"That's the kind of team spirit I like to hear."

She laughed. "You're so weird, Brody. Can I bring anything?"

"Just you, baby. Just you."

After they'd indulged in a couple of hours of "appetizing," Brody brought Faith dinner in bed. When they'd finished eating, he brought in a tray of chocolate-dipped strawberries and a bottle of champagne.

"Oooh, is this my surprise?" she said, clapping, and then sipping the champagne he handed her.

"No, this is dessert. I'm preparing to get your present now." He pulled on a pair of sweatpants and stuffed his feet into a pair of running shoes.

"Why are you getting dressed?" Faith asked, around a mouthful of chocolate and strawberry.

"Because your surprise is outside."

Her eyebrows raised.

"But first, I wanted to ask you something."

"Shoot."

"Can I keep Jason? I mean, foster him until he's ready to leave for college?"

Her eyes widened. "Really?"

"He's an awesome kid." He shrugged, chagrined. "To be honest, having him here has really helped me get my head straight."

"He's thriving, too. You and Herman have built him up so much, but it's all been organic, you know?"

Brody nodded.

"I think we could get him placed here permanently, sure. If *you're* sure."

"I wouldn't have brought it up if I wasn't one hundred percent certain."

She sighed. "Do you have to keep making me fall deeper in love with you?"

"That's the plan, yes. Okay, for your surprise. Back in a sec." And he left.

A few minutes later Brody reentered the bedroom holding a squiggly, scruffy golden puppy against his chest. "Okay, her pedigree is nil. She's a Heinz 57 mutt. But she was so damn cute—"

"Oh, Brody!" She set the dessert tray aside and scrambled to her knees, completely naked and comfortable in her own skin with him. It felt so good. "Jason's going to flip. He loves animals. You never told me you were getting a dog." She snuggled the little pup, who was at least part terrier, laughing as he kissed her chin and nose. "What's her name?"

"I don't know. She's not for me. She's for you."

Faith froze, blinking up at him. "But, I can't have a dog at my place. Remember?" She looked down into the puppy's eyes. "Now you're going to break my heart."

"I don't want you to have her at your condo, Faith. I want you to have her here."

Clearly confused, Faith continued to pet the puppy, but her gaze was on Brody. "You're not making much sense. Why don't you explain?"

Brody sat on the edge of the bed. She could sense his nervousness. "I want you, and the little pup there, to move in with me."

"Okay, but—"

"I love you, Faith. Not only that, but I told your father I'd take care of his girl forever, and he gave me his blessings." Pain crossed his eyes. "I can't let the man down again."

Touched, knowing how difficult that had to have been for him, she laid a palm on her chest. "You went to my father? Oh, Brody."

"Not to mention we can't let this little girl down." He indicated the puppy. "I mean, look at the poor thing. She has a cute collar but no name tag."

Faith clicked her tongue with sympathy and ran her fingers around the puppy's tiny collar, stopping when she felt some kind of tag attached to it. She pulled it around to look at it, shocked to realize it wasn't a tag but a diamond ring.

A gorgeous diamond ring.

Her gaze shot up toward Brody. She searched his face. "Brody?"

He kicked off his shoes and crawled across the bed to her, taking her hand in his. "I love you, Faith. More than I've ever loved anyone in my life." He struggled with his words, raking his free hand through his hair. "When I came back to Troublesome Gulch, I had no idea why, or what I was looking for. Part of me thought I'd just finally gone nuts. Now I know it was fate bringing me back. To you. Fate and Mick. So, please, please, please. Marry me."

Her eyes teared, and she bit her bottom lip, unable to speak around the lump of emotion in her throat.

He squeezed her hand. "Look, I've never proposed to anyone, Faith, so I'm not sure of the protocol or how the whole thing's supposed to go down. All I know is I will die right here if you *don't* agree to marry me and spend the rest of your life in my arms."

"Brody," she said, her tears hitching her words a bit. "I would love nothing better than being your wife."

He actually looked shocked. "Really?"

She laughed. "No, I'm lying, just to jack with your brain. Yes! Yes, yes, yes! Brody Austin, I will marry you. And…if you're okay with it, I'd like to call this little girl Hope."

"Hope." Brody grinned. "It's perfect."

"Mick would've loved it."

"Yeah," Brody said, as he slipped the ring off Hope's collar and onto Faith's finger. "I have a feeling she would've loved this, too."

Faith shook her head as she gazed at the ring. "I know it seems woo-woo, but I have a feeling the whole thing was Mick's idea in the first place. You know my sister—"

"She always wanted her own way."

They laughed.

Brody leaned in, kissing Faith gently on the lips. "I say we let Mick have her way for the rest of our lives. I owe her at least that much."

"So do I. Because I have you." Faith laid the now sleepy puppy on the pillow next to her and pulled Brody into her arms. "So I say, you've got yourself a deal."

And somewhere, in a place far away, a green-eyed angel pumped her fist in the air.

Victory.

Of course.

As if she'd settle for anything less.

* * * * *

Valentine's Fortune
by
Allison Leigh

"Miss?" The deep voice seemed to come at Bethany from a long, hollow distance. "I'm with the Red Rock Fire Department. You're safe now. Just open your eyes."

Her throat hurt. Breathing in made her nose burn. She wanted to sleep. How long had it been since she'd had a decent night's sleep? Since before…before what?

Her brain searched, but all it found was fog. Thick, choking fog.

"Come on now, darlin'. Open your eyes for me."

She was floating in the fog. Was she flying? Someone had told her if she flew in her dreams that meant something good.

A dream. That was it. She was dreaming.

"Dammit, make a hole," the deep voice barked. "She needs air."

She winced. She wanted to shrink away from the harsh command in his voice. Didn't he know she was sleeping?

"Breathe through my mask." The voice was low again. Intimate. "It'll help."

Something covered her face. She pushed at it. Tried to protest. Sucked in oddly sweet air. She turned her head away. "No." The word scraped her raw throat.

"That's it, Miss. Come on back to us. You're doing fine now."

She could follow that voice anywhere. Even up and out of her dreaming fog.

"You're safe now," he coaxed softly. A lover's whisper.

No. That wasn't right. Her lover was…where?

She frowned at the pain inside her head. "No."

"Yes, you are safe. I promise. Just open your eyes. You'll see. Can you tell me your name?"

Bethany. The name sighed through her. *My name is Bethany.*

She jerked, her eyes flying open to stare into the face of the man speaking to her.

Voices. Shouting. Sirens. Smoke. Flashing lights.

It all accosted her in that instant and fear shot through her, making her stiffen. She tried to work her hand to her abdomen, but couldn't seem to manage it. "What?"

"Can you tell me your name?"

Relief was swift, but fleeting. She hadn't said her name. Or if she had, he hadn't heard it. Not over the incredible clamoring confusion surrounding them.

She started to clear her throat. Coughed. What was the name she was using? "Barbara," she finally supplied. Her voice wasn't much more than a croak. Her brain just didn't feel like cooperating. "Burr—" *Not Burdett. Not Burdett.* "Burton." That was her borrowed name. "What happened?"

"Don't worry about a thing now, Barbara. You're safe," was all he said. "I've got you now."

He was carrying her, she realized, and just as quickly she

felt consumed with dizziness. She closed her eyes, but that didn't help. "I feel sick."

The floating, rocking motion ceased. "I'll bet. I'm going to put you on the stretcher now. Just relax."

She opened her eyes again as he settled her on a firm, blessedly steady surface. "What happened?" she asked again. He had streaks on his face. Like war paint. And shoulders wider than a linebacker. He looked armed for battle.

She realized vaguely that a large white van was next to them.

"I almost didn't find you when we were clearing the restaurant." He'd leaned down closer to her and his voice was softer. Impossibly gentle.

Comforting.

She blinked. Rubbed her eyes. Realized that they were watering.

"The smoke was thick in there. You were unconscious," he said. "They're going to take you to the hospital. Just as a precaution. Make sure you're all right."

She didn't want to go to the hospital. She wanted, she wanted…she didn't know what she wanted. "A fire," she said, stupidly. Thickly. Even now, she could see the lick of hungry red lighting the sky beyond the van—an ambulance. And beyond that, a rise of thick, cloying smoke.

Oh, God.

She slid her hand over her abdomen. Please, *please* be all right. "I came for an enchilada."

His teeth flashed. "Afraid you'll have to wait a while for that. Inhaling smoke the way you did can make you pretty woozy," he said.

It wasn't war paint on his face. It was soot. And the armor he wore was a fireman's uniform.

"*You* rescued me?"

"Yes, ma'am." She realized his grin was slightly crooked. "And you're gonna be just fine, Barbara. D'ya have someone you want us to call? Husband? Boyfriend? Who were you with at Red?"

Red. The restaurant. She'd been treating herself to the first meal out she'd had since she'd landed in Red Rock. A woman only turned twenty-five once in her life, right?

"Barbara?"

Her mind was wandering. She knew it. She just couldn't seem to make herself stop. "I'm not married." It seemed to be the only clear thought in her head. "There's no one to call."

"We've got her now, Darr." A woman and another man appeared beside the stretcher and before Bethany could marshal another coherent sentence, they pushed the stretcher and she felt herself slide smoothly into the rear of the white ambulance. The woman followed her.

But Bethany wasn't looking at her.

She was watching the fireman, still standing there.

And then the ambulance doors closed and she wanted to protest, but it was already too late, because she could feel the vehicle begin to move.

The ambulance attendant closed her cool fingers around Bethany's wrist. "What's your name, ma'am?"

Bethany closed her eyes again. In her mind, though, was the firefighter's crooked grin. His deep, gentle voice.

"Barbara." Again, the lie scraped along her raw throat. "Barbara Burton."

SPECIAL MOMENTS™ 2-in-1

Coming next month

PLAIN JANE AND THE PLAYBOY by Marie Ferrarella

When playboy Jorge shares a New Year kiss with quiet, shy Jane he is shocked, as the commitment-phobe finds himself captivated by her!

VALENTINE'S FORTUNE by Allison Leigh

After rescuing mysterious Barbara during a snowstorm, firefighter Darr Fortune found himself stranded with the pregnant stranger. Could he uncover her secrets?

LULLABY FOR TWO by Karen Rose Smith

Vince assumed custody of his friend's son after an accident, and was glad of the help of Dr Tessa McGuire – his ex-wife! Could this be a second chance for them?

CHILD'S PLAY by Cindi Myers

Pregnant designer Diana is not what head teacher Jason expects when he commissions a playscape for his school. The single dad has no time for romance...until now!

THE SON BETWEEN THEM by Molly O'Keefe

Samantha keeps JD grounded. But when he discovers her secret, things change. JD must choose between his former life and a new one – with Samantha.

RUNAWAY BRIDE RETURNS! by Christie Ridgway

Injured in a blaze, firefighter Owen gets a very special carer – wife Izzy, who had bolted after their quickie Vegas wedding! Soon Izzy realises she won't be running away again!

On sale 15th January 2010

Available at WHSmith, Tesco, ASDA, Eason and all good bookshops.
For full Mills & Boon range including eBooks visit
www.millsandboon.co.uk

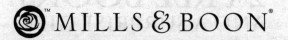

2 FREE BOOKS
AND A SURPRISE GIFT

We would like to take this opportunity to thank you for reading this Mills & Boon® book by offering you the chance to take TWO more specially selected books from the Special Moments™ series absolutely FREE! We're also making this offer to introduce you to the benefits of the Mills & Boon® Book Club™—

- **FREE home delivery**
- **FREE gifts and competitions**
- **FREE monthly Newsletter**
- **Exclusive Mills & Boon Book Club offers**
- **Books available before they're in the shops**

Accepting these FREE books and gift places you under no obligation to buy, you may cancel at any time, even after receiving your free books. Simply complete your details below and return the entire page to the address below. You don't even need a stamp!

YES Please send me 2 free Special Moments books and a surprise gift. I understand that unless you hear from me, I will receive 5 superb new stories every month, including a 2-in-1 book priced at £4.99 and three single books priced at £3.19 each, postage and packing free. I am under no obligation to purchase any books and may cancel my subscription at any time. The free books and gift will be mine to keep in any case.

Ms/Mrs/Miss/Mr _____ Initials _____

Surname _____

Address _____

_____

_____ Postcode _____

Send this whole page to: Mills & Boon Book Club, Free Book Offer, FREEPOST NAT 10298, Richmond, TW9 1BR

Offer valid in UK only and is not available to current Mills & Boon Book Club subscribers to this series. Overseas and Eire please write for details.. We reserve the right to refuse an application and applicants must be aged 18 years or over. Only one application per household. Terms and prices subject to change without notice. Offer expires 31st March 2010. As a result of this application, you may receive offers from Harlequin Mills & Boon and other carefully selected companies. If you would prefer not to share in this opportunity please write to The Data Manager, PO Box 676, Richmond, TW9 1WU.

Mills & Boon® is a registered trademark owned by Harlequin Mills & Boon Limited.
Special Moments™ is being used as a trademark.
The Mills & Boon® Book Club™ is being used as a trademark.